THE LAW OF UNINTENDED CONSEQUENCES - MORGAN OLSEN
BOOK 2

CJ Stevens

CHAPTER ONE

The Mail

Morgan opened her mailbox to find the large manilla envelope. At first, it seemed unremarkable, tucked in with all the other garbage she gets on a daily basis. Catalogs she does not want. Special offers for 'her only'. The water and sewer bill. Most of this stuff went through her industrial strength shredder and then into the recycling bin.

As she walked up the sidewalk and sorted things mentally tagging them for either opening or shredding unopened, the envelope seemed at first to be in the shred unopened category.

The only time Morgan ever uses the front door to her house is to walk to the curb to get the mail or deal with missionaries. Most of the time, they had about the same level of intrinsic value to her, except that she can schedule her trip to the mailbox around when she is working better than when someone comes to her door to share their story.

Occasionally her front door was put to a different use. One time a teenage girl brought a large yellow dog to her door and asked if it was hers. She seemed disappointed to learn that Morgan only had cats. To underscore that, Watson, the fat Himalayan cat, had peeked around her ankles curiously at the dog. To the yellow dog's credit, it merely looked back. Morgan pointed out to the young woman leading the dog on an improvised leash " Whoever owns that dog? They had cats too. This dog understands cats. I am not sure if they helps you find the owner, but good luck! Perhaps look for cats or cat furniture in a front window."

The girl looked down at her canine charge and said: "OK. That's... Interesting. Thank you."

Morgan was not against dogs in theory. It was just her life as a homicide detective did not allow for their necessary care. Morgan

1

would never have an animal member of her household she could not deliver the proper level or care to.

On her way to the bar in the Rec Room to lay things out and sort them, Morgan looked more closely at the envelope. Whatever was in it was moderately heavy for its thickness and also fairly stiff. Heavy paper or cardboard it seemed. It had been postage-canceled in Houston and had a standard issue white laser printed address sticker and no return address. Never a good sign. Morgan flipped it over and saw that, in addition to the bent metal tabs holding the flap closed, it had also been taped along the seam. Morgan concluded this meant manual envelope stuffing, not done by a machine. The postage was physical, individual stamps, not a registered meter. No machine metered postage equals less traceable mail.

Alarm bells regarding the source of the envelope went off in Morgan's head.

Morgan went to the kitchen, pulled a flashlight from the kitchen drawer. Returned to the bar. She held the envelope carefully and examined the stamps, the label, and the tape over the clasp. She could see no fingerprints on any surface that would have easily picked them up. Someone had filled the envelope with its contents rather carefully in order to not put any identifying marks upon it.

More alarm bells.

Going back to the kitchen Morgan pulled out a pair of her latex gloves from the box she kept there and retrieved a small sharp knife. Morgan sharpened every knife in her possession after every usage. A dull knife is a dangerous knife. If she was at someone else's house and happened to be cooking (Morgan would cook for a lover, but she would not make a habit of it), it was a source of frustration if she could not find a whetstone or steel to sharpen them. Morgan is not so anal however as to bring her whetstone with her 'just in case'. She gave whoever it was shit for not keeping their knives in usage ready condition. One of her lovers, DeWayne, had taken that abuse one time, and as a joke bought several different knife sharpeners and scattered them about. Morgan smiled when he pointed them out and then asked what he was cooking for dinner, only safely now that his knives were sharp.

Carefully slitting the flap, and holding the envelope well away from her face, Morgan inverted the brown paper in her gloved hands, pressed in slightly on the edges, and a sheaf of 8x10 glossy prints slid onto the bar top.

No powder. No unusual smells. No cover letter. Just pictures.

Morgan looked inside the opening of the envelope to verify there was nothing else, but it was now empty.

Setting that to the side, Morgan picked up the photographs in her gloved hands and saw her concerns about this envelope well placed. The pictures were of her.

The first picture was of her on her bike, fully set up for her ride in the MS-150 last month. She was bent over the handlebars, and the picture taken from the side of the road opposite where the bikes were running. Offset and a few feet back was Wendell, on his bike. Morgan's head was turned to face the camera, and she was looking back at Wendell, smiling. Morgan thought she looked happy.

The next picture was similar, except they were closer together, both sitting upright, and Wendell only had one hand on the handlebar because he was gesturing at something with the other. Both had open mouth smiles.

Next was a series of shots from the midpoint of the MS-150: The overnight camp in La Grange at the park.

Standing in line together to get food.

Getting food loaded onto their plates.

Sitting at a table together eating food.

Near a campfire, with beer glasses.

The last set of pictures from the campground was Morgan on hands and knees getting into the two-person tent, Wendell waiting, and then another shot of Wendell entering, with Morgan visible inside the tent reclined and wiggling out of her shower clothes.

The next series was Morgan and Wendell, in the morning, leaving her tent, in different bike outfits, eating breakfast, checking their bikes, mounted and riding.

The final series was of the end of the MS-150, where they both had hands up as they crossed the finish line, then loading their bikes into the Van for the return trip, then Wendall kissing Morgan standing next to the Van. They were the same height, and Morgan had a hand behind his head to pull his face to hers. Morgan remembered taking Wendell unawares with that unexpected kiss.

In all the pictures, they are smiling and happy and laughing, enjoying themselves and each other. The implications of the series of pictures chillingly crystal clear.

Someone stalked them during the MS-150 event. Morgan had never noticed.

This was the DeWayne situation, all over again. The hidden people in the department that did not want Morgan having a lover who is not lily white.

When Morgan's hands stopped shaking from anger, she retrieved her fingerprint kit and dusted all the pictures. All the surfaces of the envelope. There was not even a partial. Whoever sent these wore gloves, and at every step of the operation. Developing them, drying them, putting them in the envelope, stamping, addressing and mailing. All of it. So much effort just to put this hateful thing in the mail to her.

The envelope was a standard office supply store issue. The label from a laser printer meant no distinctive smudges like the good old days of typewriters. The stamps were canceled by the post office in Houston so the bastards could have dropped this in ANY mailbox. She looked at the stamps closely, because there were a fair few of them given the weight of the pictures. Whoever sent this wanted to be sure it did not have postage due.

The stamps in the upper right corner were the type you lick rather than 'peel off / stick on' adhesive, so Morgan hoped that they might have saliva she could sample and get DNA results from. All she had to do was get a lab somewhere that can run that kind of test. Morgan being a Homicide cop did not mean she could run whatever the hell she wanted through the crime lab. What case would this be for? Answer: The case where hidden people inside the department want to control her life. If it turns into more, she would have this as evidence, but for right now it was something Morgan had to control. Track. File. She would put it in her desk, and lock it at work where there are cameras and keys and she could talk to a jury someday about how this came into her possession, and how she treated it ever since then. She wrote up notes about the time and the place and signed and tucked this documentation in with the pictures.

Morgan would do everything within her not inconsiderable capabilities to be sure whoever was behind this would ultimately be taken into account, however long that might take.

Morgan reassembled everything and then put the envelope inside a bigger one so she could carry it without disturbing the evidence.

Morgan would have to call Wendell. Damn it. She had so much fun on that trip, and the two dates since then. There was no help for it: the Galveston County cop needed to know he was being stalked too.

Wendell answered the phone "Hi Morgan!"

Wendell had recognized her number the first time she ever called him. He apparently memorized it. That he knew it was her was not news anymore, but it was still an interesting data point for her.

"Hi, Wendell. I hope I am not disturbing your evening, but I needed to call. I have news. Bad news, I am afraid."

"Our date is off?" Wendell asked.

"Well. Maybe. Depends." Morgan said.

Morgan recited over the phone what she found as she went through the envelope and its contents. Her tests and precautions, and her plan to sequester the evidence until she had enough to move on... Whoever the hell this was.

Morgan ended her story with "I AM going to get these people Wendell, I just don't know when. They are careful, but they will screw up, eventually, and I WILL take them down."

"I see." Wendell said. "This is like the DeWayne thing you told me about. Some KKK dudes in the force up there are hassling you and me now."

"In a nutshell." Morgan agreed. "I am not sure of their exact affiliation just yet. KKK-like at least."

"So you want to call it off with me." Wendell said. It was very, very uninflected. So uninflected that it was obvious how much effort it took to make it that way.

"No, sir: I absolutely do NOT. That is not my choice, however." Morgan was emphatic. "While it is not of my doing, I bring this garbage to our relationship and I cannot ask you to have to deal with it. It has nothing to do with me or what I want. It has everything to do with people I cannot control and do not YET know who they are. With this new information, I suddenly became high maintenance for you, and that is nothing I can tell you how to deal with. You needed to know. With DeWayne, he is on the force up here. He was getting shit too. We mutually decided to slow roll our dating because of that. It was not just my career, but his being threatened. I do NOT care about what these people will try to do to my advancement. I am happy right where I am for now. What I cannot dictate is YOUR response to all of this."

"Always honest. I have a say here?" Wendell asked.

"Of course you do! If you did not, I would not have called." Morgan pointed out.

"True. OK. My point of view on this then Morgan is 'Fuck them'. I want to see you. Spend time with you. Take you to bed when you are interested. Same as we have been. You made it clear that you and I are not getting married and having kids."

Morgan protested that description. "I did not say that. Not like that, in any case."

Wendell returned "You said we should just enjoy each other. No strings. I inserted the ramifications. I am not being singled out. No one owns your heart, or at least not yet and I honestly don't want to meet the guy that can. I have not met them and I hate them already. Until then Morgan, I like you a great deal. You are fun. You are smart. So smart, and I love me a smart woman. You are a person I want to spend time with, sex or no sex. I hasten to add that the 'With Sex' option is better though. So: No. This is NOT up to me, it is up to YOU. You are the one with the KKK people in your department and up YOUR ass. No one at County gives two shits you and I are occasionally dating."

Morgan could not help smiling as Wendell said his piece. "You will not think me selfish if I keep seeing you, despite this? This kind of thing drove a real wedge between DeWayne and I, but he is up here on the same force I am, and it affected his job and his life. If there is a good thing about you being a long distance relationship, it is that if they come after me, so far I have seen no evidence they have enough reach to affect you. If that is wrong, you need to tell me immediately."

Wendell paused. Morgan assumed he was thinking that over. "Actually, Morgan: I don't." He said.

"What do you mean?" Morgan asked, taken aback at his tone.

"I mean all you have to know is that I wish for us to see each other when you are so inclined and our jobs and the distance let us." Wendell explained. "That's it. Full stop."

"You will not tell me if you are taking heat over me?" Morgan asked.

"I may. I may not. I will decide if you need to know based on the circumstance at the time. Works this way, Morgan. I am a Black cop. You couldn't care less about the fact that my skin is darker than yours. To you, it's pallet. To most people, it's a mark of me being a lesser human. I get grief over being a Black man all the time, and I, therefore, get to decide when and if dating a woman of any particular shade of color makes that better or worse and to a degree I find unacceptable." Wendell was firm.

"I am not a white woman, Wendell. My dad is Caucasian. My mother was not." There were times that Morgan did not like that she 'passed' for white when the standard issue bigot would declare her to be the same lesser being Wendell referred to if they knew she was half

Amerind.

"I repeat, Morgan: Any shade. You do not care about ethnicity. Neither do I. I want to see your amazing and intelligent dark blue eyes looking into mine wherever and whenever you decide that is something YOU want. None of the rest of it matters. I fade that heat all the damn time. Look: for some women, it's a fetish to date a Black guy. I have been on those dates. Not that great. Sometimes getting laid just is not worth the other BS. For some Black guys, it's the same the other way around: to date a white girl. I know one guy that will ONLY date white girls. Yes: Date is code for have sex with. It's weird, and I don't get it, but it is what it is. That is not what you and I are about. We are the ethnic flavor we are. I like that about you. Not that you don't SEE me, but that you don't care. You enjoy being with me because of who I am."

Morgan thought, not for the first time, about what it must be like to be a Black cop in the deep south, and decided that she had no place picking Wendell's battles. She would not be one of them. She wanted to be a brighter light than that in his life. She liked the honesty he gave her about the whole issue / Non-issue.

"OK. Then we are still on for Tuesday. You are coming up to my house. I drew you a map so you have NO excuse to not find it, and then we are going out. I already told Sam that Wednesday morning, at the least, is downtime for me. I anticipate a late evening. You have been warned." Morgan said.

"Good, because it has been a while since I have seen you, and I also think it will be a long night. I am resting up NOW. Hitting the gym. Getting in my eight. Done. I will see you then." Wendell told Morgan, and they hung up.

Morgan thought about that call for a while. It is not possible to not SEE what a person looks like. It is not possible to not care. In Wendell's case, she liked the way he looked when he smiled, and she liked his trim, fit body. He is sexy to her, based off ancient wiring in her brain. Another man in her life, Ken Cunningham, is nothing like Wendell. Tall. White. Slightly overweight. Intelligent. Well informed. Ken's problem for Morgan was that he wanted MORE in their relationship than Morgan was willing to give. He wanted exclusivity, in the form of marriage.

Not going to happen. Morgan was not against the theoretical concept of marriage. She knew that as much as she enjoyed Ken; he was not it. Lifemate. Soul mate. Whatever it is.

CHAPTER TWO

Homicide

Sam Parker looked up from the pictures in his gloved hands and shook his head at his partner. "Geez, Morgan. Again?"

"So it seems." Morgan gestured at the evidence. "No letter. No written warning like there was with DeWayne. Just that clear photographic message that they do not like me seeing Wendell."

Morgan sat back at her desk and watched her partner as he examined the pictures. They have been through a fair amount of crap together, especially after a few months back they arrested Bob Watts, the best Crime Scene Photographer of the department. How to make yourself Persona Non-Grata at the department: Arrest one of your own.

Sam put the pictures back in the envelope, then slid that assembly into the larger envelope, and handed the package to Morgan across their facing desks. As he stripped off his gloves, Sam said "I assume, you being who you are, you already have your next date with Wendell set. "

"Of course. I called Wendell and gave him a chance to decide if this bullshit is nothing he wanted to deal with. He demurred. Therefore: I am still going to be in late this next Wednesday."

"Good? I guess? I am glad you are not letting these people tell you what to do, but I am also worried: We have no idea who these fuckheads are. How far they will go. They followed you beginning to end on the MS-150, Morgan. That is pretty damn serious. You have to tell JJ. You kept the DeWayne thing to just us, but he needs to know."

Morgan took the evidence envelope and looked at it unhappily. "JJ will not care. It will be a 'lady problem' to him. If you were dating a black woman, you wouldn't be getting this kind of shit. As for the end-

"Get in here, Olsen. What threats?" JJ asked sternly. Now he was working his way into 'father figure' territory.

Ever since Morgan had arrested Hector, a relative JJ hated, and she was, via the legal system, getting ready to put Hector in prison for a long time, JJ has been friendlier to Morgan, but that was a matter of degree. He hated having this particular woman reporting to him LESS than he had before. He still hated it.

"I do not have the first one with me. In summary, I have been dating, on and off, an officer named DeWayne Kelly. I received a note telling me to make that a full time 'off' as it was not in my best interests to continue to see a black man. I showed it to DeWayne, and it did have a chilling effect. DeWayne, immediately subsequent to my note, also received notes about our dating. These unseen people communicated to him that our relationship did NOT meet with someone somewhere's personal ideas of propriety. Now I have received these photographs of myself, on the MS-150 bike ride with another man I am seeing. Wendell Jackson. There is no threat other than the implicit one that I am being watched."

"That them?" JJ asked, pointing.

"Yes, Sir" Morgan said, not offering them.

"May I SEE them, Morgan?" JJ asked, holding out his hand.

'Oh. Great.' was Morgan's inner thought. JJ switched to her first name. Not good. Last time he did that, she was sending Hector to jail.

Morgan handed him the package and gloves, and JJ said nothing about the fact that she had included the gloves. He worked them on to his overweight fingers, and then carefully opened up the nested envelopes.

Morgan commented along the way. "Outer envelope is mine, to maintain the evidence such as it is. I have dusted everything, and whoever sent that package wore gloves the whole time. Smudged fingertip with no definition at best. Kodak print paper, standard issue. The envelope could be from anywhere. The label was laser printed. To find anything from this, I would have to either find who printed these or run DNA off the stamps. They are the type you lick, but of course, they could have used a sponge."

JJ nodded as she pre-answered questions he might have had.

"There are a few sequences of photos. The ride out of town. The overnight in La Grange, with both dinner and breakfast at the midpoint park. The ride to Austin on the second day, and the loading of the Vans for return. The person taking these went the entire way. I never noticed them. I think, looking at the way the background appears relative to me that a long lens was used. I will show these to Bob and ask his opinion. I also think this because I never noticed anyone taking pictures of me, nor did Wendell. There are photographers all over the MS-150 however, so it is not a thing I would have been paying attention to."

JJ looked up at Morgan in some disbelief. "Bob? Bob Watts? The Photog you got fired from here?"

"Yes." Morgan agreed simply.

"Why in the hell would he help YOU? You caught his ass. You got him nailed. He is on probation for the next forever over manslaughter charges. Charges YOU brought." JJ was utterly disbelieving that Bob would do anything other than run Morgan over with a truck it seemed.

Morgan smiled at JJ's indignation. She had not expected Bob to want to ever see her again either. "Bob did not mean to kill Sally, and he was carrying around a LOT of guilt over that. He was glad I caught him, once it was out. His wife is divorcing him as well, but he does not blame me for any of that. He told me the other day he can pay for what he did, and start over. He thanked me, JJ if you can believe that."

JJ shook his head, not believing. He held up a picture of Morgan looking back slightly at Wendell as they rode their bikes along the side of the highway, smiling at each other. "I see why you were not paying attention to the world around you." He held up the one of Wendell going into her tent. "You had other things on your mind."

"Yes, Sir." Morgan replied, stifling an urge to blush and glad she had not gotten further out of her clothing at that point. Of course, Wendell had closed the tent fairly quickly. Morgan remembered that night. The sounds of the party around them in the night. Their taking it private. It had been fun. Until now.

JJ reassembled the packets. Morgan felt required to point out "I do not get this sort of thing when I see a Caucasian man. This only happens when I see men of color. In fact, when I have dated men of any other ethnicity than Black, I have gotten zero threats or pictures."

"How many other colors is that, Morgan?" JJ asked as he worked.

"All of them, I suppose? It is not really something I pay much attention to, Sir."

"Have you had long term relationships with, for example, a Hispanic man, in public, such that others would KNOW you were doing that? I ask because this is public. MS-150. DeWayne Kelly is a cop on this force. People would KNOW about it."

Morgan considered that. A good question. "I have in fact had long term romantic relationships with Hispanic men, however, I am a very private person, JJ. I go out to eat, and such with whoever I am dating, of course, but rarely is there PDA. That picture of the kiss at the end of the race there is an exception. I was being spontaneous which is not a thing I often do. That is part of why it was fun."

JJ nodded. "Morgan. I need to show you something. Sit." JJ pointed at one of his awful chairs.

Morgan perched on one. Best that can be achieved given the round top and the hard padding.

JJ opened a file drawer in his desk, and immediately and without any searching removed one that was at least an inch thick. He handed the folder over to her, then noticed he was still wearing the gloves and stripped them off.

"Newspaper clippings" JJ explained. "The life and times of Morgan Olsen. Have a look. Tell me what you see there."

Morgan saw that the oldest ones were on the bottom. She worked her way through them, scanning. Quickly at first, then stopping, going back. Reading.

"I assume you have never read your notices before, Morgan?" JJ asked, seemingly interested.

"Never, Sir." JJ may be calling her Morgan, but she was staying with the 'Sir' given this. "I do not care. I do not do this to get into print. Shit...."

"May I assume you have seen the patterns?" JJ asked, sweetly. Far too sweetly.

"Every time, from the time I have been a beat cop to now, my every single arrest, promotion, award, whatever, has been in print. Worse, when I arrest someone of color, the article is a terrible picture of them. When I arrest a white person, it is a picture of me, or Sam and I. This one, from Bob's arrest, is of Sam and I walking down the steps of THIS building, talking!"

"Got it in one. Never let it be said you are a dummy. Dummy." JJ let sarcasm enter his voice. He clearly thought Morgan had been being stupid.

Morgan held up a few. "When I arrested Hector, there are literally five different papers reporting on that! All of them have pictures of Hector except this one from the Daily News that has a picture of the BeachView Review parking lot and a caption saying this is 'where it all went down'! Great advertising for the club there."

Morgan held up an example article. "Most of the Chron ones about me, all the way back, are by this one reporter. Peter Spencer. I have never met this person, but you'd think I hung the damn moon from these. There is even an article about last years holiday party, and it is a picture centered on me, in the group! Pardon me sir, but FUCK!"

Morgan rarely cursed, so JJ just gave that a grin. "Exactly, Morgan. All the way back. The department PR machine works overtime to be sure every time you have a good shit in the can, Spencer there makes sure the world celebrates your achievement."

"Why?!?!?!" Morgan was deeply confused.

"When you joined from the academy, tops in EVERYTHING, you had eyes on you to see what you would do. You then did all of that, in that folder. When I inherited you, you came with a clippings folder. The only cop I have who ever did. Youngest detective. Highest closure rate. Take down anyone that needs it. The powers that be, both public and not so public, want to be sure everyone in Houston knows that the department is on board with equal pay for equal work, promoting women, the whole enchilada. We aren't of course. You, Morgan, are the exception. You were promoted over people more senior than you against protests. You are paid MORE than any Homicide cop with your years in. You are who they want to point at and say 'aren't we clever?'. Let us not mince words here: you are somewhat photogenic, Morgan: never hurts a PR shot. Add all that up. What do you get?"

Morgan screwed up her mouth. "I get that when I find the people trying to tell me who to date, that they are going to be bigots, and I am going to take them down, and it will be a shit show the PR department does not want."

JJ did not smile at that. He leaned back. Put his arms over his belly. "Yes: That is exactly NOT my point. Good work." JJ shook his head negatively. "Morgan: you need to be careful. This is still a southern police department, even if we are in the fourth largest city in the US. They are crafting a careful image here, and they will not take kindly with you fucking with that. That note about DeWayne and these pictures mean they are serious. If you make them regret selecting YOU for their cover girl of departmental progressiveness, they will make you regret it too. I know what I am talking about here."

JJ was topped out precisely because he was one of the people that had opposed Morgan being put on his squad, Morgan's pay and promotions. All of it.

"If they want me to be their spokesmodel for progressiveness, they would not be fighting me on actually being progressive" Morgan said.

JJ waved that away. "They are not actually progressive. The exact opposite, which is why they are doing this. Have you learned nothing in your short life? Never mistake PR for reality. Do you think the Patriot Act was about being a Patriot? Look, not everyone in the department is in on this. Most people want to go along to get along. Hit their marks. Go home at night and get laid. There are however just enough people, of enough rank, in enough places, that you do not want to get sideways with their little show. YOU are their little show. It is just a show though, so don't you forget it. You can end your PR run with a glorious 'fallen cop in the line of duty' funeral."

Morgan stood up. JJ indicated the photos in the envelope. "For a genius, you are an idiot, Morgan. I know you. You are not going to take good advice. Put those in the evidence locker, and maintain chain of custody. You might need those someday, right before they shoot you in the goddamn head."

"Yes, Sir. Thank you, Sir." Morgan said and left to do exactly that, an entirely new set of data churning behind her eyes. She needed to talk to this Peter Spencer guy that seemed to be the PR flak.

CHAPTER THREE

Friday Morning Body

It was 4:03 AM Friday morning when Morgan arrived on the scene. She walked up the alley towards all the lights and radios and unnatural early morning Sturm und Drang.

Sam's truck out on the street told Morgan he was already here, first on the scene as usual. Sam, for all his southern boy whiteness, lived in the Montrose. Morgan didn't. Given their attitudes and lifestyles, that was sort of backward. Morgan lived out in the County, he lived up in the city. Sam dressed in boots and a cowboy hat and looked every inch a good old boy, whereas Morgan with her slightly exotic mix of Norwegian and Amerind, long hair, and relaxed attitudes about sex and ethnicity fit perfectly in the Montrose. This proved to the two detectives that appearances and attitudes are not everything. Sam liked being plugged into his city, where Morgan preferred the mental space of her house away from the hustle. She could always drive into town when required. She could not throw a rock and hit her nearest neighbors house. She liked it that way.

The dumpster lined alley Morgan walked along made an 'L' with a second alley, and at the apex of those two alleys was the crime scene. Easy to see and hear up ahead. The alley was lit in pools by rectangular outdoor flood lighting. White painted cinder block walls punctuated with steel doors for deliveries. Standard commercial building alley.

Morgan paused, to look the scene over, but Sam stole Morgan's pre-engagement moment by waving at her to come over. Sam never understood Morgan's pre-scene engagement ritual. Sam is a dive-in kind of guy. Morgan compromised between her need to observe and Sam's gesticulations by walking slowly and looking around at the scene, trying to get as much situational detail into her mind before she had to plug in.

As usual, in May, it was warm and dank. The dumpsters exuded their trashy odors as organic things broke down quickly in the Houston climate. May is already summer in Houston, so it was not pleasant.

"Hey, Morgan. Good Friday morning to you! I hope you had a good sleep!" Sam chirped, looking like death warmed over, coffee cup in his hand.

Overcompensation. Morgan would have liked it better if he had just shut up and let her absorb the details.

Morgan stopped at the body. The kid was young. Morgan guessed he was not even eighteen yet. His skin a light cappuccino color. His black curly hair in a two-inch long afro style, the curls combed directly away from the skull. Black baggy sweat pants. Designer athletic shoes of some kind that would prove once again Morgan had missed a fashion trend, not that she cared. Black sweatshirt with a sports team logo, hiked up his waist slightly, probably from the fall to the ground. Legs and arms in random arrangements of death. Head to one side, a large pool of blood over his left shoulder. Head wound that bled until the heart stopped. Death was not instantaneous. It rarely is.

Morgan looked around. M.E. was not here, but everyone else was. Crime scene guys were just standing about and chatting, so she assumed the scene photos were done.

Morgan kneeled by the body, just out of the blood pool, and observed the details. The wound behind the ear was clear. The blood on the ground evidence of the body throbbing out its last goodbye as the young man lay there.

Morgan saw the places the Crime scene people took their samples. The blood gelled enough to make this obvious. The flattened arc in the edge of blood was less clear as to how it came to be there, though Morgan had a suspicion.

Morgan stood and walked around the officers at the scene. She found the footwear she was after and looked at the officers' badge.

"You were first on the scene?" she asked Officer Simmons.

Simmons was taken aback by the detectives' correct assumption. "Yes?" He answered as both a question and a statement.

Morgan pointed at the dead young man. "He was like this when you found him? You checked him for a pulse, etc.?"

"Found him exactly like this, detective," Simmons said. "I checked the pulse in his carotid, found nothing, called it in."

"You get this on routine patrol, or was this found by someone and called in?" Morgan asked.

"Routine patrol, Detective." Simmons said, still wondering how Morgan knew he was the first responder.

Morgan pointed up each alley to the streets with her hands. "You were walking by on one of those streets?"

Simmons nodded and pointed up the alleyway Morgan had come in on. "Yes, Ma'am. I was patrolling, walking along the sidewalk over there. I looked down this alley, the poor kid was clearly, even from the sidewalk, laying on the ground. I ran up here to see the blood. It was already congealing like that, so he had been here for a while. When I checked for his pulse, he was fairly cool to the touch. He had been on the ground for hours, and no one ever looked up either of the alleys and noticed him. That seems weird because this service alley is well enough lit I could see him plainly from the sidewalk. I checked his pockets for anything, found nothing. No money, no wallet, no phone."

"Thank you, Simmons. I will read your complete report with interest. Please be anything but succinct. I want everything you can recall." Morgan told him. She looked significantly down at his feet, then left him be.

"Yes, Ma'am" Officer Simmons said, picked up and looked at his feet, then saw how Morgan singled him out and cursed himself for his stupidity.

Morgan was surprised when the M.E. on the scene turned out to be her friend and the chief M.E., Cooper Johnson.

When he walked into the lights, Morgan recognized him and said in a fairly happy greeting given that this was a crime scene: "Cooper? What brings you here? I thought you lived in your morgue."

"I heard there was a body. Vacation coverage. You know... Hi Morgan. Glad it is you." Cooper explained, even as he looked down at the kid. "What do we have?"

Sam answered "No ID of any kind. We'll need dental. A single shot to the head like you see here." Sam waved at the kid on the ground, circling finger at the blood pool. "Concrete, so nothing soaked in."

Morgan indicated the blood pool. "I need to know the angle of the shot, Cooper. Small caliber, behind the ear, gangland style, but the kid was standing when he was shot. From what I can see, upward angle but only slightly. My quick estimate is that shooter is five seven or eight, but need that confirmed. Also, no in and out and small entry wound with powder stippling so guessing something like a .22 held at point blank range. Bullet still in his head."

Cooper Johnson looked down at the young, dead man, cocked his head. "Why am I here? Clearly, you have all of it figured out already?"

Morgan came over and touched her friend lightly on the arm. "I need everything I just said CONFIRMED Cooper. These are my wild ass guesses so far. I need data. Actual facts?"

Cooper looked at his favorite Detective and gave her a small grin. "I will let you know, Morgan. Quick as I can get him to my table. Your guesses are normally as good as anyone else's verified facts."

Cooper knelt where Morgan had, looking at the wound. Nodded. "Agree on your initial assessment of angle and caliber. They done with all the pictures and samples?"

Sam said "They are done. CSU was second on the scene. Before me even."

Cooper nodded his thanks, then opened his bag and started his part of the work.

"Middle of the night. No houses near here. All the businesses around here were closed by the time this went down. Canvas is probably going to be a big fat zero." Morgan said to Sam as they watched Cooper work.

"Yeah. There a couple Uni's out there trying anyway." Sam replied. He looked up one of the alleys towards the sidewalk and the look on his face and his resigned tone told Morgan that he was not holding out much hope for that activity.

Morgan looked up at the cinder block walls on all sides of the murder scene, and she started to walk along the alley she had not come up. Here and there, over steel business doors, outdoor lights, angled down so that the steel back doors were well lit. There was a variety of different signs by the doors about who to call for deliveries, delivery hours, ring for deliveries, authorized personnel only, or just the business hours. All the usual things one would expect in the back alley of a strip center.

When Morgan arrived at the sidewalk and street that ran at right angles to the street she had parked on, she looked up and down along its length in the darkness. There was an open lot directly across from where she stood so no business with a security camera pointed up the alley.

Sam came up behind her, watched her as she scanned about. Said nothing.

"Not a camera anywhere. Four-way stop on the corner there: no traffic camera." Morgan said with some frustration. "If you are going to shoot a kid in the head, this is the place to do it. I'd be willing to bet the crime rate along here is higher than average for the area."

"Yep." Sam concurred, sharing Morgan's frustration. "Before you rolled in I walked along the sidewalk here and looked in the windows of these various shops. I can see interior security systems, but for the outside? Nothing. Maybe there is a motion-sensitive camera pointed at a door. Best hope of getting something. If the killer came in from that lot across the street there is not going to be anything. I looked to see if there were any fresh prints, but didn't see anything. You might have more luck: Better tracker than I am."

It was not an oblique reference to Morgan's ancestry: Only acknowledgment of established facts. Morgan ignored that offer. Sam looked. There was a sidewalk along the opposite side of the street that the killer could have done the approach on in addition to crossing the lot, so it was all hard surface.

Morgan indicated the nearest storefront. "I guess they were worried someone might steal the cameras if they were outdoors. You know: normally I love that I do not live in a security state, with CCTV cameras everywhere, but it sure as hell makes our job harder."

"Welcome to Texas." Sam said.

Morgan looked for anything useful along the street. An ATM. Anything... Found nothing. She gave up on that hope and instead turned and they walked back to the crime scene. "We'll need some Uni's to be here as these places open and check for your motion-sensitive camera idea."

Sam smiled, noting Morgan expressly did NOT double check his examination of the lot across the street. "I'll talk to the OIC about that." He said.

Cooper looked up as Sam and Morgan returned. "Detectives. My best estimate for TOD is midnight, based on liver and air temps."

"Thanks, Cooper." Morgan then said to Sam "On my walk up and just now, I did not see any of the places being open past 10pm. Cinder block walls No windows at all along the two alleyways. You would have to be walking directly by on one of those two sidewalks to see anything. A .22 makes a tiny noise so even if someone was working late inside of one of these stores, they probably would have heard nothing. Another question to have the guys ask though."

Sam noted in his pad "Cameras. Anyone working late that might have heard anything. Also, show a picture of the victim and see if anyone knows him."

Sam cradled his phone, and frowned at Morgan across their desks. "Nothing on the Canvas, Morgan. I mean literally nothing. The guys walking around found no one to talk to at all. Literally no one. The morning canvas came back with no cameras and no late workers."

"Literally a dead zone." Morgan commented.

"Is that a JOKE?" Sam asked.

"Not intentionally no. We have a dead kid that is so far about as close to a perfect murder as there can be. Execution style at a time and place where no one would see or hear it. Even with all the alley lights." Morgan gave Sam a look the echo'ed his own feeling. "Unless Cooper gets a bullet from a gun that already has a body on it, we are going to be seriously screwed here."

"I may go back there on the way home and talk to some of the business owners about upgrading their security systems. It is like you said: perfect place for a murder. I did look up the stats for there, by the way. First murder. Amazing, when you think about it."

"Makes me think whoever did this knows the area. Something to add to the profile, but ... I don't get it. Looks like a Pro hit, but he was just a kid! What would he have done to have a pro after him?" Morgan made a few notes in her case log about those exact questions as she spoke.

"No idea. I guess we are stuck for now, till we get something to go on. I'm toast. I say let's call it a day, and maybe a weekend?" Sam asked.

"Unless we get a call-out. Agree." Morgan said. She was ready for an early bedtime herself.

CHAPTER FOUR

Janie

Morgan knocked on Angel's door. She was here to see her friend, but also see Nakoma, her friends' baby daughter.

Morgan has a single-minded goal: spoil Nakoma rotten with attention. It was partly based upon Nakoma's biological father disappearing from her life before she was born, but truth be told, Morgan just loved spoiling Nakoma. The advantage of being Mom number two is that she can spoil and run. Angel complained about this all the time, saying things like: "Sure Morgan: Thanks. Leave me with the brat when you are done with her!"

Angel opened the door. "Hey, Morgan. Come on in."

"Hi, Angel. Is Nakoma home? Can she come out and play?" Morgan asked, teasing but also not.

Angel Laveau is by all appearances a full-blooded Native American, but she has no idea what tribe. Her current last name was a gift from her Ex, and Angel was trying to decide if it was worth changing it again or not. If she changed her name, she had to change Nakoma's as well, and then the question became: To what? Morgan suggested 'Mankiller' in honor of both the famous leader of the Cherokee Nation, Wilma Mankiller and also what would happen if her Ex, Andrea, ever showed back up in Angel's life. Not because Angel would actually kill sperm donor Andrea Laveau, because that is NOT Angel's way.

Angel, proving Morgan's thinking, had told her friend at the suggested last name that: "I would not kill him, Morgan. Hurt him, sure. Kill him? No way."

"I would" Morgan said. "It is just that I already have a last name. I kill him, we tell everyone it was you..."

Angel knew her friend had been kidding when she said that. Very little escapes Angel about people. Angel is the most empathetic person Morgan had ever met. She just seems to know what other people need. Morgan wondered how Andrea Laveau had been able to slip by Angel's perceptions.

Angel waved her friend in through the doorway. "I have a surprise for you..."

Inside the house was, unexpectedly, another woman Morgan knew. She met her the same night she met Angel at the strip club in Galveston. Janie Moore. Morgan might tease Angel about her last name but she would never make a joke about Janie's, even though 'more' is a good description of her, and in a good way. Janie is an exotic dancer, and Morgan thought Janie to be the living definition of the term 'Full Figured Woman'. Go to any store that sells plus size women's clothing, and you will see a woman shaped like Janie on the signage. Morgan thought it therefore ironic (at least to herself) that Janie is one of those people that look better without clothing than dressed. Sans apparel just seemed to be her natural look. In clothes, Janie was not someone that necessarily drew the eye. Nude, she is Morgan's idea of beautiful.

Morgan, being a practicing heterosexual, was not sure why she thought about Janie's state of dress at all, but it was undeniable she did. During Morgan's homicide investigation, following a possible lead to the strip club in Galveston, Morgan had talked to Janie in both her clothed and unclothed states. Janie caught her attention far more when she was standing at her table in her natural glory. In a place with many other naked women walking around and working the room, Janie stood out.

"Janie! Hi!" Morgan greeted her "Nice to see you again!"

"Hi, Morgan! You remember my name!" Janie decided to go in for a hug, and Morgan reciprocated with a firm two-armed embrace.

"And you remember mine. It was a memorable night!" Morgan told her.

Angel explained how Janie came to be at her place. "I was just catching up with Janie on current events. She left BeachView, and has joined Evie up at 'rox' now."

Morgan thought that was good news and said so. "That is wonderful! Excellent move. I am sure that Margie treats you much better, even if the club is not as swanky as 'BeachView' is. How long have you been dancing at 'rox'?"

Janie liked Morgan's enthusiasm for her change of venue. "A few weeks now. Yeah: I like me some Margie. Former dancer, and makes sure we get treated right. She makes sure Mike lets a guy know if he is getting too... Well, you know. I don't do the sideline stuff, like Pam and some of the others do. Margie makes sure we all get treated well. Doesn't matter to her if we dance, or dance AND take on the occasional fuck. She takes care of her girls. Like those places you hear about up near Vegas where the girls like to do the sex work because they are treated right. The whole thing too. I heard her telling a new girl to ALWAYS use condoms, and how to do a DC. Sorry: Dick Check. Margie said she will NOT have her club getting a rep as being where someone caught something. Not a customer, and most especially not one of her ladies."

Janie gave Morgan a knowing grin. "Speaking of Mike, he was sorta hoping after the case was over you were gonna call him up. It's been over for MONTHS now. How are you resisting that burning hunk of man-love?" Janie asked. "I mean, holy shit girl. You have eyes."

They sat and got comfortable. Angel made a glass of water appear in Morgan's hand, and Morgan did not even ask how Angel knew she was thirsty. Hot day in May, Houston's ever-present swampy humidity, top down on the Miata, so of course, she was. Even if Morgan had a quick shower before coming into the apartment in some theoretical parking lot bathing facility, and she had looked fresh as a daisy, Angel would still know.

Morgan looked at the water and swirled it around the ice cubes. She commented to Angel. "With Janie here, it seems like this should be a Shiner Bock."

That was what Angel had served Morgan the night at the BeachView when she had been questioning the dancers there.

"It should be." Angel agreed blithely. "Later. After you rehydrate. Also, I will more than likely stay dressed, unless Janie strips and then I might."

Angel had been naked except for a gold waist chain at the club. Angel was joking of course.

Morgan addressed the open question from Janie. "Mike. Yes. I have eyes, and I use them. I am also aware he was interested in me for whatever reason. So, let me see: why I never went back? I figure that particular man, with his looks and venue of work, has, and I am not exaggerating, about one hundred women lined up for him. I do OK in being able to find people to date without that kind of grief. I do not like lines, so I never got into his. Let us face facts: Mike has choices:

any breathing bisexual or Hetero woman, plus any bisexual or gay man. According to the latest stats, that means over 95% of the female population plus at a guess another 5% of the male population. Also, stats about sex are notoriously inaccurate, so more than likely higher in all categories. You are not wrong about his animal charisma. "

Janie found that amusing "Honey, you are so right about the line. Same here: a man that gorgeous is nothing I want to compete for either, but you are also wrong about one thing. You are at the head of that line. Very first one. You show up at 'rox' and that guy is going to dive on you and leave that line standing around pouting and saying things like 'What's she got I don't'. You really impressed him. I get THAT about you too, doll. You fucking impressed me that fateful night, what with Hector and everything. If I swung that way, I'd be on you like white on rice. I don't do chicks and I am STILL considering it. Mike gets all the tail he wants, sure. What he liked was YOU."

Morgan tilted her head. Considered. "Yes, well, back at you, Janie. If I had a list for women lovers, you would be first in my 'Want' column. Regarding Mike: You know all this how, exactly?"

"When I came to 'rox', the very first thing he ever asked me was if I knew YOU. He followed the case in the paper, and he knew all about the thing with Hector. When I told him I used to date Hector, and that you took Hector DOWN that night, Mike was all like 'Of course she did' and 'That lady can do anything!'. On and on he rambled about you: I think he knows your entire resume. He has newspaper clippings about your cases and even a picture of you behind the bar. Taped to the barback mirror. The picture was from an article where you took some cop down. Right after you were down at 'BeachView' that night. Hey! I just realized: That guy on the steps in that picture next to you: It's the guy you asked me about! The weirdo." Janie gave Morgan a wide-eyed look as she realized the connection.

Morgan glanced over at Angel, who was deeply amused. "Yes, well, I never explained to you why I was asking about him, Janie. That 'weirdo' is my partner on the force, and I was looking into him as a suspect on that case. The same case where I arrested a cop and that was in that article you said is on the wall." Morgan could not share personal details about Sam but felt she owed Janie a summary at least. "It turned out in the end that my partner, Sam, was having some serious issues with women in general at the time. Personal and confidential stuff I was not privy too, but that I could see the outlines of. I was checking into Sam because I did not know about the problem until later."

"Yeah: tell me something I DON'T know. Dude was fucked up." Janie agreed.

"He is much better now." Morgan assured Janie.

Angel chimed in "He is. I know him now, Janie. He is NOTHING like that guy you described from the club. Good Cop. Always has Morgan's back, which given all the shit SHE stirs up is a good thing."

"You are a different kind o' cop, fer totally sure." Janie said. "Margie says that 'bout you too. Says she never met a cop that gave a good god damn about any of the girls before. Evie talks about you all the time. About how you took her serious and listened to her. Hell, Angel here is your best friend! You are one of a kind, lady."

"Well, that is nice to hear." Morgan's eyes sparkled as she teased Janie: "Does all this mean I get a discount dance from you next time I am there? I bet you are expensive, and I am just a Cop, on a Cop's salary."

Janie narrowed her eyes and said in a low voice "Doll, you show up at 'rox' and come see me dance? I'll give you all the dances you want for free, and I will break all the distance rules! I owe YOU after you got that Hector bullshit out of my life. I was thinking about takin' him back, and you showed me what he is. I owe you big time for that rescue. Not even Coast Guard! I mean: Shit. I was so snowed! Like I said, Doll: Free Dances for life. Hell, I'll even take you to bed. That would piss Mike off for sure. Hmmm..."

Janie looked up and touched her chin with her forefinger like she was thinking about it.

Angel grinned at that expression. "In a what goes round comes round kind of way, Morgan: Janie is the top dancer at 'rox' now. Like Sally, only way healthier frame of mind and body. Margie loves the hell out of you for her. I saw Janie at BeachView of course, and she was good there. She is better now."

Morgan looked at her friend quizzically "You have been to 'rox'?"

"Sure. To see Janie. Evie and her do a thing together too. Super sexy" Angel admitted.

"Huh. Evie did a thing with Sally. I never saw it of course, but it was supposed to be real 'garden of Eden' kind of thing." Morgan said.

"Girl: Come see me dance. I will make you switch sides, which like I said will really get up Mike's gorgeous nose because he wants you playing for the Het team. His Het team."

"I am not sure my heart can take that." Morgan admitted. "When you were naked at BeachView, after our interview? You just standing there? I thought you were the nicest looking woman in the place. Just standing there naked, you were more attractive than any of the others there dancing."

"Well, aren't you the sweetest thing?" Janie asked, grinning.

"Just telling you what I thought." Morgan said, her hands and shoulders in the 'what can you do?' position.

"Damn. I might just give you a whirl." Janie said. "I bet you are tasty when you are naked too."

"No special guy or guys in your life?" Morgan asked. Morgan, not being monogamous, did not assume anyone else was either.

"I am on a break from men. I decided I needed to get my head together. You walk into 'Beachview' and you saw what Hector was right off. Me? I was a complete fucking idiot." Janie complained.

"Janie: Hector had a line of women at 'Beachview' like no one I have ever met." Angel said emphatically, to try and get her friend to lighten up on herself. "Hell: Hector even had Morgan believing the Coast Guard BS till she looked into it. Give yourself a break. You didn't get snowed like I did either. I should know better, but look what Andrea did to me."

"Gave you the cutest little girl ever?" Janie asked.

Angel looked sheepish. "Yes, well that too."

"I take it my girl is sleeping?" Morgan asked.

"Yes, Morgan. YOUR girl is taking a nap." Angel said, then to Janie "I love working up here and working for Marvin, but I am in serious danger of losing my kid to this girl. Nakoma loves Morgan."

Janie grinned at that. "I am sure working here is way better than being a naked waitress at a strip club."

"So much..." Angel said fervently.

"You know, Morgan. You want a little cutie of your own, Mike will help you with that project." Janie said.

Angel interceded for Morgan on that idea. "Morgan has no shortage of help in that area. She talks about Mike's line like it's unique but she has a few guys around here willing to help her if she is so inclined."

Morgan added "Not sure how having a child of my own works with being a Cop, unless I keep the daddy around for the late night call-outs. Not ready to pick that man out. Eunice thinks I should just marry Ken."

Angel gave that a negative shake. "I like Eunice, but she is wrong. Ken is a nice guy. He is not your man. You like him. You will never

LOVE him. If you need to settle, take Wendell. You could fall for him, I think."

Morgan studied Angel for a moment and again wondered about her friends' ability to see things others can't or don't. That line of thought was nothing new to her. "Yes, well, since I am getting threats over him, I might have to leave the force to make that work, and then the whole point of having the stay at home man goes away. Catch-22. Also, not ready to just settle. I want to be sure."

The news about the threats made Angel sit back. "Wait: Threats over Wendell? Since when? Like with DeWayne?"

Morgan laid out the story of the MS-150 pictures and then gave Janie the background on DeWayne as well.

Janie said "Damn! I thought my life as a stripper was complicated! She-it. No one cares who the hell I fuck."

"As long as it is not Hector." Angel said firmly.

"Yeah: Ok. True. Be hard though, what with him being in the slam and all." Janie replied.

"What are you going to do about this, Morgan?" Angel asked, knowing her friend would not take anything like implied threats laying down.

"Me? I am going to see Janie dance tonight, I think. I get free dances, and she might jump me! Tuesday night, I am going out with Wendell, and then if he is interested, taking him home with me."

"Oh. You go! Right on!" Janie enthused. "Do me a large though: Don't bring your partner?"

Morgan agreed. "No. Places like strip clubs are not healthy for Sam. He has made a lot of progress, and I would not want to set him back. Also, a female cop taking her male partner to a strip club? Bad message there. Not only no, but hell no." Morgan paused, added "I think I will bring my truck. That parking lot is crowded as hell. I don't want any new door dings on my little car."

Angel laughed. "Your BABY, you mean."

"My other baby, but I wouldn't take Nakoma to 'rox' either." Morgan replied with a grin.

Morgan walked into the lobby of 'rox', and saw the only thing that had changed in it since she was last here was the lobby photographs. Some of them were new. Sally LeBlanc was gone. Janie and some other dancers pictures were now up on the walls instead.

Margie Allen had not been warned Morgan was coming, jumped up, and set her cigarette into an ashtray. "Morgan? Morgan Olsen? Who died this time? I'm not missing any girls!"

"Hi, Margie." Morgan pointed at her clothes. "I am off duty. Just came to see Evie, Janie and you. How are you?" Morgan smiled warmly and extended a hand.

"None of that. Give me a hug, if you are not here as a Cop!" Margie said firmly.

Morgan was starting to wonder about all the hugging. Janie hugged her hard when she left Angel's. Now Margie was glad to see her, at the hugging level of happiness as well?

"Really: things OK?" Morgan asked, taken aback at the warmth of the greeting.

"You got Sally's killer. Because of you, I have a new dancer that has eyeballs popping out and money flowing in. Janie dances like Sally, only better. She's a goddamn genuine brick shithouse. I loved Sally, but Janie is the real deal. Everyone likes her, and oh, by the way, since she started? Profits up nearly ten percent. Want to know another funny thing? I have not had to pay off a Vice cop in months." Margie enthused.

Morgan thought that was interesting. "Why not?"

"Don't be silly. You, girl." Margie said, grinning.

"Me? I did not do anything... Well, I sort of did? Not much though: I just went over to Vice after the Leblanc case was over to see if I could find out who was squeezing you. You know what? Blue wall, even against me. No one was talking. I pulled all the reports about here and looked through them. Clean. No violations AT ALL! You and I both know that is not true, but they had nothing on you."

"Like I said. You girl. They think YOU are taking a personal interest in here. YOU took down a cop. You have a rep: I know. I looked through Mike's clippings. It's like you have a private line to the Chron. 'Hero Cop takes down one of their own' kinda juicy headline bullshit! With press like that, no dirty Cop is going to give you a chance to take them down. I bet you all the free beer you can drink, and you KNOW what my prices are here." Margie grinned again. She looked Morgan over. "I should have known you was off duty. Look at you! Jeans and a jean jacket. It's a nice look for you but why you even wearing a jacket in this heat?"

"Even off duty, I am a Texas peace officer, Margie. That means I have a gun on me at all times, so I need to cover it up." Morgan explained. "I don't like ankle holsters, and my SIG is too big for one of those anyway. Even with a pea-shooter, ankle holsters suck. Rather just have my 9 and wear a jacket."

Margie nodded. "Well, in that case honey, it's drinks on the house. It's not a bribe if you are not working a case here. I am just glad to see your cute little ass. Well. Not that little, not like Evie's tiny buns, but you know what I mean."

"I will figure it out. Eventually." Morgan told her.

"Go on in, Hon. Janie should be up to dance soon. There is a hot bartender that will be glad to see you too." Margie gave Morgan a knowing look with that.

"So Janie tells me." Morgan shook her head. "Honestly Margie, I find that hard to believe."

"Oh, believe it Hon. You might starve as a dancer here despite your cute and curvy ass, but you turned Mikey's head, but good. He gets a royal stiffy just looking at that newspaper picture of ya. Git on in there."

Morgan followed Margie into the main room at 'rox'. The inside of the strip club was the same as it ever was, as near as Morgan could see. Tables with men. Naked waitresses milling about, squeezing by. The three-foot rule for lap dancers pushed down to inches. Loud music. Smoke that would be hell to get out of her hair, and which was why she had it in a tight braid: Minimize the follicular surface area for smoke to penetrate.

The bar had its usual empty barstools. 'rox' had been a convenience store in a previous life, and when built out to be a strip club, the bar had ended up starting just inside and to the right of the entrance to the main room. It was out of the way of traffic, and therefore no naked women brushed against you if you sat there. Morgan took a stool furthest away from the traffic patterns so she could just watch. It was like Las Vegas for Morgan: a study in human behavior.

Mike turned around and spotted her. His face split into a wide smile, revealing perfect teeth, His scruffy five o'clock shadow from five o'clock sometime last weekend. The gym-toned body Morgan remembered well.

Mike looked past Morgan, nodded, and came over to her. "Hey. Nice to see you again, Detective. Margie just signaled: Whatever you are drinking tonight is on her." Mike pretended to study Morgan. "You look like a Scotch lady, but I assume you are not drinking that hard tonight."

"Hi, Mike. Yes: I know you new headliner, Janie. Came to see her dance. I hear she is Sally level special. I never saw Sally dance, so I did not want to miss this. My friend, Angel, came here and watched our Janie dance too. Angel said I might want to take Janie home with me for a lost weekend kind of thing after seeing her dance."

Mike glance over at the stripper pole on the little stage near the TV, as always playing hardcore porn. "Yes: She is good. Best I have seen in a long time. Even better than Sally I think. More... Real? You don't get genuine in this biz often, but that's Janie. She is the real deal. Every curvy line of her."

Mike turned back to Morgan. "So. Beer? Not a wine girl. Flavor..."

"The Sierra Nevada pale ale, please." Morgan said, pointing that the glass front cooler on the back wall of the bar. "I saw it last time I was here. You saw me looking at it, Oh Carnac the Magnificent."

Mike raised a hand. "Got me. Yeah. I saw you lusting after it. Coming up. You are no fun to mind fuck at all. Who is Carnac?"

"Old Johnny Carson gag on late night TV. Before our time, but I know about it because it is a classic. In case you missed it when I was here last time, I am a Detective, Mike. I can show you my shield again even. You will have to do better than that. Also: beer drinkers tend to be whiskey drinkers when they go for harder liquor, and people that like IPA's tend to be Scotch drinkers. My personal observation only: no studies to back me on that assertion. However, based upon your little routine there, you seem to have the same opinion of who likes what." Morgan said, accepting the bottle and the chilled glass, and pouring it herself.

Mike watched, said, "You should be the bartender and I should be the customer." Mike tapped her glass on the side. "Got it. You like to keep the head down, more carbonation in the beer. Preference noted, Detective."

There were any number of much more flirtatious answers to that. Morgan chose "Correct".

Mike had to work, so Morgan watched him. Experienced bartenders are dancers of a sort. Their moves more with their upper bodies, but every time he needed the beer key, he pulled it, spun it, opened the bottle, spun it again, and slid it back into his back pocket, in lovely, smooth motions. The back pocket's general vicinity also was very nice.

When Janie came on stage to dance, Morgan waved, and Janie waved back.

Mike brought Morgan a fresh beer, already poured. Morgan assumed whenever she had a beer near Mike in the future, that was going to be how that worked, then realized somewhere along the way she already had chosen to have some kind of future with the Sexually Oriented Business Bartender and Bouncer. She guessed it was the beer key in the back pocket that put it over the top. Oh well: Only human.

Morgan wondered how the Cabal was going to like that idea. Whatever their plans for her were, did they include a man that was the 'right' ethnicity by their 'standards' but was in this particular profession? That was getting ahead of herself though. Morgan was a try before she bought kind of person. Just because she liked him, and liked the way he looked did not mean he was a keeper.

Morgan changed her focus because of why she was here. Janie was good. Her pole work was not as athletic as some but was far more phallic. Her natural body being slowly revealed in classic burlesque moves, and Janie's happy eyes as she looked around the room pulling in the audience like a magnet. The room loved her, and she loved the way the room responded to her, in a sexual feedback loop that Morgan found affecting. For perhaps the first time in her life, she understood this aspect about men, because she wanted Janie to take her clothes off faster too.

Once Janie was naked other than her heels and some flashing jewels on her neck and wrists, the hooting and hollering was louder than the music, and that was saying something.

When she was done, Janie blew Morgan a kiss and winked her way. Morgan returned the gestures. Morgan was amazed at the way she tingled. She sat here the night she interviewed all the dancers, and the same at 'Beachview' and that never happened before.

Mike came back to Morgan. He looked sad. "OK. I had you pegged all wrong it seems."

Morgan looked at Mike over her beer glass as she sipped in no little amusement. "Oh?" She asked.

"Yeah: I thought you were into men, Detective. Hell, I thought Janie was into men. That last thing that just happened there? It was like she wanted YOU. All those guys out there kept looking at you to see why she wanted one person in particular during that dance. Jesus: I may need a cold shower."

"Well, Mike, as far as I know, Janie and I are both male-oriented when it comes to our gender preference." Morgan looked over at Janie, working a table. "I will not lie, however: If I was going to make an exception to that, it would be Janie. She is as sexy as I have ever seen, and I'll try most things at least once. It is hard to condemn something for one's self if you have not tried it. I do except obvious things like hard drugs from that." Morgan indicated the empty stage. "Not to speak ill of the dead, but it is hard to imagine Sally being as good or better than that."

Mike nodded in obvious relief. "Ok. Good. Whew. May still need a cold shower...."

"That is a myth. Cold showers make you cold and horny, rather than hot and horny." Morgan inserted.

"... And. Great. Just what I needed to hear." Mike sighed in an exaggerated way.

The porn movie that had been paused during the dance was restarted. Janie was working the room, stopping and doing three minutes or so dances at a table, and getting large bills placed in a garter she had put on since the stripping. If you were the man ordering the dance, that was all the touching you got. Sliding fingers along her skin as you placed money in the garter on her thigh.

Mike said to Morgan, in slightly distracted tones as he watched the room: "I have to watch these guys close. A few try to head north from the garter, and Janie doesn't work that way. The Reg's know that of course, but they already creamed their jeans from that dance anyway, right? It's the guys I have not seen before I have to watch. She usually takes care of it, but you know. Just in case."

Morgan liked Mike's protective thing. Then she thought about that: she HATED men being protective of her, but Janie was out there naked, and for some reason that made a difference to her. She realized she felt the same way: She felt protective of Janie as well, and that was odd given how little time she has known her.

Much more thought required.

Janie was working her way across the room to where Morgan sat. That diagonal trip was going to net her many hundreds of dollars in the garter. When a song came on the club sound system, she danced with what Morgan could only call joy. The faces of the men that her hips and breasts swung near were rapt and grinning.

Mike said in a continuation of his comment "Someday, a guy is going to be needing his hands smashed up a bit. Janie is good with the come-hither expression solidly mixed with warning looks, but... Someday."

"I like that you do that. Shitty enough job without getting mauled." Morgan replied to that.

Mike looked a little embarrassed. He flipped that around. "See, that's the thing about you, Detective. You come here. You don't judge. You care about the girls, and you recognize that this job really sucks, all at the same time."

"Mike: You know my name is Morgan, right?" Morgan asked. She pointed at a newspaper clipping taped to the mirror on the barback. "Says it right there in fact." She pointed several more times. "Also there. And there. And in the caption of that one with my actual picture. See? Look. Same woman." Morgan pointed at her face.

Perfect teeth appeared. "Oh, yes. I know. I just did not want to push my luck with you." Mike said in a confessional tone.

"Why is that?" Morgan asked.

He opened his arms to include the bar. "So you will come back again. You know you are never paying for a drink here ever again. Right?"

"So I have been told." Morgan said. "Still, I do not normally drink in places like this. No offense."

"None taken." Mike said. Then "Where DO you like to drink?"

"Quiet places, where I can hear myself think. And also so I can hear my date talk." Morgan said.

Mike nodded, then nodded a different way. Towards Janie, who had arrived, and who hugged Morgan happily. Morgan returned the embrace and enjoyed not only Janie's skin but Mike's expression.

"What did you think?" Janie asked, leaning back and keeping her hands on Morgan's shoulders. Morgan saw Mike bite a knuckle.

"Janie, so much better than BeachView. This place suits you. You look amazing out there. You should never wear clothes. This is the real you. Like this." Morgan told the dancer.

Morgan grinned and bent over slightly to slide a twenty dollar bill into Janie's garter. Mike wiped his face dramatically with a bar towel.

"I need to get more change. Is there an ATM here?" Morgan said. "I was not expecting to need it like this."

"Doll, are you HITTING on me?" Janie asked. "Because if you are, like I said, I'll give it a try..."

"Not hitting on you: Paying a fine as hell dancer who just made me tingle. If I was hitting on you, according to Mike, I would head north from that garter with my fingers about four inches and then Mike, being a big old softy but a protector of you, well: he would have to hurt me."

Morgan grinned at Janie and Mike's expressions. "Also, I AM just being honest." Morgan nodded out to the table area. "You look happy out there. You have these guys under your spell. Me too. Captivating. That is the right word. You are captivating. I need more money."

"I gotta go dance some more, but you stay right there." Janie turned slightly to leave, then back to face Morgan. "You know what? Someday girl, you and I are going to try it. I want to see YOU naked, and even more, shall we say, captivated. Bet I can make you come... I KNOW you can make me come. That idea? Makes me tingly too, and I can use that feeling out there! These guys will like it that I am turned on."

Janie grinned at that and spun off back into the main room, at a different angle to harvest some more cash.

"God." Mike said emphatically.

"God? Just 'god'?" Morgan asked. "That seems like an understatement." Morgan watched Janie dance for a moment. "I bet she can make me come too. Look at her go!"

"Yeah: God. I don't have a chance with you if SHE is after you." Mike looked sad.

"Yeah. Right." Morgan said with no little eye roll to the hangdog expression. "You just want to be there if it happens, Mister. Or maybe that is WHEN it happens given that last comment. You just want to be in the middle."

"Damn straight! Then, after that, I can die a happy man." Mike enthused, then asked "Beer?"

"Not yet. Are you trying to get me drunk?" Morgan asked. "Because if I am drunk, there is no informed consent."

Mike froze solid at that comment, not sure exactly how to take it.

Morgan pointed at a waitress waiting at the other end of the bar with a tray. "I think she wants you."

CHAPTER FIVE

Second Body

Morgan yawned. Sam looked at her with no sympathy at all. "You partied all weekend. What you deserve."

"You are just angry because you didn't." Morgan replied.

"You really went back to 'rox'?" Sam was downright incredulous.

"I really did. Angel went to see Janie dance, said I should. So I did. It was nice to see Margie and Evie as well. All are well. I did not call you for obvious reasons. For one thing, your therapist, Betty, would flat kill me, and be right to do it. Not a good place for you." Morgan said, reasonably

"No. I am glad you didn't. I just can't believe YOU had fun there." Sam said "It's a strip club. Where women take off their clothes! You are a woman!"

"Sam, am I happy there are places that debase and demean women? No. Every magazine cover I see does that. Ever makeup ad. Sex sells, and sexualization of women is literally everywhere. I like tilting at windmills as much as the next costumed crime fighter, but there is also this: I like Margie, Evie, and Janie. Sue me: I just do. They have shitty jobs, but they are not lesser people because of that. Besides, I just found out this last weekend that Vice leaves 'rox' alone because they are afraid of ME. Afraid what I might find out about them if I started looking too hard. If I can protect my new friends that way, and keep their jobs from being a little less scummy, I am good with that. Do I wish Janie and Evie would get better jobs? Sure. If they want to do that, I will help there too. Also, we did not really party ALL weekend. We just sat in the club at the bar, lights up and Mike kept the beer and wine flowing after hours so we could sit and catch up. It was nice."

Morgan skipped over putting money in Janie's garter. Sam would have a coronary.

Sexual preferences and roles, plus many other things in that general area were a source of disagreement between the partners. Those disagreements did not in any way involve raised voices or over-the-top emotional remonstrations. They were nonetheless heartfelt on each side and had a long history. They were not that far apart in age, but they were light years apart in upbringing with Morgan being far more open-minded about such things.

Despite this, Sam looked thoughtful rather than disapproving. "Vice is AFRAID of you?" he asked. Of all the things Morgan had mentioned, that was what caught his attention the most.

"That is what Margie said. She has not had to pay graft since you and I started working the Leblanc case there. Seems that us arresting Bob for Sally's death has had an unintended benefit. The Cabal made me their poster child in the papers for whatever the hell reason, and I am now also apparently famous inside the force as the Detective that arrests Cops. I can use that to help people. I like it." Morgan ended that with an evil grin. "Mike has the Chron article about it, with the picture of you and I walking down the steps, so your picture is up in the club as a hero now."

"You call them the Cabal now?" Sam asked, once again selecting one of the items of interest and ignoring the rest.

"Not like they have introduced themselves. It seems like as good a label as any. If I knew for a fact they are KKK rather than KKK-like, I would call them that." Morgan pointed out.

"OK. That is funny. Also, glad this is all on your Rep, and not on mine, Poster-child. I am your silent partner." Sam said.

"You do not get off that easily, Sam. You are in the picture next to me, in the bar." Morgan said with a grin. "I plan to have lunch with Janie, Evie, Angel, my Nakoma, and Margie soon if you want to come. It would be nice if Janie did not think you are a scum-bucket."

"Gee. Thanks." Sam said. "Maybe. We'll see. Does Angel know Nakoma is yours?"

"Sure. It is a race. I think Nakoma will call me 'mommy' first."

"You breastfeeding her?" Sam asked "if not, you are doomed in that race. Sorry to inform..."

"No: Apparently you have to be the one to actually give birth to have the milk part working. Anyway: About lunch: Up to you. I know you are not comfortable with women that take off their clothes for a living, but it is not as if Pam or 'Sally Ride' or whoever is going to be there. I did not like them either. I am just amazed Pam has not landed her sugar daddy yet."

"Me either." Sam gave that a very 'who cares' shrug. "Guess even the guys that go to those places pick up on that. It's not like Pam is subtle about it. I just missed it with my wife is all. I am smarter now."

Morgan looked at her partner seriously. "Last time Janie saw you, you were a space case, so I have no idea how that works for lunch. All the girls at the BeachView thought you were a scuzzball, but that was because you would not pay for a dance. Seeing you in your natural habitat might change their impression of you, assuming you don't freeze up. Not pressuring you, and Betty may think this is a terrible idea. I just wish you could see them the way I do. Nice ladies with crappy jobs. I'm a nice lady, even if the Cabal thinks I am a slut. My job is to look at dead people all the time. Speaking of that, I think I'll call Cooper, and see if he has anything for us on that kid in the alley."

Morgan was reaching for her desk phone to call Cooper when JJ came out of his office and dropped a slip of paper on the desk, equidistant between Sam and Morgan. "It's Monday morning. You can tell because you two just caught another body."

JJ was improving. In the old days, he would have handed it to Sam, and then Sam would have handed it to Morgan without looking at it.

"Are you sure you want to park here? There is an illegal place just right over there." Morgan pointed it out unhelpfully. Sam liked to park his Tahoe just wherever, and fix the tickets if he got them. Morgan teased him without mercy about the habit.

Sam looked over at the other side of the street with the "No Parking here to curb" sign.

"Be harder to get in there than where I parked." Sam said

"Yes, but where you parked is legal. I... I don't know if I can deal with that. I mean, sure, if I was driving, this is where we would park, but it is YOU." Morgan laid it on.

Sam gave Morgan his best withering stare, to no effect. "At least we aren't in your little death trap."

"You know, You are the only man in my life that complains about my Miata." Morgan and Sam walked to the visible clump of uniformed officers, standing by an open gate in a brick wall.

"Yes, well, there is a reason for that." Sam said. He stopped himself before he said more.

As this badinage was about to come to an end as they approached the job, Morgan tossed what she knew would be the last word: "Because you are the only chickenshit."

Sam did not respond to the 'chickenshit' shot, because where it led was an old conversation. Morgan saw Sam clamp down his full response about the men in her life, and was even fairly sure she knew what it was. Sam thought she should just pick one man and stick with him for a while. He had no opinion of who that was or should be, he just thought dating should be a one person at a time activity. Serially monogamous. To Sam's credit, he did not care if Morgan saw Wendell, Ken, DeWayne, or whoever. It was not their skin color, just that women should not play the field. Could men? Well, sure because boys are boys...

Being Morgan's partner made it so Sam could not say such things with any assurance they were correct any longer anyway. Morgan had not judged HIM over his issues with women in the past, including two divorces and being in therapy. She supported him loyally and even offered to help him pay to make sure he stayed with his shrink. He could do no less for her, even if he did not completely understand her behavior.

Entering the gate, and walking up to a loading dock area, the two detectives crossed to the large dumpster, angled to be picked up by a straight shot through the gate. There was a space behind the dumpster to allow it to be lifted and angled without backing and filling. The body had been discovered here.

The young man was a slender Caucasian, somewhere in his late teens Morgan estimated. He lay on his back, the blood pool smaller than the boys from the alley had been. Morgan assumed he had died more quickly, and the asphalt surface was more porous than the concrete of the alley.

Morgan's cell rang. She looked at it, then stepped away from the body and the cluster of officers near it. "Hi, Mike. Sorry. Can I call you back? I am working a crime scene right now."

Mike Doyle, bartender and bouncer, was taken aback by the quick answer and wave off. "Uh, sure? Why did you even answer?"

"Because Mike, after last weekend I did not want you to think I am giving you the brush off. I am not: I just have a dead body here that requires my full attention. Talk later." Morgan hung up and returned to the body. "Sorry. My Dad." Morgan explained to the various cops standing around.

The call came in about the body at 8:32 AM, when Thomas Pi, the shipping and receiving clerk, had been hauling trash out from the loading dock to the dumpster.

Morgan noted that the loading dock back door and roll-up steel door were both closed, presumably to keep out the humidity. Cardboard boxes for shipping can turn to mush in Houston air, given time. She and Sam would go talk to Thomas Pi in the shipping and Receiving office in a few minutes, once she had the situation properly framed in her mind.

Morgan could compartmentalize with the best of them so Mike and last weekend were filed for future reference and action and faded from her active mind as she absorbed her immediate surroundings and its occupants. Which teams were on the scene.

No CSU. No M.E. This made sense: the Uni's, Sam, and Morgan all came from the neighborhood storefront office. The other units had farther to travel.

Morgan, careful to not touch the edges of the pool of blood, kneeled and leaned over the young man's head, trying to get a better look at the back of the skull, but that was impossible.

The blood looked to Morgan to be fresher, but the surface made that hard to know.

Close up, the young man looked even younger than her original estimate. His face had the very light down of a beard just now coming in. Light and blondish red. The same color and a similar texture to the fine hair on his head.

Close into the body Morgan could detect the distinctive coppery odor of blood, mixed very lightly with the pungent smell of gunpowder. It was at the edge of her ability to detect, but the scent was there. That meant to Morgan a close in shot, as the open air of the loading dock would have dissipated anything not actually on the body.

"Shit." Morgan said as she stood up. Sam did not offer a hand, as he knew being gallant was not appreciated in a professional setting.

"What?" Sam asked, looking down at the young face.

"Gun powder scent. Back of the head shot even if not behind the ear. No through and through. Probably a .22 at point blank again. Damn it."

"Serial?" Sam asked.

"I guess we will soon see. I wish I had talked to Cooper already this morning. Let us go there next, after here."

Morgan looked around, saw the camera mounted up on the wall between the back door and the roll-up door. It pointed at the dock, but if it had any kind of wide angle lens, it would be able to 'see' the dumpster too.

The loading dock was in an enclosed yard, therefore any cameras from the street side of things would only be able to see the gate. On the other hand, knowing who went through that gate would be very interesting. The paths to the murder scene in the alleyway had been wide, well lit, but had no cameras. The ends of the alley were open to the street, and on one side to an open lot. Here Morgan had a brick wall, an enclosed service area, a gate, and a camera. As a strictly fact-based person, Morgan tried not to feel hopeful that they had caught a break on this one.

Morgan walked over to the gate to the loading dockyard area. It was a standard sliding mechanism rather than a swing-gate, and when open ran along the brick wall enclosing the street side of the yard area. The black painted steel gate was long and had vertical bars with a single wheel at the end that ran in a depression in the ground to keep the gate lined up with the brick wall on the opposite side of the opening. A chain connected above the wheel to a vertical bar and ran through a fixed motor housing to open and close it.

Once Morgan was close, she wondered with a sinking feeling if the gate even worked. The chain was covered in rust. This type of mechanism is common in apartment complexes and other 'gated communities'. She had seen many of them in her life. They all had one thing in common: A working gate would have a greased chain.

Morgan next walked outside the gate, and around to the brick wall and she studied the keypad/call box inset into the brick. She had noticed it when she and Sam were walking up and she had been calling him a 'chickenshit'. The plastic call button was broken, and it appeared that the sun's UV radiation had over the years deteriorated the plastic to mostly looking like aged bakelite. The steel plate the keypad and speaker resided in was slightly askew as well. Morgan pulled out a penknife from her jacket pocket and wiggled her blade between the plate and the wall, and it was loose. Not secured to the wall. The plate and the box it was attached to came easily out of its recess, enough to reveal the spider nests inside. Morgan pushed it back into the wall with her knife, now closed.

Sam had watched that procedure and understood what it meant. This gate was open last night and probably has been for years.

"Traffic cam way down there." Sam pointed up the street to the nearest intersection.

Morgan looked, scanned around. Sighed. "That will be useless. No way it can see all the way down here with any resolution. At best, we get a time of death."

"Yep. Still, more than we had on the last one. Maybe." Sam agreed.

"Let us go see if we can get anything from the Shipping clerk, Thomas Pi." Morgan said.

On the loading dock via concrete stairs on one side, the Detectives found the steel back door was locked, so Morgan knocked. Then again. As she raised her hand for a third, louder set of raps, the door swung in. This revealed a man of Chinese ancestry, somewhere in his early twenties.

"Thomas Pi?" Morgan asked, holding up her badge wallet.

He nodded, said "Yes. Come in, please." He stood aside and looked past the Detectives at the cluster of people and the body.

"I am Detective Morgan Olsen, Homicide. This is my partner Sam Parker. We need to ask you some questions about when and how you discovered the body?"

"Sure, Sure. Come on in over here, and have a seat."

They walked through a second door and into the loading dock area proper. There was a tall steel desk, covered in all the usual loading dock things. Tape. Labels. Markers. A phone set with many buttons. On shelves over the desk were envelopes and unassembled boxes of various sizes. On the ground by the steel roll-up door were stacks of assembled boxes, labeled and ready for pickup.

"I'll get another chair. Be right back!" Thomas said, and left quickly out of the dock and into the hall. Almost immediately the sound of wheels to a rolling chair was heard coming back up the hall. It clacked over the threshold to the loading docks inside door, and Thomas placed it so that they could sit side by side. Their chairs were both office chairs and infinitely better than JJ's despite looking a little worse for wear. Thomas was up on a higher chair more like a barstool with a back, meant for the tall steel table he clearly worked at.

Morgan was not intimidated by looking upwards, so sat and said: "Thank you." Sam would hate this relative body position thing. He was big on the concept, whether he knew it consciously or not, of 'positional authority'. If Thomas turned out to be a suspect, they could change their relative positions easily enough. Morgan assigned a very low probability to the idea of Thomas Pi being the killer.

"Thomas, a few framing questions. How long have you worked here?" Morgan opened with.

"About two years?" in the questioning way people have when they are asked a question they are not exactly sure of the answer to, and they are talking to a cop.

"Have you always worked here, in the shipping and receiving area?" Morgan swirled a fingertip at the room.

"Yes. My father owns the building, and this is a job he gave me while I am in school. I switched to night school this last year so I can be here during the day. Also, it gives me time to study." Thomas indicated a stack of textbooks off to one side. She did not look as she had noted them on the way in and while waiting for the chair. The top one was 'Accounting'.

"You are a Business Major?" Morgan asked.

"Uhm... Yes?" Thomas seemed puzzled. She had not looked at his books when he had pointed them out.

"She does that all the time, kid. Don't worry about it. Just realize lying to her is never a safe thing to do." Sam said, rolling into the 'bad cop' role easily.

"OK? Why would I lie about something?" Thomas asked, confused.

Thomas Pi clearly had no idea that he was going to be looked at and ruled out as a suspect.

"Your father owns this building? I assume it has about eight or nine different tenants at the moment?" Morgan diverted.

That made Thomas even more confused. "Nine. Yes."

"I assume that you have some vacant space right now? Not fully occupied?" Morgan continued.

"Yes...." Thomas agreed.

"As a business major, do you know if the current level of occupancy is profitable for your father?" Morgan closed in on her first point.

"Huh... I am not sure. I don't see that part. The money things. Not yet. I think so?" Thomas was completely adrift with this line of questions and the rapid-fire correct assumptions Morgan was making.

Morgan switched lines of inquiry, now that he was off balance. "Do you know who does security for this building? Is it in-house? Or do you have a service?"

"This is the Montrose. We don't have security. Crime is not really high here, other than some tagging and stuff like that now and then. People dumping stuff in our dumpster." Thomas explained as if Morgan was new to the area. Thomas pointed at a machine on small wheels against the wall. "We get tagged, I go power wash it back off, and the brick gets cleaned. Someone dumps their trash in our dumpster, it doesn't cost us any more to have it picked up. It gets annoying when they dump a couch or something like that. Then I get to break it apart and put it inside the dumpster. You know."

"Community service trash?" Sam asked.

"Why we have the big dumpster like that. If we were fully occupied I guess we'd need it too, but this place is a grungy old building and eventually, Father will just sell it for ten times what he paid for it." Thomas Pi explained.

"That desire to sell this building is why nothing works here?" Morgan asked. "Your father is just waiting and timing the housing market?"

"Yes. You could tear this place down and build a massive condo tower here. Be worth millions."

"I therefore assume that the security camera on the wall out there is not in working order?" Morgan asked.

"It works." Thomas said, adding "The recorder doesn't. We can look at the screen and see what's going on out there. I can see who is delivering things." Thomas spun around and turned on a twelve inch screened TV set, housed in a recess under one of the shelves. It came on with a black and white image of the loading dock. A raster line slowly rolled down the screen.

"I keep it turned off till I hear a truck or whatever. The gate is broken, but the bell for the big door works too, so delivery or pick up people ring and I look and then roll up. Not like anyone is going to rob this place during the day. Or night. Or on the weekend. The nine businesses in here: none of them are cash business kind of places. Nothing anyone wants to steal unless you want Salvation Army waiting room furniture and Goodwill rebuilt computers. Why risk jail when you can pick everything in here up cheap someplace."

Morgan had been afraid of Thomas's responses to most of that line of questioning, but it was framing up as she suspected after seeing the gate and call box. A place people knew about from around the area, and that probably knew the security camera was useless. If there was a third party monitoring the camera, there would be security service signs, but they did not even have the fake ones people buy to pretend big brother is watching.

Morgan switched her line of inquiry again. "Thomas, you called in your discovery at 8:32AM. Can you walk Sam and I through the sequence of events?"

"Sure." Thomas placed a hand on the high desk. "I got in here about

8:00 AM or so. I came in through the front door, not the dock. Through that door and to the right. I had left some trash in here to work on this morning because I knew I didn't have any deliveries scheduled, and I had a test at school so I wanted to get over there and have a quick review before I took it. My girlfriend goes to school there too, so we studied there, I took my test, we went and got some food afterward. Taco Bell, you know?"

Morgan nodded to that, agreeing she did, in fact, know about Taco Bell.

Thomas continued. "Anyway, this place is a pit, but Father sells the fact that I work on the dock as a service. I'm free, they just pay for postage and stuff. That way I have a job, and he has a way to keep people here that would move out and go over to Harwin or something. You know Harwin..."

"Yes: A large number of import stores over there." Morgan said. "I bought some Sari silk there recently."

"Right! Exactly! This part of town is getting expensive so everyone is bailing. Soon it's going to be all Starbucks and stuff. Anyway, I had boxes to break down, and some other trash, so I did that, went to take them to the dumpster, saw that kid laying there, tossed my stuff in the dumpster real fast, and ran back in here and called 911 from my phone there." Thomas Pi thumbed over at the multi-button set on the desk.

"Commkey system. I assume all the various businesses in the building can call you that way?" Morgan said.

"Sure. Exactly." Thomas agreed.

"You go back out after you called 911 and wait out there with the body?" Sam asked.

"Hell no! I sat right here. I am a business major. I don't do dead bodies." Thomas scowled.

"You recognize that young man at all? See him around here ever?" Morgan asked.

"I did not look at him close." Thomas looked horrified at the thought. "I just looked long enough to see he was not breathing. Had to watch his chest for a few moments. Like that. But, No Ma'am. I have never seen him before."

"That camera screen was on or off? You watch the scene out there at all from in here? After you called?" Morgan asked.

"I didn't think to turn it on." Thomas Pi gave the camera monitor a guilty glance. "I was in here just kind of shaking at first. I have never seen a dead person before, so I was sitting here getting myself under control, you know? I knew you guys would want to talk to me, and I didn't want to be a wreck."

"How long has that gate to the yard area been broken?" Sam asked.

"I have no idea, Sir." Thomas looked embarrassed, presumably on behalf of his father. "I have been here two years. It has not worked since I have been here."

"You can see the hall and the door to the loading dock from here. Has anyone else come from the main part of the building and looked out the back door onto the crime scene since you arrived?" Morgan asked.

"No, Ma'am. Just me. I haven't talked to or seen anyone. You all got here fast!" Thomas Pi seemed amazed at the police response time.

"Our station is close." Sam explained. "Does anyone else have a key to the back door. A clicker remote perhaps to open the roll-up door? Anything like that?"

"Father has a key to the people door, of course. The big delivery door behind you there is manual. No motor so no clicker. You have to be inside to open it." Thomas pointed up to the top of the overhead door mechanism. "You have to pull those chains. It's not hard. Just takes a lot of hand over hand. I think there might be a way to stick in a crank handle up there too, but I never got up there and looked. My father told me he had to replace this door a few years ago because the motorized one was broken and cost too much to fix."

Sam looked around behind him and up at the mechanism. "Oh. I saw those green and red buttons by the door there and thought they did something."

"They used to. Like I said, now you have to be inside to open it because those chains are only in here. You undo the latch over there to unlock it, which you also have to be inside for, and then you pull on that chain. It's a loop, so to close it, you just pull on the other side." Thomas pointed as he described.

"No resident would ever enter the building this way? Via the dock?" Morgan concluded.

"They couldn't normally. If they were walking by, peered into the dockyard from the sidewalk, saw I was in here doing a delivery or something, they might use the shortcut, but other than that, no. Not saying that has NEVER happened, but it's rare. You have to be coming in at the exact right time. To go out I guess they could: the door you knocked on opens from the inside, but no one ever does. I guess they are just used to going the main route. If you go out that back way like for a smoke or something if you want back in, you gotta go out the gate, up the walk, and back around to the front."

"No designated smoking area?" Morgan asked.

"Up on the roof." Thomas pointed up. "Another selling point, actually. You can kill yourself with a view."

"You are not a smoker I take it." Sam said.

"No, sir. I was born and raised in this country, and I saw all the films at school about what that does to you. Besides, my girlfriend would dump me if I was. She says she doesn't want to kiss an ashtray." Thomas Pi explained.

"Good reasons." Sam commended.

Morgan and Sam watched CSU process the scene. Once they were done, Morgan turned the boys head to the side to see the entry wound. Straight shot to the back of the skull. Small caliber. Close range. Stippling. It was as she suspected from her earlier inspection when all she had to go on was the pool of blood and the extremely slight odor of burnt gunpowder. She looked up at Sam and he nodded his understanding of the wound.

"I know you are not a betting woman, but my money is on this being the same shooter." Sam commented.

"Probably." Morgan said standing. "Same MO. Same caliber. The same area of town. Same age victim. It stacks up as a fairly safe bet... As long as we are using YOUR money."

Morgan walked around the immediate area of the crime scene. She paused here and there, arms crossed and studied it: Looked at the body from various approach angles. It bothered her, and Morgan kept moving around until she found what she was looking for. Sam watched her process without comment. At one point she knelt and squinted. Opened her eyes wider. Tilted her head. Held her hands out to frame the body now at a distance from her. Morgan stood up and called out to the lead CSU tech, Ann-Marie Base. "Ann-Marie! Can you get this area here processed? There is blood on the ground over here." Morgan pointed down at an angle a foot or so in front of her.

Ann-Marie came over and looked at what Morgan was pointing at.

"Shit." Ann-Marie said, more as a comment than a curse.

"From here to there. Drag marks. You can see the gravel of the asphalt slightly disturbed. Very subtle, but just along there... See it?" Morgan indicated the line with gloved fingers.

Ann-Marie nodded yes. "I see it. On it. Good catch. It's almost invisible. Why did you think to look over here?"

Morgan made a face. "I did not like the setup, Ann-Marie. Not at all. Sam and I were talking about how this murder is like the boy from last Friday, but it is not the same and it bothered me. For example: the body laying on its back. That made no sense given the entry wound. On the ground over there: Not much blood for a head wound. I think it went down this way: Perp shot the kid here. The kid dropped face first to the ground, just there." Morgan pointed at a few slightly darker, barely visible spots on the asphalt. "The murderer did not want the body out here, visible from the street through the gate. They dragged him over there behind the dumpster to hide him, and they flipped him over. At that point he was still alive, but only barely. Also, when I lifted the head, I saw blood on his shirt-back and the shirt was not touching the blood pool that was over there, because the unevenness of the ground made the blood run away from the body, in the direction of the crown of the head, not the shirt. Therefore the blood on his shirt came from when he was face down, and probably his head jutted backward because of his chin." Morgan touched the bottom of her chin and tilted her head back.

"I also saw a few scrapes on the chin, but no bruising, so they occurred just prior to death." Morgan tapped her chin to indicate where.

Ann-Marie looked at the angle, then the ground. "Should be some skin just about there on the ground then. If it's there, we'll find it."

Giving the drag marks wide berth, Morgan walked along them, Ann-Marie carefully following. "Shoe scuffs here. Faint, but gravel pushed at an angle to the line of travel. Little arcs here and here and here. Rotated, like pulling weight. Not very big feet based on the size of the arcs. Matches the height estimate from last week. I guessed about five seven to five eight and Cooper gave that a preliminary confirmation. This looks like size seven or eight shoes, again at a guess. That fits."

Morgan paused to point at another item on the ground. "Some blood here again, but damn near the same color as the asphalt. Pulling his body along the ground by the arms or shoulders so the killer might have gotten blood on them from this. I think they stepped in a few drops right here." Morgan pointed.

Ann-Marie agreed. "I'll get some hi-contrast stuff going here. There. Over here." Ann-Marie waved back along their line of travel. "Damn it!, I wish Bob were here to shoot this... Opps. Sorry." Ann-Marie looked horrified at her faux-pas.

"I agree, Ann-Marie. Completely. Best crime scene photog we had." Morgan said.

Ann-Marie looked at Morgan closely to see if she was really as OK with her getting called out like that as it seemed. "Still. Sorry, Morgan. I am sure you get enough shit over that as it is. Don't need it from me too."

"For what it is worth, Ann-Marie: Bob and I are still friends. He does not blame me for what happened." Morgan reassured.

That got wide eyes. "Really? Wow. Did not see that coming. You arrest a guy, he usually takes that personally, you know?"

"He felt guilty. He killed the woman he loved. He was glad to not have to live the lie anymore." Morgan explained.

"I knew Bob's marriage was shit. He slept around a little before... Her. Sad, you know? Just sad." Ann-Marie sighed to punctuate.

"In so many ways. True story: I went out a few times in College with him. He was never my type, but I liked him. After this, he has had his world destroyed. Lost his job. His wife left him. For all that, Bob seems to be, for lack of a term, better? More real?" Morgan did not normally share personal details like this, but Ann-Marie was a good person, and a fellow cop, and she had to deal with the same sexist BS Morgan did all the time on the force.

"Well, next time you see Bob, tell him I said 'Hi'. Back to work..." Ann-Marie and her paper-booted team began processing the new evidence.

Morgan stood back and looked along the lines from where the body really went down to where it was found. It made far more sense to her now, seeing the crime scene in this way. A surreptitious meeting in dockyard with the gate that never closed? Perhaps a 'pst, come here behind the dumpster' call out in the dark. A refusal to step back there so they took a chance and killed the young man here and then hid the body quickly. Stripped it of all identification. Again.

It was cold-blooded killing, but it was also being lured here by someone. If the killer was the same as the young man from last Friday, then both boys probably knew their killer. Trusted them.

Sam crossed to Morgan and looked back at the gate and the street. He sighed. "Once again, unless someone is walking directly by on the street, no one sees this go down."

Morgan gestured at the building and upwards. "I guess they could be looking out one of the upper story windows in the building there, but they all have blinds, and they all are shut. West-facing windows. No one wants all the heat in their office. The building is old, but the windows are all sealed, so you can't open them even if you wanted a breeze, and no one would want that in May in Houston."

Sam looked up and down the side of the building. "I guess this means we go see Cooper next. The kid from the alley and this kid: Same MO."

"Your favorite place. The Morgue." Morgan said. "At least you can legally park there too unless you are careful. This might be a red letter day for you. No tickets to fix."

"I'll bite. I did not hear what you said to Ann-Marie. Why did you think the body dropped there? Why didn't you like the setup?" Sam pointed over to where a CSU tech was carefully looking at the ground with an ultraviolet light.

Morgan explained her thinking. The same thoughts she had shared with Ann-Marie.

Sam rubbed his mustache. Tilted his Texas Ranger looking cowboy hat back. Shook his head. "I got the parlor trick on the loading dock and how you knew he was a business major. You saw the textbooks. How you knew the number of residents: you read the mail slots. Impressed Thomas Pi. I missed this one. It bugged me the kid was on his back, but I didn't know WHY it was bugging me. That is how come I'm the junior partner... Let's go see Cooper, so you two geniuses can rub foreheads together or whatever it is you do to communicate."

"It is completely non-verbal, Sam." Morgan explained with the smallest of smiles. "Cooper dances in a particular way, I know the bullet came from the East or the North or from a particular patch of clover. Whatever the case is. I dance out questions, he wiggles out answers. It is very complicated and hard to master."

Morgan enjoyed Sam's look of exasperation.

CHAPTER SIX

Morgue

Morgan waved Sam inside. "Go on ahead. I need to make a call. Be right there."

Sam nodded and went in, not totally happy to be in the building without Morgan there with him. Cooper is her buddy, not his, though since Morgan explained the M.E. hated being called by Sam's nickname for him, which had been 'Coop', they had been getting along better.

Sam had also stopped riffing on Morgan's name when she told him she also hated nicknames. To his credit, Sam never tried 'Morgana' as one of the nicknames he had for her. He was moderately sure that would get him a magic wand inserted into his ear.

Morgan pressed the 'call back' button on her cell. Those were handy. She wondered what nifty feature cell phones were going to have next.

"Hi, Mike. Calling you back. Sorry. Young kid on the ground this morning. Second body in less than a week. Lots of cops standing around. I needed to focus on the job." Morgan explained her rudeness in summary form.

Mike said "Wow. I have never dated a cop before. It's a little weird, knowing while I was talking to you, you were looking at a dead kid. You know? You seem so normal. Not like that's what you do for a living at all."

"And yet, it is." Morgan said, trying to decide if she should correct the statement about 'dating' or not. They were not 'Dating' just yet.

Mike sensed a misstep along the way. "I am sorry: I hope I was not being presumptuous. I was calling because I hoped to see you again. I know one lost Sunday does not a dating life make."

Morgan awarded mental points to Mike figuring that out so quickly.

"Well, Mike. I would like to go out again, however: I do want to have a very frank conversation first. Have a minute?" Morgan asked, trying to not sound too ominous but knowing that was going to drop like a lead balloon.

Mike did not sound very sure when he said "Sure?"

"I had fun with you. I like you. You are a nice guy. Unexpected perhaps even." Morgan started.

"Oh boy..." Mike said, anticipating really bad news.

"Mike: I know you see a lot of women, and that is completely not an issue for me. I do not have a jealous bone in my body. I understand that you are nice looking and that you are surrounded by naked women that pay YOU to protect them. Not to mention whoever at your gym likes your workout program. Why we use protection. So that I am not having sex with your other women, and they are not having sex with whosoever I choose to enjoy outside of you. I am not being coy here: Just honest."

"OK... My popularity might be a tad overblown in that sentence, but this does not sound too bad yet... " Mike said. "There is a great big 'but' coming though. I feel it."

"Yes. There is." Morgan agreed. "Mike: There is such a thing as trying too hard. I am a Cop, not a gymnast, not an actress in a porn video. It is my general feeling that perhaps you wanted to impress me with your general athleticism and such? Correct me if I am wrong: I can be as egocentric as the next person. However, I do not need to be impressed. I do not like to run a marathon while staring at the ceiling. I am not interested in a coital pounding. I will not come harder because you worked harder. Not all the time anyway. There is a time and a place for everything. I want you in bed the way you are at the bar. Relaxed. Happy. Friendly. Easy going. Hey, you want a beer? Sure? Hey, how about some sex with that beer? That would be very nice. I like sex with my beer, and beer with my sex. I just want to be there, with you, and in the moment. I do not want to be Seka to your John Holmes. I think they were together. Not sure. Maybe that is Marilyn Chambers instead of Seka? Whatever. You get what I mean. Kapish?"

"Oh. Wow. Ok. Got it, Morgan. Yes: Guilty as charged officer. The thing is Morgan? I could not believe my luck. That you were interested. Hell, Margie told me I needed to play my cards right with you. So: yes. I wanted you to be impressed because I wanted you to want to come back to bed with me ... Other times. Many other times. You know? Seems like I did the opposite? I guess what Margie meant about not screwing it up with you was... Not do what I did." Mike sounded both relieved and chagrined.

"You get a lot of practice with others that want different things than I do." Morgan teased, but also underlined the fact they were not exclusive, all in one comment. "I thought that perhaps the 'Hey: Slow down' thing I said at one point might have been a clue, but you were on a mission. Mike: I only have sex with men I like as a person first. No mission over-screw required. Really: Try to screw me and I don't like you? That gets you arrested and the potential for you to join the alto section in the choir. I had to take a guy down a few months ago for that, and he is doing serious time for it."

Morgan shifted the phone a bit. "You would know if you were not welcome in my bed, even if it is one I rented. I liked you that first night I met you. I could not ask you out, because I was working a case. Once the case cleared, I thought about going back. More than once. Angel and Janie put it over the top, and when I saw you again, I liked you still. I wanted you to be there with me, or I would not have taken the hotel room, and dragged you to it. I am flattered you even want to be with me, given what I know about your social life. I know there is a line of some nice looking ladies. However: could you save the gymnastics for them? I want you and I to be as friendly in bed as we are in every other situation. It is not love and it is not porn. I just want us to relax and enjoy each other. OK? Look: If that is how you like to have sex, so be it, but can we at least try it the way I like it from time to time? Next time?"

"I understand. I promise I will do better by not trying to do anything other than just enjoy you and us in the sack." Mike said "You can't see it, but I am holding up my hand to swear it. I like you, Morgan. A lot. I would be really unhappy if I screwed it up with you."

"Next time then, I will lead. You just lay there and enjoy. I will show you what I like. No trapeze involved." Morgan said, reassuringly. "After that? Well, let us see how that goes. You may decide you want more Seka and less boring old me. That is fair too. At least we will know."

"Yeah: Not likely. Next time is 'go slow and enjoy' and thank god there IS a next time. Are you sure about the cold shower thing? Because it's really hot in here." Mike replied "Whew!"

"Unfortunately, I am very sure. I will call you when I know my schedule better around this case. OK? I have two dead kids. I have to take care of that before I take care of me. Us. What I want does not always come first, as I am not THAT selfish, but this next time with you? What I want completely will. After that, we will see what happens. Like I said: You may not enjoy the more relaxed, friendly thing. Not everyone does. If we like it enough, we can alternate. It is all good."

"Morgan: I promise you that I will LOVE taking it slow. So very much. OK. I look forward to then. Meantime, I am trying the shower anyway." Mike said

"Take one of your ladies in there with you. Shower sex is good. That should help." Morgan said and then hung up. Morgan looked at her phone for a moment, thinking various thoughts. You do not tell a man what you want, you never get it. One hopeful sign: Morgan said she wanted them to enjoy each other, and Mike repeated that. Ken would have glossed over such a statement because it declared in the same sentence it was not love.

Sam would be doing backflips at the very idea of a woman telling a lover things like this. Sam had two failed marriages under his belt, and Morgan had zero marriages, so she was sure her way is better. Time enough for marriage later.

Maybe. That sort of assumed finding 'the one' and Morgan was not sure that the whole idea of 'the one' is a real thing and not just a product of the romance book industry.

Cooper Johnston and Morgan looked at the body on the roll-out tray. Sam stood on the other side of the gurney and two steps farther back. He was not gloved up as he had no intention of touching the body. He could if required. A crime scene? Need to roll the body? Sure. For some reason, once they were on the slab and opened up, Sam had a mental aversion. He told Morgan once he liked the insides to stay on the inside.

Morgan looked at the insides of people and wondered why some people thought they were not animals, just like the rest of the animal kingdom.

Morgan pointed at the entry wound with a gloved finger, asking a question without words. Cooper nodded. "Your guess about the height of the shooter is good. Making a few assumptions about relative body positions and the fact that the kid never seemed to know that the shot was coming, I would say the shooter stood directly next to him, raised the weapon up behind his back and out of sight, shot him behind the ear. You are what... Five ten or so, Morgan?"

"Little over. Give or take. In these shoes add another half an inch, so call it five eleven right now." Morgan said.

"When I stand all the way straight up, proper posture, then I am five ten. Make a gun finger, raise it up alongside my back while we are standing side by side..." Cooper instructed.

Morgan did as instructed, and Cooper said "See? Almost a ninety-degree Z-axis angle into the head. This young man is a few millimeters over six feet, and the upward angle, assuming the same arm extension as you are at now, and a short barrel .22, at point blank range according to the stippling? I have the shooter as five-six to five seven, in whatever shoes they were wearing at the time."

Morgan touched her shoulder to ask "Secondary powder residue on his shoulder?"

Cooper nodded. "Correct. Side spray from the cylinder-to-barrel interface worse than average, so probably a Saturday night special. Also how we know the barrel is short. Ammunition used was a .22 Short, 27-grain bullet. Not a Long or Magnum. A light load for a crap gun, but at point-blank range that is still over a thousand feet per second and over seventy foot-pounds of muzzle energy. One shot, the bullet went directly into medulla oblongata and severed the brain stem almost entirely. The poor kid would have dropped like a puppet with his string cut. While no death is instant short of a nuclear explosion at ground zero, he never knew what hit him."

Morgan screwed up her mouth. "Gangland style execution with a cheap gun. No gun recovered so they kept a what? Hundred dollar murder weapon?"

Cooper looked at the kid on his table. "The young man is probably seventeen or so years of age, and in good shape. Runner or perhaps aerobics instructor. Perfect health. Taller and more than likely stronger than who shot him."

"So he knew and trusted his killer enough to let them stand next to him, in an Alley, and they took him out in one move. That does not add up with the other part at all. You do not let a rival gang person stand next to you. You face them, or they take you down to the ground and shoot you while you are down. Execution style, he would have been on his knees. I assume no bruises, signs of any kind of resistance? Nothing under the nails?" Morgan asked

Cooper shook his head. "Nothing. No fibers not his. No skin under nails. No bruises that are fresh. Just the day to day, I banged my knee kind everyone has."

Morgan looked at Sam. "Anything?" She asked.

"I assume nothing back on Dental or fingerprints?" Sam asked, knowing Cooper would have led with that.

"No. Nothing. Seems like the kid has never been fingerprinted. His teeth are in good shape, no cavities, so he lives someplace they have fluoride in the water. That is almost any good part of town. That is odd, because in most good parts of town they have children identification programs, so why no prints? He kept the teeth clean. Healthy gums. He clearly flossed regularly. They are aligned nicely. I don't think he ever wore braces: that leaves behind marks, changes in color that I could NOT find. No evidence of malnourishment ever, even though there is also not an ounce of extra fat on him either. His heart was strong too. I bet in life it beat at less than 60 per minute. Like I said, runner or something very aerobic. If he is a jock, he has fewer bruises than any jock I ever saw. The only anomaly is some evidence in his knees of repetitive strain injuries, but like I said: Runner."

Sam shook his head. "Fast kid. If he ran just a few steps away, the .22 would have been about useless."

Morgan lifted the sheet, examined the knees. Nothing externally obvious: no cuts so Cooper had to have seen the enlargement of the knees he mentioned on an X-Ray. She looked along the body.

"No chest hair?" Morgan asked.

"Well, yes. He grows it. Not a huge amount, it is just that he also shaves it all off. Don't ask me why." Cooper replied.

"After our last case, where you clued me in on bondage, I thought you knew everything about alternative lifestyles." Morgan poked at her friend.

"Shaving your body or not is a grooming choice, not a lifestyle." Cooper said gruffly. "It's not like the kid is a model or anything... Is he? You would already know who he is if he was. Right? You know, like how TV stars with their shirts off shave off their chest hair?"

Morgan gave that some thought. "Seventeen? Maybe he just got started in his modeling career. Worth checking into. There is a big modeling agency over on 610 West we can start with."

Morgan opened up the plastic bag with the kids' effects and spread them out on an empty gurney. "No underwear?"

"No." Cooper said.

"Weird socks." Morgan held them up. Black footies. "Runners usually do thick athletic socks. I think. I am not a runner. These are like the kind some women wear so you do not know they have socks on."

Morgan looked over the shoes. Black with swirls of yellow. Yellow laces. They made Morgan think of a bumblebee. The soles had almost no wear on them and very odd patterns. The soles were very thick, but the shoes were light. The prominent logo, rendered in the same yellow as the swirls, was a big sports equipment manufacturing company named 'Lydee'. Morgan pulled out the inner sole and found that it removed easily, so she assumed it was designed to be taken out and washed separately from the shoe. The other shoe was the same. No hidden anything. No wear.

"Brand new shoes. I assume expensive based on the name alone." Morgan said, holding one up. "I was looking at this brand in a store once when I was shopping for some new workout shoes. Comfortable but more money than I wanted to give. Also, they do not seem to be able to make shoes that are not garish. Just like these are."

Cooper picked up the other shoe and pulled the tongue out to show Morgan a label. "I tried to find that model number, like this one on the bottom of the tongue of the shoe in their catalog. Nothing matches. I even tried doing YOUR job and called a sporting good store and asked if they had the model number. They said it was not a current model, but these shoes are brand new. You may want to call Lydee and find out what is up with these because my guess is that this is a model they have not shipped yet."

Morgan thought about the new dead young man. Similar shoes. Not the same designs and different colors, but this brand, and now she wished she had looked more closely at them.

"Cooper: You are getting a new body in a while. Another kid. Another .22 to the back of the head. Very similar shoes to these..." Morgan started.

"I will move it to the top of the list." Cooper finished. "You thinking serial killer?"

"Two dead young men in short order does not necessarily a serial killer make, however, the same kind of gun, similar MO, though this body was moved postmortem in the new case. The same brand of shoes, on a dead young man of a similar age. Similarities in the crime scene in the sense that both were nearly perfect places to kill undetected. Both young men let their killer get close to them without suspicion. I doubt it is a coincidence."

Morgan looked at the entry wound one more time. She imagined the gun coming up, and firing, angling the bullets trajectory up slightly and into nearly the center of the head. Lucky shot or professional hit.

She was liking the idea of a professional less and less. Who targets a middle class or better, young and healthy kid in an alley in the Montrose?

Morgan replaced the effects in the bag after looking at everything one more time.

CHAPTER SEVEN

The Stowell Agency

Houston does not have a single downtown area, but several islands of tall office buildings, separated from each other by massive flat planes of suburban housing. People that come from cities with zoning laws and restrictions on available land find this odd. Houston has twice the square mileage of New York City but only one-quarter of the population so Morgan was used to the idea that she could drive at freeway speeds for over an hour and still be inside the city limits and just running from one island of office towers to the next.

One such island of office towers are clustered on the West side of the innermost loop of three built or planned loops. This is the 610 loop and this office-island sat just South of Interstate 10, the highway that gave the loop its name...

Morgan and Sam found 'The Stowell Agency' on the 14th floor of one office tower in this cluster of buildings, and it seemed to take the entire floor.

The receptionist gave the two detectives a very big smile as they walked up to her desk. Her desk nameplate identified her as 'Irma Singleton'.

"Hi, Irma." Morgan said. "I am sorry, but we are on a sort of wild goose chase here. Shot in the dark kind of thing." Morgan showed the woman her badge. "I am working on a homicide of a young man, no identification at all on him, and there are some indications that the young man MIGHT have been a model. We came here only because I knew this place was here from some signs I have seen driving by on the loop. We are looking for advice? How would we know if someone was a model?"

The receptionist leaned back to give that thought, and it seemed to also mentally deal with the odd nature of the request.

Morgan asked the woman while she processed the first question: "Are you a model?"

That got a toothy smile. The woman was well dressed, her hair in a medium length natural afro, her skin the color of dark chocolate. Her makeup was well applied and seemed professionally done to Morgan, though she admitted to not being an expert in that area. One side effect of being raised by her Dad. She asked him when she was twelve if she should wear makeup, and he said "Well, your mother never did, though she was pretty and did not need it and you are prettier than she was, so I am not sure why. I can take you to a place they can teach you if you that if want, but it would be a bit like spray painting gold paint on the Venus De Milo."

That comparison to her mother had put her off the very idea of it. Later not wearing makeup became a point of pride.

Irma leaned forward. "I guess everyone here wants to be a model, but no. I haven't got the looks. I won't starve myself like I need to, among other things."

"You are a good weight for your frame." Morgan commented. "You look very healthy."

"Oh dear. Models are NOT healthy, officer." Irma air quoted. " 'Camera adds five pounds' is not a lie. But you are sweet. So: without a name what you are asking is hard. Even with a name a lot of kids don't use their real one, in case they make it big time or whatever. Modeling is a lot about 'a look'. A client wants someone that looks a particular way, and so that leaves you with the portfolio books."

"The books?" Morgan asked.

"Collected portfolios of the current talent. Say you were wanting to do an ad for jeans, and it's a line for teenagers. You would come here and say "Can I see all your teenagers that would look good in jeans?" and we would pull out a book of teenage models. If you were looking only for girls, they would be in one or two of the books. If you wanted boys, they are in other books. Like that. If you are selling makeup to mature women, you ask for the face shots of the models over fifty. That would be a much smaller book." Irma grinned.

"Ok. So I could tell you I am looking for a model age seventeen, black, athletic, male, you would have that sorted into just a few books?"

"Be a few books, but yes." Irma agreed. "These are big books though."

"Do you think Sam and I could see them? Pretend we are clients?" Morgan asked.

"I am sure we can set you up." Irma said. "Let me call one of the agents, and get you in a conference room."

"Thank you so much, Irma. Big help." Morgan said.

As promised, Irma arranged it all. A conference room, with a long, wide table. An agent who said they would be happy to show them modeling books for the age range but would have to check on release forms to know what they could tell the detectives if they saw who they were looking for. "Underage kids have Hollywood parents" the agent explained.

Morgan was starting to think that in order to work at the modeling agency you had to be a potential model. Their agent was a young man, thin framed, expensive haircut, fitted suit, clean shaven, bright-eyed, energetic and eager to help. His name was Lester Kaufmann, and Lester left the detectives alone in the room after piling one end of the table with portfolio books and placing a coffee carafe, cups, and all the coffee modifiers one could ever hope for from cream, half and half, milk, four artificial sweeteners and three varieties of real sugar: white, brown, and turbinado. He also left two water bottles and glasses to pour that in.

"Well, crap." Sam said when Lester had gone "These people are being so nice I feel like now I have to hire a model to do something." He poured himself some coffee.

"Truly." Morgan agreed. She pointed at the setups. "If you have milk, and cream already, can't you make half and half? Or do I not understand some secret coffee thing?"

Sam sipped. "Far as I know, that is true. I drink skim in mine, so they missed one."

"A shocking oversight." Morgan said, sipping at her cup. "Pretty good coffee though. Better than that over-roasted and expensive stuff you get."

"It is." Sam took an appreciative sip. "I need to ask where they get this."

"Place over on Fondren. I saw the bag in the cabinet when he pulled it out. The same place where I get my tea." Morgan told him.

"You KNEW about this place and never told me?" Sam complained.

"Yes. I did not think you would want to go to the trouble to make it correctly yourself. That place is for people with burr coffee grinders because the impact ones heat the beans too much and cause the oils to break down. People who don't read sell-by dates but inhale from the bag to see if the essential oils went off. They have professional grade brew pots that brew at the correct temperature, which is 202 degrees Fahrenheit or slightly less depending upon grind and how bright you like it to be. I have been in your apartment. You do not have a burr grinder or one of those good brewing systems."

Sam looked at Morgan, shook his head, and sipped. "You don't know about milk. You do know about brew temperature. That is so you."

Morgan spread her hands. "If the coffee is not worth drinking black, it is not worth drinking. I am a coffee snob when I drink it. I admit this fully."

The partners opened books and flipped through them. The only picture they had to go off was taken by Cooper, so it was not a flattering likeness, and required study from time to time to be sure the picture of the model was not the picture of the dead young man.

It never was. They processed the stack of portfolio books carefully. Slowly. In the end, no one even required a second look.

Morgan closed the last book slowly. "Oh well. It was worth a look, even though it was really a Hail Mary pass. I suppose we can do this same thing at all the agencies, but we are just guessing about the modeling idea. Not every good looking kid that shaves their chest and wears short socks is a model."

"At least we got to sit in better chairs and drink better coffee than at the office." Sam pointed out.

"True. Or have to perch on a chair in JJ's office. Even worse." Morgan agreed fervently.

CHAPTER EIGHT

Morgue, Trip Two

Tuesday afternoon Morgan's cell rang.

Morgan looked at the little screen, recognized the number. "Hey Cooper." She answered.

"Morgan: can you swing by? Have some preliminary results that should interest you." Cooper told her.

"Already?" Morgan said.

"Already, but ... Well. Just get here." Cooper said enigmatically.

"On the way. Sam's driving, so clear out the sidewalk." Morgan said and hung up.

"I do not drive on the sidewalk." Sam protested his verbal abuse.

"I meant for you to park on." Morgan replied.

Morgan thought Cooper must be very excited because he met them at the door and took them directly to the morgue.

"Going to see if you have been reading your textbooks." Cooper told her, and he flipped the sheet back to the waist. "What do you notice here?" Cooper asked.

Morgan bent over and closely examined the young man and assumed that whatever was interesting was below the neck because she had seen his young face at the scene.

"No 'Y' incision?" Morgan asked as she studied.

"I have not gotten there yet. I did the X-rays on the head first, because I wanted to verify the angles and bullet size. Looks the same as before on the film, but need to take it out to be sure. Matches up to being a .22, 27-grain bullet at a guess. Bullet hit no bone and looks to be largely intact. Accounting for differences in height, the upward angle on this young man means the shooter was about the same height as the first young man. My preliminary conclusion on that: more than likely the same killer. I'll know more when I have the bullet."

"This young man had chest surgery." Morgan said, pointing at some scarring with her gloved fingers.

"Why I wanted you to see this before I went in. Now, this." Cooper said and took the sheet completely off.

Morgan's eyes went to the genitals. Then she quickly leaned over and studied them more closely and with obvious interest, which made Sam say "Uhh?" in confusion.

"May I?" Morgan asked, indicating the penis with the back of her gloved fingers.

"Sure. I have already processed there. Pictures. All the samples. Etc. It is interesting." Cooper said.

Morgan probed lightly, moving the body parts and the light over the table to get a detailed examination.

Sam bit his lip.

Morgan looked up at Cooper. "This is amazing. I have never seen a post-operative transsexual man before. Just... amazing. I cannot think of any other word for it."

Sam took a step back, irritating Morgan immensely, and earning a glare from Cooper as well.

Cooper leaned over and put his face down by Morgan's. "Me either. Rare as hell. Far more common for a mis-assigned male to take the corrective surgery and become female. The success rate for this female to male procedure is only about fifty percent. Not cheap either: pubic phalloplasty can cost upwards of ninety thousand dollars in the US, assuming it was done here. Not sure how I can know that yet. Perhaps the pump assembly will have serial numbers I can trace." Cooper pointed at the young man's testicles when he mentioned that.

"How does that work exactly?" Morgan asked curiously.

"Prosthetic testicle here... " Cooper pointed. "... That is a squeeze bulb style pump that was implanted. It moves saline water from a bag in his abdomen out into his penis." Cooper pointed to the penis. "Here there are two expandable long, skinny bladders either side of the new urethra and they fill with the saline when he inflates his penis. This is not unique to gender reassignment by the way. There are similar procedures used in the case of extreme cases of erectile dysfunction. With that set up he could get it up and stay erect for as long as required, assuming he can find a sex partner not freaked out by him being a transsexual. Not your dumb-ass partner, obviously."

Morgan gave Cooper a smile. "Obviously, though to be fair, he identifies as heterosexual male so it would not have been his cup of tea in the first place. He would want a female end result." Morgan pointed along a white scar line. "I cannot imagine the process that allowed him to become male as being easy." Morgan said. "So many nerves here."

"Oh no. I don't know if this is the single most painful thing a person would have to endure to become themselves, but it has to be in the top two. There is a reason most transsexuals argue that genitals are not the same thing as gender. You are looking at it. Expensive AND painful in the extreme, just to fix mother natures mistake."

"I can imagine." Morgan looked again in amazement. "Still, it is wonderful we are even able to do this. Could he have an orgasm? Not a seminal ejection, obviously."

"Maybe?" Cooper stood up and considered. With a wave of a hand over the lower abdomen. "Nerve rich area, as you said. Would just depend. A great deal of sex is in the mind, and ALL of gender preference and identity seems to be. Some people can experience an orgasm from nipple stimulation alone, for example, and that also might be a possibility." Cooper replied. He looked down. He said with obvious sorrow "Someday Morgan, we'll be able to fix all this in the genes, not with knives and pumps."

"That will be a good thing. Assuming some religious group does not take over the government and shut all science down in the meantime." Morgan looked down at the body. "I hope it was worth it for him. He had no time on this world to really enjoy finally being who he was supposed to be."

Morgan squared her shoulders and looked back at Sam who was angling his head in curiosity at the young man but from his safe distance. "Really?" Morgan asked him in disgust.

"Anything else interesting?" Morgan asked Cooper.

"Same shoes." Cooper said. "Not exactly the same, different color, but same unknown model number thing."

"OK. That is interesting too." Morgan agreed.

Cooper handed Morgan the personal effects bag, and she pulled out the shoes and looked them over. Very lightweight. Same construction and materials. No wear on the bottom to speak of.

"Sam: Shoes are not threatening to you, are they?" Morgan asked.

"No." Sam said, irritated at being called out over his reaction.

"Good. Then can you call Lydee and get the megacorporation that made these things to tell you what the hell is up with these model numbers?"

"Sure." Sam agreed, feeling like he was being punished by being assigned the grunt work.

"Thanks, because I have a date. I hope." Morgan had a thought. "Geez: JJ is going to flip his lid on this new angle."

"Glad you get to tell him." Sam said in slight triumph.

Briefing JJ went about the way Morgan expected, and Sam did NOT come into the office to witness because he had 'important phone calls to make'.

"So: Same shooter." JJ concluded looking deeply sour.

"Cooper still working on that but that is his preliminary conclusion and I agree it seems likely. Same caliber. Same weight bullet. Approximately same height shooter. Back of the head kill-shot, if slightly different placement. Both boys about the same age. No struggle. If this is different people, Sam will eat his cowboy hat."

"Where IS Parker?" JJ asked.

"Sam is trying to dig his way through the layers of a multinational company, Lydee, to ask them about their secret shoes." Morgan said.

JJ raised an eyebrow. "He piss you off?"

"Oh, yes." Morgan agreed. "So very much."

"Over the second body?" JJ asked, one eyebrow raised quizzically.

"Yes again." Morgan said.

"Then perhaps I should not piss you off with MY attitude about it." JJ said. He shoed at her with his hands. "Go the hell away."

"Leaving." Morgan said, and she was. She had a call to make.

"Hey Morgan" Wendell answered."

"Please tell me you did not catch any bodies or flying saucers or anything requiring you to be down there in your County tonight?" Morgan asked.

"No... Still on, if you are." Wendell replied. "Looking forward to it."

"You know how to get to my place?" Morgan asked.

"Let me see. You drew me a map. And explained it. In detail. So, no: I have no idea where you live. North Houston... Right? Near a truck stop?" Wendell teased.

"Sure. See you soon." Morgan hung up and wondered about just how absolutely clear she had been on how to get to her place with him. Not like her. Maybe she was more excited about his first trip to her house than she realized.

"Sam: Late tomorrow. See you when you see the reds of my eyes."

Morgan said with a jaunty wave and she bounced out of the station. 'Yeah.' She admitted to herself. 'looking forward to the evening.'

CHAPTER NINE
Date Night.

As Morgan is naturally a neat, clean as she went type of housekeeper, she had very little to do to get her house ready for guests. Angel dropped in at her place any time and Morgan never felt embarrassed about the mess, because there was not one. She showered and changed into her date night civilian clothes, which was pretty much her "I am not at work' clothes: Jeans, and a T-shirt. Tonight's shirt was a BB King shirt she bought when he performed at Rockefellers, and the dark blue background went with her cobalt eyes.

With a two-second glance in the mirror, she thought to herself 'Never let it be said I cannot mix and match clothes.'

Morgan heard Wendell's car pull up around back by the garage, and that reminded her she told him to come to the back door in her apparently extensive instructions. Morgan felt a little embarrassed suddenly.

She went to the back door, opened it, and watched her friend and lover getting out of his car. "Welcome to North Houston." Morgan called.

"Thanks. You know, I always heard Houston was a big-ass city, but I got here way faster than I would have thought possible after having to drive to South Huntsville."

They were at the stage of their relationship that Wendell got a warm welcoming kiss at the back door.

"Hi." Morgan said.

"Hi yourself, Detective. Are you ... Blushing?" Wendell asked.

"Yes, because. Well. You'll see." She took him by the hand and led him inside. Through the kitchen. "That's my kitchen. It has pots and pans in it."

"OK..." Wendell said.

Morgan kept dragging.

"This is my Rec Room. Show you it later." Morgan said. "Those are stairs over there. We are going up them now."

"Nice bar..." Wendell said as they went through the room.

"Thanks." Morgan said.

When they arrived on the second floor, Morgan continued her tour. "This is the upstairs hall."

The pair went through a door. "This is my bedroom. That thing with sheets on it is my bed. End of tour: Get naked. Now." Morgan said. She pulled off her T, slipped off her jeans and was naked. "Like that." She said. She watched as Wendell stripped, tapping her toe in impatience.

"Sorry if you wanted to eat first. Food, I mean. Thank you for indulging me." Morgan said in post-coital bliss. That encounter was what she had hoped Mike would be for her but had not been yet.

"No problem, Morgan. I can always skip a meal or six when you are on the menu." Wendell assured her, in a happy tone of voice.

"OK. Let us go rinse off. I put a nice big shower up here when I built the place. You'll like it." Morgan said.

"If you are in it, and rinsing off, it is a place I like. Call me crazy, but I like you when you are in this mood."

"Not being too pushy about the sex? I really wanted to get laid, if you didn't notice." Morgan asked. They moved to the bathroom and Morgan started the water.

"I noticed. Not being pushy. A man likes to feel wanted every now and then." Wendell stroked her skin lightly with his fingertips. "Are you having a bad week or something?"

Morgan made a throaty sound at the caress, and then they stepped into the shower together.

Morgan offered Wendell a washcloth and some liquid shower soap. She turned around and pressed against him with her back. "Yes and no. Two kids. Same killer. No ID. As sad as that is, I am homicide. I signed up for that kind of shit. What bugged me was that today the second boy turned out to be transsexual. Been post-op for a while, but shit. All that pain to get to who you need and want to be, and then killed before his real life could even be enjoyed. Just made me angry. Also grateful."

Wendell stopped washing Morgan's back for a moment. "I imagine that Sam is having some difficulties there?" He asked.

Morgan was holding her hair up on her head with both hands and turned to face him. She gave Wendell a look. "It amazes me you know him that well. Front, please? I have to hold my hair up here you know, so I need to borrow your hands. Yes, Sam tried to control it, but when we were looking at the body when he found out the poor guy was trans, he took this step back. I know he fought it, and tried to stay engaged and interested, but his first reaction was disgust, and then my first reaction at HIM was the same. Disgust."

"What did you do to him?" Wendell asked as he worked.

"You know ME well too. I gave him a crappy job. He is calling up a huge international conglomerate sporting wear and shoe company called Lydee and they will NOT want to talk about their unannounced shoe model. We have to find out more about it." Morgan said and tried not to feel a little guilty about that job.

"Explain?" Wendell requested, and so Morgan gave him all the relevant details and enjoyed being washed at the same time.

They dried and dressed and went downstairs to the Rec Room, Morgan bringing Wendell up to date on the case along the way. She asked him to leave his underwear off 'for speed reasons later'.

They perched on bar stools to talk. Morgan switched from the current case to the one that ended up with her buying the deceased woman's bar. Wendell had been involved in that one and knew most of it already, so she just filled in about seeing the bar in the Condo when she first arrived at the crime scene, and then later finding out it was being auctioned and buying it for herself.

Morgan patted the polished top. "It was the many god's own hell getting the thing in here. The good news is that the delivery people helped, and it was already in parts. Still, took me a while to get it back to where you can't see it was ever apart, and then polish it to a shine."

"It's huge." Wendell said. "Seems unlike you in a way. You are normally so practical."

"It is like my Miata I guess. Nothing practical about that either." Morgan said.

"True. Still, an interesting insight into the mystery that is Morgan Olsen. Do you keep actual drinks in the thing?"

"How am I a mystery? I am literally the most 'what you see is what you get' person there ever was. And of course I do. Are you saying you would like a drink?" Morgan asked, hopping down and going around behind the bar.

"Yes, well, I would not be averse to a whiskey with a side water unless you are making me drive home tonight, in which case, just the water."

Morgan pulled out bottles. "Ice?" she asked

"Yes, please." Wendell said.

"So, you are sort of jumping ahead in my scheme for you for this evening, but no: I was rather hoping you would decide to spend the night so I can have my way with you a few more times. I told Sam I was coming in late because I wanted to see how you are with making love in the morning too. All in the interest of science, you understand." Morgan handed Wendell his Whiskey, a double, with a large cube, and a tall glass with water and ice. He sipped. Looked at the drink. "Wow. What the heck is this?" He asked.

"You said you wanted Whiskey. Is that not OK? I can make something else. I have others." Morgan looked concerned.

"No, it's very nice. Leave my glass alone till it's empty and no one gets hurt. I just never had one exactly like this before. Smooth as hell."

Morgan pulled the bottle back out and handed it to him. "I'm a Scotch drinker, but I talked to the guy at the store about what to lay in for a bourbon consumer, and he suggested that one. I went with it because what do I know about it? I tasted that stuff before I served it to you and thought it was good. Not Macallan good, but good."

"Makers 46... And you think you have something better than this?" Wendell gave her a disbelieving look.

"Better for ME. Like I said, Scotch drinker here." Morgan explained, tapping her collar bone to indicate who the Scotch drinker might be.

"Show me the Scotch, lady." Wendell challenged.

Morgan had poured a double for herself and held out her glass to him. "Here: Taste mine. After that lovely sex, I think we can safely share a glass."

"Loving cup." Wendell sipped, looked thoughtful. Sipped his. Drank some water. Tried Morgan's again. "Ok. I conclude you have different taste than me, both are good, and I like the one you bought to get me drunk so you can take advantage of my willing nature better. PS: I am consenting now, in advance, to any and all lechery you have in mind for us, in case this gets a little crazy later." He held up his glass to indicate how it might get crazy.

Morgan sipped his drink, his water, then hers. "OK. Good. The guy at the store knew what he was talking about. That is not bad. Also: thank you for your consent. I shall be using it. Before we dive headfirst into this, what do you want for dinner?"

"You?" Wendell ventured. "I love me some tasty Morgan."

Morgan smiled warmly and did not mind the slightly possessive and completely lecherous look directed at her body either. "I, sir, am the appetizer. And also the dessert. You need fuel because I want repeats on my dessert."

"OK. Well, I don't know this part of the world. Anything good near here? I would like to stay close and maximize the time we have in your bed."

Morgan place the flat of her hand on the bar. "I was thinking of trying it on top of the bar next. Yes: A few places. A family style place just up the road. A local pizza / Italian place that is good. Most of the Mexican is Tex-Mex, but there are a few places better than the chain stuff at least."

"Any seafood?" Wendell asked.

"No idea. We can look in the yellow pages. Copy over there by the phone." Morgan pointed. She worked really hard to keep any idea that seafood was not her first choice out of her voice, but her word choice was all Wendell needed to key on.

"No idea? Why no idea, oh delicious woman of mystery?" Wendell asked.

"Well. I don't eat Seafood, so I never looked." Morgan admitted, still trying to wiggle sideways away from it. It was useless and demonstrated why there is a reason she likes Wendell so much.

"And why not? Are you allergic?" Wendell asked.

"I don't like it." Morgan confessed.

"I have heard of people that don't like Seafood, but they don't live in Galveston County." Wendell said.

"I live in Harris County." Morgan pointed out.

"True. But curious: Why?" Wendell probed.

"It smells like a latrine. OK?" Morgan said, defeated in trying to not be judgmental.

That honest answer got an energetic 'no' shake of the head from Wendell. "I eat seafood, I smell like that to you? Forget I asked. I don't like it THAT much."

"No, if you want seafood, I'll feed you seafood. You just have to put out is all." Morgan teased.

"I'll put out to YOU for just a cheap chain hamburger. Just the promise of one." Wendell said. "Let's be honest here."

"Italian? They have scallops and such things." Morgan asked.

The Law of Unintended Consequences - Morgan Olsen Book 2

"I like garlic..." Wendell warned.

"I do too. Good. We will both have garlic breath. Let's go. I'm driving." Morgan headed for the garage.

"This guy you were talking about earlier. You said he was post-op? I am not sure what that means exactly. Does that mean they found a penis donor? Was he able to sexually function? Sorry if that is a dumb question. Other than Mardi Gras, I mostly see drunk cowboys and fisherman out my way." Wendell asked Morgan as they cuddled together.

Morgan snuggled in a little, adjusting herself. "Post-Op just means that they literally built him a penis out of other parts of his body. Skin grafts and various procedures to form a penis, extend the urethra, and some human-made things to allow him to have an erection and such. Cooper told me that these procedures are rare and fail literally half the time, but this kid was a fully functional male. From what I can tell, however, even if you never choose to do the surgery, and there are SO many reasons not too, Gender is not genitals. It is who you are in your head. I am a woman. You are a man. Our bodies match our gender. We are very lucky that way. It is a thing we forget to be grateful for sometimes. That is what I meant earlier when I said I was grateful."

Morgan decided to tease Wendel slightly. "In fact, this young man, according to Cooper, could have an erection, and stay that way as long as he liked. One way that perhaps going through everything he did to get his body to match his gender made it so he had an advantage over guys like you that were born with the matching parts. Gender and body matching I mean."

"Sounds nice." Wendell said. "Sorry if I disappoint."

"We will just have to keep trying, lover." Morgan said, then wanted to clap her hand over her mouth.

"Well, good news, I think in a few more minutes, we can make another attempt." Wendell reported.

"That is good news." Morgan agreed, happy he had not jumped on her word slip.

Morgan lay there considering the idea that maybe instead of calling Mike when she had a spare moment next time, she should drive to the next county south. Then, pissed at herself for thinking of Mike at a time like this, Morgan rolled on top of Wendell and said in a low voice "While we are waiting for your blood supply to move to a useful

72

location, let us neck."

"OK... But I may have been wrong about that time frame..." Wendell said after a few long moments of deep kissing.

"So I feel. Still, I want to kiss you some more." Morgan returned to her kissing and enjoyed herself. Affection was becoming torment as well, so she had mercy after a while.

Morgan sat up and reached over to the bedside table. "Supply mission. I will put this on you when I am down there and done with the kissing. It will be a while yet, because I am not done with the kissing up here just yet, and there are some between places I want to kiss too. Deal with it."

Wendell responded by reaching out to her and pulling her face back to his.

CHAPTER TEN

Bug

Morgan rolled into the office in a solemn but happy mood. The ride in had been nice if warm: her little air conditioner had worked hard to extract the water from the air, and drop it on the road, and with the top down, it never stopped. Her little cars cooling coils hard at work turning humidity to liquid water, dropping it on the concrete so it could evaporate back from whence it came. Morgan knew it was silly: Like having a fireplace in this town when you have to run the HVAC to be able to tolerate the heat of it.

Morgan was solemn because it had been a good night, and a good morning, but it was over and now she had to get back to her job. There was always a mild pang of a guilty feeling when she allowed herself to be human and have pleasure when others needed her to be solving the murders of their loved ones. In this case, people that still had no names, but that would not last. Sam would get the shoe angle solved: Morgan had faith in that. Also, someone would report them missing, and they were watching the missing persons reports like hawks. Sooner or later these two boys would be reported, and then they would know where to start digging for their killer next.

Morgan was also slightly sad because she had been so tempted last night to skip the safe sex: She was protected against unwanted pregnancy. It would have been SO easy to rationalize it. She was happy with just Wendell. She could talk to him about being exclusive, and if he was interested then they could lose the extra protection. She could tell Mike it was a one and done after all. That she had decided to try not 'playing the field' for a while. Ken would be unhappy about it of course, but... They were never going to be serious, so maybe that was a good ending?

Sated and slightly unhappy about her state of mind, she was happy to have the top down so she could roll in to work, reflective but free, at the same time.

This mood evaporated the minute she reached her desk. Sam pointed at her inbox wordlessly. Eight by ten paper, folded in half. Gloves and fingerprint kit at the ready.

"Tell the darkie to lose the directions to your house.

The bartender is not a huge improvement but at least

he is a white boy. Teach him what you want instead,

slut."

Morgan began to shake, and the paper rattled in her hands. She set the paper down and closed her eyes as the shakes proceeded through her entire body.

Sam, observing that reaction, slipped on some gloves and picked up the note and read it.

He looked at Morgan. He did not completely understand that note, but it was clear how it was affecting his partner. She was flushed and shaking. He had never seen her like this. Sam looked back at the note, then proceeded to dust it for her since she was fighting for self-control in a way that terrified him.

Sam has seen that face before, just never on her. The last time it proceeded a vase being flung at his head by his ex-wife, right before she took their daughter and left.

Then, like now, Sam was not exactly sure what the cause was. He completely understood the effect. Morgan was in a rage.

"No prints" Sam reported, then tucked the note into an evidence bag, noted the time and date and circumstance of it arriving, but not how it had sent Morgan over into a speechless amount of anger.

"I'll take it to evidence. Put it with the collection." Sam said, trying to frame her world with some normalcy.

When he returned, she was seated at her desk, still gloved up, her phone apart. She was using a small set of computer tools she kept in her desk to disassemble it. Neatly arrayed in front of her were the battery cover, the battery, a thin plastic looking shape with wire traces visible in it, and in a coffee cup, screws were being dropped with regular little ting's.

"You think they bugged your phone?" Sam asked.

"I know they did. This thing right here." Morgan tapped the plastic shape. "It was laid in behind the battery, and these two little traces Vampire tapped the power of the phone. I imagine it had a pretty good range and probably let them track me too. It is custom to this model of phone, or at least all phones that use this battery type."

"I assume you said something on the phone that they let slip in that note, telling you they overheard?" Sam guessed.

"Two things. Yes." Morgan looked up at Sam. He could see her rage was gone cold now. Enraged she was terrifying but this was now an even more scary Morgan. The people behind that note had annoyed her with their threats up to now. Now they had a committed enemy.

Morgan decided to tell Sam the clues. "I complained, on the phone, to Mike about our first time together. Details are not important. Only that I complained. Referenced in the note in the second sentence. Yesterday, when I called Wendell, I was being silly about if he knew the way to my house, and he mentioned I had drawn a map AND explained it. Referenced in the first sentence. I was talking on the phone in two different physical locations and with no one around me either time. My conclusion is that they either had a long ear trained on me or my phone was bugged. Given the labor involved in putting a long ear on me, I assumed phone tap. Sure enough: there it is. Part of it anyway."

Still wearing his gloves, Sam picked up the flat plastic device and studied it. He got out a jewelers loop and looked at it more closely. There were tiny numbers on the central rectangle inside the plastic, but they were meaningless to Sam. There was a whirl of traces around that, and two traces that ran to the edge and peeked out of the insulating plastic. The battery taps, with small '+' and '-' symbols printed inside the plastic.

"I assume this is the transmitter part, and you are looking to see how they got your voice?"

"Exactly right." Morgan agreed and then said, holding up her open phone so Sam could see the guts she said "Tap on the earpiece here. I wonder when the hell they were able to get my phone for long enough to do all of this. Even a pro would need a little time to take it apart and install all of this. The ear bit needed to connect to these wires! That is not ten-seconds work. This set up would take a while to install, but it would be fairly long range and never need batteries to be changed."

Morgan regarded her phone sourly. "I wonder how much better my battery life would be without this garbage in here."

"Maybe they switched it?" Sam said. "Not as if that Nokia model is uncommon. They are everywhere. Unless you marked yours in such a way as to know it was switched, how would you know? They clone your address book and settings, and it looks like your phone. Right? They have those machines at Cingular where they just park your old phone and your new one and it copies everything over. If they have access to that kind of bug tech, surely they can do that?"

"Yes. That is also a possibility. It means the Cabal has resources. Money. Contacts into the surveillance state I did not suspect." Morgan picked up the flat plastic transmitter. "I should have suspected I suppose. They clearly watch me. I just thought it was via people in the office or at the paper. Human Intelligence. Not this."

"What will you do now?" Sam asked.

"Well, Three things. Dust this thing, but I bet there are no prints. Then put my phone together. Then drive over to Cingular and get a new one. Check the new one for bugs. Can you cover the office for a while longer? I'll call you when I am done." Morgan asked.

"Sure" Sam agreed. He did not like the look on her face. She was talking like all was normal again, her detective hat back on, but Sam sensed lurking danger.

Morgan called Sam about thirty minutes later.

"Hey, Morgan. New phone already?" Sam answered.

"About to cut over. Last call on this unit. Just wanted to tell you I'll be offline while I move into the new phone, and also, to the people listening to this call, fuck you."

"Understood." Sam said. Morgan cursed so rarely that hearing that made him inwardly cringe above and beyond the way she was challenging these people. He was very worried about his partners' safety.

Morgan watched with interest as the store technical staff used their in-store machine to copy her address book and settings over to the new phone. She thought about what Sam had said. Had they replaced her phone? Would she know? Since she kept hers in good shape, and in a case if it was the same model, would she be able to tell? Part of why she was getting a different model now. That and they changed the phones every year. She was not sure she thought this one was all that much better in technical terms, but at least it was different. Even the battery was different and that meant the bug they had used would not work in this one. Its little power taps would be in the wrong place.

Back in her car, Morgan sat with the new Nokia plugged into the twelve-volt power to charge it and sighed before she made the call she did not want to make.

"Hey, Morgan." Wendell greeted. He sounded happy to hear from her. In his world, they had gotten up, made love, showered together, had breakfast, then he had gone to work late in Galveston while she went to work late in Houston.

"Hi, Wendell. I have some really crappy news." Morgan said, not wanting to end that happiness he clearly felt. That she had sort of felt this morning, amid her melancholy.

"Uh oh?" Wendell said. He knew that there were classes of things she was not calling about, such as her being pregnant, but that left all sorts of other bad news. Wendell would actually not classify her being pregnant as bad news in any case. He just would never let her know that.

"I heard from the Cabal today, and they warned me again about seeing you. They let me know my phone was bugged even, and I found it when I took it apart. This is a brand new phone and I checked it before I called you. I have no idea if your phone is tapped or not as well."

"I see." Wendell said, a cold pit forming in his stomach. "What are you going to do?"

"Depends on what you think." Morgan said.

"Let me check my phone. I would rather not broadcast what I think. Where was your bug, exactly?"

Morgan described it in detail.

"OK. I'll look. Shouldn't take long to at least check the battery part." Wendell told her.

"OK. I am in my car in the parking lot, charging the new phone so I'll wait here." Morgan replied and hung up. She stared off into the distance, feeling rage combined with warmth from their previous night.

Wendell called back in about five minutes. "Nothing. If mine is bugged it's totally inside the phone. I'll look when I can find some tools with the right screw heads."

"Possible it is still bugged, but I am guessing these people work up here, not down there." Morgan said.

"So: what do you want to do about it." Wendell asked.

"I told them on the bugged phone to fuck off. I cannot tell you what to do." Morgan said. "These are my tormentors, not yours."

"Morgan. At the risk of sounding too serious about you because I know you hate that, if they are bugging you, they are bugging me, in the literal and figurative sense of that. I want to be with you. What WE do about this situation... well, that ball is in YOUR court, girl. I'm in if you are, at whatever level you want." Wendell felt his way through that answer trying to be clear and at the same time not push Morgan away.

Morgan decided Mike was going to have to wait. "What I want, Wendell, is that when this case is over, how about I take a couple days, and we have a four day weekend somewhere? My only specification is no phone, no laptop, no tech at all, nothing. Barely any clothes, and only then to be able to eat out because I am not cooking and neither are you. Also, no fish." Morgan tagged that last part to make what she wanted sound lighter and more frivolous.

"If you are sure you want to be that in their face about it. After last night and this morning? I would LOVE a four day weekend like that. More recovery time."

"I would too, and Wendell, not because it is a big 'up yours' to them. It's hard to maintain a long distance relationship, especially between two cops, and I think this is how you do that. By scheduling time to be with each other. Maybe even doing something other than screwing now and then."

"I assume that is how you are supposed to do it. First time I ever had one. Not a cop relationship, a long distance one I mean. Screwing or sitting on the roof: Don't care. I just like being with you." Wendell said. "However, I do like the screwing. Please do not misunderstand."

"All your other women are local or imports you kept around once you seduced them?" Morgan teased.

"Every single one of them. All of them. You keep running away North. Not sure what I am doing wrong there. Will need to check my spell book later. Maybe I am not using enough eye of newt? Worked on ALL the others though. Humm... You are a mystery." Wendell agreed, and in a way that left how serious that answer was open to question.

After they hung up, Morgan wondered out of idle curiosity how many other women there actually were in Wendell's life. Did they even have to all be women? It was possible she was the only significant other. It was possible the number was similar to Mike's. Wendell is a good looking man and a cop. His opportunities would be many. Morgan had no way to know short of asking a serious question about it and that led to a whole other place. Morgan did not do 'possessive'.

To inquire about that meant she was thinking about being 'serious' though. She was not sure she was ready for that.

Oddly that made her think of Janie. Wendell and Janie and herself: Now THAT would be a wild weekend unlike any she had ever had.

What would the Cabal have to say about that? Hopefully, nothing, because they would have dropped dead from prude-shock, if that is a thing. But hey: They said she is a slut: Maybe she should own that word, and put it in their faces.

That led Morgan to think about the way the Cabal had been leaking all her cases to the Chron and building her up. The progressive face of the department, when the reality was that inside the force in some locations and in some commands it was nothing of the sort. Could she feed things to the Chron too? Would they publish things that she intentionally fed them to tear down part of that clean-faced image? Her beat is The Montrose: Surely no one would blink an eye at a story about her being out on the town or attending an orgy. That didn't even have to be a real thing. Supermarket tabloids proved that.

Was that a way to get the Cabal off her back? It is not like she cared what others thought. They obviously did. Morgan started her car and headed back to poor Sam. He would flip at the idea of her intentionally making herself appear to be 'less' than what she is, even if the definition of 'less' was in the eye of the beholder.

'Honest Cop Who Solves Cases is Secret Slut.'. Maybe not: Might be a few drawbacks: the other Homicide detectives at the office for example. She could see it now. 'Hey Olsen, is it our turn with you yet?'.

Not of this harassment would never happen to a male on the force.

Why was it so hard to just be a good cop?

Morgan came back into the office subdued.

On her desk was an evidence bag, timestamped and explanation about the bugged phone filled out.

Morgan looked up at her partner. "Thank you, Sam. Very considerate."

She dropped the bugged phone, still assembled but turned off and the battery removed, into the bag and sealed it.

"If this keeps up, we are going to have to switch to a larger evidence locker." Sam said.

Morgan smiled, and it was her old smile, peeking through the cold. "Be right back."

When she returned to her desk from the evidence room, Sam

decided to share his concerns. "Morgan: you need to be careful here. These guys have been after you for a while, they are not backing off. They are escalating: they called you a 'slut', meaning they have zero respect for you and what YOU want. You are the bravest person I know, but... Don't be stupid. OK?"

Morgan considered that. "Thank you, Sam. I get it. I am concerned as well. I just cannot let these people win. If I leave the force, they win. If I do that they want, they win. I do not know why they want me to behave. Not at all, in fact: I cannot connect to how their brains work in any way. I intend to be inconvenient as all hell for them though. Maybe I can get them to make a mistake that will reveal themselves to me, and then I can take them down."

Morgan paused, her more somber expression from earlier returning. "Sam, this is my problem. I understand if you want to get a new, less troublesome partner."

"No, Morgan. Not what I am saying at all. You are one of the bravest, most fearless people I know, and no matter what, I have your back. Promise. I just want you to be careful is all. Drive that little car with eyes in the back of your head, because I can see them deciding to just run you off the road with a truck."

Morgan considered that comment, and thought it is easy to be brave when you have a trust fund you can just leave and go to a different job and not worry about eating in the meantime. Morgan wanted THIS job. It was the one she trained for. She would not give it up without a fight.

Morgan gave Sam a very serious look, Met his eyes. "Thank you, Sam. I really appreciate all that. It means a lot to me."

Sam smiled, then looked off in the general direction of the evidence room. "I hope people with these kinds of resources don't just pluck all that out of the evidence room. They have to know we are logging it all."

Morgan agreed. "Yes: I considered that as well. On the other hand, taking things FROM evidence without being tracked is hard, and perhaps that is a bread crumb they will leave that lets me find them."

"Us." Sam corrected. "Us find them. Partner. Remember? By the way, while you were out playing phone tag, I swept our office here. I don't have a scanner or anything, but I could not find any evidence of a bug in here. As small as that one was, that is not a certainty.

Morgan looked around in thought. "You take apart the power strips?"

"No. Had to leave something for you. Did not do the phones either, since those can be tapped up at the switch, not here."

"Yeah: I assumed already those are wired. I just never thought they could get to MY cell phone. Bastards. OK. Bugs need power, so let us check the outlets."

Thirty minutes later, they concluded that nothing was there. JJ came in and stopped. "What the hell? Why are you taking apart your office?"

Morgan looked up from under her desk, where she was screwing things back together. "Hi JJ. Found a bug in my cell. Just looking for more." Morgan said casually as if bugs were things people found all the time.

JJ stood there frozen for a few moments. "Those people again?" he finally asked.

"Without a doubt." Morgan agreed.

"Jee-Suus, Olsen. You couldn't have your enemies be like the Girl Scouts or something? You had to go piss off the CIA?"

"The Girl Scouts ARE my enemy. Those damn caramel and coconut cookies: I am powerless against them. Anyway, these guys are local, not Feds. I don't know who they are exactly, but they are almost certainly well connected old white men who think they need to be calling ALL the shots, and who do not like uppity women or probably Hispanic men if I had to guess. Racist, misogynist assholes, for sure." Morgan lightened up her response but leavened it with the knowledge that JJ Alvarez was someone they would not like either.

"I am sure you are right." JJ admitted. "... But they never came after me like they are you."

"Because YOU are not an attractive young woman, JJ." Sam said from under his desk.

"Thank god for that!" JJ said fervently.

CHAPTER ELEVEN

Serial Killer

Morgan decided to run out for a late lunch and get a small amount of shopping done. A case for her new phone. Another charger. Spare battery. Things she could buy less expensively on Harwin Street than she could at the Cingular store. Sam called before Morgan could return to the office.

"Morgan? We have another one. Same MO. Young kid. Headshot. Body in Hermann Park this time. That big park area right near the planetarium."

"Well, shit. Meet me there." Morgan said, and mentally rerouted herself to try and figure out the best way to get to the park. Traffic is always a beast around that park since it houses the zoo, the planetarium/science museum, open fields, picnic areas, a lake with swans. Even a tiny train that wound around the lake.

When Morgan arrived at Hermann Park on the entrance near her favorite attraction, the planetarium, it was easy to see where the excitement was. Numerous emergency vehicles with flashing lights pointed the way. Finding parking was the challenge she expected it to be, but Morgan imagined Sam would just pull up onto the grass or sidewalk. Even if she were so inclined, her low slung car would not work well for that. Curbs have real meaning to her when she was in the Miata. She drove a fair ways away from the flashing lights to find open parking and started her walk back. Sam would beat her here given his starting at the station and his parking habits, but with the time of day and the wide open space of the park, this would allow Morgan time on her walk up to observe the setting. She slowed as she approached the main cluster of police officials to look over the nearby park benches and paths, thinking about visibility and chances anyone saw this one.

She saw an M.E. vest, but it wasn't Cooper this time. Day shift person. Ronald... Something. She could not pull up the last name immediately. Cooper always called him 'Ronald' and never 'Ron' and Morgan had paid more attention to that. Cooper disliked anyone calling him by a nickname, but Morgan knew Cooper was a stickler for calling people by whatever their preferred name is. Sam is 'Sam' not 'Samuel'.

Morgan felt the usual mental shift as she entered the fray and assumed the lead.   Another reason her whole destroying her reputation that the Cabal had built would not work: Here she had to be the detective in charge, and that meant all of these people needed to listen to her. This was another place her arrest of the police photographer, Bob Watts, had a side effect. The people here knew not to screw with her. Morgan did not like that for some the respect came from fear rather than her competence, but on the other hand, it was better than no respect at all.

She stopped at the edge of the cloud of Cops and looked around. No body was in sight. There were more officers up in the woods, and the ones there had more stripes, so she headed over.

Sam was there, standing behind the huge tree and why she had not seen him right away. On the ground, face up, was a very young man. This was more gruesome than the other two dead boys, in that the gunshot was directly into the right eye.

"Sam" Morgan greeted.

Sam gave a greeting nod. "Morgan. I assume you parked in Timbuktu?"

"A suburb of there, yes. Timbuktu needs better urban planning." Morgan looked around at the ground and noted a few things of interest. "What do you know so far?" she asked.

"This one more brutal. Shot in the leg there for example." Sam pointed at the lower left thigh, just above the knee. "Small caliber. Guessing .22 from the entrance wound. No stippling, so also guessing far enough back it was a 'lucky' shot if you want to call it that. You can see the kill shot in the eye. Stippling, so point blank on that one."

Morgan swiveled to look at Ronald, standing back talking to another officer. "M.E. already did their thing?"

"Yeah: TOD about one AM, give or take," Sam said.

"Help me roll the body?" Morgan asked, and they gloved up and squatted.

Holding the boy on his side, Morgan noted two more entrance wounds. One on the left shoulder, one just above the belt on the right side. A closer look at the buttocks showed there to be a third wound, right side gluteus maximus.

Morgan let the body roll back flat and stood, and started to walk along the path that caught her attention. Tiny scuffs in the dirt, like toes catching in the grass during a stumble. Drops of blood that started at the next large tree over. Morgan stood there, looked back at the body.

Ann-Marie Base walked up to where Morgan was standing. "Just got here. What have you got for me, Morgan?"

Morgan pointed out the scuffs and blood spots she had observed. "Maybe more, Ann-Marie. I just got here too. My initial assessment is that they were standing approximately here to start, then the young man saw the gun, turned to run, and the killer opened fire at him retreating. He was struck three times, and one of them made him stumble, right there. See that divot looking spot?"

"Yes." Ann-Marie agreed. Walking along either side of the path or retreat, Morgan looked at the ground. "I think this is the toeprint of the pursuer here." Morgan said, pointing at a triangular indent in the ground. "They were in full pursuit. They hit him with shots there, then there, then there." Morgan indicated each location on the ground. Ann-Marie nodded her agreement.

Morgan proceeded slightly further, pointed at the ground. "He then tripped here and fell. Ended up face up. The killer fired again, hit him in the leg, just above the knee. Assuming this is the same garbage .22 as the others, the distance between killer and victim is close, but just outside the range where there is GSR or at least much of it. Then, now shot four times, He scooted along on his back, kicking with his uninjured leg. I think these depressions are from his elbows. The killer moved in to point blank range and shot him in the face there. Hunted him. This killer is stone cold."

Ann-Marie cocked her head, looking at the young face. "Where is he from, you think?"

"Polynesian ancestry. US clothing. Lightweight cotton appropriate to the Houston climate. Also the South Pacific." Morgan answered.

Morgan bent over and looked at the watch. Very bright. Plastic case and band. "Swatch Watch. I think these are very popular right now. First even semi-identifying thing on this case."

"No wallet?" Ann-Maries asked.

"Not that I saw, but I did not check the pockets yet. I am guessing 'No'. I think the killer takes that kind of thing to try to hide who their victims are. Delay us. Anyway, to finish answering your question, my guess is that he is from Hawaii. I understand those watches are popular globally, but the clothing is pure middle class, linen/cotton mix shirt. Very tropical, but nothing someone could afford without a middle-class income at least. I am not married to this theory, but it is where I would start."

Sam commented "I saw all that of course. While you are tossing around theories, how are you on mine that this is the same killer as the other two kids."

Ann-Marie walked away as more of her team arrived, and started telling them what to cordon off, and what to label.

Morgan looked down and considered. "I think so, but obviously we'll need more from Cooper." Morgan indicated the dead young man's feet. "I assume you saw the shoes. Look the same to me. No major wear on the bottom, so brand new, and similar patterns. The model number probably nothing announced yet. I do not like that apparent escalation of violence here. Five bullets this time. Chasing him down to kill him. I think point blank in the face is a lot colder and more calculated than the back of the head shots where you are not looking your victim in the face as well. So much anger or hatred or pure psychopathy. What I would like to do to the Cabal."

"You would chase them down and shoot them in the face?" Sam asked.

"Only if they tried to get away." Morgan said.

Sam looked back along where the Crime Scene Unit was marking out the path the young man had been chased down. "Like this?"

"Of course not. I have a well maintained and accurate 9mm and I am a much better shot." Morgan said darkly. "This close in? Double tap to the head. Done."

"You scare me." Sam said.

"Why? You are not Cabal." Morgan said.

"No, and thank god." Sam said fervently.

While CSU processed the scene, they found a few more places where droplets of blood had fallen to the grass. A bullet strike with this caliber gun did not equal instant blood on ground results. Instead, movement and panic'ed blood pressure forced it out farther along the line of retreat.

CJ Stevens

Sam and Morgan watched from the sides, occasionally being called over to look at a new scuff or toeprint. Nothing found argued against Morgan's initial assessment, and in fact, appeared to support it entirely. The killer had cold-bloodedly taken this poor young man down like a trophy hunter.

"Hmmm." Morgan mused as they watched and she replayed the scene in her head.

"What?" Sam asked. Curious what Morgan was going to come up with next.

"I am changing my profile of the killer. I had it originally, with the first boy, as a professional hit. Then the second kill started to move me off that. This one? Moving me off that even farther. This is sloppy. Cold, but sloppy. The second thing I assumed was that the killer was known to the victims. This death and how it occurred makes it seem like they were not expecting the killer at all. We assume the killer is the same person, from the wounds, therefore, the type of gun used. Add in the weight and height estimates from the various scenes. Same size killer. This now feels more like that while they were lured here somehow, perhaps it was under false pretenses. That perhaps this young man did NOT know who killed him or at least did not to the level that they trusted them."

"You think that trail from first to final shot here supports the weight and height estimate of the killer from the other murders?" Sam asked.

"CSU will be able to give us scientific data, but at a guess, based off the divots, it looks like about the same width foot to me. They will know more once they have soil type and moisture content and such to know how much weight it would take to do that, but my initial guess is same as the loading dock in terms of foot size." Morgan said.

Sam walked over to one such divot, knelt and studied it. "Yeah. Looks the same to me too."

He stood. Looked back at the body sprawled out. Sam indicated the feet. "Also, let us not forget these shoes. Lydee's again."

"You get anywhere with the shoes yet?" Morgan asked. "I assume this kids are the same as the others in terms of being unannounced models, and if so they are becoming ever more key."

"Some progress. Not there yet." Sam said with a negative shake. "I called the sportswear company, and after major stonewalling, hangups, and threats finally got a call back from a marketing person this morning. They said that model is top secret and in the process of getting a national marketing campaign built around it. It is lighter than previous models, etc. He has no idea how the kids came to have them. Says that samples have been sent out to partners for local advertising but that local and regional chains, while they have restrictions on dates and presentation formats, are not restricted in the exact nature of the ad. It just had to be approved at corporate before it ran to be sure it met the highest standards and conveyed the brand message and ties in well with the national campaign. These local stores get 'guidelines' to follow. All that BS. I have the list of the local stores that carry them and triaged it by which ones would be big enough to run a tie-in campaign. Only two of those. Lydee's are high end: not the kind of shoe you would get at a place like Walmart or Target. Takes a specialty store. One that is big enough to afford advertising one specific product at a time, and will get enough traffic on that product to make it worthwhile, although it also seems like there might be a bit of a 'Halo product' thing to it. You know: We have this super-duper shoe, and people come in and buy something, if not the expensive shoe. These shoes on these kids, when announced, are going to cost over two hundred a pair."

"Ouch?" Morgan said. "I did not pay that for the bike shoes I use on the MS-150 rides, and they have special little bits to clip in the peddles."

Morgan looked over at the CSU team working away. "Ok. How about when we are done here, since we have to wait for Cooper, we pick one of those two stores you triaged, and go to their local HQ? See if we can find out what ad campaign they might have in the works."

"Sounds good. We can take your roller skate back to the office and leave it there. It is on the way since the bigger chain and the one that should have the bigger ad budget is in the next building over from The Stowell Agency."

"Worst case then, we can drop in on Irma for some coffee." Morgan agreed.

CHAPTER TWELVE

Sporting Goods

The reception area for University Sporting and Outdoor Equipment was located on the 19th floor. According to the directory in the lobby, USOE had three floors: 19, 20, and 21.

The receptionist on the 19th floor looked to be of college age, fit and wearing what appeared to be a sort of dressy tracksuit. The USOE logo was on her left breast where the pocket would have been if she had been wearing a suit rather than a track jacket. The visible white shirt had the 'SO' center part of the logo visible. Her permed brown hair was in a poof on the crown of her head, and she wore rather thick glasses, somewhat detracting from the overall theme. Morgan assumed she wore corrective goggles or contacts when out playing whatever sport it was that she used to maintain her rail-thin body.

"Hi, can I help you today?" the young woman asked very happily. Morgan assumed her joy was from the endorphins from her last run that were still kicked in. Either that or she was being a little judgmental because she was still angry at the Cabal, and had just seen another murdered boy. Could be that.

"Hello. My name is Morgan Olsen. This is my partner, Sam Parker. We are with Homicide." Morgan displayed her badge. "We need to talk to whoever it might be that would work on advertising campaigns here, specifically for new, unannounced shoes. Lydee shoes if that matters."

"Golly." Her eyes widened behind the glasses. "I have no idea who that might be, but I can start you with one of our marketing people and see if they might know who to talk to. Let see... Gaby Sprengle just went by a bit ago. Let me try her."

"Thank you. Yes. That would be a good start." Morgan said. She had no idea who Gaby Sprengle was or her place here, but it was forward motion.

The receptionist, whose nameplate identified her only as 'Patty', which went with the ethos of wearing a tracksuit to the office Morgan thought, started making calls.

While they waited Morgan imagined her desk plate saying only 'Morgan' and liked it. She never cared for the times JJ or one of the other Homicide detectives called her by just her last name. 'Olsen' as a single name form of address was somehow almost as bad as Sam's old crappy nicknames had been. Being addressed as only 'Olsen' is something Morgan never really fought though: Last names as only names are common when a lot of the people you work with are ex-military, as many cops are. Further, there was just a similar culture to it even without the military connection. Uniformed officers name badges were frequently just a last name. Rank was displayed elsewhere on the uniform so you could be 'Lt. Smith' by merely adding together a few things.

On the phone, Patty explained to someone she assumed to be 'Gaby' that Homicide detectives, and yes, there were two, were here and why, what was needed. Patty was told to call another person. Then a third. Morgan and Sam exchanged semi-amused glances but were not unused to the idea that when a homicide cop or two was standing in your lobby, that had a tendency to both be avoided and kicked up the line.

Ultimately a very elegant looking woman appeared. She was not dressed in a tracksuit, but rather standard issue upwardly mobile dress: a blue pinstripe skirt, jacket, oxford blue shirt with button down collar, red ribbon style tie. Directly from the Brooks Brothers catalog. Her straight brown hair, with just a few distinguished grays, was past her shoulders, curled on the end back into her body, and worn with long, carefully swept bangs. "Hello." She said, extending her hand to Sam. "I am Leanne Montgomery, VP of marketing. How can I help you, detective?"

Sam shook her hand, then said with a sweep of the hand at Morgan: "Well, you'll have to ask my boss, Ms. Montgomery." Sam tipped his head at Morgan. "This is Morgan Olsen, and this is also her thing. I just fetch her coffee." Leanne Montgomery went a little pale at her mistake. "Oh, my sincere apologies, Detective Olsen. Stupid of me to assume! I should know better!"

Morgan shook, and skipped past the apology, at the same time giving Sam a look of gratitude. "Ms. Montgomery, my partner and I are working a very difficult set of homicides. All three victims were wearing distinctive and unannounced Lydee sports footwear. Sam traced the advertising campaign that product would receive to here, and so we wondered if we could see any campaigns that might feature young men you may have underway, that would feature in particular a new shoe line for Lydee? I can also provide a model number for the shoe."

"Oh! My. Well. Please, come to my office, and let me see how we might be able to help you. Again, I DO apologize."

"Please: Sam is always having to focus people. I know I do not look like a lead detective." Morgan let her off the hook, sensing that even though this woman is marketing and therefore not required by her job to be sincere, she was genuinely distressed about this particular mistake.

They entered an elevator and went up to the 22nd floor. Morgan commented on that. "The lobby sign only indicates you having three floors, the top of which is 21."

Leanne Montgomery laughed. "It takes forever to get signage changed. We moved some of the executives up to make more room for the creatives. Our company is growing, and business is good. In fact, it is amazing we are doing so well since the national chains are always trying to get a piece of the market. We are just super well known here in town, and in the Texas Triangle, and people prefer our much more specific focus on both affordable and higher-end sporting goods. You can buy a five hundred dollar canoe from us, or a two thousand dollar one, for example. We are negotiating for the 23rd floor here as well, to build a new studio for commercials. Something bigger than what we have. Then we can turn over that space on 20 to be made into offices. Another reason to wait I suppose, because they would just have to change the signage again."

"I see." Morgan thought about that in terms of how accurate some things are in this world. It had no bearing on this case, but might be useful someday to know that the lobby sign is not necessarily the entire story.

"I assume that by the Texas Triangle, you mean Houston, San Antonio, Dallas/Fort Worth?" Sam asked.

Leanne Montgomery agreed "Yes, though it includes other places too. Austin. New Braunfels. San Marcos. Temple. Waco. College Station. Arlington. All the suburbs of those metros. We also have a few places down in the Rio Grande Valley. Looking at El Paso. We are stretched along I-10 all the way to Florida. Almost two hundred stores in all. We'll open store two hundred and fifty by the end of next year."

Perhaps the reason the VP's moved up was so more of them could get windows, Morgan thought. Leanne Montgomery had a large office with a wall of them, overlooking the 610 Loop, the offices buildings on the other side of the loop, and far off in the hazy distance, the main, original downtown area.

Seated, Morgan pulled two pictures out of a folder, explaining as she did so. "We have three young men, all shot to death in execution-style murders. Each was wearing shoes like these. You can see the model numbers from the inner label: As I said, it is not an announced model. A third boy was found just today, wearing these shoes. Why we are asking you about them is this: These young men have no identification on them. None. Whoever is killing them is taking it, and the only thing we have to go on right now is that this footgear it utterly unique. All three wearing the same model of unannounced footwear is not a coincidence."

Sam took up the narrative. "As you can see, those are made by a sportswear conglomerate. Lydee makes everything: Shoes, socks, underwear, tracksuits, every kind of implement used for sports: bats, rackets, gloves, you name it. They even plaster that name on things not specifically sports related. They have some major sports celebrities doing their advertising. When I talked to their marketing people, they said this particular model was distributed to partners, and that there is a coordinated set of advertising. They do national things, and then companies like yours advertise that you carry them, and put your own spin on it."

"That sounds accurate." Leanne Montgomery agreed. "I know of our upcoming shoe campaign of course. Not the details." She tapped the picture. "This shoe is being marketed specifically to upwardly mobile kids. Fun patterns and functional characteristics. Very light. Cross Sport competition treads so that they can be used to run or play tennis or whatever. Most kids that buy them will never use them for anything but walking between classes."

"So you are planning tie-in advertising?" Morgan asked. "The local tie-in to the national campaign Sam just mentioned?"

"Oh, absolutely!" Leanne Montgomery enthused. "Lydee thinks this shoe line is their next big product. I saw very convincing presentations on that during a closed-door event in Las Vegas a few months ago.

There is also an element of exclusivity to this particular line. You can purchase Lydee products all over, but not these when they are released. For the first six months of availability, only a few national and regionals will even have them. This line will never be available at mass market stores. To support all of this Lydee will be running a national set of print and video ads and during big events like the World Series and the Superbowl next year. The print campaign will be in not just sporting related magazines, but fashion ones. Lifestyle magazines. Even 'Cosmo' and 'Playboy', if you can believe that. We need to be ready on our end to move these. In store, we'll have end caps and a dedicated set of shelves, with signage to match the campaigns. Other Lydee tie-in products, like sports socks and outerwear for the active lifestyle. Lydee wants young people to wear them on dates even. If you can only have one pair of shoes... Like that."

Leanne Montgomery looked at the pictures. "We have in-house talent to make the commercials and the in-store signage using Lydee approved logos and such, but of we work with local talent agencies to recruit the faces for the signs and the actors in the commercials. One particular meeting I went to about this campaign said they were thinking about trying a new thing: going to a local high school and having open auditions. It would be a big school to be sure there were enough kids responding and that had the right look. Just a moment: let me get Darren in here. He was in charge of this."

Leanne Montgomery called on her desk phone and moments later a besuited middle age man appeared.

"Darren Fischer, this is Lead Detective Morgan Olsen, and her Partner Sam Parker. They are with the police, in the Homicide group, and need to ask some questions about the Lydee campaign."

Morgan tried not to smile at that very specific introduction. Also that 'Homicide' was a 'group'. Ms. Montgomery was not making the mistake about Morgan's rank twice.

Whatever Darren thought he was being called into the office for, that was not it. "Err: OK? That commercial is not even out yet. Won't be for weeks. Last I saw, Dick was still cutting it because he was just not happy with the flow and music sync. He and Sarah are butting heads over it too. Also, he is about to fire the voice-over talent. Said they sound like they are selling cars."

Morgan stood and used her five foot eleven of height to look directly into Darren's eyes as she shook his hand. She wanted him to focus on her problem, not his. "We are not here to discuss that particular set of logistics. Sam and I are after names of kids who were in the commercial, to see if they line up with the faces of three young men that have been murdered."

Darren made his mouth into an 'O' shape. "I see. Well... The Lydee stuff? How do you want to do that?"

"If you have a casting book with photos, that would be handy. Worst case, we watch the commercial as currently cut and see if our victims are in it." Morgan said.

"Sure. I have the casting list with the pictures. We cast that thing at a high school. A 5A school called 'Ronald E. Evans'. You know what? Never again. It is bad enough working with kids with controlling parents. At least the ones that work in the business know the ropes. How things work. I got so tired of explaining over and over why we did not use little Johnny or little Sally for the final cut."

Morgan tried to look sympathetic. "That does sound tiring."

"Let me go get the book. Also, see if Sarah Luchs is available. She directed that commercial and cast it. I was just there, and mostly went with what she wanted in terms of look and such."

"Very nice. Thank you." Morgan said, and Darren exited quickly. It seemed he did not like self-confident Homicide police officers looking in his eyes.

"Let's use my conference table." Leanne Montgomery said, pointing at a round table behind the two chairs Morgan and Sam sat in. It had six chairs, a speakerphone in the middle. "That way you can spread out as you look. Also, would you like anything to drink? Excuse my manners. I am really off my game today."

"Do you often deal with Homicide detectives appearing in your office?" Sam asked as they stood to move over to the table.

"First time." Leanne admitted. "So, water? Juice? Coffee? We have a well-stocked kitchen just up the hall."

"Water would be fine for me." Morgan said. If Angel were here, she would know Morgan did not really want refreshments, but she was afraid Leanne was about to start apologizing for something else. Accepting hospitality usually eased things.

"Same" Sam said.

"I will be right back" Morgan had expected that to be a 'buzz the secretary' situation, but upon review decided that both personal service and being able to escape were goals of Leanne's.

Leanne returned with two chilled bottles of expensive spring water, imported from an island on the other side of the world, two glasses, and coasters imprinted with the company logo.

"Thank you." Morgan said, opening it and pouring some into her glass. "Nothing for you?"

"I had a big lunch." Leanne explained and Morgan doubted that. You do not wear expensive clothes like hers and risk changing sizes. Leanne Montgomery is in the Marketing profession and at an executive level. Appearances are reality in that world.

Darren reappeared with a large book. "Sarah said she'll come up here in a bit. She is talking to someone on the phone about... God knows what. Here is the casting book." Darren laid it on the table and then topped it with a printed list of names. "That's all the kids we cast from the school. Not every single one is actually in the commercial because cutting room floor things happen. We do a lot of takes and mix up the faces, and then go with the ones that we like the look of on tape, or whose movements matched the music at that spot or whatever."

"How were the kids paid for this?" Sam asked. Morgan had that question on her list too.

"It was one day of work. A Saturday, over at the park. The one near the zoo?" Darren asked.

"Hermann Park?" Sam asked.

"Yeah. That's it. First time I was ever there. I don't have kids... Anyway, we paid them with the shoes. They got to keep them. Plus a bunch of other Logo stuff. A gift card to the store. Like that."

"Is that normal?" Morgan asked.

Darren shrugged "Is casting your commercial at a high school full of kids that never acted for a day in their life normal?" and seeing the look on Morgan's face hastily amended "Yes. If they aren't professional and the release forms are like just for that day's work and such, they often do stuff like that. Payment in kind. They aren't actors or models with contracts or guilds or whatever. A lot of them are hoping that this is how they get INTO the business. A few even looked like they could make that cut, but the whole idea of this one was to make it look totally real. Real kids doing real things, in these shoes. These shoes fit their lifestyle. On like that."

Sam tapped Morgan's shoulder "Morgan?" Sam pointed at a picture. "The second kid. His name is Neil Armstrong Snyder."

Morgan gave Sam a light, happy fist to shoulder. "You did it, Sam! You found the connection! Excellent work!"

Darren and Leanne exchanged looks of deep dismay "Oh. Crap." Darren said and sounded positively horrified.

"What?" Morgan asked. "This is good. It means we know where the killer found their victims. Maybe how. Maybe we can stop it from happening again to one of these other kids on this list." Morgan tapped the list of names Darren had provided.

Leanne gave a poisonous look at Darren. "Darren knows we can't use that commercial any more."

"Oh. I see." Morgan said, and she did see. She also thought it very small of Darren to be worried about that issue at that particular moment. So far, it seemed Darren spent a lot of time worrying about how HE was personally affected by things.

Sam kept flipping pages in the book. Stopped. "Morgan: The kid from this morning."

Morgan read out loud "Ailani Aquino"

After some more flipping, Morgan said before Sam could, but it was close "First kid. Derek Jefferson. We need to get over to that high school fast. Warn them."

Leanne Montgomery said "Let me help you out there, Detective Olsen. Darren, get copies of those pictures for the detective, please. Also their release forms: I assume that they will need to notify next of kin. That should be on there."

Morgan had a feeling Leanne Montgomery was going to make up for Darren worrying about the ruin of his commercial by being as helpful as she could. She used the phone to call her administrative assistant. "Gladys, would you get the principal of the Ronald E. Evans High school on the phone, please? No call backs: if Paul demurs tell him this is critical. Life or death kind of critical. Seriously. Thank you, dear. Put it through to the conference phone. Thank you."

Three minutes later the phone came to life. "I have Paul on the line, Leanne." Gladys said.

"Thank you, Gladys. Paul?"

"Life or death, Leanne? Really?" the principal of Ronald E. Evans asked, apparently everyone on a first name basis.

"Paul: really." Leanne Montgomery used her Vice President of a big company voice to nail that down fast. Her next words underlined it for the man. "I have Homicide Lead Detective Morgan Olsen and her partner in my office. It's horrible, Paul. Three kids from the school have been killed. Here is Detective Olsen to explain." Leanne shimmed Morgan into the conversation quickly.

"Detective?" Paul asked. It was a sort of 'this better not be a joke' tone of voice. Seems Leanne's VP voice had not completely sold it yet.

"We have had three young men killed in the last few days, Principal." Morgan said in her voice that brooked no arguments. She made 'Principal' sound like 'Young man' when he had been a kid and being lectured about his bad behavior. Leanne gave Morgan a shrewd look. "Until today we did not know who they were, but we have just learned their names are Derek Jefferson, Neil Snyder, and Ailani Aquino. All were shot, execution style, and their bodies left in various locations in and near the Montrose. I hear your skeptical tone, and I understand since what we are discussing here is so very serious, however, if you need to, I can give you my badge number, and you can look up the phone number for Homicide and verify my identity. Leanne has seen my badge, however. She would not have called you like this if this was not deadly serious. We need to be sure your students are warned, as we are not sure how the students are being targeted, other than they all go to your school, and all were in the Lydee shoe commercial. So far, all are male as well, but there is no way to know if that has meaning or not."

Sam added "My name is Sam Parker. The killing patterns suggest that whoever is killing these boys is familiar to them. It could be anyone they know either from the school or the commercial. We need to warn everyone there without delay."

The Principal of Ronald E. Evans High was quiet the entire time. "How soon can you get here, Detectives?" he asked. It seemed verifying Morgan's identity was not going to happen. Morgan assumed from his tone of voice he had changed mental lanes and was already processing how to proceed.

CHAPTER THIRTEEN
Ronald E. Evans High School

Sam was running the magnetically attached emergency light, and his siren as they raced into town and the campus of the school.

Morgan's phone rang, and she was loath to answer it as it meant she had to let go of the grab handles. The number on the LCD screen was Cooper's however. Morgan would always take his call, even when dangling from the roof of the truck.

"Hi, Cooper." She said over the wail of the siren.

"Thought I would tell you I have a name on one of the kids. Neil Snyder. I was able to trace back the serial numbers on the pump I mentioned."

Morgan said "Thanks Cooper, but Sam already found that out. Your first kid is named Derek Jefferson. The kid from today is named Ailani Aquino. They all go to the same school, and were all in a TV commercial about shoes together."

Cooper gave that two beats of pause. "Sam Parker found out the names before I did." He said in a sort of grumpy disbelief.

"Sam beat you bad on this one, Cooper. Sorry." Morgan enjoyed the look of satisfaction on Sam's face when he heard that.

"Well, fine. I guess I'll go get the bullet out of Ailani's head then. By the way, the first two kids are 100% match. Same gun. I have a lot of bullets to pull today, but at the very least, one of the ones in the thigh or the glut should be intact. I am guessing the same. Entry wounds look like .22. This kid looks like he was hunted."

"I think he saw the gun and tried to run and whoever it was shot him over and over till he slowed down enough they could shoot him in the eye. None of those hits were fatal before that one." Morgan explained her theory of the crime scene. "Let me know what you find,

Cooper. I need to call JJ and let him know what is up." Morgan said, and they hung up.

Morgan called her boss next. "JJ, Morgan. We have names..." Morgan knew with a break in the case she could be 'Morgan', not 'Olsen' for the purposes of the call. Morgan fully reported the break in the case, and again mentioned it was Sam's 'shoe leather' that got it done.

"We are on the way to the school now to meet with the principal." Morgan leaned into a turn, holding the phone tightly. "I am sure they are going to go on some kind of lockdown, activate their emergency protocols, call all the parents, all that."

"Sure." JJ agreed. "Call me from there after you talk to the school people. Morgan: Excellent work. Both of you. Also, thought you should know, Derek Jefferson just showed up on the missing child sheet. I just looked at the picture while we were talking. It's the first dead kid."

After she hung up, Morgan resumed two-handed clinging to the handle and said "This was destined to break today no matter what. Cooper had a name. Derek showed up on the missing child report just now. We were ALWAYs going to be having this ride to the high school today."

"I bet you wish you were driving." Sam teased.

"So very much..." Morgan agreed. "I have never been to this school: I hope they have a nice runway for you to park on."

The Ronald E. Evans High School campus went vertical whenever it could. Where most schools are two or three stories tall in Houston, this one was five. Student parking was a parking garage, as was teacher parking. They had to make room for the sporting complex somehow, Morgan assumed, because everything around it was typical Houston short and wide. The pickup and drop off lanes were clearly marked, and led up to a portico. Sam pulled up to the front, his spinner dramatically flashing light off the windows and doors on the front of the building. There were five adults waiting at the front of the school. As school was not out yet, they were either all in class, or the school had been placed on some sort of 'keep kids in classes' alert.

Even as Morgan and Sam stepped out, marked four-door police cruisers came screaming up to the building, presumably sent by JJ.

Morgan flashed her badge as she walked up. The man in the center of the five people stepped forward "I'm Paul Rafferty, principal. This is my staff. Detective Olsen..."

"Sorry to be meeting under this circumstance." Morgan said, then waved "My partner, Sam Parker."

"Come to the office." Paul Rafferty said, and they headed into the school. His staff waited behind to talk to the new wave of police officers.

"Derek's parent just reported him missing today. You have to wait..." The Principal started to explain.

"Yes: we identified the young men only shortly before that report came in. Sam was able to trace them through their shoes." Morgan said. "Had we literally not just figured their names out, we would still be here now because of that report. Also, the M.E. just discovered Neil's name forensically."

Paul Rafferty's office was nothing like Leanne Montgomery's. It was good sized, but being in the center of the building, had no windows. The white walls were covered in pictures of various school-related activities. Sports teams and certificates of achievement for things. Paul was just finishing up explaining the school was on a sort of hold, and teachers were rotating through in the auditorium being updated on emergency procedures.

"I have already made the all-school announcement about the loss of these boys. Everyone needs to understand why we are activating all this. No child will leave this school in an unusual way today. Bus drivers are being told be sure that they watch the kids more closely than ever as they leave the bus. All children are being reminded to not trust strangers. You know the drill."

"Been a few years since I was in school, but I get the general idea, yes." Morgan agreed. "The department will take care of family notifications for these three young men. I presume classes will not be held tomorrow, and that you will have counselors available?"

"Classes will not be held, but the school will be open for families for whom their situations do not allow for their kids to stay at home. There are a lot of families where both parents work. Also, none of the boys was killed here. Maybe this is the safer place?" Paul Rafferty wondered aloud, seeming to want input on that last idea.

"With everyone on high alert like this, I would think so. What we need to further this investigation is to talk to the other children that were in the commercial. Thus far, only kids from that commercial have been killed and it is a reasonable next place for us to look for motive. As it stands right now, we do not know WHY these three boys were picked out. We were looking at the idea of a serial killer until all of this came to light. Now that we know that they all went to school here, and they all were in this commercial, that changes the optics for me. This could be personal."

Morgan slid the pictures Leanne had made for her. "Do you know these boys at all?"

Paul Rafferty shook his head very slowly left and right, but it seemed to be sadness, not negation. "I know Neil. His family came in when he started here and explained a few private things to me about him. I can't share why, but we created a special gym program for him so that he never had to be in the boys' locker room."

"Because he was transsexual and you were afraid that other boys, upon seeing him naked, would figure it out?" Morgan asked.

Paul looked up from the picture. "Of course you know. Sorry. Yes. Exactly. We tried to accommodate him. I was clear that Neil is a 'him', and his route to becoming a male was not known outside this office. Myself and the school counselor were it. Oh, and the nurse. Just in case."

"In case of some jock kicking him in the groin because he was not in gym class?" Sam asked.

Paul gave Sam a pained expression but agreed. "Yes. Children can be cruel about differences. Special treatment."

"Yeah. I don't miss high school." Sam said.

"Do you have a fax machine I can use?" Morgan asked. "I need to send the contact information over to my boss so he can arrange notifications. I assume you did not release names in your all-school announcement."

"Yes: It's right out there behind the receptionist station. And no, of course not, but Derek's name is being widely tossed about as everyone knows he has not been in school and many know he was reported missing. He was a popular kid. Track star." Paul said.

Morgan faxed her stack of paper to JJ. Pictures. Name list of every student in the commercial. Release forms with contact information. It took a few minutes, as fax machines are slow to scan and transmit things over phone lines.

When it was done, Morgan called JJ again. "Hey, boss. I just sent you all the details on the three young men. Pictures. Contact information. The names of the other kids in the commercial. Everything we developed today."

"Thanks, Morgan. I think. I'll have some Uni's go do the notifications at their homes. I will let you know when that is done." JJ assured.

"Thanks, boss." They hung up, and Morgan went back into the office. Morgan was still 'Morgan' to JJ, so she was using 'Boss'. He liked to be called that.

"Notifications are underway. Uniformed officers will be sent to each home." Morgan reported. "My commanding officer will let me know when that is done. I will tell you so you know so you can orchestrate releasing the names according to however that works here. In the meantime, we need to work with you to set up interviews with this list of kids."

Morgan handed over the list of all the kids in the commercial.

Paul Rafferty scanned the list. "That is going to take a while. Some of these kids will want to have their parents there or the other way. Most of these kids are between sixteen and nineteen years of age, but most are under eighteen, so I can't haul them into a conversation with the police without parental consent."

Morgan understood the principal was thinking about his problems at the school now, but she needed to catch whoever was doing this so she said very firmly: "Principal Rafferty: Whatever it takes. We do not know WHY these three kids were killed, and anyone on that list might be a target. I need to talk to them. I need to understand WHY. Now that we know the 'who' of this crime, we need to prevent this from happening again to one of those other people. The best way to protect your students is to help us catch who is doing this."

He heard the tone, and presumably as principal was not used to people taking it with him. Morgan had taken parental/authority type intonations with him twice in one day. Morgan watched his face change as various reactions to being told what HE had to do flowed through his mind. He landed on "Paul, please, Detective. We are going to be working together on this. I was only trying to let you know that it will take some time, NOT that we would not be in full and complete cooperation with you on your investigation. We will help you in every possible way, within the legal limits we have, and perhaps bending those if need be. I will take this list, and work with my associate principals to develop an interview schedule. We will make all the calls to get students in at their appointed time. As you say, we will be closed for a few days, but that gives us a chance to schedule students in to talk to you in a more private way. How much time should we set for each student on the list?"

"I would allow at least two hours. It will not run that long for most of them, but if we find someone that has useful information I want to be sure we have time." Morgan glanced at her partner, and Sam nodded agreement to that timeline.

Paul smiled at that "Well, that will help with setup time as well. There are seventeen names here, not counting the three boys, so that will take three, maybe four days. The older ones we can get in first, and work out a way to the ones that need more time and a parent to set aside time to be here." He paused. "In fact, we can probably get two or three in by tomorrow afternoon."

"Excellent. Thank you." Morgan scribbled on her card. Handed it to him. "This is my information. Office and my personal cell. I have also added the information for my Lieutenant. JJ Alvarez: He can help you with various things like campus security and police interactions. I assume you will want a uniformed police presence for a while until we can resolve this."

"Absolutely." Paul Rafferty agreed.

CHAPTER FOURTEEN

Breaking and Entering

On the way home, Morgan used her new wired headset with her new phone to call Wendell.

"Hey!" He said, clearly happy to hear from her.

"Hey back. Just want to let you know some things going on up here. Break in my case."

"Oh? Tell me!" Wendell said, and Morgan realized one nice thing about dating another Cop is that she could talk about work, and have it be understood. She had missed that aspect of being with DeWayne without really realizing it. Morgan proceeded to relate everything that had happened since and included Sam's work to get the names.

"Wow. Good work Sam!" Wendell enthused, as if Sam was there to hear it.

"Yes: I felt slightly bad about giving him that crummy job because I was angry with him, and not that I told HIM that, but man! Did that ever pay off!"

"You start interviews tomorrow it sounds like." Wendell said.

"I'll call Principal Rafferty tomorrow to see what he has been able to arrange, but yes. That is the plan. With any luck at all, I may have that long weekend soon."

"I can't wait." Wendell said.

"So: I did all the talking so far and you listened nicely. I was excited about the idea we might get that weekend so I had to share. What was your day like?" Morgan asked, and felt slightly shy asking. She wondered about that.

"Well, let's see. I broke up a fight in a bar on the seawall. Woman did not like her drink, and came over the bar at the bartender. Got a domestic disturbance call in the Painted Lady district. Little dude was getting thrashed by his boyfriend. Pulled over a car weaving around on I-45. There turned out to be a girl who was having sex with the driver. Not oral sex: Intercourse. Little bitty slip of a girl so he could see around her, but let's face it: Distracting."

"Much better than DUI." Morgan commented.

"Oh?" Wendell asked.

"Impaired driving is impaired driving, but sounds far more interesting and fun to be having sex than to be drunk. Maybe that is just me." Morgan teased.

"No: I agree. I just think the car should be stopped is all. If they had been on the side of the road, I would have said 'have a nice day and be safe out there.' But they were weaving all over. I had to cite for reckless endangerment. I did tell them about a nice place they could pull over and finish what they started though."

"You are a giver." Morgan told him, smiling. "I guess you take all your women there?"

"Not ALL of them." Wendell replied.

"Have to work your way up to that, I suppose. Like a merit badge." Morgan teased further.

"Nope. Just have to be physically IN the County and also in the mood for some outdoor loving. I am an equal opportunity roadside lover." Wendell teased back. A reference to them being a 'long distance' relationship.

"Oh. Ouch. Well, at least I am in the same category as all your out-of-town lovers." Morgan said.

"Yes: Although at the risk of sounding like I am falling down on the job, you are currently the only out-of-towner, so only you have deprived me of that experience. Oh: By the way: I took my phone apart the other day, it is not bugged, or I would not be HAVING this conversation. I marked it too, so that if it IS bugged, I'll know it. Hair on the door kind of thing. They take it apart, I will know."

"Oh: good idea. I will do that too because I like being able to tease you over the phone." Morgan said, happy to know this. She was also kicking herself for not thinking of making it obvious if her phone was tampered with again. Not like these guys can be trusted at ALL.

Morgan studied her new phone closely and decided that the classic hair trick would work. She raided her hairbrush and cut a strand down and after several tries, was able to get two short strands to lay between the two halves of the case and just barely protrude near the upper right and lower left corner of the candy bar shape. She then screwed it back together and studied the tool marks she had made to be sure she remembered what they looked like, in case those changed as well.

She did the same thing with the battery cover, then slid the candy bar shape back into the new leather case which would cover the even minuscule hair protrusions. She then plugged that into her charger, and set it on her bedside table. Every day from now till she took the Cabal down, she would check that.

In theory, it is impossible to bug cellular signals. The CIA or the NSA probably had the tech to do it and it was top secret, but the way spread spectrum calls worked meant that it would be VERY hard to merely possess a radio in the right frequency ranges and try to intercept and put her signal back together. She moves around with her cell phone, which means her tower changes too. Each new connection is a new arrangement for her signal as they negotiate the best way to communicate.

The Cabal could, in theory, bug all the cell towers themselves, but that is massive scale, not to mention having reach far beyond what Morgan thought they had. Morgan would be the first to admit it is JUST a guess, but she felt from the way they communicated that they were local to her. Maybe even only inside Homicide, but more likely the department as a whole, spread out. Some associated places in Houston. Maybe Fire. Friends in media to be sure. Galveston County seemed to be free of their pestilence though. Wendell once told her that the only shit he got about her was standard macho bullshit about 'How did HE get so lucky to be dating the hot lady detective.' And so forth.

Morgan had scoffed at that. "You are seeing a HOT lady detective too?"

"Morgan." Wendell had replied. One impatient word.

"I truly do NOT think of myself as 'HOT'" Morgan replied back, irritated at his ability to rebuke her like that.

"Lady. False modesty does NOT become you." Wendell had said.

Morgan still did not view herself as anything other than just being herself, but she had not pressed the point then. It did not matter. 'Hot' or not, they were seeing each other, and he was very much 'hot' in her mind. It was about so much more than looks at this point for her. She thought he felt the same.

* * *

Morgan was not sleeping well. Her mind was churning and ricocheted from topic to topic.

There was her complicated love life. Not for the first time she wondered if she should simplify it. Maybe the reason people are monogamous is just to keep things simple?

Then there was the Cabal, and who they were and why they had picked her for their attention. That was anger and some fear mixed together in her uneasy mind. Morgan did not want people like that to win, or to even exist, but at the same time, it would be SO easy to just say 'screw it' and go back to school and learn a different career. It was not as if she could not do pretty much anything. Hell, with her computer minor, she could just switch to programmer NOW and be done with it.

Or she could go private. A PI license would be trivial to get. Then she could investigate cheating spouses instead of murders. That had no real appeal. Be nice if she could go private in such a way as to still be doing important work. Work that mattered, in the same way that what she did on Homicide mattered.

Morgan had firm ideas for what kinds of things are important in this world. What things are trivial and useless. Cheating spouses came under the general heading of 'Who cares' for her. If you suspect they are cheating, and that bothers you, then you are already in trouble. Solving murders and trying to get justice for the families is important. Finding a cure for cancer is important. Discovering a new form of matter. Important. Who won last nights sports match? That got a big shrug.

Bubbling around in between all of the personal topics was this case. What was the motive? Why kill three young men from this commercial? What kinds of questions did she need to be asking the other kids in the commercial?

Morgan sensed someone was in her room. She slept alone other than her cats, and her cats spent the night on her pillow or her feet or both. Tonight one was in each place, and she was not sure who had won the toss for the pillow. They have normal spots, but sometimes they change things around. Cats figure out such things between each other. She opened one eye and in the moonlight from the window saw it was the usual occupant. Watson, her overweight Himalayan cat. That made Spicy the one in her usual foot-of-the-bed location. Whatever woke her, it was not cat wrongness. Or maybe it was. Watson was fully awake and staring at something in the dark. She listened. She felt the air stir.

The window was open.

Morgan did not sleep with the window open this time of year. Even if the air was cooler, it was still humid. That was her second clue to things being amiss. The air smelled wrong. It was outside air. 'Fresh' air to the degree that is a possibility in summertime Houston. At least she was not near the ship channel and all the chemical plants over that way. The smell of freshly made synthetic rubber would wake her for sure.

Morgan could not sense movement in the shadows, but waited, and finally caught the sound of the lightest 'whish' of fabric against fabric.

Morgan rolled and caught the shadow against her moonlit window. Tall, thin, male, dressed one hundred percent in black. A stealthy hand reaching for her phone on the table. He froze realizing she was awake, and then he was rolling backward trying to avoid the sheet of the bed being thrown over him. Morgan had her gun out of the top drawer and holster before the sheet fully fluttered to the ground, and was crouched to minimize her shape in case the man in her room was armed.

He was diving to the window rather than pulling a weapon.

"I am armed. Stop NOW or I fire." Morgan warned, saw no slowing, and with no hesitation center-mass shot at his back. Double tap.

Texas laws are fairly relaxed about shooting people in your house. A man on the second story that came in through the window, dressed entirely in black approaching a naked woman in her bed would not cause any legal concerns at all. That Morgan is a peace officer? Even less.

That is not the same thing as Morgan wanting to shoot someone. Before tonight she never had. Just person-shaped targets. Friend-or-foe obstacle course scenarios. She was trained to act correctly in the moment. She was not thinking about any of that as she fired. She was letting her training have full rein.

The dark outline of the man-shape pitched forward and out the window, and to Morgan's instant assessment, it did not look like a controlled exit. She mentally played back the sound of her two shots landing and decided the man was wearing a vest.

Bulletproof vests do not mean that there is no feeling the impact of a round. Morgan fired her gun at a range of less than ten feet, and her 9mm slugs were jacketed hollow points, to minimize the chance of a through and through and injuring someone on the other side of an intended target. At 147 grains and nearly one thousand feet per second, they impacted her target with over 300 foot-pounds of energy and she hit him twice. At the very least they knocked the wind out of him, and the slugs might even break some ribs despite the body armor. A vest spreads the energy, but it has to go somewhere.

Morgan moved quickly to the window and looked out, seeing that a black ladder leaned against her house. At the base of it, sprawled in an unnatural way, the black outline of a body against her lawn.

Morgan grabbed her new phone, and raced down the stairs, dialing 911 as she went, only going slowly enough to keep from falling in her unlit house.

Banging out the back door, and turning to the right Morgan moved quickly and carefully to the bedroom intruder, her gun ready. Her eyes were dark-adapted from having been asleep, and in the moonlight, she could see the unmoving figure was face down. His head was cocked at an off angle, and now she had a choice as 911 came on the phone.

"911: What is your emergency?" came the operators' voice.

"My name is Detective Morgan Olsen, with Houston Homicide." She replied and gave her badge number. "I have just shot a bedroom intruder at my house, and he fell out of the second-floor window as I did so. Please wait for a moment. I am standing by the man and have to put the phone down to check for a pulse. I am still armed should they try to do anything."

"Absolutely, Detective. I am scrambling emergency response to your location." The 911 Operator replied in a calm voice.

Since Morgan was NOT going to set her gun down, she laid the phone down in the grass and used her left hand to lift the neck edge of the mask and check for a pulse. There was none. Morgan verified that he was, in fact, wearing a bulletproof vest, and felt for where her shots had landed. Either side of the spine, heart level. One of the hollow points was embedded. A quick glance in the grass found the other, the shiny copper colored jacket glinting in the moonlight.

Morgan removed the ski mask by grasping the place where the knitting converged at the crown of the head and looked at the dead mans face. No one she knew. Black hair. Heavy brows. Short cropped black beard. She guessed him to be in his thirties.

Morgan picked up the phone. "The intruder broke his neck falling out of the window. He was wearing a bulletproof vest, and my rounds did not penetrate. We will need the M.E. here, not an ambulance."

"Understood. You are OK, Detective Olsen?" The calm 911 person asked.

Morgan thought about that. "I am physically unharmed." She

replied. There was no point in sharing the outrage and violation of having someone break into your house.

"I am going to call my partner on the force now. I will remain with the body until your response teams arrive. Have them come around to the back of the house. That is where I am." Morgan told the operator.

Before she called Sam, Morgan decided to put down her gun and phone and check his pockets.

She found a small toolset and a fresh phone bug. Of course. The Cabal.

Morgan called Sam, and it took him a while to answer.

"Morgan?" Sam asked.

"Hi, Sam. Sorry for the call at this time of night but I thought you would want to know. The Cabal sent a guy to my house to do some B&E, and re-bug my phone. I shot him, he fell out of the second story bedroom window and broke his neck. He is very dead."

"On my way." Sam said, instantly awake, and he hung up before Morgan could say anything else.

In a snap decision, Morgan went inside and placed the toolkit and bug in a kitchen drawer rather than tell Harris County law enforcement about it. Morgan lived in the County, not the city. While inside she grabbed her 35mm film camera and some scotch tape and went out and took her own set of crime scene photos, glad the batteries in her electronic flash were fresh. She concentrated on the face, holding the camera at a strained angle to get the face as full on as she could, given the grass. Next, she lifted a set of fingerprints after removing the dead man's black gloves.

Morgan slid the gloves back on to the body and took everything back into the house, and returned again to the dead intruder. She picked up her gun and phone from the grass and stood there thinking about the fact that she had shot at a living human for the first time in her life. She had threatened to before, but never had. In one place of her roiling thoughts, she was glad to know that, when push came to shove, she could actually do what she needed to. It is a thing about yourself you can never really know until faced with it. Morgan had not frozen. She had not flinched. She warned and she fired.

Given the phone bug, there was zero doubt that this action had been taken by the Cabal, and she had no idea if they had Harris County connections. Morgan was not taking a chance they did. This was a violation of her home, but it was also a break. They made an overt move against her.

A Harris County Sheriffs department car came racing into her driveway, light bar ablaze but not running siren. Her car and truck were in the garage, so they came all the way to the back, and hopped out quickly.

The officers walked over, and Morgan greeted them "Morning." She said, omitting the 'good' since obviously when you kill someone at your house there is nothing good about the morning.

Morgan knew both cops by name but not well. Charla Pitt and Kelly Ginsberg. This area was their beat in the County.

Charla nodded in response. "Detective Olsen. Hell of a thing. We are here if you want to go put some clothes on now. Kelly doesn't need any more wet dreams than he already has."

"Err.." Morgan looked down and realized she was naked except for her gun and phone. "Well, damn." Morgan said. "In all the excitement. Well. Obviously. Be right back."

Kelly complained to her "You are gay and you liked that every bit as much as I did."

"I know." Charla said. "It's OK if I have dreams about her. Just not you."

"How is THAT fair?" Kelly complained.

"You are a pervert, where I am classy." Charla told him.

"Sez the woman that screwed our Hooters waitress recently..."

"She was cute, interested, and had a nice lady-friend to join us." Charla tormented.

Morgan thought they had been partners for a while.

Morgan is not deeply body conscious, but she is aware that society expects people to be clothed in certain situations. Dead people in your back yard is one of them, and she imagined that she just started a story that would make the rounds of County and probably get into the city department as well.

Take THAT Cabal. A naked detective story that won't be salacious, since it is from the death of their operative.

As Morgan went inside, the partners fighting good-naturedly about who liked Morgan's body more, Morgan heard more cars arriving. The chatter of the car radios as well as the belt or shoulder units. It was like one of her crime scenes, except she WAS the crime scene this time.

Morgan got dressed in jeans, tennis shoes, and a ZZ Top "Antenna" tour T-Shirt. She clipped her badge on her belt, and tucked her gun into a holster and clipped that on too. This was her gun, not her service weapon. It was deeply unlikely that the County officers would want it for testing, but she would have it should it come up.

Morgan returned to the back yard to find eight officers standing around the body. She knew most of them.

Charla watched Morgan approach. "I won't say that is BETTER, Detective, because it totally isn't. Less distracting for sure."

Her partner Kelly said "Though with a body on the ground, distracting is good too. Some of us don't see deaders every day like you do."

Morgan smiled. "It is not every day, Kelly. Just a lot of them recently, it seems. We can all go to a nude beach later and compare moles. Start some nice juicy rumors that way too."

Charla gave Morgan an appraising look. "You don't HAVE any moles I could find. I looked. I do though. I'll show them to you."

Morgan considered Janie at a nude beach for a few microseconds. Smiled. Mentally switched to Wendell. Liked that even better.

As they sat around chatting and Morgan telling the story of how she woke up and saw the intruder, and several officers scribbling away in notepads, Sam arrived. That meant he had broken every speed law there was between his house and hers. He was running his mag-mount spinner. That thing was getting a work out lately.

Morgan introduced Sam around, and Sam squatted to look at the body. "This guy was in your bedroom?" Sam looked up at the window and the ladder.

"Yes. I woke up, felt the air moving around when it should not have been, rolled, got my gun from the top drawer of the bedside, warned, and when he continued to flee, fired. He fell out the window he was headed to anyway, and you can see the result."

Morgan was already tired of telling this story.

"Broken neck, obviously." Sam stood.

"My guess, looking at the vest and where I hit him with the two rounds is that the impacts stunned him, and he fell uncontrolled and face first. A second-floor fall is not usually fatal, and especially not if you are loose and falling to grass, but look at his mask there. Dirt and grass stains on the chin. I think it just snapped his neck, impacting in that way."

"Good riddance. Nice grouping by the way. Tight. Centered." Sam said, pointing at the back of the vest."

"That is what I was going for: A high score on my gun range test." Morgan gave Sam a very mild amount of gallows humor.

The next arrival was the Harris County Coroner with their body wagon. The night staff looked over the body, took measurements, looked at the angle of the ladder, and pronounced "Broken neck from falling out of that window."

Morgan and Sam looked at each other, and suppressed smiles and looks to the skies.

The Harris County Coroner loaded up the body in their wagon and headed to the morgue.

Cops dispersed since the excitement was over. It was not even a righteous kill as the bullets had not been the direct cause of death. An intruder in a bulletproof vest entered a cops house and died. They had everything they needed. There was no mystery about who killed who, or how the dead body came to be in the back yard.

After everyone had left, and the dawn light painted everything, Sam asked with a glint of amusement in his eyes "You were really naked when they got here?"

"Yes." Morgan said. "I had to be told I was. I was focused on other things. Charla and Kelly had a small argument about who liked me naked better."

"You are never going to hear the end of that." Sam told her.

"I know. In this one case, I am actually fine with that. The mashers at the office will be pissed off they missed it, especially the unholy trio: Gilbert Swanson, Hector Munoz, and Tom Le, and isn't THAT just too bad. So: You have never been to my house. Any trouble getting here?" Morgan asked.

Sam shook 'No'. "Nah: Out here in the County. Easy to find."

Morgan led the way to her house. "Come on in. I'll make some decent coffee, and show you my bar."

"That's RIGHT. I forgot you bought that thing!" Sam said. He tentatively added "Uhm: Morgan? Would you prefer to grab some things and come doss on my couch? House broken into and all that?"

"Nah." Morgan waved that offer off but appreciated the sentiment behind it. "It was Cabal again. Hopefully, they are done for the day. I just cost them a guy, so if they are too pissed off about that, they can find me anywhere."

"How do you know its Cabal?" Sam asked as they sat at the bar and Morgan fired up her coffee grinder. A burr grinder Morgan could not help but point out.

Sam ran his hands up and down the bar. "This thing is so nice. I am glad you bought this from Sally's estate. She never knew you, but I bet if she had, she would be glad you have it."

"Thanks. Yes: I do love it. Rearranged this whole space for it. So: Cabal. Dead guy was here to bug my phone again. I found him reaching for it. I found the new bug and the tools on him."

Sam sniffed the air in appreciation of the coffee. "That was not mentioned to me out there. All they talked about was the dead shot bullet cluster and the naked detective. Pretty sure a bug would have come up, even if AFTER you being good with a gun!"

"And naked. Yes: They don't know. I have pictures, and fingerprints, and the bug. Also the toolkit."

Morgan set the coffee to brewing and went to the kitchen and retrieved the bug and the tools. She had them wrapped in cellophane now to not add any more prints than she already had. Laying that on the bar, she pulled out her phone and popped the battery cover. She tracked the hair to the bar for replacement.

"Damn. They know what kind of phone I have NOW. Different battery contacts means a different shape of the bug power tap. Shit!" Morgan said.

Sam frowned. "These guys send a guy, break into your house to place a bug. Know what your phone is. They are connected in some deeply scary ways, Morgan."

"I know. So, what are my choices here?" Morgan asked.

"Knowing YOU, stay the course, find out who they are, and take them down. Not like you will do what they want." Sam said. He added "Maybe you shooting your first guy in the line of duty will slow them down? Or make them shoot you first..."

"Wasn't line of duty. Home invasion. Wasn't my service gun either. I fired my personal 9. My service record is intact. No weapons discharge in the line of duty." Morgan said, slightly smugly.

"Because they care about that in the Cabal." Sam said in return. "Nice coffee by the way."

Sam settled slightly, asked "You think it was a good idea to keep this bug evidence from County? Above and beyond that you clearly did it so you must?"

"Sam: I am assuming that the body is not IN the morgue later today. So yes. I think it goes this way: clean shooting, no charges, clear home invasion. None of the guys here this morning will be investigating anything about it. Right? They file their reports, no one reads them, done."

"Right. It is clear you killed in self-defense and also home defense. Also, You did not kill, it was the fall. You contributed, but were not the direct cause of death. So, no investigation." Sam agreed.

"No County cop here tonight will ever go to the morgue. Not their beat like it is ours. They will never know if the body is there or not. Someone out of curiosity might ask if it was ID'ed, and get back a 'No', but where does that take them. Do you think anyone will get stirred up enough to take it to the next step? If they get back a 'what body' answer, then do they care enough to launch an investigation or do they assume it is just a screw up that does not matter anyway because it was a John Doe and a home invader of a cop. Do they care?" Morgan asked.

"Probably not?" Sam replied.

"Body goes missing, and a few months from now, maybe someone asks about it because it came up during lunch one day, and the morgue says 'Oops: We misfiled it and it must have gone to crematorium un-identified. Sorry.' That is the end of that." Morgan said.

"You think they have reach into County." Sam said.

"Cabal does not have to have any real County pull to make this work. All they need is a second person willing to break into the morgue and take the body." Morgan pointed out. "THAT is assuming the body even gets there. Maybe the wagon crew stops at 'House of Pies' for coffee and breakfast, and they come out to find the body gone. Or they get a call, respond, run around a location looking for who called, and get back to a missing body. That one is less likely. I bet it is taken from the Morgue and the paperwork on it zero'ed."

"You are getting cynical in your old age." Sam told Morgan.

"Do you blame me?" Morgan asked.

"Not really, no." Sam said and sipped.

"How are you going to run those prints?" Sam asked.

"No idea. Keeping Wendell out of it for sure, and he is my best out-of-the-office law enforcement contact, but I am dating him: not using him as my private backchannel guy. I need to know someone at Interpol or the FBI or something."

"Time to make new friends." Sam paused, looked thoughtful and slightly amused at a thought. "You do seem to know how to make new friends."

"I am going to spit in your coffee if that is a reference to me being naked." Morgan grouched.

"It completely was. I'd drink it anyway. It's good." Sam smiled evilly, holding it out to her.

CHAPTER FIFTEEN

Morning is Broken

Morgan rolled into the office by 10AM. She was running on about two hours of sleep, and two gallons of coffee it felt like.

Sam was already in, of course, his traditional large cup of expensive coffee on his desk.

"I could have made you more." Morgan said, pointing at the cup.

"You needed to hit the rack, Morgan." Sam said

"Like you didn't? Thanks for coming out last night though. I appreciate it. More than I can say." Morgan told her partner very gratefully.

Sam shrugged. "You would have done the same. What partners do."

Morgan's desk phone rang. "Detective Olsen" She answered.

It was a distorted voice. Probably male. "You are turning out to be more trouble than you are worth, Detective."

Morgan went cold. "Yes, well, Good. I never asked to be your poster child or whatever it is you want me to be, so expect that to continue, asshole."

"You do not know your place." It was hard to tell because of the distortion, but they did not seem happy with Morgan's defiant answer.

"Standing on your head? Over your dead body? Something along those lines?" Morgan asked casually.

Morgan was keeping her voice very carefully neutral to slightly sarcastic, which in no way reflected her inner dialog. Fear was rearing its ugly head as this Cabal shit just kept getting deeper and more serious. She wondered again if being a Cop is worth this.

The line went dead.

Morgan looked at Sam darkly, who was wearing an expression of the fear she felt. She pulled out the phone book, found the number she wanted, and dialed it.

"Harris County Morgue." The person answered, and did not self identify.

"Hello. This is Detective Morgan Olsen. I am calling about a body you have there. A John Doe. Would have come in this morning."

Morgan gave her badge number and a description of the corpse.

"Just a moment, detective. Looking."

Morgan heard some paper moving about.

"No bodies came in last night. Are you sure this was Harris? Not Houston?" They asked.

"It should have been. Thank you." Morgan hung up.

Sam having heard only half of the conversation still understood the result. "That is just great!: Good work knowing you should have palmed the evidence that you in fact did. Bad news: You have enemies that can take bodies from official custody. So: what next? You going to try and track the body down?"

"No. No point. That second story man, literally, was hired help. There is no WAY these guys risk one of their own. I have pictures and prints of him if needed and assuming I find someone that can run them OUTSIDE of Cabal influence, but I am fairly convinced that, as hired help, he would neither tie back to the Cabal or any other useful thing. To go after the world of hired assassins and other professional criminals would require a task force, and I am fresh out of those." Morgan sighed. "I will go tell JJ what is up."

Sam followed her into JJ's office, and JJ waved them in.

"Nice break on the case. I assume you are setting up interviews?" JJ asked.

"Yes: the principal at the school is handling that actually so he can make sure parents are there if needed. All of that. We have seventeen kids to talk to assuming the idea that this is related to the TV commercial turns out to be true. As we perform the interviews, we will get a better idea about that. Hopefully, it does not expand the scope as that is a 5A school, which means we have a student body of around two thousand students. Obviously, we have other ways to triage that if needed, but this seventeen is our starting place."

"Bueno. Understood. The school is cooperating?" JJ asked.

"Yes. Morgan had to get a little hard ass with the principal, but he understood the need." Sam answered, knowing Morgan would not blow her own horn.

JJ nodded. He then asked with narrowed eyes: "Is there a reason you two look like shit?"

"Someone broke into my house last night." Morgan explained. "Sam came out when I called to tell him about it."

JJ looked at her dumbfounded and momentarily wordless.

Sam added, tossing a nod at Morgan: "She shot the intruder. Twice. Double tap with a nice tight cluster in the back between the shoulders. The intruder was wearing a vest so in theory, it just hurt like hell. Can't ask the guy because after they were shot they fell out the second-floor window. Face first, so they broke their neck. Died in her grass."

JJ stared at Morgan, eyes trying to escape his face. "You did not START with that? Why didn't I hear about it?" JJ tapped some papers on his desk. "I have nothing in any report from last night. Why isn't this on the news? TV? Chron? Something?"

"Many reasons. First of all, it was a righteous shoot. The County guys aren't filing and in fact, could care less. A fellow cop shot a dude in a bulletproof vest in her bedroom and he dies falling out the window. The body either never made it to the morgue or was taken from there. The on-scene cops will file their reports, but the DA isn't going to do anything with it, and unless they check as Morgan did, they won't even know the John Doe body is gone." Sam explained.

"Fucking hell! No one noticed a body go missing?" JJ was incredulous.

"It's all about paper. Reports will be buried. No reporters were there to cover it. Middle of the night. Body is gone, and the morgue day time crew does not even know there was supposed to be one. Also, the Cabal called a short while ago regarding the events of the evening and told me I am more trouble than I am worth. I have little doubt based upon that call that this Second Story man John Doe was their person in my house. Given the way the body faded, they seem to have some reach over into County. That or a second person was on standby, took it, and the County people have no idea their paperwork was erased." Morgan said.

"Fuck. When you make enemies, you don't fool around, Olsen. You came in to work WHY?" JJ asked.

"Three dead boys." Morgan replied as if that was obvious.

JJ rubbed his forehead. "You are fucking unbelievable, Olsen. I mean just … no other word for it."

"I have it on good authority that I am more trouble than I am worth, sir." Morgan agreed, and felt a little surge of pride at that. A badge of honor, even if this meant her life was probably in danger if they

CJ Stevens

decided their pet project really is of no use to them.

"You think this means they are going to back off you?" JJ asked, hope in his voice.

"I was just wondering that myself, Sir. Could be. I am not sure how big their operating budget is, but having the hired help killed has to be expensive. Next guy they try to hire for B&E at my place will ask what happened to the last guy, etc. I have an alarm system, I just never use it. Stupid, I know, but when you live out in the County, you tend to think you are away from the big city issues. I will use it now, of course. Maybe I will add some video. My system has that as a feature but I thought I would never need such a thing. Silly me. I should also mention that I had a feeling this body going missing was going to happen, so I got pictures and prints before Harris County came. Obviously, I cannot run them where these Cabal assholes can see what I am doing."

JJ pursed his lips. "Let me see if I can find another way on that. I don't have contacts at the FBI, but I know someone that does. They are female and Hispanic so I DOUBT they are hooked into these shitheads, but I will try to check that out first. It's time we take this to the feds anyway. This is more than just some rogue cops sexually harassing you. If they have reach into County, we need help."

"I am not sure it ever was rogue cops. I am not sure what this is, other than it feels like some part of a larger plan, and they have me cast as a pawn."

JJ found that idea amusing for some reason. "That is stupid as that shit gets. Either they did not know you, or they decided if they can get YOU to behave, they can get anyone to do it. You are a fucking pain in my ass."

"Yes, sir." Morgan said, in faux meekness that JJ knew was not sincere in any way.

CHAPTER SIXTEEN

Drama Department

Morgan and Sam arrived in a different school than the day before. No flashing lights. Echoing halls.

They went directly to the office, and Paul Rafferty was waiting for them. With him was another person.

"Detectives Olsen and Parker, this is Jana Judd. She is the head of our drama department. She worked with representatives from Lydee, as well as the people at University Sporting and Outdoor Equipment. I thought that perhaps starting your conversation with her might give you some ideas about where to take your conversations with the kids later today."

Morgan approved of that idea. "Very good. Ms. Judd: sorry to meet under these circumstances."

Jana Judd nodded back and she and Morgan shook hands. "Agreed. I am horrified by all of this of course, but so happy you all are on this now."

Sam shook next, saying "Please be assured that Morgan is quite literally the best Homicide Detective that we have to offer in this city, and that we will figure out who did this. It took a few days for us to identify the bodies, but I think we can see now why they went to efforts to hide their identity. With your help, this will be solved soon, I feel quite sure."

Morgan found that more loquacious than normal for Sam and looked at Jana Judd more closely to see if there may be some hidden attraction. She looked nothing like either of Sam's Ex-wives. Sam had a type, and Jana was not it. Medium height, very thin, dressed in black slacks, a striped blouse, a matching silk striped neck thing that was either a scarf or a really fat tie: Morgan could not be sure which it was supposed to be. Her short dark hair was streaked lightly with gray, and the cut was lopsidedly asymmetric. She looked to Morgan to be the prototypical head of the drama department right down to the upright way she carried herself as they stepped into Principal Rafferty's office. As they sat at a new table that was not in the office the day before, Morgan could see Paul had rearranged the space slightly to get ready for the interviews. This was to be the venue. The tiny table had four chairs around it, and there were several more against the wall that could be moved into service as required by however many people were in the room. For this interview, the four arrayed themselves in a circle around the table.

Morgan opened this conversation with courtesy. She felt she owed that after having to assert her authority with the Principal yesterday. No point in him thinking her a complete jerk. "Paul, thank you for setting this up, and for letting us use your office like this. I am sure you and all your staff have had a harrowing night talking to parents. Making alternative care arrangements. Grief counselors. All of the numerous things that you have had to do OTHER than deal with this."

"No problem Detective." Paul Rafferty said, and the warmth of his tone made Morgan look at his left hand in her peripheral vision. No ring.

Jana Judd made a gesture with both hands. "First names already!" She proclaimed. Morgan received a look that was presumably meant to X-Ray her, but that Morgan was already starting to interpret as stagecraft.

Morgan skipped over that as irrelevant and went directly to the heart of the problem. "Ms. Judd, could you please describe for Sam and I the way in which you worked with the company to find and cast the commercial?"

Jana Judd touched the back of Morgan's hand lightly. "If he is Paul to you, then I am Jana. Please. Well, that is pretty easy. I went to school with the director of the commercial, Sarah Luchs. We were lovers for a while as well and remained friends after. We did not break up so much as just move on. You know how that all goes."

"I do" agreed Morgan.

"So anyway, what happened was that out of the blue Sarah called me up and described for me the idea the shoe people had for their new line. They were doing this integrated campaign, where they showed celebrities using the shoes to do all sorts of things: everything from participating in various sporting events to going out on the town. The new dressy: tennis shoes! Sarah said that if they could film people making love with just their shoes on, they would do it. They wanted ALL of it. The shoes were for EVERYTHING. The local campaign was supposed to show that not just celebrities, but everyone could have the lifestyle. For the local commercial, a thirty-second spot, they wanted kids shooting hoops, running, playing in the park, etc. They wanted good looking kids of course, and they wanted it to hint at the idea that the kids were going to go off into the trees and have sex with their shoes on, without ever saying or showing it of course. Sex sells. Like that. Being kids of course, it could only ever be implicit, not explicit, and being a globally respected brand, that was all handled the way they usually do that kind of thing: Beautiful people dressed to the sky and yet looking at each other as they played as if there was just one more thing they wanted to do."

Morgan allowed what she thought of this to show on her face and in her voice. "Sex sells. Something that I personally find distasteful given the way it objectifies and clouds the open and healthy discussion of sexuality, however, I find that I am being quixotic when I complain to anyone about it."

"I could not agree more, and since I am gay, it is in some ways even worse for me. If I try to put on a production that has anything remotely open and honest in it about sex, I would be lynched! But if we throw in a few sly nods to sex, or use Shakespearean language to cover it up, applause!" Jana clapped her hands once to demonstrate.

"How did the casting work? How do you balance that desire for the good looking kids against the fact that many were under the age of eighteen?" Morgan asked.

"That went this way. Sarah decided to try and cast the entire thing here so that it could be a one-stop shop. No having to deal with multiple schools, multiple PTA's, all that. They brought the idea to the PTA and it was approved there, though not without some discussion. Parents that were against it were told to just not allow their children to audition. Just don't sign the permission form. Simple as that." Jana shrugged.

"After it was approved, we put posters up all around the school for open casting..." A dramatic swirl of a finger to include the school "... and over two weekends we have tryouts. Another weekend for callbacks if needed. Just as if we were casting the senior play! Sarah and I sat in the auditorium, with other people from USOE and even someone from Lydee, and had the kids read things, and bounce balls, run from one side of the stage to the other, and the like. The reading thing was useless because there were no speaking parts. It was just tape of the kids doing things, with voice over. Standard stuff: Shoot hours, cut it down to seconds."

"There were twenty kids cast in all? Out of how many?" Sam asked.

Jana looked at Sam, and Morgan got a hint of an attitude that Jana thought that he should just let the girls talk. "There were one hundred and fifty-three people signed up. Most of those showed one of the two weekends: One hundred forty-two in all. Of those, there was a number that showed the first weekend that did not have the correct permission forms filled out and on file, and at the end of the second weekend, there were one hundred twenty-seven total kids that tried out and had permission to do it. From that, we cast twenty kids and four alternates in case someone could not make the taping dates for some reason. An even split of girls and boys."

"I see." Sam nodded. "Thank you, Ms. Judd." And with that, he signaled that Sam understood he was on the outside looking in on this conversation.

"Were there any controversies around any of that process? Who was cast? Who was not?" Morgan asked.

Jana Judd grinned at that. "You know, the thing about anything like this is it brings out the absolute worst in people! Parents turn into assholes instantly. Why didn't my kid get more screen time? Can they have a copy of the tapes with their kid on them so they can submit them to agents? All of that. Not EVERY parent of course. Some went the other way and had complete disinterest. I am sure you understand."

"In a way. I had a band in high school, and of course, we tried out for things like talent shows and such."Morgan explained. "Our parents were of the 'indulge them and they will grow out of it' mold. My dad always thought I had greater things ahead of me than the lead guitar in a cover band."

"Oh? And is he proud of you now?" Jana asked.

"My dad is always proud of me. I literally could do nothing wrong as a child. While he does not like that my job has dangers associated with it, he is proud of Sam and my record, and how we have achieved it." Morgan replied, and ignored the look Jana was giving her. "Back to the commercial, so there were no issues in and among the kids with each other? No jealousy. No yelling. Nothing?"

Paul laughed at that one, and Morgan gave him a quizzical look.

"Jana was not happy with all of the casting from the start, were you?" He said. "Some rather heated words in the hallways outside the auditorium."

Jana did not look happy about that coming out. She did not quite glare at Paul, but then looked sheepishly at Morgan. "I did not like all of the people cast. In particular, one of the dead boys, Derek. Such a Jock! Could not act to save his life. His reading was the WORST. He stood up there and said 'I can't say that!' when it came time to read some lines. Some stuff from Romeo and Juliet. Really dramatic. We used it to see if they had any range. Derek didn't. Good looking kid, but just a terrible actor. I thought there was another kid that was just as 'jocky' looking and far better at his lines, but Derek had the look. Frankly, they wanted a black kid. Part of the commercial: diversity. He looked right, so he got it."

"Anyone else you disagreed with?" Morgan asked.

"Darla Odean." Jana said instantly and without having to think about it, and then she waited as if she had explained everything with that one name.

"What was the issue with her?" Morgan asked.

"Do you know who she IS?" Jana asked. Incredulity in her voice and her shoulder set.

"Off the top of my head? No idea." Morgan said, then asked "Sam?"

"Only Odean I ever heard of is the one up on the billboards at the church out on the West side."

Jana pointed triumphantly at Sam. "Exactly right! She's ON some of the billboards: The ones with all three of them. Father, Mother, and Daughter. All holier than thou."

"Your problem with Darla Odean was that she is religious?" Morgan asked, puzzled.

That got a solid belly laugh. "Darla Odean is a little druggie and a slut. If she is religious, I am a gay Morman priest. My problem with her is that there were other girls, IN the drama department, that look as good or better, and who actually want to be doing this kind of thing. Work for it. Odean waltzes in, tosses off her lines, struts her curvy ass across the stage, and Sarah goes apeshit over her. I mean just turned her head. If I did not know better, I would have thought Sarah was going to make a pass at her, but Sarah would never do that. She's thirty years older than that tramp, and besides, she is in a relationship. Still, it SEEMED that way to me."

"I see. Anyone else?" Morgan asked.

"Those two I really did not like. There were others that were judgment calls. I would have gone a different way, but it's her commercial. You know what? Lydee loved Sarah's casting, so she knew her customer better than I anyway. Even Derek and the tramp. Hell, both USOE and Lydee loved Darla, because she just has the look they wanted. Her inner tramp comes through on tape, and that is what they were after. What a distraction. On filming day, all the boys were glued to her ass. The straight ones anyway. Drugs and sex. All they were missing was rock and roll, but that was added later with the voice over."

Paul added "All of that about Darla is 'allegedly'. We have never found any drugs on her."

Jana snorted. "Not that you tried all that hard. Her big important daddy and her mommy on the PTA, damn near running it. Going after Darla would be a real problem, wouldn't it?"

Paul agreed. "Yes. It would be, but that does not mean we have not looked. We have drug-sniffing dogs. We have checked ALL the lockers. We have found drugs, but never on her or in her locker."

"Because that little bitch is too clever by half." Jana said.

"No issues with the other two boys? Neil Snyder or Ailani Aquino?" Sam asked.

Jana returned to the conversation. "No: I thought those were great calls. Neil had a really nice look to him and Ailani could act just fine."

Next in to see Sam and Morgan was the school counselor.

Paul introduced them "Detective Morgan Olsen, the head of this investigation. Her partner, Sam Parker. Detectives, this is Gail Samolinski, our school counselor. We have several others in her department, and they are very busy as you might imagine, setting up outside grief sessions and talking to parents. I asked Gail to make herself available to you for these sessions. There are some parents that requested that both myself and Gail be here in their lieu as they are both working, in some case not in state or country. We have faxed permission forms going out all over the world on this. Some parents absolutely will be in attendance, however. The students you are seeing today are all over eighteen and do not need parental permission to be here. We are not hiding this process however, and all families are fully informed."

As Morgan shook hands with Gail Samolinski, she was thinking that any sessions that were without parents or authority figures were the most likely to be of use. She left that unexpressed and instead said: "Ms. Samolinski, thank you for your assistance in this investigation. I know this is a very trying time for you and your staff."

Morgan was repeating that particular refrain with no small amount of frequency. It seemed to her that schools are nested fiefdoms. Paul Rafferty had his staff, the assistant principals of each grade. Gail had her team of fellow counselors. There were head coaches and junior coaches just as surely.

Gail said as she shook with Sam "I am glad to be able to do whatever I can to help. This is a very difficult time for the students, of course, and it is times like these that while difficult, are why we are here. High school is such a difficult time for growing minds and bodies, and inserting things like death and most especially murder, can really take some of our children here down a dark path. We have to be ready."

There was just enough self-important smarm in it that Morgan fought down dislike for the woman. "Before we interview any of the kids, I wonder if you have any observations about of them? Their dynamics. Conflicts. The way that the various social grouping interact? I am referring to things like how the athletes get along with kids from, say, the drama department, and so forth?"

The four took their seats, Gail sat where Jana was earlier.

"Well, our school is like most any school of our size, as you might expect. The athletes are not even a homogenous group, in that inside the larger athletic world, there are football players, basketball, swim team, baseball, track and field, and so forth. In that hierarchy, the football players reign supreme, and while I could not tell you why, I have observed that to be true at most schools. The issues we have is the typical 'boys will be boys types of things. Teasing weaker boys. Silly pranks. The usual things. The coaches run around like they own the place of course. The number one complaint I get from parents is about how badly the coaches teach academic subjects. I am sure you are aware that you can't JUST be a coach, but you also have to teach classes. Many coaches just read from the teachers' edition, and administer the tests. However, the BEST freshman algebra teacher is also a coach, so it is not universal."

"We called them Jocks." Sam commented.

Gail agreed. "We all do. For many, that is all they will ever be. The trick is to find the ones that have the potential to be more. Encourage and nurture them. Worse, to my way of thinking is that being a cheerleader, a baton twirler, or on the drill team is the same pinnacle of social success as being a football player, with a similar disregard for education. Again: Not universal. True enough to be frustrating, however."

Gail then ticked her fingers to enumerate other groups. "Then there is band. Choir. Orchestra. Jazz band. Same stratifications: you are in freshman band or choir and move up to JV, then Varsity levels of each. Jazz band is the pinnacle of musical success, and Orchestra is where all the invisible musicians go to disappear. All the musical performing arts are raided for marching band during football season other than most of the orchestra, as there is no marching Violin section."

Gail was amused by that idea, and actually, Morgan rather liked the mental image of marching violins and violas.

"They do share some of the percussion students, however." Gail added. "Then we have the other performing arts. Drama. That includes speech, one-act play, debate, all of that. Jana opens two plays a year for school wide auditions, but of course, it mostly ends up being cast with her students. The two performing arts groups have some interaction: there are kids that play instruments AND act, for example. Not many."

Jana ticked off another finger. "Then we have the intellectual clubs, like physics and chess. They hang out together, debating the nature of reality and such. Our chess club won its last three tourneys. The student body greeted them as conquering heroes. By that I mean they ignored it and them completely. It got a morning announcement. In general, being a geek or a nerd or whatever is always treated that way I think. That was my group at school, as I am sure you can figure out."

Another finger. "Unlike a more rural school, our FFA group of future farmers is tiny. To be a redneck here mostly means you listen to Country and Western rather than rock and roll. Maybe you work at the Houston Livestock Show and Rodeo. Something like that. We also have a very small ROTC. We do not seem to be training many soldiers here for some reason."

"Last two are the druggies and the kids that are not really plugged into much of anything. The drug users are mostly kids that come to class stoned or high, and you can smell it on them. We don't have a huge problem here with harder things. Heroin or opiates. Mostly weed. Alcohol. Valium. Things like that. Unaffiliated sort of speaks for itself." Gail concluded.

"There was a prostitution thing last year." Paul reminded.

Gail looked at her hand as if she needed more fingers. "Oh. Yes.

Well, that was taken care of last year." Gail met both detectives eyes. "You see, there were some kids in fiscal trouble, and some men took advantage of it. Recruited here. Five girls ages sixteen to nineteen were connected to a call-out service. For clients that like their women young, you see. We were lucky they did not get any girls that were younger. And who knows? Maybe they did? They did from some other schools. That was the last time we had detectives here, in this office, and frankly, I am not sure which is worse. Those poor girls selling their bodies, or these poor boys losing their lives."

"What can you tell me about Neil?" Morgan asked.

"Nothing." Gail said firmly.

"Ok. Good. I assume from that response that students here were not aware he is transsexual. Therefore no one teased him about that. It is a relief to know that there are absolutely NO issues of ANY kind that Sam and I need to know about as it pertains to his death."

Gail narrowed her eyes at the way Morgan leaned into her points, and then consulted Paul silently with her eyes. "I can tell you this: No one was aware outside of this office. When we set up the special gym program for him so that he could get PE credits but never have to go to the locker room? Well, that required Paul to intervene quite strongly."

Morgan swiveled her attention to the principal. Paul shrugged. "The head coach thinks that boys should just all learn to buck up and be boys. A kid has an issue with another kid, he would rather they punch each other a little and get it out of their system. I had one boy with a huge bruise on his arm. I asked him about it. He said the kid that was next to him in PE, in the changing room when they were dressing out, hit him every day. Same place on the arm. I asked why the coach did not stop it, and he said the coach told him to just hit him back. I asked if he did. He said no: he was not raised to hit people. I went to the head coach, Beau Evans. Asked him what the entire fuck? He said that a kid that can't defend himself deserved to get hit."

Paul looked disgusted. "I am pretty sure I can take Beau. I was sorely tempted. Being principal, I instead pissed Beau off by moving the boys to different periods. I support anyone that does NOT want to fight but would rather find a peaceful resolution to things. Beau was never going to let that happen. Gail mentioned the 'boys will be boys' thing? It starts with Neanderthals like our beloved head coach. Regarding Neil: when Beau found out there was a kid he was NOT going to have in his class, he went apeshit. Wondered why I was coddling him. All that. You know: He is a winning coach, depending upon the sport, but a total jerk. I told him to back off, and if he EVER bothered Neil, Neil was under strict instructions to tell me immediately, and I would suspend Beau without pay and without question, even during football season. I will not have a kid in my school harassed like that."

"Paul Rafferty: you are my hero." Morgan said with true admiration. "I can take care of myself, but it is a shame I have to. I learned to fight because of my chosen profession, and I can take down any man, short of an MMA fighter at least, and those I can shoot. That I had to do all that is because there are not more people like you."

Gail raised her eyebrows at that statement. "You know, detective, you are somewhat unexpected as a detective as well. I would not have come into this room, knowing I was about to talk to homicide cops, and think you would understand ANYTHING about Neil."

Sam laughed at that. "Gail, I am learning from her in painful ways ALL the time. There is a reason she is the lead, and I am her flunky."

"That you can learn and are willing to is all it takes, Detective." Gail said, warmly.

"Sam." Sam amended

"Sam." Gail said, and her look told Morgan that they were in danger of setting up a double date with the people in this office if they kept on this course. Her dislike for Gail had abated. Morgan realized Gail came into the room with pre-conceived notions about what talking to Homicide cops was going to be like, and she wondered who she had dealt with in the Vice squad that left such a sour taste in her mouth. She would revisit that someday with Gail, because that tied in with Vice and them suddenly leaving 'rox' alone as well, possibly.

"So, Gail, Paul. Next up we dive deep into the young lives of the kids here, looking for the WHY of this thing. Here is what I have: Three dead boys, all in a TV commercial for tennis shoes. Well, technically, cross-trainers I am told. While the way in which they were killed suggests familiarity with their murderer, we have no idea WHY they were killed. In terms of Means, Motive, and Opportunity, we have very little of that. What Sam and I will be trying to get to are any ideas that any of these kids might have. Who might have done this and or at least some idea of why? When we have a place to look, we might see who has the murder weapon or at least access to it."

Gail was looking at Morgan oddly. "What?" Morgan asked.

"You know Eddie Christman on Vice?" Gail asked.

"No. I do not actually know ANYONE on Vice all that well, though I have recently learned that they fear me. Why do you ask?" Morgan was now very curious.

"He just runs his investigations very differently." Gail said.

"Gail: is that Call-out ring actually shut down?" Morgan said out of sudden suspicion. "Or do you suspect that Vice just moved the operation to be under their control?"

"No. Not that exactly. I think that it is more likely that Eddie Christman is having sex with a girl they busted during it. Underage, even now. I can't prove it. I just suspect it. From the way she is acting. The way she reacts when I say HIS name to her."

Morgan moved up her mental timetable for looking into Vice here. "Gail: If that is true, I will find out about it, and I will arrest him. He will go away for a very long time." Morgan nearly growled the last.

"She will, too." Sam said. "Only if I do not beat her to it, however: given that she is the genius, I would bet on her getting there first. That may also be a good thing, as she probably would not kill them. I make no such assurance."

"You all are Homicide, not Vice." Gail said, looking between them.

"And?" Morgan asked, slightly coldly, but only because she had a very dark foreboding. It was not her intention to arrest her way through the department, but it still all tied back to the kind of cop SHE wanted to be. The kind where she was not walking into meetings with people at schools and having them think she was not going to take the same care of their kids as they would.

Gail heard and understood. "I see. Very different kind of detectives indeed."

CHAPTER SEVENTEEN

Kids in the Commercial, Day One

The first student to enter Paul Rafferty's office after lunch was very tall. Morgan estimated he was at least six or more inches taller than herself. Also thin in the same whipcord way Sam is, with floppy hair and a prominent Adam's apple.

Paul introduced him. "Rob, this is Detective Olsen. The homicide lead investigator. This is her partner, Detective Parker. Detectives, this is Rob Wodzinski. Rob is a senior and plays on the basketball team. He is going to The University of Texas next year on a sports scholarship."

Rob had chosen that no parents or special presence was required for his interview, so the four of them sat down.

"Rob, you are our first student interview. Please be assured that Sam and I have no specific focus with this interview other than getting to who killed these three young men. I'd like to start by asking you a wide-open question: Can you think of ANY reason someone would want to kill these three particular people?" Morgan asked.

Wide open questions are not always useful, since they do not help people focus, but Morgan could narrow it as they went along. Sometimes not having a target illuminates one for her.

Rob wiggled in the too-small chair, but not out of any anxiety. It was just too small. His entire school life is probably misery for him, Morgan thought.

"Well, let's see. I only kinda knew Derek. Track guy. Good dude. Easy going when he was not on the track, but a good competitor too. Kinda shy with the chicks, which is funny, since they liked him. I didn't know Neil at all. Nice little guy, it seemed, but I only actually met him on the day we were shooting, and I didn't really talk to him much. We weren't in many scenes together. Same with that other guy. I... Started with an 'A'...."

"Ailani Aquino" Sam supplied.

"Yeah. That dude. New kid. Just transferred here recently I think?" Rob said.

Paul nodded. "Yes. From Hawaii."

"I didn't know him either. We all kinda talked during breaks on the shoot, and at the party, but other than that, I didn't know those guys. After the commercial experience, we nodded in the hall at each other between classes. That kind of thing. Same with anyone you were in the commercial with. Not going to be all stuck up after."

"Ok: Focusing on Derek: You say he was easy going. Girls liked him. Anyone NOT like him? Did he do anything with a young lady that might have pissed off someone else?" Morgan asked.

"Like I said, Derek was kinda a shy guy with girls. When Darla hauled him off during the card game to the closet, I thought he was gonna turn red." That thought seemed to slightly amuse Rob.

"Darla Odean?" Morgan asked.

"Yeah. Total babe. Sorry, Principal Rafferty..." Rob looked suddenly stricken.

Paul Rafferty waved that off.

"So, this card game. What was it exactly?" Morgan asked.

"Kinda like strip poker, except when you lost, it was the lowest boy hand and the lowest girl hand, and instead of stripping, you went away together to a bedroom or a closet. There you talked or whatever, and then when you came back you pretended you made out like crazy."

"Pretended?" Sam asked.

"Sure. For one thing, who can get it on in like ten minutes? Maybe you kiss if you are lucky. Darla kinda broke that time rule. Kids were knocking at the door to get them to come back out, and they came out grinning, like they had played the best joke on everyone, but really. They called it 'Seven Minutes in Heaven', but it was never that. Never seven minutes I mean."

"Poker based hands. Interesting. I thought that game was played like 'Spin the Bottle'. Who dealt?" Morgan asked.

"That was Darla's idea. She said it would make it more fun, and it did. Dealer rotated around, just like Poker. Everyone took turns. People came and went. Some of the kids were out back, where the burger pit was. A few were dancing. Because it took so long, there were two bedrooms and a big ass closet being used to go away into, so you know: six at a time. But a lot of people brought people, so it was a big party. Supposed to be a 'plus one' thing? No one cared if you brought more. Some people brought just themselves too."

"Whose house was it in?" Sam asked.

"One of the drama kids. Her parents were around someplace too, to make sure it didn't get too wild. No drinking or smoking allowed or anything like that. But they seemed pretty cool. They cooked and kept the snacks loaded up on the table and other than that watched TV in their TV room. They had a media room: Very cool. They didn't care about the card game."

"No arguments? No jealous plus ones? No one unhappy that their date just disappeared into a bedroom with someone else?"

"Not that I saw or heard, man. Worst thing I heard was when Darla went off with Neil someone said something like 'what a lucky little fucker that guy is'. Or something like that. Sorry, Principal Rafferty."

"Rob: we are after the truth here: Please do not apologize for telling it." Paul said.

"Yes, sir." Rob said.

"Wait a minute. Darla went off with a second boy during this game? Neil?" Sam asked.

"Yeah. Like I said. Three rooms. If you come back and rejoin the game after your trip and lose again, you go again, but with a different person. Darla wasn't the only girl that lost more than once. Or the only guy. Some guys, like me? We kept winning, and we were talking about making it so that the two HIGHEST hands got to go, but then... Well. It was random. You weren't sure you were going to get Darla or anything. And it could be like you said: What If I went back there with the girlfriend of a guy on the team? We ain't gonna do nothin, are we?" Rob complained. "You were asking about people being angry? That's how it was never angry. People there in serious relationships didn't do anything unless they went back with their boyfriend or whatever. And then, what the heck is the point? You already are with them. That games supposed to be about having fun. Getting to know people. Breakin' the ice. I left the game after that. I wasn't losing, so I wasn't going to the bedrooms with anyone. I went outside after that and shot the shit with some other people. Ate some burgers. Like that."

"You said some of the other girls were losing more than once?"

Morgan asked.

"Yeah. Debora Gomez for one. On the drill team. Her boyfriend wasn't there though, so he didn't know she was off with other dudes." Rob said.

"You don't think he could have found out?" Morgan asked.

Rob shrugged. "Debra was kinda pissed he didn't come. I bet she told him. In fact, she said something like that when she lost the first time. She took the guy by the hand and said loudly 'Just wait till my boyfriend finds out. Let's give him something to be mad about. You know how that all is though. I bet they didn't do shit."

"Debra go off with any of the people that were killed?" Morgan asked

"Not while I was in the game." Rob replied. "I did not stay to the end. It was clear I was never going to lose, IE, win, so I ate and then I went to a different party."

"What was that?" Morgan asked.

"UT thing. For incoming sports scholarship people. Just a 'get to know you' thing. Nothing weird." Rob said.

"Dancing. Music. Food. A card game. Anything else happening at the party?" Sam asked.

"No. That was about it. Maybe later, but not while I was there." Rob looked a little bored now.

"No one had cross words or issues during the shoot. Or tryouts?" Morgan asked.

"The audition thing was a piece of shit." Rob said, slowly shaking 'no'. "You sit in the auditorium all damn day watching people try out till they call your name. You go up there, do the same stupid thing they all have been. Then you leave. Boring and the seats in there are crap. The day of the shoot, that was mostly at the park. They set it up, did a bunch of takes, and then set up the next thing. So, like me, they wanted to pretend I was doing pickup basketball, and we played a while, and they shot it all and said they would recut it and put music on it, and it would look cool. You knew it wasn't a real game because they mixed it up, dudes and chicks, and some of them were short, and couldn't sink a shot to save their life. They just kept saying to go with it, and have a good time, and they kept shooting. I went up, came down on top of this one girl accidentally, and we rolled to the ground and laughed and they ate that up. Loved it. Wanted us to do it again. The first time you do that, it's funny. The second time, it's not, you know?"

134

"I can see how that might be, yes." Morgan said.

"There was a funny thing they did." Rob said, looking more interested. "It's a commercial about shoes, so they put the camera on this cart thing, and it had this weird device that held the camera steady as it bumped along, and they had us run around, and they ran between us pushing that camera cart and zigging and zagging as we ran around, filming our feet going all over the place. It must have been crazy to watch. The way the camera didn't move? That was just weird. It was like it hovered on the cart."

"Did you film anything else?" Sam asked.

"Yeah, sure. All day. They only had twenty of us, so they moved us around to change who was the main focus. Like Derek: He ran through the park holding hands with like four different chicks, and they re-filmed it on this track thing as they ran along, and we were all in the background pretending to be doing picnic things on blankets or reading, or whatever. Feet up, shoes in sight, of course. You know: I did hear one of the girls get a little pissed about that. She ran along with him first, but when they shot Derek and Darla, they were jazzed. I heard the director saying "That's it! That's the one!" and the first girl was kinda pissed. Said 'She is such a cunt!'. Sorry, Ma'am. Just what she said." Rob looked very embarrassed.

"You don't call me that, we'll be fine, Rob." Morgan said. "Who was this girl?"

"Cheerleader. Gabby Lloyd. I don't think she liked it much that Darla was getting more love than her. The people in the commercial just really got into Darla's fine as hell look, and a lot of the guys did too. I would not have minded being the guy that went off with her, lucky Derek and Neil. Just being honest, ma'am. My opinion, but I think Gabby hated that about Darla. She is used to being the queen bee, you know?"

"So we have a reason to hurt Darla, not three boys." Sam said.

"Sorry, sir." Rob apologized.

Sam raised a hand "No worries, Rob. You saw what you saw, heard what you heard. Not your fault you did not walk in here and hand us this on a silver platter."

"If I knew who did it, I would have said already." Rob defended himself.

"That's why the genius and her sidekick are in here talking to you and everyone else." Sam said.

* * *

There was a space of time before the next interview was scheduled. Morgan used it to talk to Paul and look over the list of people he had assembled so far.

"The next person is Terry Pfeiffer. One of Jana's drama kids. Senior." Morgan noted flipping papers. "We don't talk to Debora Gomez till tomorrow, and neither Darla Odean or Gabby Lloyd is on the schedule yet. Say's here 'permission pending'. Obviously, after what Rob just told us, they are both people we'll want to speak with."

Paul shifted in his chair to lean forward and tap the page. "Well, Morgan, Debora Gomez is first thing, and I think we can get Gabby in right after that in this slot. Her parents will want her in here because they want to be sure that nothing soils her good name, etc."

Morgan read from that statement Gabby Lloyd was not going to be a comfortable interview, with lots of parental interruptions. "Great." Morgan said with audible sarcasm, and Paul smiled at her in understanding.

"Darla is another thing entirely. Her mother is a high muckity muck on the PTA and her father being the preacher at that mega-church, it might take an act of Congress to get her in here."

"Have they refused?" Sam wondered.

"No, but they have not said 'yes' either." Paul said. Paul looked over at Sam and asked "I understand that your partner IS a genius, however, I find it interesting you just told that to a student. Not as if it is not obvious, but ... I think you have another reason perhaps?"

Sam's grin crinkled the corners of his eyes. "You are correct sir. A: She IS a genius, and I peddle hard to keep up with her all day. However, the 'B' of that is this: As the kids talk to each other about these interviews, it will not hurt to have them think they are up against a Homicide detective genius. Make them a little nervous and put them off their game."

Paul gave that an understanding nod. "I see: Bad cop, genius cop." He summarized.

Morgan heaved a sigh. "I just thought Sam thought I was smart..." But gave her partner an upturned corner of the mouth. Why they worked well together as partners.

Terry Pfeiffer was six feet tall and weighed at least two hundred and forty pounds. Some of it was frame, but some was a clear love of food. He had longish hair and was dressed in a 'Social Distortion' punk band T from the 'Mommy's Little Monster' era of the band. A skeleton sitting watching an 'A' bomb explode on an old style TV, with a kid on the arm of the chair next to the skeleton wearing a voodoo mask and pouring a bowl of cereal. Morgan thought it an affectation, and said nothing, assuming it was his parents T or he found it while searching second-hand shops, perhaps up in Austin.

"Terry here is the lead in the senior play this year. Tevye in 'Fiddler on the Roof'." Paul introduced

Morgan skipped past the opening niceties. "What roles did you play in the commercial, Terry?"

Terry cocked his head slightly, not ready to jump so directly into the case. "Well, funny about that. I was always in the background. They wanted athletes mostly on the foreground, and let's face it, I am not one of those, as you can see." Terry presented his body and waistline, ending with a little wrist flick. "Also, they wanted this to be a straight kids thing, and I am a good actor and all, and I can play straight, there is no competing with the real things sometimes. They want a boy and girl to run around holding hands, I can do that, but not when they have a track guy and a buncha straight girls to fawn on him. So, in the commercial I am always the kid on the blanket, chatting with friends or whatever."

Morgan accepted this as a statement meaning to cause a reaction and gave him nothing.

"Were you at the party?" Sam asked, also not reacting.

Terry was having trouble reading the room apparently and looked at Paul like it was somehow his fault the two detectives were not reacting as they should.

"Yes, Detective, I was at the party." Terry said, not amused at the rapid change of subject.

"Did you participate in the card game?" Morgan asked.

"Oh, Hell No! Straight kids rules. Why would I want to go off with a chick to a bedroom?" Terry asked, insulted at the very idea.

"Now that I am aware of your gender preference, which I was not previously, I cannot think of any reason why you would." Morgan agreed equitably. "So, what did you do at the party? Did you bring a boyfriend and neck out back by the BBQ grill? Did you stay in and observe the card game just to see what occurred? Dance in a large group? Go into the media room and watch a show? What did you do to entertain yourself?"

Terry now understood that his being gay was neither going to shock Morgan or pull her off her mission to ask questions about things OTHER than him.

"Well, it is as you say, Detective. I was not sure why I came. I brought my boyfriend and it IS the Montrose so no one thinks anything about that, but for a performing arts activity, it was dully straight. Watching the breeders go off to screw in the bedroom was boring. We danced. We went outside and ate. Good BBQ and burgers. Got bored pretty fast, and called it a night. Heard lots of giggling and shit from the house, but did not pay it much attention."

"As you are making abundantly clear: given that you were on the outside looking in, your opinion, please. Any observations of stress. Jealousy. Hatred? Any reason at all that someone might want to kill someone else?" Morgan asked.

Terry looked at Morgan with respect and no little amusement. "Damn, Detective. You don't take shit from anyone."

"I do not." Morgan agreed.

"So, let me see. Only thing I really saw was a few of the guys being disappointed they won, which of course meant they lost. The point of that game was to go into a bedroom or closet with a stranger and get to know them, biblically if at all possible, and I think that in some cases it was possible to get to 'know' someone." In a way Morgan found far too cutesy, Terry gave the 'know' air quotes as if she had not understood the 'biblically' reference.

Terry continued: "That chick on the drill team, Debora Gomez. Made a big deal about her boyfriend not being there, and going off with a guy. Did they do it? I'd guess yes, but what do I know? She seems to be like that kind of person; gets even by fucking someone else." Terry made an upward pointing gesture and said dramatically "That'll teach 'em! They don't come to MY party, then I am going to BE the party!" he pronounced in a stage voice.

"Debora Gomez was the party. Got it. Her boyfriend was not there to care, and it is my understanding that the boy she went away with was none of the three that were killed. Did you observe anyone unhappy with those three?"

Terry frowned, realizing his act was crashing and burning with this audience. "Only one of the guys that died that I saw was the track guy that got it. Him and the PK going off together. Really lost interest after that."

"PK?" Sam asked

"You know. Preachers Kid." Terry said as if that was obvious.

"So, you saw Darla Odean and Derek Jefferson together." Morgan prompted.

"Not together together. I saw them lose a round early on, and her take him by the hand and lead him to his straight fate. He looked a bit nervous, to be honest, but she looked like she had just won the lottery and he was her yummy prize. Derek is a nice looking guy, so I was glad to see it looked like he was going to be properly appreciated."

"Almost as well as you could have." Morgan noted. A simple statement with no spin.

"That is no lie." Terry agreed.

Once Terry had left, Paul Rafferty looked at the door and said in some disgust "That was useless, if dramatic."

Morgan touched his forearm "Not useless. Irritating perhaps, but not useless. We have corroboration on the fact that Derek went to a private area with Darla Odean. That was not in doubt from Rob, but it is nice to have two witnesses. It means nothing yet, but it does present at least a possible motive: Someone not liking Derek being with Darla."

Paul was not so easily appeased. "Well, I am also not happy to be finding that my students are off having parties like this."

"Paul. Really? Do you think high school age kids are all sweetness and light when they leave here? It was not a school-sponsored event. No one has brought out ANY questionable activities during the school parts of this. Not the tryouts and not during the filming of the commercial. Not as yet anyway. If you think a simple 'Seven Minutes in Heaven' game is bad, you will not like to hear about the parties after the various performances of the Jazz band or the senior play." Morgan teased. "Lead guitar player in a high school cover band: I know whereof I speak."

Paul Rafferty gave her a pained expression. "Do NOT remind me. I have enough problems with the pregnancy rate as it is."

"Does this school not have a sex education program?" Morgan asked.

"Of sorts. It's the South." Paul said. "I am always tempted to move someplace with more forward thinking on subjects like that."

"I do not know about YOU, Paul, but I enjoyed high school immensely." Morgan said, and while not coy it was also clear what she meant by 'enjoyed'. "Teenagers are bundles of hormones, and Nancy Reagan's 'Just say no' as applied to sex? Never going to work."

"I know. I know. There are just limits to what we can say and do. Pain in my ass." Paul said. He then added, "I think if YOU had been one of my students, I would have no hair."

"You are not that old, sir." Morgan told him.

"Just in mileage." Paul rebutted.

CHAPTER EIGHTEEN

Weekend

There was nothing to do for it. No more students were scheduled to be in Paul's office until Monday morning, and that left Morgan and Sam with a weekend. Weekends are normally things to treasure when you are a homicide cop, but Morgan, for her part, was ready to get on with it. She did not like that she still did not know why three young men had been murdered, and that lack of knowledge meant that there was a good chance another might be killed before she could figure it out.

On the other hand, everyone at the school was warned and on high alert. Cops patrolled the campus, and all weekend activities there were canceled. It was not just Morgan and Sam that had a weekend on their hands, everyone at that school suddenly did as well.

Morgan considered calling up Mike to see what he was up to but decided against it. In deciding against that, she was deciding something else that made her nervous and required some honest self-examination.

Morgan cleaned and generally puttered around her house Saturday morning till she realized she was just putting off doing what she wanted to do and why. The realization came with resignation: it is what it is.

Maybe the whole idea would be a bust. It was unplanned as hell, and that sometimes works out well, and sometimes is a disaster. It was an odd sort of win-win. If the plan did not work, she was saved from admitting she might be getting too serious and could just relax. If it did, then she was going to enjoy herself and worry about the why of it later.

Morgan drove down to Galveston. Top down. Air Conditioning on. If nothing else, it would be a nice drive.

The City of Galveston is a historic place. From the days of cotton and slavery through the Civil War and its 'cotton-clad' battleships and 'the Battle of Galveston'. The city nearly destroyed by a hurricane in 1900, with somewhere between six and twelve thousand fatalities. Then there is the Balinese Room in the '40s and '50s. Frank Sinatra played there, and illegal gambling took place, the room out on a pier long enough that by the time the law reached the room, all the gambling gear was hidden. ZZ Top had a very famous song about it called simply 'Balinese' , and Morgan had covered it with her band. Galveston's current status is as a port and a tourist destination (when you only had a weekend and lived in the Gulf Coast area). Morgan was in a historic AND tourist location, the Hotel Galvez. After she checked in and was in her room, she called Wendell with some apprehension. She did NOT want to feel like a stalker.

"Hey. Just thought I would tell you I ended up unexpectedly having a weekend. So I drove to The Galvez and checked in. Just going to spend today and tomorrow here, in case you have some time and want to drop in."

Morgan was very careful to sound casual and gave him her room number. She did not want Wendell to feel ANY pressure from her.

Wendell paused. "I can be there in two hours. Just need to take care of something."

Here was the danger of being spontaneous. Morgan hastened to explicitly underline her point: "Wendell, if you have plans, don't worry. No pressure from my end. I came here on the offhand chance you might have some time and want dinner or something. If you do NOT have free time, do not worry as I can find plenty to do. Go to the railroad museum and stuff. You know I like museums. Again: If you have other plans, a date or something, no worries. Really. I just did not expect to have this time. I came here 'just in case', you know?"

"Morgan: I just need to get someone in to take part of my shift. At least five people owe me. Give me two hours." Wendell said.

"Oh. OK. If you want or need to work, I am here all weekend." Morgan said. "Really: this is just a last minute, unplanned thing. I get if you cannot get free."

"Morgan. Two. Hours." Wendell sounded impatient with her now. "I was not aware you had hearing problems. We may need to get that checked. I'm concerned."

'We?' Morgan thought. "Ok. Well, in that case, let me see. I think I will go for a walk on the Seawall. Take a shower after that, because, well, humidity. Galveston has it. Meet you back here in two hours?"

"See you then." Wendell said. "Wait on that shower though, please. You need help with that."

"Need my hearing checked. Cannot take a shower by myself. Geez." Morgan said, adding quickly "Fine: I can wait on that. Just make sure you do a good job. You know how picky I am about my showers."

'Picky in that I like to take them with other people in them.' Morgan mentally added. Even in her own mental dialog she forced that to the plural 'People' from 'Wendell'.

"If I do it wrong, I'll do it over and over till I get it right." Wendell said.

Sometimes not planning leads to a lovely weekend.

CHAPTER NINETEEN

Kids in the Commercial, Day Two

Morgan and Sam appeared in Paul Rafferty's office at 8:00 AM. The third student from Friday's interview schedule had been a no-show. The majority of the interviews stretched ahead of them and was longer by one more.

Paul greeted them. "Good morning, detectives. I hope you had a good evening and in fact good weekend."

Morgan, in fact, had a lousy evening after her return from Galveston. No one here needed to know about her nice weekend. The bad part had started when she had pulled all the documentation on her alarm system, seeing how she could add Video. It wasn't that old a system, but the company had moved on to new models of everything, which left her with an out of date system that she could not buy the video components for new. The aftermarket would have everything, and she could assemble a system and the company she bought her system from could install her upgrades and put it on a support contract because people would have the model system she has for years to come. They just had no stock to sell her as new.

Morgan had called the alarm system's twenty four hour support hotline and asked the man on the phone at "If you can support these things, does that not mean you HAVE all the components in stock?"

To which he replied "They are all tagged for support, and committed to people that have bought a contract. We can't raid that stock or we would not be able to support these systems down the road."

This made sense. Morgan liked, at one level, that they would shelve things to be able to take care of customers. At the same time, she was pissed off because they had dumped her model system without warning. Or maybe they had warned her, and she had just shredded it thinking the mail looked like junk mail. It all meant a long evening researching sources of used alarm parts. Morgan was tempted to just replace the whole thing, but that would be giving in, and that is not a thing Morgan could do easily.

So, even as Paul seemed fairly chipper, and his greeting warm and genuine, it took a fair amount of mental gear shifting to get into the moment.

"Good morning Paul. My evening was... Suboptimal. I hope yours was better." Morgan managed.

"I read my divorce papers over again." Paul said, and one-upped her without even trying.

"Then why are you so chipper this morning?" Sam asked.

"As I said: I read over my divorce papers." Paul repeated. "I wanted this divorce, and so did she. The papers are all above board and what we agreed on. We have no kids, so it's a pure property split thing, and she is a businessperson. Makes more money than me and not by just a little. It's equitable and fair and I am happy to be putting this part of my life behind me."

"I have two ex-wives, and neither was equitable in the divorce. Two daughters, both gone from my life. You are very lucky." Sam said. "I spent the evening in, watching TV, and thought I had the best evening till you said that."

"I am sorry, detective. That can't be easy." Paul was genuinely sympathetic.

"It is horrible. I COULD find them of course. I am a cop. They made it clear they did not wish to be found and to not try." Sam plopped heavily into a chair and looked at his coffee cup. "Sorry Paul: I did not think to bring you any coffee. Rude of me."

"We have coffee here. Little coffee machine back by the office equipment. We drink a great deal of coffee around here, and so its always on and usually fresh. Nothing fancy though. Just store bought tins. Nothing like that."

Morgan pointed at Sam's cup offhandedly. "That is over-roasted, but at least it is expensive."

"My one indulgence." Sam said. "It's not as good as yours. I admit."

"Why was your evening, as you say, 'suboptimal', Morgan?" Paul asked.

"I am upgrading my home alarm system, and it is turning out to be a much larger project than I thought it would be. It was a good and expensive system when I built the house, but it turned out to be the last year that particular system was made, and the new systems are very different and video parts are not necessarily interchangeable. Or they work, but you lose features. I spent the evening looking into it, and it seems that there is a lot of proprietary componentry to these things. Looking through various forums, I found several pushes underway to standardize and also a huge 'roll your own' group out there. Now I am trying to decide if I buy used parts from systems being upgraded elsewhere, and do the work myself, replace the whole damn thing, and switch alarm companies so as to not reward them for their planned obsolescence, roll my own out of off the shelve parts, or what. Right now I am leaning to the latter. I was a computer major, and I know how to do everything required. Then it just becomes WHEN I do it."

Morgan, of course, did not share WHY she was doing all this.

Paul listened intently and said "Ok. That does sound like you win the worst evening contest, however, I do have to admit to being impressed that you can build and install your own alarm system."

"There is a great deal to it. Design choices to make. How many hours of video do I want to keep? That affects how I record the video. Someday that will all be digital but right now it is all tape. How many cameras? Motion sensitive lights near the outside camera's so they can see in the dark. Wired or wireless sensors? Wired or wireless communications back to a monitoring service? Do I even use a monitoring service, or do I set it up to just page me? On and on." Morgan explained.

"Like I said. Impressed." Paul said. "Far more complicated than who gets the couch."

"So, who DOES get the couch?" Morgan smiled and asked.

"I do. She wants a new one. So did I, but I just lost my excuse to get one." Paul said.

"No, you did not. Once you are all done, have a garage sale, and restart your life with all new things. Keep what you want, reboot the rest. If nothing else, if she ever comes over and says 'Hey, where did that thing go?' you can say you never liked it and sold it." Morgan advised. "Not that I have ever been married, more or less divorced. Take my advice with a huge grain of Sodium Chloride."

"I tell her that, it's the best, most effective communication we ever had." Paul said. He tapped a small sheaf of papers. "So, as these things often go, people are calling and rearranging. Life intersects all things. Our first student today is one you wanted to see though. Debora Gomez. Her parents were going to be in with her but could not make it at the last minute. She is nearly eighteen, and they agreed to have Gail in here during the interview instead."

With Gail in the office, it was not possible to put the chairs on a circle and have them near the little round table, so the table formed the hub of a larger wheel. As Morgan took all her notes on a PDA, and Sam in a little notebook, neither needed the table as a place to write on. Instead, school photos of the three young men were placed there and oriented to be facing Debora Gomez's chair.

After the introductions, Paul said "Debora is on the drill team, and is a junior. Because of how her birthday landed, she is one of the oldest students in her grade and nearly eighteen. Her parents have agreed to let her be here for this interview with Gail and I as monitors."

Debora Gomez, as her name implied, was of at least partial Hispanic heritage. She had dark eyes, hair, full lips, and was wearing clothing to accentuate her drill team physicality. Debora looked strong. Broad shouldered. Perhaps she was the one at the bottom of the various formations drill teams often did, Morgan thought. Her round face was at odds with the rest of her.

"Debora: How well did you know any of the boys there?" Morgan indicated the pictures.

"I knew Derek of course. Track guy. They don't have the drill team out at track meets or anything, but you know. Nice guy. A little shy. Good on the track. He won a few of the recent events he was in." Debora said.

"You do not know the other two at all?" Sam asked.

Debora gave that a small, noncommittal shrug. "Well, I know OF them of course. I saw them at auditions. I saw them during the commercial. I saw them at the party. I didn't go out of my way to avoid them or anything. We just didn't hang in the same circles. Way I hear it, that Neil guy was kinda weird. A bit... solitary? He didn't do sports or anything. He didn't date anyone I knew. The other guy? He was new to the school, and I didn't have any classes with either of those two, so I just didn't know them. You want to talk to someone that knew them, you need to talk to Darla Odean."

"Oh?" Morgan asked.

"That chick knows everyone. Never met a guy she did not like." A catty remark like that required followup, and Morgan thought she would return to that later, but wanted to focus in on the events in the bedroom first.

"You played the 'Seven Minutes in Heaven' card game, and lost a round, and went away to a room with a young man. You were angry at your boyfriend and said in general that you being in the bedroom with this young man was what your boyfriend deserved." Morgan stated, looking for a reaction.

Debora heaved a single breath of amusement and said "Yeah. Grant Peters. Cute guy. Nervous as hell to be in a bedroom with a girl from the drill team. All that. Had NO idea what to do with that opportunity."

"You showed him, however." Morgan said.

"Some. We didn't have sex if that is what you are saying.". Debora gave a quick glance over at Gail, and it was not clear if that was a worried glance or a 'are you going to allow this' type of look.

"I was not implying that you did." Morgan said. "It was just clear that you were angry with your boyfriend and that you planned to have some sort of comeuppance."

"I'm not proud of that, but yeah. I was mad. He wanted to hang with some of the other guys of the football team, not be out with me. What kind of guy does that?" Debora let some of her anger enter her voice.

"So, you let Grant do some physical things with you. Did you tell your boyfriend later?" Morgan prodded. She was trying to find anger or hate or resentment here.

"Yeah. Look, I lost twice. Two different guys, OK? I let both of them touch my tits. Took off my bra and everything. I play by the rules, and I am not a tease. You lose, you go off to the room, and you do NOT talk about the weather. So, I told him."

"What is your boyfriends name?" Morgan asked.

"Matt Kaur. He is a lineman. Big guy." Debora replied with a slight cat that ate the canary grin.

"What was his reaction when you told him about the two young men?" Morgan asked.

"He was pissed off. Wanted the names of the guys. I told him 'no'. That it was NONE of his business since he couldn't be bothered to come to the party. We had a fight, and then we made up. He made me promise to not be letting other guys be touching my body when he wasn't around, and I made HIM promise to put me above the guys on the team. Win-win."

"So, you gave him no more details about the party? The game? The other kids that played it?" Sam asked.

"Naw. We were making up. Look, Matt knows all the kids in the commercial, or he could if he cared at all because they posted the final cast list in the school newspaper. Doesn't matter, because most of the people at that party brought other people, and he doesn't know who they are mostly. I mean, if Neil there brought a date? I don't know who they were even and I was there! Derek brought a girl, but she was 'just a friend'."

Here Debora shook her head slowly and sadly. "That guy. Good looking shit. Tight little butt, runners body. He had chicks all over the school that wanted to date him. He could screw a different girl here every night if he wanted, but he never did. He had no idea how good looking he is, or how many different girls would have jumped his ass if he gave them a chance. Hell, if I had lost with Derek and gone to the bedroom with him? My boyfriend would have had something to be mad about because I would have ripped Derek's damn clothes off. No lie. He is that cute. Was. Darla had to drag him off to the closet when they lost together, and I will bet you twenty bucks they did it. They were gone extra long, and he had the look. Well: He looked at HER like they had just done it, and you know how a guy is that has had sex with a girl. He looks at her different. Not in a bad way different: Just different. Not all possessive, because no one possesses that girl. Just like they hope they will get another go. She looked back and winked too: he was going to get her again, someday. Not that night though."

"You seem quite open to discussing this." Sam commented.

"Look, if these two don't know what is going on in this school, then ... Whatever." The 'These two' were Paul and Gail, as indicated by a wiggled index finger. Paul and Gail did not react. "All the cheerleaders and most of the drill team are sexually active. The few that aren't are 'saving themselves' or have some religious thing going on. Just how it is. I pity you guys trying to find out why someone killed someone around here because, by the time you connect all the dots of this many people, it's going to look like a spider web."

"You played the game the entire evening?" Morgan asked.

"Most of it. I danced a little. Ate some. The game was the place where all the yucks were. Lots of laughing and teasing and having a good time. Get right down to it, this was the first time a lot of us even partied together. Most of us just don't hang." Debora said.

"You lost twice. Darla also lost more than once. Anyone else?" Morgan asked.

This caused Debora to stop and consider. Her eyes went up and to the right. "Let's see here. Darla lost four times. I lost twice. I can't think of anyone else that lost more than once. No. Weait. Yeah. Gabby. She lost twice too. Darla had these three guys here, plus another guy. Swim team. Shawn Pascolla. I know him too, of course. I asked him later if he did it with Darla, and he wouldn't answer but he blushed like hell. I think he did."

Morgan leaned forward. "To be clear, Darla Odean lost four times. Each time to a different young man. Derek Jefferson the first time, Neil Snyder the second time, but also she went to the bedroom with Shawn Pascolla and Ailani Aquino?"

"Yes. In that order too." Debora agreed.

"How did that work exactly? Who was dealing?" Morgan asked, then as an aside to Paul asked: "Also, can we get a picture of Shawn Pascolla?"

Paul nodded yes, said nothing.

Again Debora looked up and away. Thought. "Well, Darla was dealing the cards when she lost with Derek. I remember that because we made a big deal about it. You know: Derek lost, and he was going away with the school tramp to his fate, and SHE had dealt him his fate. All that kind of stuff. No one said much when Neil lost because no one really knew him that well. Just a few kinda 'Have fun' remarks. Shawn, being swim team got more reaction and teasing. Someone said something like he and Derek could compare notes later. It was the end of the party pretty much when she hauled Ailani off to his fate. Long night. Long game. Lots of couples going off. Hard to remember all the details. I got some shit about it of course, but I was not the only popular girl there. Not to sound too egotistical or anything. Gabby Lloyd was pissed she was not losing more than her two times, and that Darla got both a swim team guy AND a track guy. Gabby was pissed during the commercial shoot too, because the Director loved her some Darla, and made her front and center in a lot of the shots. She was dressed kinda slutty I thought for a commercial. Not just a short skirt. She had on one of those shirts that they professional tear up to look like they are rags but aren't. I don't get them. I think they are from that store at the mall that sells all the punk rock stuff. With Darla's boobs, the tears in the shirt were a bit... Stressed, shall we say? She had on a little jacket over it all, but like in the scene in the park where she and

Derek held hands and ran along, she was damn near flashing the camera, and even with those big ole boobs, she didn't have a bra on. The guys were all drooling. Well, not a couple of the gay guys of course. You know what I mean."

"I believe I am clear on what you mean. If I may ask, do you know Darla well? You have called her 'tramp' for example, but you have not really put any...heat into it." Morgan thought that lack of emotional energy interesting, since usually when insulting someone there is some anger to it.

"Well, you see: I feel sorry for Darla" Debora explained with a 'what can you do?' gesture. "I know other kids of ministers, and they are all like that. Rebelling against their parents. Doing drugs. Sleeping around. Darla's Ok. We aren't friends or anything, and as far as I know, she never goes to any school sports activities. I kind of envy her a little even. I have to be all aligned with the image of the drill team, and we get told everything we have to do. The captain of the drill team and our sponsor are ALWAYS on my shit about my weight. I barely made the squad and I have to eat like a damn bird and work out all the time, and still, I am too big. My boyfriend doesn't care. More cushion for the pushing he says. He is always shoving Pizza at me, the asshole." Debora replied.

"Do you recall who was dealing the other three times Darla lost?" Morgan asked.

"Darla was at least one of the time... Maybe all of them? I wasn't really paying that much attention. I know one other time for sure because I hate to deal, and she offered to take my turn for me because I said that. She immediately lost to Shawn that time and took him off. She never viewed it as losing. She always gave a little whoop of joy and said something like 'comeon dude, let's get it on!' or something like that. That is a girl that knows what she likes, and it is boys. Every kind. All flavors, colors, and walks of life. She was just as happy about hauling off Neil as she was Derek, which I thought was weird a little because Derek was a total babe, but Neil was kinda laid back and shy. Hey. You know what? They had that in common. Derek was too. He was just unaware of his babacity. Neil was cute enough: don't get me wrong. Just didn't have the same body at all though." Debora looked wistful. "I can't believe Derek got it."

When Gabby Lloyd entered the room, Morgan thought this interview was going to be useless. For one thing, she was dressed in her cheerleader outfit, and Morgan could think of no reason for that other than her wanting to underline that she was Elite.

Worse however was Gabby's mother. An older version of Gabby herself, she wore an expensive watch, a huge diamond wedding and engagement set, a diamond tennis bracelet, expensive and form-fitting clothing, down to the thin button front sweater that fit as tightly as the top underneath. The tennis skirt displayed well-toned legs. Overall, Morgan got the idea that they were here under protest and meant to show off their position in the school.

Paul Rafferty thanked them for coming in, but Morgan's read of him was that he was having the same reaction to them that she was.

"Mrs. Lloyd. Gabby. Thank you for coming in today. Please meet Lead Detective Morgan Olsen of Homicide, and her partner, Detective Sam Parker."

As they shook hands, Mrs. Lloyd went for a firm grip with Morgan, which she returned in kind, at the same time thinking that this was a game men usually played. As they shook with Sam, Morgan noted Mrs. Loyd expressly did NOT try to squeeze his hand as firmly: She watched the skin on Sam's hand and there was no white around her fingers from the pressure. Aggressive with women, not men. Interesting.

Paul continued as seats were taken. "We have been assigned the finest Homicide team the city has to offer. Detectives Olsen and Parker have the highest case closure rate in the department and a reputation for not allowing anything to stop them from getting to the criminal. They even have arrested other police officers in the pursuit of justice. I tell you all this so that you can know that we are doing literally everything to be sure that our students are safe and protected."

Morgan resisted giving Paul a quick glance, but she was sure that there was more to that introduction than simple reassurance. He was putting Mrs. Lloyd on notice.

Morgan went with it. " Mrs. Lloyd: as we have learned in these interviews, there are topics of discussion that are going to come up that are of a prurient nature. There are certain behaviors that will be described that are matters of fact, not opinion. At no point are my partner and I interested in anything other than apprehending the person or persons that killed three young men at this school. That is our ONLY concern. We have discovered many things not related to this murder, and if they do NOT illuminate a motive, we do not care. Do you understand?"

Mrs. Lloyd narrowed her eyes. "Are you implying that Gabby might have been involved in some of these... Things?"

"I am implying nothing. I am telling you directly." Morgan replied.

"What are these things that you THINK my daughter did?" Mrs. Lloyd.

"Know." Sam said, simply.

Mrs. Lloyd looked at him. Leaned back in her chair. "Let's get on with it." She said.

Morgan looked directly at the cheerleader. "Gabby: In the course of making the TV commercial about the shoes, you called Darla Odean, and I quote here and please do not bother denying this, 'A Cunt'..."

That was as far as Morgan got before Mrs. Lloyd exploded. "What does that have to do with ANYTHING?"

Morgan raised one finger, in Mrs. Lloyds general direction. She waited until Mrs. Lloyd looked at her face, her finger, her face again, and then leaned back, arms crossed. Morgan said nothing. Mrs. Lloyd read Morgan's expression and decided wisely not to fight that battle.

"Again, Gabby. You do not care for Darla Odean and during the day the commercial was filmed, you were quite vociferous in your language about it."

Gabby looked at her mother, who was stewing but silent, then said "Yeah. So?"

"So, Gabby: Seven Minutes in Heaven." Morgan said. She let the implication sit there between them. Morgan met Gabby's eyes.

Gabby went through a series of answers that Morgan could read flitting across the cheerleaders face. She picked the worse answer. "Yeah. So?"

"Who did you go off with?" Morgan asked with a glance at the table and its pictures to let Gabby know she already knew the answer. She didn't actually, but Gabby was off balance now.

"Neil one time. Shawn the other." Gabby said. Stopped.

"And?"

"And nothing." Gabby replied with defiance.

Morgan studied Gabby for a moment. "You are sexually active." Morgan stated, flatly, lifting her finger again to forestall Gabby's mother.

Gabby looked at her mother, then back at Morgan. "What about it?" She asked.

Morgan watched Gabby's eyes flick to the table. The pictures.

"So, you are a cheerleader, and you like athletic young men. What about it is that you had sex with Shawn."

"We didn't SCREW!" Gabby was livid.

"There was not enough time. I know." Morgan agreed.

"There was if you are Darla!" Gabby reached out and tapped Derek, Neil, and Ailani's pictures. "She fucked these guys AND Shawn that night. I mean... SHIT! I asked Shawn if he wanted to finish what we started in the bedroom and he said 'yes' but wanted to know if we could wait a little because Darla drained him and he needed to recover a little. I was like 'screw that: You fuck her, you are NOT fucking me.' You know?"

"You gave a young man an opportunity with you, and then you found out he had already been with Darla." Morgan concluded.

"I don't walk around letting just any guy have sex with me. I am a damn cheerleader. I can get anyone I want. I do not need Darla's sloppy seconds."

All of this was leading up to this question for Morgan. "So, now that we are being honest in her with each other, Gabby: can you think of any reason someone would want to kill these boys?"

"I can see why someone would want to beat the living shit out of Darla..." Gabby started, then leaned back. Shook her head. "I wanted to beat the shit out of Shawn."

The thing so far in this interview that Morgan found interesting other than the main line of questions was Mrs. Lloyd's reactions to them. She was neither shocked nor upset by the idea that Gabby was sexually active, or that she had offered to have sex with Shawn.

"You went off with Neil as well." Morgan said.

"Nice little guy. Really. We talked. He asked me what it was like to be a cheerleader and did I have a lot of guys hitting on me and stuff like that. Said he was not going to be one of them. I gave him a quick kiss when I time was up. That was it." Gabby said.

"You missed out then. Rumor has it he was a very good kisser." Morgan said. She had no such rumor but felt like Gabby needed to be taken down a notch.

Gabby looked sad. "I can believe that. You want to know something funny? I kind of wish he and I had done ... More. I date jocks. All the time. Most of them are dumber than dirt or all into themselves. I can see why a little guy like Neil would be different. Better. Listen to what you have to say. Like that."

That was the first unexpected answer, but Morgan liked hearing it.

"Variety is the spice of life." Morgan replied. "So: no reason you can think of? No one you know who would have had it in for any of these young men?"

Gabby shook 'No'. "Derek was popular and a track guy. I never got with him. Before, during, or after. Neil, like I said, was just a nice guy. Ailani seemed nice but lonely. Transfer kid. He was in Drama, and I think that was to make friends more than he was into acting or anything. Just an impression. I talked to him a little on the day we were shooting the commercial over in the park. You know: Cheerleader. Got to be reaching out to everyone. I don't mind. It's part of the gig, but I like it. So: A jock, a drama kid, and a nice but quiet kid. They didn't run together at school, and as far as I know, the only thing they have in common is being in the commercial. Derek got a lot of attention in the commercial: the Director really liked him. Neil and Ailani were more just background people all the time, other than that thing on the basketball court where we all ran around. Why we had time to talk: The Director kept putting Derek and Darla at the front of stuff."

It was already established that the preference of the Director for Darla had made Gabby unhappy, but Morgan could not see any point in raising that here. It was a motive to hurt Darla. Not these three boys.

"Anyone comment on that? The Director's preference?" Sam asked.

Gabby rubbed her nose as she considered. "Well, one guy. The one that is always the lead in plays and stuff?"

"Terry Pfeiffer?" Sam asked.

"Yeah. I was talking to him and he did not like what the Director was doing. He said to me that he understood how I felt, because he was used to being out front too, and it was hard to see Derek and Darla getting all the attention. God. Their names even work together..." Gabby shrugged. "Terry was right. I didn't like it. Neither did he. Funny thing? When Darla took Derek away at the game? Terry didn't like THAT either. He even brought his boyfriend, and he was still a little jealous. Derek may be shy with girls? He was not into guys at all, I think. No WAY Terry was going to get with him. I don't know: Maybe Terry thought Derek being shy was a sign? If so, his Gaydar is busted as shit, because when Derek came BACK from the room with Darla, all he could see was that bitch. Rest of the night, Derek's eyes were on HER. Terry never had a chance with him."

"So, in your opinion then, Terry might have been jealous of Darla and Derek?" Sam asked.

"Maybe. I guess. Terry is an asshole though. Ego. I can't see him letting anyone get to him. He's always in charge. You don't want to fuck him? That's OK, He didn't want to fuck whoever anyway. Like that." Gabby gave a quick look at Paul, then her mother, but neither reacted to her language. For her part, Mrs. Lloyd seemed to be happy none of the current questions went to Gabby's motives. Also, these were Sam's questions, and Mrs. Lloyd responded to him far differently. Everything in her body language was different when Sam was asking versus Morgan. It was very weird.

Morgan recalled from the release forms for the commercial that Gabby's father is a British businessman, a Senior Vice President to a large oil-related company. He was not here today because he was in the UK. Mrs. Lloyd was strong and hard charging and ran her daughters life, but more than likely deferred to her important and rich husband. Morgan thought Gabby to be the product of an absentee father and a driven mother.

"Terry or anyone else ever say anything about the other two boys in your presence?" Morgan asked.

"Not really. Rob called Neil a weird little dude once, but it was not harsh. He just wondered why he didn't have to take PE. Said his coach was PO'ed about that. I don't know why. One girl, a drama girl, was watching a scene being shot. Kids kicking a soccer ball around. Ailani was out there and doing pretty good. Fast. Good with his feet. Clearly played before. Anyway she asked no one in particular 'I wonder where he's from?' and I guessed it was because he looked like he was from the Philippines or something. That's a US place, right? Like the Virgin Islands are?"

"No. It is a Republic and a founding member of the United Nations. A great deal of turmoil there over the recent years, and there DID used to be a US base on one of its thousands of islands." Morgan said very gently. "Ailani and his family come from Hawaii, however."

"Oh..." Gabby replied, embarrassed.

"I did not know that about the Philippines: Founding member?" Sam asked. Morgan thought he was softening the blow.

Morgan smiled at Sam. "1945. Funny thing is that they were not recognized as an independent nation by the UN until 1946."

"Treaty of Manila." Paul added.

"Though I can understand the confusion." Morgan said. "One of the most famous recent presidents of The Philippines is named Corazon Aquino. Same last name as Ailani."

Gabby brightened at that.

The next girl that came in was in the choir and the band.

Paul introduced her proudly. "Karen Khan here is a prodigy. When all the dust settles, she'll be the one you hear about ten or twenty years from now. At Carnegie Hall perhaps. She sings, she plays trumpet and sits first chair in Varsity Band and the jazz band. She also plays Viola in the orchestra."

Morgan gave the young woman and impressed look. "That is not easy: Crossing from brass to stringed instruments. Completely different muscle groups and skill sets. Different clefs even. How did you find time to do a commercial? You must practice every waking hour!"

Karen's parents beamed at Morgan's understanding of their brilliant child. Morgan thought her mother was probably Indian, from the Indian subcontinent, and that was partly based off the Sari, as she wore no caste mark. Her father MIGHT be as well but was probably of Muslim descent rather than of one of the Hindu branches. He wore a well-trimmed but very thick and dark black beard. He was dressed in traditional business wear as if he was headed to the office after this meeting. Morgan was glad to see parents taking an interest in their child, but given the accomplishments listed also wondered if perhaps they might be overbearing. She would watch them closely for reactions during the interview, as a point of curiosity.

Karen's voice was rich in timbre, and Morgan could hear the singing voice behind it. "Why, how do you know such things? Yes, I DO practice a great deal, but ... Music is easy to me. All of it. I wanted to try a different area of performing arts, and my parents said I could try out for the thing. It was only a small time commitment. One weekend to try out. One weekend to shoot the actual commercial. It was very interesting to see how the Director worked. See how all the parts fit together. I talked to them when they had spare moments and they shared how they were thinking about this and that as they worked, and so I understood why they were putting the camera where they were, and why they liked the look of one set of kids over another for any given scene. So interesting."

"I know a tiny fraction of what you do about music. I was in choir and had a band in school. Rock and roll though. Nothing like your accomplishments. I was never good enough to do Jazz guitar, for example. That is just way out of my skill set. I studied Clapton and

Stevie Ray Vaughn and ZZ Top. Muddy Waters. BB King. I kept my stuff more three-chord blues and worked on pitch bending and trying to get the passion into it, but... I am just not a natural performer. I still practice with my friends from the band, but it is just a thing for us now. At the same time, it lets me understand just how special YOU are."

More beaming from the parents. Karen smiled warmly too. "I am glad you have kept with it. Music is special, and even if you are not performing, it means something."

"It does, and it is a nice escape from my day job." Morgan said.

Karen gave that a very curious look. "That is interesting to me. You solve murders. You are the LEAD. Yet you are a young woman. I find THAT inspiring to me. It is not easy to be a talented woman."

"No. It is not, and it never gets easier as near as I can see. Sam and I are very successful as detectives, but I would be lying if I said that success has bred broad respect. In fact, it seems to have, in some corners, had the opposite effect. Still, stay with it, and do it for yourself, not them. Not anyone else." Morgan advised.

"I will." Karen said.

"So, our questions. From what you have said, I wonder if you had a similar observational look at your fellow cast-mates as you did to the production itself. In particular, any and all interactions with those young men." Morgan gave a slight wave at the table and the four pictures it contained. They had added Shawn Pascolla's. Karen looked alarmed. "Has something happened to a fourth boy?"

"No, no. Not that we are aware of. At this point in the investigation his name... " Morgan pointed at Shawn's picture "... has come up and we plan to be talking to him later today in fact.

Karen gave Morgan a very shrewd look. "The four boys that went into the rooms with Darla Odean, you mean."

"I do mean that. Yes." Morgan admitted. "So: what can you tell me about how your cast mates felt about any of those five people? Let us add Darla Odean to your observational reportage."

"First of all, there was the cheerleader. Gabby Lloyd. She did not like that Darla was getting more attention from the Director, and being put into more of the scenes and shots up front. The Director said she liked Darla's look on camera. She was the most natural. The most relaxed. Darla didn't care about the lens, and so she didn't act like it was there. Darla was interested in other things. Derek for one. That came through on the camera too, and the director loved it. I was really interested in what she was saying about it. The difference between a performance, like what a lot of the drama kids were doing, and just having a blast. Funny thing about that is that other guy, the lead in the senior play? He didn't like Darla getting the Directors attention either, but it was because he wanted to be up front. The director didn't like him as much. She said 'yeah, he can act, but it looks like acting, especially since we are not going to be on any one thing very long. It's all fast cut, and focuses in on the shoes, not the kids.' Like that."

"Are you aware of Gabby Loyd having any issues with any of these boys?" Sam asked.

"Not really. Gabby and a few of the other girls were jealous of Darla is all I could see. She had the Directors attention. She had the guys attention. That's just Darla though. She moves through life like that."

"Can you expand on that?" Morgan asked.

"Oh, you know. Darla is a free spirit. She does what she wants when she wants to. No one at school is above her, and no one at school is BELOW her either. She takes no guff, but she gives none either. She has been to our concerts because she likes music, and I know it's her out there even if I can't see her because she cheers the loudest. Stands the longest. If she likes you, you know it. If she doesn't like you, she just ignores you."

"Which of your many genres did Darla like best?" Morgan asked.

"Jazz band for sure, but she came to the band concert and the choir concert and even sat in rehearsals for 'Fiddler'. I'm playing Viola in the pit orchestra for that. After she always tells the orchestra guys they did great. It's funny because it really bothers the Director sometimes. They like to be the one tell you when you did great."

"You were at the party?" Morgan asked.

"Yes." Karen said though she stiffened ever so slightly.

Morgan read that warning sign as 'My parents cannot know what happened there.'

"Are you vegetarian?" Morgan asked, to relax her a bit.

"No. Not at all. I don't eat a great deal of meat, but I can. Why?" Karen asked.

Morgan was extremely casual with her answer. "I was just curious. Not germane. I have heard the menu several times during these interviews, and I know that there are many ways the dietary restrictions are interpreted, especially in this country, and so I just wondered. In India, it is my understanding that all red meat is Halal, for example. That is not always easy to find here. I am like you: I can eat meat, but I restrict it for health reasons. When I do eat meat, I prefer

Halal if at all possible, not for religious reasons but for personal ones. Humane treatment of the animals is important to me."

"Oh..." Karen said.

"As I said, it was just curiosity. I hope I did not offend." Morgan continued. She could see in her peripheral vision that Sam had no idea why she was saying these things but was, as usual, following her lead.

"No, no. Not offended." Karen waved back at her parents with a half turn. "Mom will eat chicken and seafood, but Dad won't eat most seafood, so we eat a lot of Veg. We have multiple pans. Red meat must be prepared in separate pans from Veg or chicken, but my parents worked all that out long before I came along."

"I see. Thank you. I find that very interesting. Sorry for the sideroad."

Mr. Khan smiled and had bright white teeth. "Not everyone understands our dietary restrictions, Detective. It is nice to meet someone who does."

Morgan gave him a slight bow of her head in return. "So, to the party. As I understand it, there was a card game. A sort of poker, with no money involved. Just the kids having fun."

Karen looked at Morgan in such a way as to communicate deep gratitude.

Morgan continued. "As each round was played, the losers were roundly teased and made to sit out a hand. Each of these boys lost one hand. They were teased. Here is the point of this question: Based upon your observations about the teasing, was anyone giving them a harder time than anyone else?"

Karen gave that thought, translating it to the real game. Sam gave Morgan a lightly amused look as Karen considered. "I can't think of anyone. Darla came in for the most teasing because she lost four times. I lost once too. No one really said anything especially mean, or whatever. It was all just a game. Darla did not care at all, because. Well. Darla. Water off a ducks back."

"I get the impression you admire Darla." Morgan said, and that got another look. This one contained fear.

"She is so... Free. You know. I like that about her. I wish sometimes I could care a little less about what other people thought about me. Not that I do things to have people thinks poorly of me or anything, but... Her lack of fear. It's impressive."

Morgan saw the parents were not at all following the second level conversation she and Karen were having.

"For whatever it is worth, and I have not yet talked to Darla so I could be completely wrong here, but I know kids who are the children of clergy. Many of them are a lot like Darla. Free spirits, if you will. When I talk to Darla, I will know for sure, but it often happens that the social pressures and expectations of being the child of clergy leads to various forms of rebellion and so this freedom has a cost. I admire someone for the same reasons you state, but be prepared to learn there may be a darker side. A cost for her to be this way." Morgan finished.

"If that is true, and Darla needs a friend to talk to about that? I will listen. I get energy from her, so it is only fair to give it back. That is how we should get through this world. Supporting each other." Karen said.

"Indeed. I could not agree more. Mr. and Mrs. Khan, you must be extremely proud not just of your daughters' talent but for the human being that she is."

"We are, Detective, we are." Mr. Khan said, and his wife bobbed her head and smiled.

When the Khans had left, Sam gave Morgan a hard time. "A harmless card game?"

Morgan grinned. "Yes, well, wait a minute or two. I am guessing we will get a little more information shortly."

Sam gave that cryptic remark a look.

"I thought that very kind of you. They are a very traditional family, and knowing the truth would have hurt their daughter." Paul commented

"Thank you. Karen has done nothing wrong and in her own way has the same types of pressures as a child of clergy. She did not deserve to have this investigation cause her issues with her parents. Please excuse me for a few moments." Morgan stood and left the office.

Morgan went outside the school offices and slightly away from them to the empty hall that led to the front door of the school. She waited. As she had hoped, Karen came running back up to her, slightly winded.

"Detective. Thank you so much for what you did there. I was so scared all that was going to come out!" Karen said. She waved back to the school entrance. "I told them I forgot to tell you one thing. I did not forget. I just saved it."

"First of all: You are welcome. They did not need to know unless you did the killing. They do not need to know you went away with a boy, what you did with that boy, or that you have had sexual relations with Darla either. That only is important if YOU did kill three young men, and then it would not matter, would it? I am moderately sure you did not kill though."

"How can you tell I didn't do it?" Karen asked.

"You and Darla had your fling. I am guessing an experiment, at least the first time?" Morgan asked.

"Yes. I ... Just like her." Karen admitted, looking down.

"I understood that immediately. What about the boy you went to the bedroom with?"

"He was nice. I like boys too. We fooled around. Same as everyone." Karen said.

"What was the thing you were going to tell me that you saved?" Morgan asked.

"Every time Darla lost, which of course meant she won, she was dealing the cards. I think she cheated. I don't know how. I think she WANTED to go off with those guys. Those times she and I were together, she talked about her lovers. Not JUST them but guys she wanted to get with. We giggled about it. She would say something like 'I want to fuck Derek, don't you?' and I would say I wanted some guy in the band or whatever, and she would ask why, and I'd say 'because of the way he plays French Horn: He must have nice lips' and she would say 'Oh, I never thought of that!' and we would laugh and agree to him too. That's just how she is, you know? She plays the field. Tries everyone on. A nice rear end there, nice hands on that guy there, or aren't his eyes soulful, or whatever."

"So you and Darla are together, on and off, and have been for a while." Morgan said.

"Yes. It is just a thing we do sometimes. She also teases me about how dark my nipples are or about how my parents would hate knowing we are having sex, and then say 'but they are never finding out, are they?' and I would agree they weren't and she would grin and dive in to my body like she was starving for me. We even talked about having sex with a guy together, but we never have. Yet."

Karen tilted her head. "Doesn't the fact she and I are... Together? Doesn't that make ME a suspect? Aren't you looking for someone that would be jealous of her having sex with those boys?" Karen asked.

Morgan smiled at Karen in a reassuring way as she explained. "Karen: you killed those three boys, and only those three boys WHY? You just said she told you while you were being intimate that she talked about other young men she wanted to try out in bed. That your relationship pre-dates the commercial. You would have had to kill how many people if you were a jealous lover?"

Karen looked impressed. "That is very true, Detective. Very true. Well, I have to run. Here is my phone number. Call me if you have any questions and need to ask them when my parents are not around. Thank you again." Karen zoomed away.

Morgan went back into the office to two pairs of expectant eyes. "Karen came back and told me that Darla was dealing every hand she 'lost'. She was cheating, and Karen does not know how, but Darla Odean targeted these four boys for sex, and three of them later died."

Sam waited for a heartbeat, then said to Paul with a sigh: "You see? I deal with this all the time."

Paul looked steadily at Morgan. "You knew Karen would come back and tell you that."

"No. I was moderately sure she would come back and tell me something. I had no idea what it would be. That was it though." Morgan replied.

"HOW did you know that?" Paul asked.

"Karen told me during that conversation she had more to say, but not with her parents there. As you say, a very traditional family, but she was born in this country, and like most children of immigrants, there is divergence. Karen idolizes Darla Odean, but knows her parents would HATE her."

"That conversation just there. That Sam and I both listened to." Paul rubbed at his forehead. "You want Gail's job?" he asked rhetorically.

"Not even a little bit. Besides, Gail is doing an excellent job." Morgan said. She switched to a teasing tone. "Besides, after this case, she wants to date Sam and I do not want to mess that up for him."

Sam looked at Morgan in stunned disbelief. "Gail told you that?"

Morgan waved that off. "No, of course not."

"Then..." Sam started.

"Sam. Trust me on this one. I promise. Ask, she'll say 'yes'. Once the case is over though, OK?" Morgan.

Paul agreed to Morgan. "Yes. I think she will too."

"I'll be... Something'ed. Not sure what." Sam said.

"You know nothing about women, Sam, so just go with it." Morgan assured him.

"Clearly. Nothing." Sam was utterly nonplussed.

CHAPTER TWENTY

On the Third Day, They Rested

Shawn Pascolla rescheduled to Tuesday, but he did make his new appointment. He had gotten his parents to agree that they only needed Paul and Gail there with him.

"Shawn: Thank you for coming in. As this is day three of this, I assume you are aware from talking to others about the general nature of what we are talking about in here." Morgan opened, once all the introductions were complete.

"Yeah, sure. I talked to a couple of the guys." Shawn agreed.

"I appreciate you talking your parents into NOT coming." Morgan added. "Though I am sure you did not want them knowing what we are going to talk about."

Shawn Pascolla looked at the floor and nodded. His chlorine bleached hair included his eyebrows. Either that or he was the blondest young man Morgan had seen in a while.

"Yeah. The party." Shawn said.

"To dispense with a few things: We know about Darla of course, and also that you managed to make Gabby Lloyd unhappy with you."

"Yeah. That was dumb. I should not have told her about Darla. I thought it might make her jealous, but it turned her off big time. I shoulda just shut up. Coulda been the best damn night of my life."

"You played that wrong for sure." Morgan told Shawn. "I am very glad you are not denying anything or being coy about it here."

Shawn found that amusing.

"Something funny?" Morgan asked.

"It's like you said. I talked to some of the others. Karen said you are the smartest lady she ever met and knowing Karen even a little bit? That's saying something. Gabby said you were a hardass stone bitch.

Rob said you were OK but went right in and didn't fool around. Karen showed me some newspaper articles about you and your partner. She went to the library and printed some off. Seems like it would be kinda dumb to come on here and try to get away with shit. You'd just nail my ass to the wall."

"That is quite true, however, this will save us time. Let us begin then. You went away to the bedrooms with two different attractive women. Did you get any grief from ANYONE about that?" Morgan asked.

"Hardly. First of all: Darla? You seen her? Oh my god. And it's not just a body that won't quit, its that Darla LOVES to... You know."

"Have sex?" Morgan offered.

"Exactly. I mean, she digs it. Kinda sweeps you along with her. It's like having sex with a hurricane. In a hurricane? Something."

"And so no one said anything about that?" Morgan asked.

"Sure they did. I mean, Gabby was pissed for one thing, but the guys were like 'you lucky dog' and stuff like that. I didn't tell anyone anything, other than Gabby. They just assumed. Even better? Darla wanted to do it AGAIN sometime, so you know what? Gabby is no great loss. Would have been fun, but really? I can't see her being anything like Darla. Gabby would be all like 'I am doing you a favor, letting you screw my cheerleader ass' but Darla would just be a hoot. Will be, I hope. Unless this whole murder thing screws that up."

Morgan was glad Shawn had his priorities straight. More worried about how murders killed HIS chances at a repeat with Darla.

Sam said as much. "Shawn: are you saying you are worried that you may not be having sex again with Darla because three boys died and that might make it so she isn't in the mood anymore?"

Shawn blushed. "It did kinda come out like that, didn't it? I didn't mean for it too, I ... Just. I know I am supposed to be all popular being a Jock and stuff, and I do OK? Maybe? I think? I don't know how much the other guys really do it. I think they all say they do a lot more than they REALLY do though. But Darla, man? I have never been with anyone like her. I just haven't. It's hard to explain."

"Do you think anyone that has been with Darla in this way would want to kill other people? Jealous? Want her all for themselves?" Morgan asked.

Shawn turned beet red. "Meaning me." He said.

"I did not mean you in particular, but I am treating you here as the subject matter expert. Have you heard anyone ever say anything like that?" Morgan revised.

"From that party, I am the only guy left alive. I have been afraid I was next. The question you are asking is one I have thought about a huge amount, detective. Like every waking moment since this came out. I have replayed every conversation I can remember about her with anyone. I can't think of anyone like that. There's the people that like her, like Karen. The people that hate her, like Gabby. The people that could give two shits, like Terry or maybe Debora some. Then there are the guys that just want to have sex with her. They don't like her or hate her because they don't KNOW her. They just know her rep and see her body, and they just talk about wanting to screw her. Stupid shit, most of that too. You know. 'I could show her what a real man is like' kind of bullshit. They have NO idea. She would show THEM. Then there are the people that have been with her. They are like me mostly. They want her again, sure, but like... So, Derek and I talked the next day, and he was like me: He could not wait till he had another chance with her. Hell, I even talked to that Neil guy, and I barely know him, but I knew he had been with her and he was all like formal and stuff about it, but it was still 'yes. I would very much like to enjoy her company again.'. I knew what he meant. Point is, no one, and I do mean NO ONE I can think of ever said anything like wanting to kill her lovers. You know what, at this point, that would be a LOT of killing too. Darla is ... Generous."

Morgan did not interrupt Shawn's rambling, because this was very interesting to her and Shawn had clearly thought about it. This was the best insight she had so far into Darla and possible motives, even as Shawn was not actually giving her any.

"Are you in love with her?" Morgan asked, very low key.

Shawn looked back at Morgan for the first time. "Maybe. I don't know. I always heard you aren't supposed to confuse sex and love, but... Hell. She is all I have thought about since that night, one way or another. Either wanting her or being terrified about being the last guy alive. If that had not have happened? If everyone was still alive and I was just living for the moment she and I could be together again? Maybe? It's hard to know because that isn't what happened, is it? Also, while she NEVER says it, and she is totally in the moment with you, at the same time you know putting your heart out there with her is a good way to get it hurt. Destroyed even."

Shawn looked far away. "So yeah. I could be. And yeah: I can see someone getting totally lost in her and wanting to kill for her, but that would be one sick bastard. Someone that just does not get her." Shawn paused. Added "I am not even sure that makes it a guy. Chicks fall in love with other chicks, and what if one of them does not like that Darla likes guys? I mean really likes them?"

At the end of the third day of student interviews, Morgan and Sam sat in Paul's office with Gail and went over their results. Morgan consulted her PDA, which she had reorganized every evening at home to summarize and place related facts together.

"We have now talked to fifteen kids. Of the original twenty, three are dead, and two of the kids do not have parental permission to speak to us. One of those two is a young man that, by all reports, did not go to the party, and was in no school organizations at all. No one seems to know anything about him other than they saw him at auditions, and they saw him during the commercials. Between takes, he read a book, but it seems that it was homework: Orwell's 1984." Morgan started.

"He did it. It's always the quiet one." Sam said, but in a tone to let everyone know he was kidding.

"Well, you laugh, but I do actually hold him in reserve." Morgan said.

"Why?" Sam asked.

"Because I know almost nothing about him. He has a solid 3.5 GPA. He is on early work release and works at the convenience store up the road. Is he secretly in love with Darla? Seems a fair number of the young men here either like her or hate her, and it pivots off whether or not they have had sex with her. In one case, they had sex with her, and she did not want seconds, and that pissed him off. That band kid, Charlie... Err.. " Morgan looked at her PDA. "Charlie Brodsky. Tuba player. Unhappy because Darla was one and done with him."

Paul looked at Morgan and pursed his lips. "How did you get all that from that interview? I sat right there in the same room you did."

Sam lifted some fingers "Oh, I got that too. That's not Morgan Magic: That's just obvious jealousy. When we asked him how many times he had dated Darla, he blushed and said, and I quote, 'Oh, lots of times: you know!'. Translation. One time. Body language. Tone of voice. All of it."

"I thought he really had..." Paul said.

"That is because you think Darla would do that." Morgan said.

Paul looked like she had just kicked him. He did not reply immediately. Thought it over. Slumped. "No. You are right. Not proud of that."

"The problem with the, and I quote here, 'school tramp', is learning she has values, even if you do not understand what they are."

"You do?" Paul asked.

"I have not met her yet, so no. I don't. However, some consider me a tramp, and it is largely because they do not understand MY dating and relationship criteria, so I do identify." Morgan said.

Gail gave Morgan a look that she read as 'Girl, do NOT be telling the guys about the things they do not understand'

"This last three days has been one of the most eye-opening experiences of my life, and seems I still have more to learn." Paul said.

"When we stop learning, we start dying." Morgan noted.

"In that case, I will be alive forever." Sam added. "Thanks to you."

Morgan ignored that particular repartee. "What we have at the end of all this is that no one seemed to hate these three boys at all. Many of the young women would have liked to have been the one in the closed room with Derek or Shawn. The two athletes. Fewer cared about the transfer student Ailani Aquino because they did not know him or Neil, who they also seemed to not know well. All the kids are physically attractive, which is why they were all cast in the first place. No one thought a thing about the idea Darla might want to take them to the bedroom. Opinions about Darla vary based on their relationship to her. The young ladies liked her far less than the young men, with a few exceptions. The gay girl from Choir, Susan Kohowski, would have liked to gotten to know Darla better but never has it seems. The rules of the card game were such that only heterosexual relationships were occurring." Morgan said. She paused, seeing the expression on Paul's face.

"Susan Kohowski is gay..." He said, dumbfounded.

"Yes." Morgan said and decided Karen Khan's assignations were not going to be mentioned here. "As motive and as Shawn pointed out, it is interesting to consider the idea that the jealous person here might be a woman that was in love with Darla and hated the way she spent time with all the young men. However, if that was a true motive, then the murdering would be of more boys than this, and would not be limited to the ones in the commercial."

168

"Unless this is just the beginning." Sam said.

"Then you still have to address how the first three were all in the commercial." Morgan pointed out.

"I was kidding." Sam said, surrender hands.

"Three of the dead boys went to the bedroom with Darla. That has to mean something." Paul said.

"I am sure that it does. I am just not sure what yet, though obviously Shawn Pascolla needs to be very careful. All the murders were about being lured to a killing field. He needs to NOT be going around without others with him at all times. Given what he said, he seems pretty mindful of the danger. Still, you may want to remind him."

"I talked to his parents once it was clear that three of the boys had been in the bedroom with Darla. I did not say WHY I was worried about him, just to make sure he never goes anywhere alone. What will you do about Darla? Her parents have completely refused to bring her in here for questioning."

"That means she is coming to MY house for questioning instead. I will talk to her." Morgan said.

When Paul and Gail exchanged confused glances, Sam explained the parlance: "Morgan means they will be questioned at the station. Our house. In an interrogation room."

"How will you arrange that?" Paul asked.

"I will let them, Darla and her parents, know that if they do not appear and talk to us there, then I will arrest her, here, in front of the entire school. They are trying to hide behind their social standing and money. I will not have that." Morgan said.

"You can just arrest kids?" Paul asked, struggling with the concept.

"No, Paul. Not JUST arrest them. There are procedures to follow before doing such a thing. I know what they are. It should be very clear after the last three days that Darla is at the center of this. Somehow. I do not know how yet, but Sam and I will figure it out." Morgan said with firm assurance.

"Now you seem more like the Vice cops." Gail stated in disapproval.

"In what way?" Morgan asked, offended.

"They were all high and mighty too. Had power, and loved to use it." Gail replied, slightly cold.

"The difference is, I will go to a judge and get a warrant, I will not just impose my will." Morgan assured Gail. "I have zero interest in power and every interest in finding who killed three young men. Also, I am the one that will be arresting some Vice cops soon if it turns out they are doing what you suspect."

"Not Sam? Just you?" Gail asked.

"I like to ask him if he wants to come along on my little side trips into career damage hell first." Morgan explained. "Maybe Sam too. I just don't want to speak for him."

"Arresting Vice cops can damage YOUR career?" Gail wondered, seeming to not believe that idea.

Sam explained. "Yes Gail: Cops don't like to arrest cops. That whole 'Blue Wall' thing you hear about is real. Morgan and I have done it and so we have a rep to maintain, and also there is that I like working with a clean cop like her, so of course, I will be there. If these scum are doing ANYTHING to harm underage girls... Well. I have two girls. I work with a woman. She will have to keep me from doing more than just damaging my career if this is true."

Gail gave Sam a school counselor sourced look. Reading him. "Detective Sam Parker: I will pay your bail if so." She said.

Morgan could tell by the way Sam's neck muscles flexed he was avoiding looking at her in an 'A-Ha!' moment. Morgan also assumed that Sam would ask her out at some point.

CHAPTER TWENTY-ONE

New Covenant Abundant Light Church

Sam insisted on driving because Sam. Morgan often wondered if his professed dislike of her little car was an excuse for him to 'be the guy' and drive. In Sam's upbringing, men were the drivers. Sam had told her once that his father (the quintessential 'thundering hand') would never let his mother drive. It did not matter that Morgan was a better driver (much better: She had trained at a driving school in hot-rodded Mustangs, just for fun) or that she parked in legal parking spaces. Morgan was fairly sure every time Morgan drove the two of them someplace, Sam was feeling like she was doing something that he was supposed to be doing. Programming from his youth he has not yet escaped. Not an emasculating thing exactly, but definitely a gender bias from his horrid youth.

Morgan considered it horrible, in any case. It was nothing like the relationship she had with her Dad. It is inside the realm of the possible that Sam really was terrified of the little car, but it was just more likely that if he was driving there would be no issues for him at all.

Morgan would NEVER let Sam drive her beloved Miata. It was easier to just call him a 'chickenshit' and give him the driving chore.

Morgan did not care in the slightest about being promoted over many of the older, more experienced men in the department, however, it was different with Sam. Sam always supported her, and never challenged her as the senior member. He followed her lead. They were a good and successful team because of Sam's ability to put his ego in check when required. It was easy to give him this one. Besides, it gave Morgan time to think or read or whatever was required on any given case and at any given time.

At the same time, if Morgan ever met 'The One' he would be a man that let her drive without argument. Silly, but true.

Driving West on the freeway and looking south at the church campus, it was hard to understand the scale of the building that the New Covenant Abundant Light Church occupied. It was set far back from the road and had a parking lot that would make a Walmart or even two of them together proud. That perception did not change as they exited the Freeway, and turned south and under the overpass. Morgan tried to remember if this overpass had been here before the church building or not. Did they build here because there was an easy exit? Or did they build and easy exit because they wanted to put the megachurch here? Morgan was not sure how that went.

As they entered the concrete expanse of the parking area, Morgan wondered if they ran trams during services to get people from the far reaches of the massive expanse of concrete up to the building. The parking lot lights had section numbers on them. It was like being over in Astrodomain. Morgan liked roller coasters and went to Astroworld to ride them with more frequency than most grown women she knew. This was like that to her.

Sam drove his truck to the front row and parked in handicapped parking, of which there was a huge number of slots, and very few cars in the lot. Given the time and the day there would not normally be any other than church staff and people taking meetings about various things. Texas ADA code for a parking lot of this massive size is to have 20 close-in slots, plus an additional slot for each one hundred regular car spaces. Even as massive as this parking lot is, Morgan thought that perhaps they have set aside MORE ADA spaces than required. Perhaps the church had a larger elderly population than average.

Despite the huge ADA car parking set-aside, there was a section of non-ADA spaces right next to the door for 'Church Staff', and a very new Nissan Altima was parked there. Morgan stopped and stared at the handicapped sign, then at Sam, then the sign again.

"There is no one HERE Morgan." Sam complained at her unspoken but obvious criticism.

"God knows we could not have walked from right over there." Morgan pointed at a parking space in the second row of painted spaces. "Who knows? Maybe Odean does faith healing in his off hours and can heal your handicap."

"If these slots fill up, I will come out here to move the truck." Sam said stiffly.

"Just humor me and move your damn truck, please? Park in 'Church Staff'. I will not say a thing." Morgan said.

"Fine." Sam got in, saving Morgan the trouble of demanding the keys and moving it herself. She would have.

While she waited, she scanned the lot. There were a few cars dotting it here and there, presumably members of the church that had left them here for one reason or another. Maybe they broke down, or maybe they had too much wine with their services and got a different ride home. As often as it rained in Houston, this parking lot would be a bitch to run from a car to get to a sheltered location. They should have built a parking garage. In Houston, it is wide open spaces and long uncovered walks most of the time. Land is cheap. Parking garages are not.

Morgan noted a sign on a lamppost that said trams ran every ten minutes before services. That explained the covered bus stop looking structure off to one side of the building entrance as well. That was all well and good, but the parking lot needed covered bus stops spread out in it to make that tram really effective. To Morgan, it said 'We love you only this much and no more.', Perhaps there was a church fundraising drive going to add shelters. It was hard to know. Yet.

Close up, the scale of the building was impressive. Not quite as large as a sports stadium over in the Astrodomain complex, but nearly, or so it seemed. There were eight doors, and a sign that read 'West Entrance'. That implied to her that as one went around the building there were other big entrances: at the very least one more.

Morgan avoided organized sports with the same alacrity she did organized religion, but she found this parallel in the physical structures interesting. The two activities both ran on belief in things that she did not understand. She wondered how does one pick a sports team and declare 'This is the one I support' over another. What differentiates them from each other? They both play the same game in the same stadiums supported more or less by the public in the same way. It all seemed mostly harmless unless you were in a stadium that collapsed or there were riots in it. Tickets were crazy expensive. Her weekend at the Galvez cost less than good seats at most games.

Morgan did the MS-150 because it supported a good cause. If the proceeds of a baseball game went to a worthy charity every single time, then she would have a selection criteria. She could decide what team to support based off what charity or charities it supported. There are a huge amount of worthwhile charities, so that may not work much better. At least it would be SOMETHING she could think about and understand though.

Sam walked back up as she stood thinking about the doors and sports. "Happy?" he asked.

Morgan saw the truck parked in the first row on non-handicapped parking, and replied "Yes, Sam. Thank you very much. I appreciate it." Morgan put no spin or sarcasm into it.

This defused Sam. "OK. Sure. Whatever." He said.

The Detectives entered the edifice through an unlocked door, after trying a few of them. For Morgan, the interior appearance of the entrance area moved the building design ethos away from Sports arena over to large performing arts venue. Wortham Center scaled up. There were posters featuring upcoming events on the walls and on stands.

Electronic signage abounded also announcing this new series or that. Things such as 'Searching for a new job with God's help' or 'Gods plan for your Prosperity, are you listening? A four-part series' and 'When you give, you get more.'

Next to a large set of double doors, there was a family portrait, top-lit, of Joseph Odean, Deedee Odean, and Darla Odean. Close up it appeared to be an oil painting but from any distance back it looked like a photograph. The plaque at the bottom of the painting read 'Welcome to our family of faith. A new hope for you and your family await you within these walls. The Odean Family.'

They pushed open a door and entered the Sanctuary. It was a cross between performing arts and sports arena inside. There was a richly colored red carpeted ramp with rows of stadium seating on either side, done in a sort of 'Theater in the Round' fashion, except it was an Octagon and only seven eights of one at that. The final eighth appeared to be a service corridor up to the stage, as well as a place to hang massive blank screens and ancillary stage support items.

As the pair walked down the ramp to the stage, they looked about. There were blank screens everywhere, and once they were into the room enough to look up and back, they could see camera emplacements lined up over each section so that the stage could be filmed from seven long angles. Up by the stage were more cameras on platforms, managing to make front row seats terrible in several places. At the end of each aisle, there were steps up to the stage.

The room was even larger inside than it appeared outside, due to the way the ramps dipped down. They had taken a fair number of steps up to the doors from the parking lot, but this went much farther down than ground level. Morgan thought about the location out on the West side of Houston. The elevation here was about fifty feet above sea level, and they had gone down at least that far. It would take nothing to turn this place into a swimming pool during a hurricane. Morgan assumed that, given the expense of the building, they had paid attention to both sealing the concrete from below to prevent water from bubbling up, as well as making sure they had sump pumps with generator backups.

The pair went up the steps. This was where people came up during services to join Joseph Odean and talk about how their lives were so much better since the believed in the message, gave money, and were rewarded tenfold. Morgan researched this place before she came here, and she watched a few recordings of services. The theme was always the same: give to get. Many variations on that, but at the end of the day and when semantically analyzed, that is what Joseph Odean's message to his flock boiled down to. He was not a faith healer, so much as if you needed more money for being healed at the hospital, give to God and be rewarded with resources from directions you had no idea were possible.

Up on the stage, Morgan looked back up at the seating, and the way the lines all converged on the stage. She had read that the facility supported over twenty-thousand people at a time per service, and that matched her quick estimate from the stage.

Morgan paused to wonder if, during a service with stage and spotlights in operation, was any of the room even visible? She had performed on much smaller stages with her band in school, and knew the stage lights made the audience a swath of blackness that sounds came out of. Hopefully applause. According to Karen, she could hear Darla out in the darkness whooping during Karen's performances.

Of course, they left the room lights up during services, so that was different. In the recordings Morgan had watched, when Joseph Odean called people up, he would say a name, and often follow it with 'Are you out there? Come on up here!' That implied to Morgan he could not, in fact, see the faces in the audience very well. It was hard to know what was show though, as Odean had a solid patter down to fill time as things took place.

As the partners surveyed the room from the stage, Sam asked Morgan "You told me once you tried out a bunch of different churches.

Ever go to one like this?"

Morgan looked over at her partner and nodded yes. "Not this one. A different one up near town, but the same idea as here: Prosperity Gospel."

"And?" Sam asked.

Morgan felt like laughing sarcastically but didn't. Sam was asking her a straight question. Not trying to provoke anything. "Well, I never went again, but after attending the service I did feel the need to hit the gym, go for a bike ride, get laid, and have a shower, in no particular order. I felt similarly after watching Joseph Odean's recorded services, but it was worse being there, at that place in person, in the middle of it all."

Sam looked around the huge space. "I can see that. You try a sweat lodge to get it purged out? You are part Amerind, after all."

Morgan did give that a short amused laugh. Sam trying to be funny. "That is a stereotype. Not all American Indian tribes have a sweat lodge practice or tradition. You are not wrong however, in that I would have tried anything to get that experience out of my head."

"What worked best?" Sam wondered.

Morgan debated that answer briefly, went with honest. "The sex. Perhaps not for the reason you might think. Or in addition to that reason. Churches often use their so-called moral authority to dictate how people have sex, though that is from my personal observations less true in this type of church than some of the traditions it grew out of, say the larger Charismatic movement for example. Still, controlling sexual behavior allows one to control everything about people. It is not that they do not still have sex, and in ways the church does not approve of, it is that they feel guilty about being human and having natural desires and needs, and then a large number of churches manipulate that. I had sex. I enjoyed it. I did not feel guilty about it. It was not just that the sex was intrinsically enjoyable, it was also just a great big 'up yours' to any institution that tries to control me."

Morgan shrugged as she reflected on that particular sexual experience. It was ironic because, in her need to cleanse her mind of the experience and replace it with a positive one, she had also been in the mood for and delivered the kind of 'shagging' that night that she had just complained to Mike about. To be fair to herself however it was not as if she did not warn Ken in advance it was coming. The conversation with him afterward as they rested went 'what brought that on?' and Morgan had simply explained 'I went to church' and left it at that. Ken asked no further questions, that had either been a satisfactory answer or one so filled with landmines he avoided it completely.

Sort of the way Sam was accepting her comment and asking no further questions now.

From the stage, it was easy for them to see the corridors that led away to the support area, and they walked back that way. Somewhere back there would be the offices they sought.

Backstage reminded Morgan very much of being a standard performing arts setup, full of various props and furniture, all on wheels and ready to be rolled out to reset the stage based on what was going on out in front of the curtain wall. Except it was not a curtain wall but a fixed in place multi-media wall. It could have been ripped out of the Astrodome or the new baseball stadium downtown, Enron Field.

The detectives walked down some stairs to a hall and looked left and right for signs to the church office. Presumably, there had been another path to this hall but Morgan was glad they had taken the one they did. It was illuminating as to the scale this church operated at, and the money it had to work with.

They came to a glass double door that said 'Church Office' in gold lettering on the door, with posted office hours. They entered the sumptuous room. A woman in her late thirties looked up at them as they entered. She was well dressed, but not in such a way as to hide her physical attractiveness. The engraved sign on her desk read 'Assistant to Joseph Odean' in larger letters, and 'Cathleen Gray' in smaller letters on the second line. The disparate font sizes alone told a story.

"May I help you?" Cathleen Gray asked pleasantly, clearly used to people she did not know entering the office.

Morgan flashed her badge. "I am Morgan Olsen, Homicide. This is my partner, Sam Parker. We are here to speak with the Odean's about their daughter, Darla? I am sure you have read about the killings up at her school by now?"

Cathleen gave that a sad expression, sincere Morgan judged, and she nodded. "Yes, of course. So horrible. I am afraid neither of the Odean's are here yet, but I can offer you a comfortable place to sit. This is the outer office, mine is through there next to the Odean's offices, and I have a lovely couch you can sit on. I can get you something to drink as well. Water? Tea? Coffee?"

Cathleen stood and waved them into the next room. It was about the same size, decorated with many pictures, a huge overstuffed leather couch, coffee table, small drink bar with coffee maker and various boxes that Morgan assumed were for tea. Below that was a cabinet that probably hid a refrigerator.

The desk was covered in neat stacks of papers, pictures, and at the front edge, an empty spot to put the desk nameplate from the outer office. Morgan assumed she moved it, and that there was a receptionist normally out there rather than Cathleen.

"Nice couch." Sam said, looking it over with obvious appreciation. Morgan guessed the couch cost more than all the furniture in Sam's apartment put together and then some.

Cathleen found that amusing. "You should see Joseph's office. This is nothing."

Morgan perked up at that and treated it like it was an offer. "Can we? Just to look. I promise not to touch anything."

Cathleen hesitated but apparently saw no harm in the ask, and took them on through into a much larger office. The office was as Cathleen said: It would have been at home in Buckingham Palace if the British Royals went in for putting pictures of Joseph Odean on every wall and flat surface. He posed with all sorts of people. TV Stars, President's, Senators. Even sheiks, based on the garb and the beards.

Morgan found the pictures very interesting. They told a story, and she was sure she was reading a different version of it than most people that looked at the room and its multitude of grinning faces in all sorts of places and with all sorts of people posed to either side of whoever Joseph Odean was posing with.

"Thank you. This is very impressive." Morgan waved across the wall above the massive leather couch where many pictures hung. "So many important people here."

Morgan could really care less about how important the people thought they were, but she knew this was the expected thing to say. Besides, it IS possible there were actually important (by Morgan's definition of the term) people somewhere in that mosaic of photos. Doctors and Nobel prize winners perhaps. Someone from CERN maybe?

Cathleen looked at the pictures with a happy smile. "Yes: Joseph knows everyone it seems like to me. All over the world!"

The three went back to Cathleen's office and Morgan reexamined the pictures displayed here with new eyes. They are all of

Cathleen and Joseph in various places, and rarely featured anyone else but the two of them. They were from all over the world, however.

Morgan, still standing, indicated some of Cathleen's pictures. "I am curious: How long have you been having sex with Joseph?"

"What? I never..." Cathleen blustered.

Morgan made calming gestures with her hands, adopting a reassuring tone. "Cathleen: Please. I am a detective. Do not answer if you do not wish to: it is not an official question at this time. It was only idle curiosity. At the same time please do not try and pretend you are not sexually involved, and for many years, as that will be a dishonest way to start this conversation. You are an adult, Mr. Odean is an adult, and your current sexual relationship with him is not important to me unless it is directly germane to the Homicide investigation. Should your love affair become important for some reason as the investigation unfolds, I will need to know more about how you came to be involved. In that case, it will not serve you well to try to lie to me about it."

Cathleen glowered at Morgan. Morgan returned the look impassively. Cathleen looked at the floor next. Shrugged. "A while. Maybe six years or so." She reluctantly admitted.

"Does Deedee Odean know you two are seeing each other romantically?" Morgan asked, again pitching it to sound as if it were only idle chatter.

Cathleen laughed at that question harshly, and with far more emotion than how Morgan had asked. "Deedee? You have to be kidding me. Deedee was the one that strayed from Joseph first. A long time ago, and with so many men! We should just put a revolving door on her office. Poor Joseph." Cathleen looked in sympathy at a picture of herself and Joseph Odean standing on a peer near water someplace.

Cathleen looked at Morgan, a sort of pleading tone entering her voice. "They just have to leave the marriage like it is for another four months, until Darla is eighteen, goes away to school, and then they can get a divorce. We'll have to wait a decent interval to go public but then Joseph and I can finally be together. In public I mean. We already are together in every way that counts but one."

Cathleen narrowed her eyes, even though Morgan had not changed her expression in the slightest. "I know you think I am a foolish woman to think that he will divorce Deedee and marry me, but Joseph already gave me the ring."

Cathleen went to her desk, opened the top drawer, pulled out a ring box, and opened it, showing Sam and Morgan a massive engagement ring.

"Very nice." Morgan said, never really sure what to say in moments like that. Morgan was sure she would never be one to prance about showing off her ring, should that time ever come. Would she even want a ring? Not for the first time, Morgan thought that it seemed more likely SHE would be the one asking and that may imply SHE was the one that needed to have a ring ready.

"It will be you up on the billboards?" Sam asked an upwards wave to indicate how high the freeway signs are. "You and Joseph peering down at the traffic on I-10, 45, and 59?"

Cathleen shrugged noncommittally. "I don't really care about that. In private, Joseph and I don't even talk that much about the church. Mostly we think about where to go on our next trip, or what to do if we have a free moment to spend together. You know: Deedee out with one of her men, and Darla off at a school thing, or something like that. Joseph has a very high-stress job, and he needs his time with me to be about relaxing. Decompressing."

"Are you religious?" Sam asked, and he did a good job of leaving all judgment out of that question.

Cathleen considered. "I believe in God. Yes. I believe he wants me to be happy. This is what makes me happy. God will reward me being patient by giving me the man I love."

They heard the outer office door open, and Deedee Odean stepped into Cathleen's office, curious who she was talking with.

"Oh. Hello." Deedee greeted the two detectives noncommittally.

Morgan stood and introduced herself and Sam, and badged her so that Cathleen was saved the introduction and explanation for their presence.

"We have been having a little trouble having a conversation with Darla about the events at her school. Sam and I thought that perhaps before we go and get a material witness warrant and arrest your daughter, at school and in front of everyone, Drag you down there and to the courthouse and all of the various inconveniences that process would bring that instead we thought we'd talk to you first. Try to minimize the public embarrassment."

Deedee frowned at them but waved them back into Joseph's office, not her own, which was connected to Cathleen's office through a door in the wall behind her desk. Morgan thought that placement interesting: Cathleen could look in and see Joseph at his desk through the door when it is open, but Deedee's office being behind Cathleen, she would have to stand and walk over to the door to observe Deedee's space.

Perhaps that is handy if you need to have a revolving door for your paramours installed?

"Who knows when he'll be in? Sit!" Deedee waved Sam and Morgan at the bed sized couch and perched on an armchair on the other side of the hand carved coffee table.

"As I said, we are here to avoid having to arrest Darla. Based upon our interviews so far, we have far more than enough to get a material witness warrant issued. Any judge in the city no matter how strict about the requirements would issue one based upon the information we have." Morgan said.

Sam underlined it. "There are some judges that are real sticklers for the types of situations they will issue such a warrant under. DA's often have to shop around to find a friendly judge. For this one, we would not have to."

"Why do you want to talk to my daughter?" Deedee asked, clearly irritated at the implicit threat.

"Darla is the last person to see the dead boys alive." Sam replied.

That was not accurate of course, since they had not all died that night but one at a time and days later. Still, it was succinct and effective at making their point.

That received a scoff and a dismissive wave. "Boys? That one kid wasn't even a boy" Deedee told Sam, very snotty and derisive.

Morgan took that one."Yes, he was Deedee, but if you are referencing the fact that he is transsexual, then how did you come to know that?"

Morgan was very interested in the answer to that one because in every interview they had done so far, all the kids referred to Neil as 'him'. No one said anything about sexual reassignment. Neil's transsexual status was absolutely not common knowledge, but Deedee knew of it?

"Everyone knows. Don't be silly." Deedee said, again hitting 'dismissive' squarely.

"No: They do not, Mrs. Odean. How did you come to know that?" Morgan asked more firmly.

"I am on the PTA. I do fundraisers for the school all the time. I know EVERYONE there. I know things that would curl your hair in fact. I know that it was not a boy. How I came to know that I do not exactly remember, but honestly, the things that go on in a public high school. I should have insisted more strongly we send Darla to a private institution, but no: Joseph said that his little girl needed to be seen in public and to not be getting special treatment just because she is our daughter. That she would learn more about the way the world works 'out there'. Well: We see what Darla has learned, haven't we? There is so much sickness in the world, and we should have done a better job protecting Darla from it, not immersing her IN it. In a private school, they would never have tolerated all the goings on. In a public school, ANYONE can go there, and you just have to put up with it. Even in the damn commercial: All politically correct casting, Black kids, a girl pretending she's a boy so hard she carved herself up, a chink, and a few white kids, like they are seasoning on top of a politically correct cake. Probably not even the sickest thing that happens in that place. Who knows? It's not like kids tell you everything they see and do when they get to that age. Thank god that school is up in the city so that there aren't farms and animals there, like some other schools around this city, or they'd be screwing the damn horses and pigs at recess."

Deedee made a grouchy 'Harumph' like noise. "Anyway: it's not like Darla tells me anything these days."

Sam and Morgan glanced at each other.

Deedee looked at Morgan intently "I am not proud to say this, but my daughter and I are not close. Ever since puberty, we have grown apart. We barely talk anymore in fact. I have no idea what goes on her life, and isn't that just ironic? I know more about what happens at her school than I know what happens with her. Still, only child, and a girl. Classic, right? Darla is much more Joseph's daughter than mine these days. Daddy's girl."

Cathleen came into the office, but only barely. The tension between her and Deedee was palpable. "Joseph just called. He is going to the hospital to visit several people. Some church members were in a multi-car accident a few days ago. They need some reassurance."

Deedee grinned. "Reassurance that their new car will be bigger and better than the one they just wrecked."

"God makes events into opportunities." Cathleen said, and it sounded like a quote. Cathleen added, "I told him you were here waiting to see him, Detective Olsen, and he asked that you speak to his Lawyer rather than him since he was not clear what exactly a 'Material

Witness' warrant even is."

Deedee stood up, went over to Joseph's desk, and opened up a Rolodex. She spun it around, saying "I will get you the name of the firm, and our Lawyer there. I am not clear on what that means either."

Morgan stood. "It means Sam and I talk to a DA, who talks to a judge, who is requested to approve an arrest warrant, and who that warrant is for and which then becomes a matter of public record. The warrant gives me the right to arrest, detain, and interrogate the person it names. Newspaper reporters literally stand around the courthouse looking at new filings to catch the news first, not to mention platoons of OTHER lawyers who have staff onsite watching the warrants and related arrest paperwork flow by to see if they can drum up business. Darla Odean, in particular, her LAST name, being a name on that paperwork will catch fire quickly as it is a name and a face all over town on billboards, not even counting the TV commercial. I am not sure it has aired yet, or now if it ever will. That aspect will be newsworthy as well, of course. On a slow news day, I have seen a warrant turn into a news story in less than twenty-four hours, and in this case, it might be front page and accompanied by a picture of the entire family, since you have provided them one already up on the billboards. I am trying to AVOID this, which is why we are here."

Morgan pointed at Deedee. "Your lawyer will understand the subtleties of the law since Darla is not a legal adult just yet, but none of that matters if your goal is to keep this a more private conversation. I will speak to the lawyer, but only one time. If he gives me any stalling, which Lawyers LOVE to do, then I will forgo the concept of your privacy being important to you and proceed however I need to in order to find out everything I need to know about the night in question. Answers only Darla can give me."

Deedee handed Morgan a slip of paper. "Understood, Detective. I do appreciate your efforts to keep this civil. I do. I wish I could be more help here, but as I said, Darla is Joseph's darling, and he always thinks he knows best, about everything. I will tell him I think he needs to cooperate with you, and let you talk to Darla. From where I sit in this family, that is about the best I can do for you."

Morgan read the slip, then put it in her jacket pocket. "Thank you, Mrs. Odean. I appreciate your candor and any assistance you can provide getting Darla to talk to us."

"Anything I can do..." Deedee Odean promised.

Cathleen followed the two detectives back to the church office.

Morgan paused, hand on the door handle "Thank you as well, Cathleen."

"No problem, Detective." Cathleen looked back into her office to see Deedee Odean going past Cathleen's desk and into Deedee's mostly unseen office and then closing the door.

Cathleen looked visibly relieved. She turned to Morgan. "I will talk to Joseph. Deedee was right in that Darla is more his daughter than hers, but actually, I am the one that has been taking care of her for a while. Darla doesn't call me 'mom' or anything but helping with her is just another thing I can do to take the stress off Joseph. I doubt he would listen to Deedee about it, if she even really calls him, which would be somewhat shocking. More than likely she is in there with the door closed to be calling Larry. Lawrence? Someone. I forget who the current guy at the gym is."

"Thank you, Cathleen. Anything you can do to help. Also: best of luck to you with... All of it." Morgan gave a significant look back at Deedee's office.

"Thank you, Detective. I appreciate it. It will be fine. Just need to be patient." Cathleen Gray held the door open for them as they left to make their way back to Sam's truck.

CHAPTER TWENTY-TWO
Darla

Sam was quiet on the drive back, saying at one point "That place gives religion a bad name."

Morgan decided to not reply to that at all, because she had yet to find one that gave religion a good name, despite a lot of looking. Morgan figured the problem was not that she was looking for answers FROM religion, but was trying to figure out what sorts of answers others had sought and found with it.

Morgan knew from other discussions that Sam had been brought up in the Southern Baptist church. He did not attend and had not for many years, but he believed in a Christian version of God. It was nothing they talked about in any depth since talking about religion at work was something Morgan had down as a bad idea. They had already discussed it more on this case than they normally did. Sam accepted Morgan had no religion. Morgan accepted Sam did. They left it there.

There was one stop for an expensive coffee for Sam, and Morgan decided to get a large unsweetened black tea, no water, easy ice so that she would not have to make and chill something at the office. Sam seemed to like it when she got something too, and Morgan assumed it made him feel less guilty about his guilty pleasure.

Once they arrived back at their desks, Morgan saw an eight by ten single sheet of paper, folded once, on the top of her inbox tray, and sighed. She gloved up and picked it up. Sam, seeing the gloves go on, perked up and paid attention. He also pulled out a fingerprinting kit from his desk in a sort of automatic way. Gloves, notes, look for fingerprints. How that worked these days.

"What's it say?" he asked, sliding the kit over to her.

"Odean is under our protection. Tread very carefully, Detective." Morgan read out loud. She held up the paper at an angle to the light, and shook her head, but proceeded to dust it for prints anyway.

"Well, at least they are not telling you who to date." Sam said, not seriously.

"Just who I can arrest." Morgan griped. "No prints." She reported.

Morgan pulled out an evidence envelope and put the latest message in it. She noted the date and time on the outside and put a short paragraph in a text area about her finding, reading, and dusting it. She waved it at Sam "Going to go put this in our collection in the evidence room."

Sam nodded acknowledgment.

When Morgan returned, she pulled her desk phone over, and the paper out with the Odean's lawyer's number. "Going to call the Lawyer now. Stand by for threats." Morgan told Sam.

"I'll get the fire extinguisher ready." Sam replied. Using the desk phone meant Morgan was telling the Cabal to get stuffed.

The phone was answered on its second ring. "Daniel Moritz" a confident baritone voice answered.

"Mr. Moritz, my name is Morgan Olsen. I am a Homicide detective and I was given your name to call in regard to bringing Darla Odean in for questioning pertaining to the recent murders at her high school."

"I see. Yes. I spoke to Joseph a few moments ago in fact." Moritz reported. That held no meaning as yet since Moritz did not say what they talked about. Morgan was assuming mistresses for now.

"I would like to avoid going to the DA for a material witness warrant. I am trying, based on the very public visibility of the family, to keep this quiet. However, I have three murders to solve, and I am done with not being able to talk to Darla Odean. I want you to bring them here, to my location TODAY, or I give up. I will let this go wide. As a person that gets their name and face in the paper far more often than I like, I am sensitive to the downsides of notoriety. However, as I said, I am done." Morgan sounded quite done. Sam gave her a thumbs up.

"I see..." Moritz tailed off, not quite as confident sounding as he had been.

"I have been warned to tread carefully where the Odean's are concerned. This is me treading carefully." Morgan told Daniel Moritz, just in case he was aware of the note in her inbox and thought it gave him some sort of cover.

"You believe you can get this warrant, detective?" Daniel Moritz asked, some of the silk returning.

"Mr. Moritz: You clearly are not familiar with me, which means you do not read newspapers. The ones the Odean's are about to be in. I never think I can do a thing. I know I can do a thing, and one way or another, I will get that warrant. You can take that to the bank. My partner and I have far more than is required to get the worst DA and the strictest judge to see they need to issue it, and if I come across a political block rather than a technical one? That will be dealt with too, quickly and without the regard I am currently attempting to extend to the Odean's here. Stop stonewalling, and advise their clients they need to get here, TODAY, or they will be responsible for what happens next."

"Is that a threat, Detective?" Daniel Moritz asked.

"No. Not at all. I do not make threats. I do however make promises and commitments and I follow up on them. My duty here is the get justice for three dead young men. Darla Odean is the last person to see all three of these young men alive in some very important ways. I will detail these ways on the warrant. You will then know WHY it would be far better for you to just get her here. Did I mention TODAY? Sorry if I overlooked that detail." Morgan was letting her disgust for the worm on the phone come through. That was intentional.

"I will call you back. Number please?" Moritz asked, and Morgan gave him her desk phone direct number, and they hung up.

"You really hate lawyers." Sam commented.

"That is not true." Morgan replied, glaring at her phone. "I think everyone is entitled to having a good lawyer. I am not trying to arrest Darla for the murders here. I am trying to get her damn story. Keep fighting me like this, and it sure starts making me wonder if there is something they need to hide. Lawyers are a necessary evil. They designed this system to make sure they were."

"Having been on the receiving end one of your crusades for truth, that guy needs to just come in with Darla. Otherwise, you are going to know everything about him, including his favorite food and sexual position."

Morgan grinned back. "I do not know that about you."

"Only because it never came to that." Sam said ruefully.

Morgan did not reply, because her desk phone rang.

"Wow. That was quick." Sam said as Morgan answered.

Joseph Odean, Darla, and their attorney, Daniel Moritz (of Moritz, Grant, Neumann, and Moritz) appeared at the Homicide office that afternoon after school was out.

Morgan knew after some quick research that Daniel Moritz is the second Moritz in that law firms name. His father, still at the firm, is the first Moritz. It is an old, well connected and fairly large group of lawyers, covering all aspects of civil and criminal law. They covered the gamut from personal injury lawsuits to high profile defense. Going into the courtroom against the firm was fairly widely feared and usually resulted in settlements.

In cases Morgan had testified in where a Moritz, Grant, Neumann, and Moritz attorney was present, and treating her as a hostile witness (since she was an arresting officer and they were defense) Morgan found that she could hold her own, though she could also see that someone not utterly prepared or easily intimidated might not fare so well.

Morgan knew that it is not just about how good the lawyer is in a courtroom. How well a judge rules during pre-trial and trial is more influential in how a case turns out than most anything else. It was the things allowed and disallowed as evidence in all the pretrial hearings that set the stage, and it was rarely about the performance before the Jury. It was what the jury was able to consider.

In cases where Morgan had been allowed to testify, she had done well. That was an amazingly small number of cases. To her and Sam's credit, their conviction rate was in part fear of how well they had built their case. A slam dunk more often than not turns into a plea deal. How the system works.

After all the introductions were made, and everyone was settled into the Interview room, with the door open so that it was less intimidating, Morgan laid out the current situation. "I want to be very clear right now, especially as you are here without having been arrested, that at this point in time, Darla is a person of interest in the murders of Derek Jefferson, Neil Snyder, and Ailani Aquino. Material witness, not current suspect. That means if you have not been so advised that we, Sam and I, feel that Darla has information vital to the solution of this case. I appreciate you being willing to come in and answer questions without the ugliness that would have ensued if we would have had to go before a judge. It would have only been a formality as even with certain protections you enjoy, we have a preponderance of evidence indicating that Darla is key in solving three murders. This will help Sam and I arrive much more quickly at who performed these crimes."

Daniel Moritz lifted some fingers to speak. "You really did not give them much of a choice, detective. You were quite clear on the phone. Also with his wife up at his church."

"Cathleen I presume you mean?" Morgan said, to forestall any idea she and Sam were not aware of how that really went. "I did not give you any choice, and that was intentional. I do not like being stonewalled. I am after a person or persons that killed three young men in the prime of their lives. That is my only concern. That being said, I still prefer to keep this civil and not resort to arrests and the hostility not to mention public scrutiny they engender." Morgan said.

"Understandable." Moritz said. "We are here on the assertion that you have more than enough evidence to get the promised warrant issued. What exactly are we talking about here, Detective Olsen?"

"As there had been no arrest, and this is not a trial, I do not have to share all the details of that with you, however, most will become clear as we talk. You can force me to make the arrest if that is your preference, however since you are here to advise your clients in real time, why don't we talk and not waste more of that time?" Morgan spoke with a great deal of confidence because her witnesses from the party were remarkably consistent on the facts as they pertained to Darla and the dead boys.

Moritz nodded "Very well, Detective. I will answer your questions. Darla and I have spoken of the events of the evening in question. Ask what you need to know, and if it is something we can answer, I will."

Lawyer filter. That is never optimal, but at least Sam and Morgan could watch Darla as the questions were put forth and answered and get a second level of answer to them. Daniel Moritz's weasel words and Darla's reactions to the questions and his words.

Joseph Odean inserted "So just be quiet Darla."

Darla gave her a father an 'eat shit and die look' but she said nothing. She did not agree or disagree with her fathers' stricture. Morgan thought that rebellion in this situation was interesting. Darla was angry at her father but not intimidated by either the interrogation room or the process that had landed her here.

Morgan started in with a question designed to elicit a response. She looked at the teenager rather than the lawyer as she posed the opener. "Darla: When did you learn to deal off the bottom of a card deck?"

Clearly, that was not the expected opening question, either by

Moritz or his clients. Darla and Daniel Moritz looked at each other, and Darla's eyes were asking him a question, and she managed to insert sarcasm in her expression. A sort of 'Now what, genius?' type of look.

This was the first time anyone from the Moritz and Company law establishment sat across from Morgan and Sam in an interview room or they might have known that the lawyer and his clients were not the only ones to have a pre-meeting strategy session.

Sam added in a very casual way: "It was very well done, I must say Darla. Clearly a great deal of practice and skill involved."

Morgan and Sam planned that additional compliment to forestall any idea that Darla had NOT actually been stacking the card deck in her favor. Her 'favor' in this instance is to lose and then go off to an assignation with the person of her choosing.

Daniel Moritz did the standard issue lawyer splutter of outrage with an associated hand gesture. A delaying tactic as this line of questioning was obviously not something Darla and Moritz went over in their talk. "How could that ... Act, shall we say, if true, possibly be pertinent to the case?"

Morgan stifled a sigh of impatience that would have been over the top and instead gave the fake-outraged lawyer a stoney expression. She let contempt for Moritz's intelligence enter her voice, but only at the edges. Not straight up, in his face. "Mr. Moritz, it is. That Darla did exactly as we just inquired about is also not in any doubt, so save your canned bullshit for the courtroom. Answer the question, as it has been posed, or I arrest Darla right now. Right here. Also, before you get all up in your nose about it, you should know the Chron has been asking some questions regarding this case and very specifically about how the Odean family is related to these murders. I have not answered of course, but once again I remind you they are interested and that means they are watching the courthouse. Why I want to know these things will be detailed therein and on the front page the day after that."

Morgan waved over at Joseph Odean, who was looking somewhere between indignant and confused at this turn. "Mr. Moritz, it took Sam and I about ten-seconds, tops, to find out that Joseph AND Deedee are both having extra-marital affairs, so I imagine the Chron will get that information if they stay interested in this case for more than a few days."

Morgan next pointed dead center at the lawyer. "You, Mr. Moritz, and the family want this all to go away quickly, and that means you answer our questions. We solve this case, and if Darla did not kill the three boys, and I am NOT saying that she did, then the Odean family names are not the headline, are they? The real murderer, who-so-ever that may be is the headline. If it was, for example, a fellow student at the school, then the news story moves off to talk about violence on campus and all the related stresses of school, and Darla fades from any public attention, and therefore Deedee and Joseph Odean's extra-curricular activities remain undiscovered by the fourth estate."

Morgan glanced at Darla next. "If Darla DID do these murders, we will find that out too. You, Mr. Moritz, walked in here with a reputation, but Sam and I have one too. We close cases. If you did any research on us before you entered the room, Mr. Moritz, and at your firms' rates that is a near absolute certainty or you are not worth what Mr. Odean is paying you. Taking that as a given, you know Sam and I will find out who did this, no matter who it is, or who they THINK is protecting them."

Morgan again pinned Moritz with a pointed finger. "You cannot put the fix in via your connections either. We already heard from them and they already told me to back off and instead, we are here, and we are doing this. This is how we back off. So: Your. Choice."

Sam added to Morgan's speech "It is as she said, Mr. Moritz. Morgan arrested a Cop who is also a friend two months ago, and that was not popular around here. We do not do popular. We do not respond to pressure. Many cops in this station are more pliable about political and personal stress applied from above, however, it is your bad luck that WE caught this case. Mostly her. Morgan never is pliable when she is after a murderer. She may not care who you are having sex with, but if you kill someone than your ass is grass. The best you can hope for is to hang on for dear life. I do not lie."

Moritz looked down at the table, then nodded acknowledgment. "Yes, Detectives. I am familiar with your work. Your reputation is that you are both a sort of rogue set of cops and frankly that you are straight shooters. Honest, fair, but also quite relentless. I have in fact heard that you do not respond to intimidation or political pressure. You survive here only by virtue of being correct so often."

Daniel Moritz then said to Joseph Odean with open palms: "This is what I told you about, Joseph. The firms clip-file on Olsen and Parker is extensive. They also seem to have strong connections to the Chron. Their cases always get coverage. Always. In particular, if Detective Olsen goes to the holiday party, they cover that she had beer instead of eggnog. It's absurd, but how it is."

"I like beer better." Morgan agreed, to underline it.

Darla exploded over all the drama. "Oh, for fuck's sake. I learned how to deal in Las Vegas when I was like ten. We used to go there all the damn time. I met a card dealer, they showed me how. Part of my 'entertainment' while Mom was off gambling with one of her lovers. Not the current main guy of course: They don't last that long. Different guy."

Moritz said warningly: "Darla, we talked about this..."

"Oh Fuck off. I'll be eighteen in like four months, and then Detective Olsen can come at me as an adult, so let her ask her questions. It is not like I killed them. Jesus on a pogo stick."

"Darla..." her Joseph Odean started in nearly the same warning tones as Moritz.

Darla cut him off abruptly. "Oh, fucking hell, Dad. Can we not pretend in here you care even a little about using the Lord's name in vain? I bet the detective knows THAT about you already too."

"I do." Morgan agreed.

In actual fact, it was a supposition Morgan had formed based off the church she had seen and the Prosperity Religion tenets she had researched that led Morgan to assume that Joseph was a con man. A very good one.

"Look: Joseph, I do NOT care about the church, who is having an affair with who there, one at a time or in a big pile all at once up on the stage after you turn off the cameras for the broadcasts. Snake dances or orgies are irrelevant to me. Nor do I care in any way about the underlying religion and who are its adherents. None of that goes to any motive we have discovered. Sam and I care only about solving three homicides from one high school. Can we return to that?" Morgan asked.

"True: Morgan walks into churches and strip clubs, and it is all the same to her." Sam supported. "Takes some getting used to." Sam added as if he was confessing something.

Joseph Odean said in no little irritation. "My daughter did not kill those boys."

That statement led to Daniel Moritz getting annoyed. "Joseph. Darla. Please let me answer the questions. Do not volunteer anything."

"Darla: you specifically targeted Derek Jefferson for your first trip into the bedroom and subsequent seduction. Why?" Morgan asked.

Daniel Moritz suddenly got wide-eyed at the question as he connected it to the first. "Detective, I am sorry, but I am going to have to instruct my client to not answer that."

Darla rolled her eyes in a fine display of teenage sarcasm at adult stupidity. "Fuck you, Moritz. I picked Derek, Detective, because, well, you saw him. Right? Cute much? Jock. Nice body. That was the cool thing about this whole commercial thing: a chance to get with guys I never would have been able to. Jocks run with the jocks, you know? They ain't going to be interested in a stoner chick. I wanted to try out a Jock or two."

"I see." Morgan said. That was a very believable statement. Morgan appreciated the honesty and the underlying motive. Morgan was inclined to think it was the most honest thing that had been spoken in the interview room so far. Morgan also doubted Darla's father would appreciate the candor and she was correct.

Joseph Odean exploded "Darla!" and he was verging on apoplectic. Morgan thought it interesting that her revelation of his or his wife's affairs had not received anything like that level of reaction.

Daniel Moritz jumped in quickly. "Darla: Please. As your Lawyer, I advise you to not say any more!!!"

Darla ignored them both and continued on conversationally "Some Jocks are kinda overrated actually, as it turned out. Nice body and so nice to touch and shit, but he barely lasted five minutes, you know? I don't think he had been with a lot of chicks before me. Either that or I really turned him on, which would not be a first either." Darla shrugged. "He was nice though, so I asked him if he wanted to try again later, and he said yeah. He'd love to try again. I figured maybe if we did it a couple of times in a row he could slow his roll, you know? That would be the hot setup: Nice guy, nice body and last a little longer. Be sweet as hell."

Darla enjoyed tormenting her dad, Morgan decided. This was a thing Morgan never understood about some parents. A 'do as I say, not as I do' ethos. Darla saw BOTH her parents having sex with multiple people down the years, yet she was not supposed to emulate that? Based off of what? Had there ever been an honest, heart to heart about the consequences of sex inside the family? That seemed unlikely, based on what Morgan knew about these people so far. In fact, Morgan wondered at the fact that Darla was an only child. Had Darla herself been an early 'consequence'?

"After you returned to the game, and the cards came around to you again to deal, you next picked out Neil." Morgan stated.

Darla nodded affirmation. Joseph looked ready to bust a blood vessel but managed to not say anything. Nor did Moritz, though in his case it was more resignation than outrage.

"Yeah. I thought he was damn cute. There was a reason for that: it turned out he used to be a chick! When we got into the bedroom and I started stripping right away he told me that all confessional-like. Nervous as hell, you know? He thought I was going to freak out or something. Said he was post-op and had been for years. I told him I didn't give a shit and to get his damn pants off so I could see his dick because we didn't have that much time. Neil was all kind of embarrassed and shit and he stripped off kinda slow, but that just sorta made it a striptease, you know? I'm standing there naked, waiting and helping."

Darla looked down and touched her chest between her breasts. "Neil had chest hair and a beard, you know. I ran my fingers through it. I like chest hair. It was all soft like he conditioned it or something? Some dudes are like that. Instead of the hair being all wiry and stiff-like, it's like baby soft. Love it. As Neil got his pants off, I looked him in the eyes and reached down and grabbed hold. Neil said four years ago he did the whole sexual reassignment thing, and they built him this cute dick. He kinda looked like a dude that hadn't been circumcised. I asked if he could screw me with it, and so he showed me. He blew that cock up by squeezing his balls to show me it worked. I am holding it and it got bigger in my hand, just like Derek's had. I was like 'that is so damn cool' and then when Neil finally understood that I wanted to have sex for real and I wasn't making fun of him, we fucked like bunnies. He never goes soft! It was fucking amazeballs! I loved it. It was like being with a dude, but also kinda like being with a chick. He knew exactly how to make me come too. God: it was great! I mean fucking great."

Joseph dropped from apoplexy down to looking at his daughter in stunned amazement. Morgan assumed this whole situation was news to him based on that reaction.

Daniel Moritz apparently gave up trying to do lawyer things for Darla and leaned back in his chair, clearly wondering why he was there. Morgan assumed at this point he was just thinking about his hourly rate and wondering if it was high enough.

"Next you picked out Shawn Pascolla. Another athlete." Morgan said

"Yeah. Variety is the spice of life, you know? After the balling Neil gave me, I thought I'd try a jock again. Swim team this time. He was

OK too. We both got off, and I had to rinse off in the shower. You know what? One nice thing about Neil? Not messy at all. Bad thing is: he can't get off. Well. Maybe. We were going to try again when we had more time too. He was really jazzed I liked fucking him. I think that maybe I was the first chick that really dug him like he is. Was." Darla looked suddenly unhappy at that last word, Morgan assumed that was Darla realizing she and Neil were never going to happen again.

Morgan also found it interesting that Darla went back to talking about Neil when the subject was Shawn. From what Morgan could see in her peripheral vision Joseph did not find that nearly as interesting.

"Your final assignation of the night was Ailani Aquino." Morgan asserted

"Yeah: only so much time in one night! I might have picked Neil again but Ailani just moved here from Hawaii. His Dad is a chef, his mom had some big job with an import/export company and they transferred here, to the damn ship channel. His mom was SO pissed about the move, but they pay her a fuck-ton of money so they decided to do it for a few years and then move back home. They didn't even sell their house in Hawaii. They're just renting a Condo here."

"Why do you know all this about the family?" Sam asked.

Darla gave Sam an open-palm gesture. "He was a new kid, ya know? He looked lonely. I talked to him at school. Nice thing about being a stoner: We ain't threatening to no one. I thought Ailani might like a nice warm fuck to feel more welcome. He did, in fact. He actually thanked me. Not many guys thank you for sex, but Neil did too. Thanked twice in one night. I felt like a fucking angel, right?"

"Ailani was in the drama department." Morgan noted.

"Yeah: the people doing the casting for the commercial picked kids from all over the place in the school. It was a commercial about shoes, for Christ's sake! They wanted the ad to look like a cross-section thing, you know? They had Derek run across this field in the park with three of four different chicks, just to see what they looked like together. They picked the shot with me in it for the commercial. They liked the way I looked with Derek. Skinny runner kid with a curvy chick. I was running along while they were filming and the Director was shouting shit at us and I was ignoring them because I was thinking about how to get Derek's fine ass in bed. That is how it looked to them too: seems that is what they were going for. Sex sells. I wanted sex. That showed up on the recording. I was undressing Derek with my eyes the whole time so makes sense."

Joseph found his voice. "God. All these boys, Darla. Please tell me you used protection."

"Naw. I'm on the pill. You know that. Fucking Cathleen took me to get the script what... Two or three years ago?"

Darla said in a sort of confidential aside to Morgan "I got pregnant when I was fifteen. You know. Young and stupid. Dad and Catherine fixed it all. All on the down-low because god knows no one at the church could find out I'm a druggie slut."

Morgan got the idea that Darla did not actually think of herself as she described, but rather how Darla thought others might react to what she was saying.

"What about STD's?" Joseph Odean asked.

"That's why they have antibiotics!" Darla said as if that was stupid.

Darla said again to Morgan in another aside "I got the clap two years ago. Dad fixed that too. Well, Cathleen did. I think Dad likes to send her out to take care of shit so he can get some fucking in with this other lady at the church."

"Darla!" Joseph Odean tried to sound affronted.

Darla was having none of her dads BS. She said in an 'aww shucks' way: "You know it's true, Dad. Not like you are really going to marry Cathleen once you and mom get a divorce, is it? Too bad really: I kinda like Cathleen. Not sure why she puts up with your shit, but love is love I guess."

Morgan felt she needed to intervene in a non-Detective way. "Darla: Your fathers' point is well taken. Antibiotics are becoming less effective. There are resistant forms of Gonorrhea for example. The so-called 'Super-bugs'. Further, Antibiotics are useless against viral infections such as HIV and Herpes. Herpes is the most common STD out there. There are no cures for either of those things. Not yet. Perhaps not for decades. There is only prevention."

Joseph Odean actually looked gratefully at Morgan for that intercession. Moritz, on the other hand, rolled his eyes very slightly.

Darla was scornful of Morgan's statement. "HIV is a gay dudes thing."

Morgan shook her head 'no', sadly. "No, Darla: That is a myth I am afraid. A very sad and dangerous one. I am sexually active myself, so I am familiar with the data and statistics, as I do NOT wish to be on the wrong end of them. As of December 31, 2000, 774,467 persons were reported to the CDC with AIDS in the US. Given that a little time has passed since then, it has gotten WORSE. In that report though, 448,060 people have already died. Two-thirds of the infected are dead. To your point: 41% of those three-quarters of a million people were infected through male-to-male sexual relations. A high percentage to be sure, but not exclusively a gay male disease by any means."

Morgan decided to NOT mention that the next largest category of HIV infection is drug injection with dirty needles. Morgan knew that Heterosexual transmissions are not only possible but were on the rise because of attitudes exactly like Darla's.

Morgan instead added: "The most effective way to avoid ANY STD is a condom. I know that most people, especially men, do not like them. Personally, I am not a fan either. On the other hand, I will never be with a lover without one. I do mean that in an absolute way. Never. I have plans for my life. Do you, Darla? Because what I am picking up from you is that you spend a great deal of your time not worrying about what tomorrow may bring you. I understand living in the moment: I do. One can do both things. Live in the now AND plan for later."

Morgan looked at Darla directly, trying to make her see the importance of what they were talking about. "It is not a question related to this case, but ... I like you, Darla. I like your attitude. You are clearly a very good person. You are my kind of person and therefore I would like to see you still here, on this planet, ten years from now. Longer than that."

Darla was very taken aback by that statement. She did not expect Morgan to say anything remotely like that, and Morgan suspected what she usually got from adults is disapproval.

Joseph Odean felt Morgan's comment required a profession of his own. "I love my daughter. I do. Sometimes I do not like her, however. She is a willful child. I am curious: Why do you think she is a good person?"

Morgan's already low opinion of Joseph Odean dropped further with that question.

Darla agreed with her dad. "Yeah: Why, Detective Olsen? Did you miss the part where I'm trouble at school? A stoner? Sleep around? Cheat at card games to get laid by the boys of my choosing, including a former chick who is now a dude?" Darla sighed. "Was a dude?" she appended.

Morgan shrugged noncommittally to both of them. "I will answer that, of course, as it is a fair question that I am sad even requires an answer, however before I do, let us finish the interview, so your lawyer there can go stare off into space in a different clients room and on a different clients dime."

"Are you going to charge Darla with ANYTHING here today, Detective?" Daniel Moritz asked when Morgan referenced him.

"Mr. Moritz, as I made clear at the start of this interview, I would have arrested Darla on a material witness warrant, not a criminal one." Morgan waved at Darla. "I do not at this point in time suspect she killed these three boys. I want to talk to her about them and find out who might want to. Further to that, I do not think it likely that Darla knows who did it or that she is hiding anything. She is quite refreshingly open and honest. I do however think Darla can give Sam and I information that will lead us to who did these crimes. 'Material Witness' means exactly that. That is why you are here today. That is the ONLY reason you are. I am not playing games. I am a homicide detective. I am not Vice. I am not looking for misdemeanor crimes." Morgan air-quoted the word 'crimes'.

Moritz looked unconvinced. Morgan proceeded to explain. "To my point about Vice and misdemeanors. I could very literally care less if, for example, Darla smokes marijuana. I am not saying she should light up a spliff in here, however, marijuana is a stupid drug to make illegal in the first place." Morgan then indicated Darla's arms on the table top. "I can see her arms. She has no tracks: I do not think she is going to OD on speed, heroin, cocaine or any other such thing here in my interview room. Again, looking at her arms, I do not think Darla uses any IV drugs, even as she calls herself a 'stoner'. Darla is a good person, trying to deal with a bad situation. She has two parents having affairs, and pretending to be married. She is not good at having to maintain the public face of being the preachers' kid. That is not unusual even: She never asked to have to lie to people about things, such as her religion or answer forty-thousand peoples inane questions like 'Oh, aren't your parents the best. So inspiring' etc. etc."

Morgan saw Odean start at that number and suppressed her irritation. "Yes, Mr. Odean, I do my homework. I checked how many people attend services at your church, not even counting all those that watch your Sunday broadcasts."

Sam laughed at Odean's reaction. "Morgan said 'we', but SHE figured out you were having an affair just by being in your church, Mr. Odean. Just being there and looking at it. Finding the killer will be a little harder, but Morgan and I will do it. You can take that to the bank."

Joseph thought about what Sam said. Joseph Odean then asked about what was really bothering him: "You believe that I did it, Detective?" and he addressed that question to Morgan.

Morgan shook 'No', as she considered her response. "Do you, Mr. Odean, have a possible motive? Maybe? No evidence points your way at all, Mr. Odean. In fact, given your obviously dysfunctional relationship with Darla, perhaps it is the opposite: It is not clear you even care enough about her to kill for her. In any case, I wanted to talk to your daughter today. Not to you. I am not currently looking at you at all for anything related to the homicide. Unless you think I SHOULD be digging into your life for something?"

Morgan decided to add "As we have stated, I do not care about your sexual affairs. People get wrapped around the axle on sexually related issues. I do not unless they are a possible motive that I need to look into. Your sexual relationship with your assistant does not even rise to the level of being characterized as an 'affair', because your wife is fully cognizant of it and could care less about it. You have an open marriage. You are polyamorous even. That does not take us to you killing three high school kids. No: My problem with your sexual activities are ONLY the negative degree to which it has impacted Darla, and that is primarily because of the public lies that you make Darla party to, not the private behavior. As I mentioned, I like Darla, and I do NOT like that you have hurt her in this way. To your credit, Mr. Odean, you have taken care of her: Well, had your lover take care of her when she needed help. You LOVE your daughter, even if you do not like her. I can live with that. Darla will soon be able to leave your influence. Go away to school. Far away, I assume and I also sincerely hope."

Joseph Odean thought about Morgan's words, absorbing Morgans censure of him. Morgan doubted Odean was used to being on the receiving end of judgment and having to take it. He stood abruptly and said to Daniel Moritz "OK. We are done here, Daniel. Darla, get a ride home when you are done talking to the detective. Call a cab or something."

Darla looks utterly shocked. Moritz said even as he stood up: "I strongly recommend against this course of action, Joseph. Cops lie. It's what they DO."

Odean looked at her daughter and asked: "We'll stay if you want us to Darla, but I assume you would rather talk alone to your new best friend?"

"No, Daddy. I'll be fine." Darla agreed.

As suddenly as that, the two men left leaving a strange feeling of Vacuum in the room.

Darla grinned at the empty door frame, then turned and settled into her chair. "That is the most beautiful thing I have ever seen, Detective. What do you want to know?"

"As it is just us, call me Morgan. Please. This commercial-making project crossed the student population of the entire school. Various normally closed groups or cliques were thrown together abruptly and in a new and strange situation. Did you see anyone ever get into a conflict with ANY of the boys that were killed, and for any reason?" Morgan asked. "I am inquiring because the motive for killing these three young men is just not at all obvious, and so far the only common thing we have been able to find is that you had sex with them. It seemed like it would be possible there was someone else that would have liked to either not have YOU with them, or wanted them for themselves."

Darla waved her hands. "Nah. It wasn't like that at all. There was some teasing at the party. The swim team came in dead last in their last meet, for example, so some kids were giving Shawn some shit over that. Derek was track, and pretty good. No one ever gave him shit about his records or meets or whatever, but then there is that it's the track team, right? Not like a glamour sport. I don't know how it is at other schools, but at my high school, even swim team gets more respect than track because they do shit like shave all their body hair, even their heads, and devoted crap like that, before swim meets. Our sports tiers: Football is the top of the heap even though our team sucks, then basketball because they do OK, then Baseball, then swim team and bringing up the rear is Track. No one goes to those meets but the parents and the other teams. Oh. Soccer is in there someplace too, but that seems to be getting more popular, fuck if I know why."

"Any of the other girls at the party jealous about you getting all the male attention?" Morgan asked.

"Shit, man! I wasn't. Look, there were three rooms that had people in them all the time. Two bedrooms and a big closet. Right? When I was off with one guy, they kept playing. It was a BIG group of kids, and lots of people kept playing. So that means people kept losing, and going off to the rooms. Musical chairs, if the chairs are places to make out. I don't know if everyone was getting busy or anything. I bet a lot of them were. Then, on top of that, there was music and dancing. There were people out back smoking some grass. Probably going off into the bushes, I don't know. I dig getting high and getting my balling on so I ain't no judge. It was just one of those good kinds of parties. We were all in a commercial together. Some of the kids were hoping to get discovered or some such shit, as if. That modeling agency had all our pictures and now we have experience. All that. Fantasy BS like that and they'll be doing porno's in no time." Darla laughed at that last idea.

"I am just curious."Morgan said. "Not at all germane to this investigation. Do not answer if it bugs you, but are you bisexual, by chance?"

"I have tried out chicks. Sure. I'll try anything once, you know. I like chicks. I like dudes more though."

"I gathered." Morgan said with a smile to take any judgment out of it.

"Why?" Darla asked

Morgan skipped over Karen Khan as not relevant. "Well, you seem utterly unbothered by Neil. No judgment at all about it. I have to think that is at least somewhat unusual, especially at your age, and yet no one we have talked to seemed to know his status. Other than your mother. I assume you told her?"

Morgan did not buy Deedee's line about 'everyone knowing'.

"I like that you call him 'him' without pausing or thinking about it." Darla replied, not answering directly.

"He is a him. Sexual identity is a complicated thing, but you are born who you are. Gay. Straight. Bi. In the wrong body sometimes. I can only imagine that last one is hell. I am lucky: I am female, and I enjoy being female. It is who I am. I like men, at least some of them, and I enjoy the ones I like too. I realize not everyone is so fortunate." Morgan returned to her question. "How did your mother come to know Neil's transsexual status, if no one at the party or in the class did?"

Darla looked abashed. "I told her. I was fucking with her. She was pissed I was out all night. I told her about everyone I fucked. All the details she didn't want to hear. Derek's fine ass body. Neil's awesome as all hell loving. Shawn's swim-team body and him making a mess on me. The sweet loving with Ailani. All of it. Mom was beside herself."

Darla looked at Morgan, felt the need to defend herself. "Mom was so pissed, and I was pissed because she has had more men than I can count. I would say it's like a collection but it's more like they come for the sex with the nice looking church lady, and then leave when they realize the sex ain't worth it. But, mom was pissed at me for being out late, so I made her MORE pissed by telling her the gory details about balling guys I actually liked. Mom was all like 'you can never see them again' and I was like 'Bullshit: I am going back for MORE because they all wanted more and so did I'. I was being honest, but I was telling her all that because it was like icepicks in her eyes."

"Do you think she was angry because someone at the church might find out? She was worried about her personal reputation? Was worried about STD's? Something else?" Morgan watched Darla closely as she offered each of these options.

"It's my mom. You just have to know her. She's like all 'do what I say, not what I do' kinda bullshit. She can go off and fuck this guy or that and take trips with lovers but if I have sex with a guy, I'm a slut. Or if I fuck a girl, I am sure I'm a lesbo slut, though I never told her about any of that. I kind of figured she'd fly even farther off the deep end if she knew I had gotten some lady love. My dad is a lying bag of garbage, but my mom is worse."

Sam asked, "Can you explain that?"

"I was wondering if you talked." Darla snarked, which of course was unfair since he had asked questions and made comments. Morgan did not choose to defend Sam at the moment since Darla was about to unload more possibly useful information. "So. My Dad. He fleeces the people for their money. Good work if you can get it, and not counting Catherine, he lives that shit he talks about most of the time. You hardly ever see the real him, behind the facade. When I was a kid, I thought he believed all the stuff he preaches. But he doesn't. Not really. Mom though? She is a judgmental fuckin' shrew. To your face, she is all 'hi, how are you, so nice to see you, Mrs. Johnson. I really enjoyed your casserole at the pot luck Mrs. Johnson.' and the minute she gets alone it's all 'That Mrs. Johnston is so FAT. Can you believe she let herself GO like that? Joseph, you HAVE to get more money out of her: She clearly can afford too much food!' and on like that. Just nasty." Darla assumes a shrill voice when quoting her mother. "Giving mom credit where it is due: In a church that fucking big, she remembered Mrs. Johnson brought a casserole, not cookies. Still, man: There is no one safe from that judgmental bullshit. Not anyone in the congregation, not Dad, not me."

Darla paused. Went on. "Mom works out like a crazy woman. She spends like three hours in the gym every day. She doesn't get that not everyone is rich like she is and can afford three damn hours a day in a gym. Mom also hates that I came out this way" Darla indicated her body. "I don't work out at all and I am a damn Siren. Mom had to pay the doc to get her tits and they still aren't as good as mine. Just being honest."

"Yes, well, I have to work out all the time too, but I'm a cop. Different reason." Morgan said "Also, I hate it. Every minute of it. You are young and can get away with extra calories. Me? I have a beer, that's that much more time on the bike, or on the weights, or kickboxing or something."

"You can always fuck it off." Darla said.

"At best that is two hundred calories per hour, and I am more of a person that likes to relax and enjoy rather than competitive lovemaking, so not really going to be able to lose weight that way. No: I hate the gym, but I prefer to work out and then later relax and enjoy my dates without having a pedometer in the bed."

"I like that you know how many calories sex uses." Darla told Morgan with a smile that verged on slightly shy.

"If you knew her as well as I do, you would not be at all surprised Morgan knows trivia like that." Sam commented.

"You are all right for a Cop. So: Tell me. Why do you think I am a good person?"

Morgan shrugged, realizing that Darla was correct. She had no more questions for now. "That is easy, Darla and should not even have to be explained. You made Neil feel accepted. I promise you, that is unique. You cared about the fact that Ailani was lonesome. You have empathy, and you did not JUST have sex with them. You made both of them feel accepted and welcome. In both cases, you asked if they wanted to do more. Later. That being with you was not a one time thing for you. There is nothing a man wants to hear MORE than 'let us do this intimate thing AGAIN'. It was sweet and caring."

Sam sighed. "You know what? Morgan is not lying. We really are that feeble. We really do give women that much power in our lives."

Darla looked at them each in turn. "Huh." She paused. "I did not think of it that way."

"Another way we know you are a good person." Morgan said, a flick of her hand upward.

"Damn." Darla said, in apparent revelation. "I am a fucking saint. Literally!"

CHAPTER TWENTY-THREE
Late Night Guns

Morgan arranged a cab ride for Darla. She spoke to the driver after reading his unit number out loud and flashing her badge to let the cabbie know he had precious cargo. She told Darla that she would 'call later' where the driver could hear as well. The threat was implicit. Morgan knew where and how to find him. Darla would report any wrongdoing. Darla grinned at Morgan but said nothing about it.

All cabs are bonded and the drivers have had background checks, so it was not that Morgan did not trust the driver. Morgan would have thought nothing about getting in a cab herself. It was about Darla knowing Morgan was extending her protection. It was about consideration, which Morgan felt was a thing sorely lacking in Darla's life.

Morgan and Sam sat at their desks, talking quietly to avoid being easily overheard by people in adjacent cubes.

"That was a fat lot of nothing." Sam said. "Our main suspect? I don't think she did it."

"I never thought she did." Morgan replied. "I mean, I was willing to add her to the suspect list, but she did not go into that interview as one for me."

Sam looked disgustedly at Morgan at that revelation. "Why not?" He asked, sounding peeved.

"Darla targeted each of those boys for sex. She was dealing the cards, so she wanted each young man to be her lover. From my point of view, if a woman targets a man for intimacy, her next reaction is not to want to kill them. Think what you might about the fact she wanted multiple lovers: I have no stones to throw in that area. I just could not see going in why she would want to kill them after she deliberately targeted each of them for intimacy?" Morgan shook her head in the negative. "It makes no sense to me. Unless you think Darla is a black widow, and while that IS possible and not unheard of, in that case, why not Shawn? Also, the psychological profile of a female serial killer did not really fit Darla: She had abuse in her life, but it was at the hands of her parents, not men in general. Still, it was clear from our trip to the church that it was a suboptimal childhood, so I was willing to be wrong here: Facts are all that matter. As you say, after that interview, I am disinclined to suspect Darla."

Sam thought about that. "I guess not." Though he did not sound happy at that admission, even though it supported his just expressed point of view about Darla not being the murderer. "With that scenario, it does not seem like Darla was trying to get one kid jealous over another either. Anything like that. The game was more of a sexual smorgasbord of different flavors of willing males."

Morgan agreed with that assessment. "If you are a heterosexual teenage male, and you have a chance to be with a girl that looks like Darla? I believe the term is 'built like a brick outhouse'? There would very likely be no resistance. No: I wanted to know if Darla stepped on someone ELSE'S toes, but these kids were partying. They came from all over the school. If someone was unhappy because she stole their boyfriend, why not kill Darla? Even if they killed their boyfriend, we would be looking at someone that dated all three boys? Surely we would have come across something like THAT by now?"

Sam agreed with a frustrated gesture. "So we are back at ground zero."

Morgan disagreed. "I do not think so. Not really. I am fairly sure we need to look at Darla's mother very closely. You saw her at the church. She is the correct height. She is young for a mother of a girl Darla's age and she is in good shape. She reacted very badly to knowing Neil is transsexual. She thought Ailani Aquino was ethnically Chinese? Deedee doesn't know the difference between Chinese and Polynesian? Really? Is she that stupid or is she that bigoted? My money is on bigoted. Deedee could probably lure those boys to those locations, either as herself or more likely pretending to be Darla. We have not turned up HOW she did that luring just yet, but we have not found their phones, have we? Want to bet there is a message on them, saying it is Darla, and to meet her at a place and time for a repeat of the Seven Minutes in Heaven encounter, only longer and better? Or Darla saying something else, like she is pregnant, but that does not work with Neil.

Or Deedee saying she has news about Darla. Or Deedee using her own sexual attributes as a lure. Or Deedee threatening them to come because she is a big deal in town and she is pissed off about what they did with Darla and wants a word. Who knows? I can see all sorts of variations of those themes that Deedee can play to get them to the killing field."

"I like it. Makes sense. Darla said she told them she wanted repeats. Either she is pretending to be Darla wanting another round, or it is Deedee as a MILF with a seduction plan or playing the angry mom. We need to warn Shawn to be careful about calls that seem to be from Darla, or her mother." Sam said.

"We absolutely should in a belt and suspenders way, but I doubt he is in the line of fire. White kid. The three that died were all kids that would not meet with Deedee Odean's view of a proper world."

"If Deedee is the killer, where did she get the .22? They have no guns registered to them." Sam asked.

"If it is a Saturday Night Special? I am guessing out of the trunk of a car." Morgan said with open hands. "Not sure how we find out about that."

"Let me check with a person I know over at ATF. They might have some ideas about how to find out." Sam said.

Sam, being older and more experienced than Morgan, despite her promotion over him, often had very useful contributions to the partnership like that kind of networking.

"OK. Sounds good. If we can at least find out if she HAS bought an illegal .22, then we can focus our efforts in the right way."

"I'll let you know..." Sam replied, picking up his desk phone, stopping, then saying "You know what? I think I'll check my cell for bugs, and then call from outside someplace."

Morgan nodded. "Good plan."

"Before you go, let us give JJ an update. He will want to know what we are up to, especially since we are about to go up against the Cabal's desires." Morgan suggested.

The two detectives stepped up to JJ's door. He was not on the phone and waved them in. "Have something?" he asked.

Morgan gave a quick summary of the interview and their conclusions. Sam bobbed his head in agreement at critical points but as usual, he let Morgan lead. Both Sam and Morgan were convinced that JJ's recent tolerance of Morgan was delicate and it would take nothing for him to revert to trying to just deal with everything via Sam.

Morgan gave a very edited summary, leaving out most of the details about the later conversation.

When Morgan was done, JJ, in fact, looked at Sam for confirmation, got the single nod, and heaved a porcine sigh. JJ leaned back, opened up a desk drawer, pulled out a single piece of paper, and handed it to Morgan.

"Got this in my inbox. I already checked: nothing usable like a fingerprint."

Morgan read the laser printed text. "Get Olsen off the Odean's." It was not signed or postmarked. Morgan handed it to Sam.

"Yes: They wrote me too." Morgan said. "Seems the Odean's are under Cabal protection if not actively part of the organization. Given what we know of Deedee Odean's views on people not of her own ethnicity, I cannot say that is a shocking revelation. Racist assholes need to hang together."

JJ pursed his lips. Since he was ethnically Hispanic, he was on their hate list too. "I assume you plan to pay about as much heed to this as you have all their other BS?" JJ asked.

"Correct, Sir." Morgan went with the 'Sir' since she was needing to underline that while she intended to be disrespectful to some faceless person somewhere in the department, it was not JJ, unless he forbid her continuing the investigation.

JJ looked pained. "Watch your back, Morgan. I do not know who these people are, but they are not going to take kindly to being ignored."

"Yes, Sir. You watch yours as well. You have delivered the message to not do this: These people should know me well enough to know I do not listen. As I mentioned, after the incident at my house, they told me I am more trouble than I am worth."

"You should have that printed up and made into a banner to put over your desk. Be careful. Both of you." JJ said.

Sam looked like he had not been to bed. He rarely rolled in late, but he was almost an hour tardy, and had two cups of coffee in his possession, and offered neither to Morgan. The first cup he drained and tossed into the trash can at the side of both their facing desks. He took a long pull at the second, sat down, and rubbed his eyes.

"Good morning, Sam. You look like shit." Morgan greeted. She pointed at the trash "I assume you got a buy one, get one free?"

Sam glared. "I wish. Two for the price for two. And you look like you had a long night in bed."

"I did. So: cough it up, furrball. What is up?" Morgan semi-quoted the Star Wars movie line.

"So my friend at ATF gave me some ideas about where and how to look for someone selling guns. It is very much a 'you have to know where to look' as well as a 'who to call' kind of set up. To say that they are suspicious and well armed would be an understatement." Sam started.

Now it was Morgan's turn to glare. "Wait: You went out without backup? Without ME?"

"I did indeed. You want to know the results or do you want to get all self-righteous?"

"Both." Morgan said, tapping her desk twice for emphasis.

"Well, as I have learned from your self-righteous ass, I'll just ignore that part and tell you what I found." Sam said with a red-eyed look that he was not backing down.

"To be continued. Fine. Tell me what you found out." Morgan was not happy to think Sam was out on a solo mission like that.

"As you might guess, there are people and places that one can go when they need unregistered weapons. Not just gun shows. In my case, I spent most of the damn night hunting for a particular 1977 Chevy Impala. Why that kind of car? Big ass trunk. This one is owned by an upstanding citizen that goes by the name of, and I kid you not, 'Jimmy Drag'. I think I would have called him 'Jimmy THE Drag', but I wanted to get information out of him."

"I see. Did you look inside the trunk of your new pal?" Morgan asked mischievously.

"No. Did not ask. After I badged Jimmy, I explained I was not looking to bust him, that I was with Homicide, etc. etc. Took a while to convince him I was not going to roll him in. I showed him a picture of Deedee, and he said 'That's that babe from the church billboards' or something like that. I agreed it was. I asked if she had perhaps bought a gun from him for personal defense reasons."

"I see: giving him an out." Morgan said in approval.

"Exactly. And after lots of hemming and hawing and more reassurances about no arrests and ratting him out or making him testify and all that, Jimmy said that Deedee had, in fact, bought a crappy gun. Here is where it gets good: he asked her if she was looking for a concealable weapon, why not get a .40 or a .380? She wanted to know if he had anything cheaper. Oh: Forgot to mention, she told Mr. Drag this was for her daughter because she was getting harassed at school."

"Deedee told an illegal arms dealer she wanted a cheap gun for her daughter for school...." Morgan said incredulously.

"Yes. About Jimmy's reaction: famous face up on a billboard, cheap when it came to her daughters' safety. He shows her a piece of junk .22 he picked up as part of a larger shipment, tells her fifty bucks, and she takes it after being reassured it had no serial numbers on it."

"Come with Ammo?" Morgan asked.

"Your honor, Counsel is leading the witness. My next thing. I asked, and Mr. Drag says he does not carry anything like that and tells her to go to any sporting goods store to pick up some cheap. If she wanted ammo immediately, buy the .380."

"Nice: So we MIGHT be able to find her buying the ammo someplace if we can just figure out where in this city she did it. Assuming it is cash, we'll need a video for store security." Morgan said.

"Yeah. Not looking forward to that part of the investigation for sure." Sam said.

"Your guy say how it is that Deedee Odean found him?" Morgan asked.

"I asked. He said he didn't know. She didn't say. She walked up to him around midnight one night when he was minding his own business over in the third ward. He thought it was weird as hell. Nice looking woman, out late at night, unarmed even AFTER she got the .22 without Ammo. He said maybe God was protecting her. I called my ATF friend to thank her for the info and asked just how well known Jimmy Drag is, and she said he is super-well known in the illegal gun world. Most any cop that works that end of things would know who he is."

"If Deedee asked someone in the Cabal, they might send her Jimmy Drag's way."

"Likely." Sam agreed.

"He say when this all happened?" Morgan asked.

"A few days before Derek was killed." Sam said, putting the ribbon on it.

"Great work, Sam. I am buying your next coffee. So, it is almost certain that Deedee Odean did the crime. She has the gun. It is her daughter. She is ethically challenged to say the very least."

"We need to go get GOOD coffee. Not the shit here." Sam lifted his coffee cup "Yeah. Problem is, proving it. No way Jimmy Drag talks on record. No way we can get a search warrant with this: not given the headwinds from above."

"We need to not only warn Shawn but Darla. Her mother is a killer, and Darla needs to be careful. If nothing else, if she does anything like this again, her mom could be out there again."

"That sounds... Not fun." Sam said.

"I'll tell her. Unofficially. My turn for a solo outing: Hopefully one with fewer guns. " Morgan said. "Let us go get you some good coffee somewhere. You can even drive since I am in my good car today."

"You are being so nice to me..." Sam replied, standing up.

CHAPTER TWENTY-FOUR

Help

There are small businesses that place themselves near high schools to capture the off-campus lunch business, as well as the after school, stop and chat crowd. They specialize in food items like Pizza and often have yogurt or Ice Cream soft serve machines.

The name of the place just off campus from Ronald E. Evans High School was 'Mr. MgGoos'. A name that made no sense to Morgan, since the school is named after an Astronaut and the school mascot came from the flight patch of Apollo 17. However out of the blue the name of the place is, the decor was pretty much exactly what Morgan expected. Lots of pictures of various sports teams from the school, pictures from Apollo 17, and the school mascot (The Fighting Falcons) also figured prominently. A CD jukebox playing current top 40 such as Destiny's Child, Creed, Madonna, U2, and the like was against one wall. There was both indoor and outdoor seating in abundance so that students had plenty of places to sit, talk, and absorb the empty calories. Being a place designed for the High School clientele, there were no alcoholic beverages.

Morgan bought an unsweetened Iced Tea and selected an outside table to wait at. She tried not to feel old, and it mostly worked. Morgan loved music and still played so she knew all the current acts. She was more Rock and Roll than pop, but she kept up. Her current dress was a Stevie Ray Vaughn T-shirt, jeans, Denim jacket and boots, so she was very fashion neutral. Morgan looked around to see if any teachers were obviously present but saw no one her age or older.

Darla came up, dropped her school backpack on the table and said "Hey!"

"Hello, Darla. Thank you for coming." Morgan replied.

"No problemo. Be back..." Darla zoomed inside. Five minutes of waiting were filled with increasing dread because Morgan realized that a teenage boy was looking at her from across the covered patio and appeared to be working up the courage to come over. Morgan spent the time waiting for Darla by coming up with easy let-down lines. Which one she used depended on the young man's approach. A crude pickup line would get a harsh response, but a shy and gentle one an easy let-down. Morgan did not believe in ageism in either direction for herself, but she did draw the line at still being in High School. No one under twenty-one and it would take an exceptional person of that age to be of interest since Morgan's taste ran to men that already knew who they are and what they wanted. She was not looking for any 'projects'.

Darla came back and spun with practiced ease onto the bench seat on her side of the table. She set a large drink on the table and held on to a small ice cream cone. The young man that was considering a pass at one apparently available woman decided two was out of his range and went back to reading a book.

Darla had an energy to her that Morgan found interesting. Here in her natural surroundings, she acted like she owned the place. Who knows? Maybe her parents had diversified from fleecing sheep?

"The things that I wanted to talk to you about are difficult. I mentioned this on the phone. I hope that this setting will be OK for you. I did NOT want to deliver what I have to say at the station, because it is unofficial." Morgan opened "If at any point in time you feel like we need to change venue, please let me know."

"OK. Yeah. Sure." Darla said, giving Morgan her full attention with her intelligent hazel eyes.

Normally, during an active murder investigation, one does not do what Morgan was about to do. Without the gun or a reason a judge would support to get a warrant, Morgan could not prove her suspicions. With the Cabal running interference for the Odean's, getting a warrant was orders of magnitude harder. Morgan was concerned now about the risk that Darla, in an act of further rebellion might involve another person that Deedee disapproved of strongly enough to kill again.

"During the course of investigating the murders of your three lovers from the party, I have arrived at the conclusion that the person most likely to have killed them is your mother. I have tried to think of some way to sugar coat that, but that is not your and my relationship." Morgan said as gently as she could.

Darla was not as rocked by that statement as Morgan might have expected. She nodded. Licked her Ice Cream Cone. Looked over towards the High School, visible on the other side of a grassy field and a parking lot. Nodded again.

"I can believe it." Darla said finally.

"Why?" Morgan asked.

"I kept finding my phone moved. All my IM's deleted. Mom was like 'Oh, you know how crappy Cingular service is...', And like that, and I didn't really think anything about it till now. Why do you think she did it?" Darla asked.

"Sam found a gun dealer who sold a .22 to a woman that looks like Deedee, or as he put it, the church woman from the billboards. This is an untraceable sale. He'll never testify about it. There are no camera's on the transaction. No paperwork. The gun is not registered. The gun dealer assured the woman most likely your mother that the gun did not have serial numbers, because she asked. Traceability seemed to be important to her, as was the caliber. It is much harder to do ballistics on a .22. We might get lucky and find your mother at a store buying ammunition, but that is a low probability task. Too many stores sell that ammunition. Houston is a huge city. We assume Deedee was smart enough not to buy her ammunition close to home."

"I bet mom knows where. She buys workout clothes at sporting goods stores, and they have guns too I think." Darla replied. Darla wore a half smile. "I doubt she is stupid enough to buy close to home but hell: USOE has places all over town, don't they?"

"There are three things we look at when we are trying to solve a homicide: Means, Motive, and Opportunity." Morgan explained. "The .22 is the means. Your mom has the gun or one exactly like the murder weapon."

Darla was letting her ice cream melt and run over her fingers, as she seemed to be absorbing the impact of that revelation.

"We never had guns in the house. Dad would never let them in. Not a religious thing: They just scare him. He worries all the time about someone in the church assassinating him. He's up there screwing the people out of their bucks, fucking around on his wife, all that. A lot of the people that go to the church are true believers. If they found out he isn't... Well. True believers are the ones that chase you around with pitchforks and shit, right?"

Morgan agreed with a shake and continued. "Motive I think you know. Your mother is a bigot. Everyone we have talked to on deep background says it. She may be OK having her affairs, but I noticed ALL of them are Caucasian. Add in some things she said, and some other things she stopped herself from saying. Well: To put it kindly, it adds up to your mother not being tolerant of ethnicities other than hers."

"She is a racist asshole." Darla said with some emotion. "This won't make me sound great, but one of the reasons I picked those guys because I wanted to throw that in her face. I liked them too, because, well, you know, who wants to fuck someone you don't like? Still: I wanted mom to KNOW I screwed a black guy. A Polynesian dude." Darla looked at her ice cream, then tried to lick up the drips on her fingers.

"Your mother called him a 'chink' at one point. She thought he was Chinese apparently" Morgan pointed out.

"Yeah. For mom, there is white and not white. Dad screwed a woman from the congregation years ago, and she was like this super light skinned woman. Maybe a quarter or less black based off her skin color? I don't know for sure but damn near passing, other than her hair. Mom was furious when she found out. Not about the affair, but because she was part black! It was a gross fight. Shit like 'You are not putting that thing in me after you had it in a ... black girl'. She used a different word. I can't use it."

Morgan smiled at that to reassure Darla she understood her reluctance. "Yes: very ugly, and not anything you should ever have been subjected to. Deedee also seems to confuse transsexual with homosexual and self-mutilation." Morgan noted.

"I didn't know about Neil. None of us did. But yeah: Mom was shitting bricks over the idea I had sex with a woman." Darla looked down. "I did this, didn't I? I have been trying not to think about it, but ... It's my fault these guys are dead. I wanted to fuck with my mom. I never thought about this happening."

"Darla: Absolutely NOT." Morgan said with vigor. "Your motives may not have been pure as the driven snow, and you may have been using the boys for your own purposes, but they went willingly into the room. You did not RAPE them. The reason I am telling you all this, however, is so you understand from now on that you need to keep such things to yourself. I have no idea what your mother is capable of. I do not even personally understand her motives, other than to know that they are what they are. Again: not your fault. You offered, they went willingly. No one held a gun on their head, and they could have chosen once in privacy to NOT engage with you physically. That is not uncommon even. Not every kid in the game had sex just because they went to the room. Some engaged only in talking, kissing, heavy petting. Again: you offered, they accepted, and as you stated, they wanted to try again under better circumstances."

"No... They were all pretty willing. I got undressed, they couldn't wait. Well, again, other than Neil stopping to explain. Once he knew I was down with it though, we went for it." Darla agreed. "Boys are easy, aren't they?"

"That is my observation." Morgan agreed. "Sex IS intimate, and perhaps more intimate for women than men. They are IN us, after all. I do not think you would have taken these boys to the rooms if you did not like them. Again: you are not responsible for what your mother did. If anything, I see your rebellion against her bigotry as a positive sign about who YOU are, deep down. If you were a bigot, you would not have done this."

"You look at the world really weird, but I like it." Darla said, still looking like she felt guilty about the results of her actions.

"At some point, you tell your mother about your adventures..." Morgan started.

"Hah! When I got HOME." Darla barked. "I was out all night. Mom was waiting. She gave me the third degree, I told her I was out all night having sex with some boys, and I tell her who. Just names, but mom is PTA and she knows my classmates, and she was all Hollywood mom for the commercial. I tell her 'Derek', and she screams 'The Black kid?' at the top of her lungs. Except like I said she does not use the word 'black'. I get mad about that, and so I tell her about Neil, to really get into her face, and she is like all red and furious, and I tell her he was the best lay and I am going back for MORE, and she is like 'Not and live HERE' and all that usual bullshit. She takes my phone away, but I find it later on her dresser and just take it back."

"You exchanged contact information with them? Derek, Neil, and Ailani?" Morgan asked.

"All the kids in the commercial, not just them." Darla answered.

"All stored in your phone?" Morgan asked.

"Of course. If I ever lose that phone I am like so screwed, you know?" Darla appeared horrified at the idea.

Morgan held up her PDA. "How I feel about this, except it's backed up to my computer. Twice."

"I need to get one of those. You know, for an adult, you are pretty cool." Darla said, and Morgan considered that she was not even ten years older than Darla, and she was somehow in the same classification as her parents.

"I am not a religious person, but I am also not a judgmental one about most things." Morgan explained. "I have an intense dislike for hypocrisy. I do not care in the slightest for example that your parents have outside lovers, as I feel that is their business and something they need to figure out inside their relationship. I have never heard your dad speak at church, and I do not know if he holds out marriage as some sacrosanct thing between a man and a woman only, as some churches do, or if he spends more time doing the standard prosperity gospel riffs. The recorded services of his I watched for the background were of that type. The 'God wants you to be wealthy in this lifetime, so believe God will deliver the goods' talks. That sort of thing."

Morgan was working completely off her feeling for who she thought Darla is. She hoped such an open statement of her opinion would not be insulting.

It wasn't exactly insulting, but Darla seemed to take an odd umbrage at the wording. "Dad is WAY smoother than that, but yeah. He gets up on stage during services the people that came to him for God's blessing and they testify how they used to be deep in debt but now, thanks to God's blessings, they have six-figure jobs and can afford the good things in life. That kind of stuff, with people from the church Dad picked out. Dad is really good at reading the room, you know? He plans his sermons around themes like jobs and money and success and shit. You know what's funny? He met Mom at a hellfire and damnation church revival. They kind of built this place together, as they figured out the good money wasn't doing the roadshow and tent circuit." Darla explained.

This led to a point of personal curiosity for Morgan. "What was it like growing up in that situation?"

It was intentionally not leading. Morgan wondered what the thing Darla would pick out might be.

"It sucked." Darla started. "I can't remember a time when I was a kid that I did not know my parents were bogus. I can't remember a time Mom didn't have over some lover or another when Dad was at the office, talking her shit about .. Everyone. Just a hateful bitch. I was closer to Dad, not that saying that means much but he was at least the one that made sure I saw the Doctors and shit. Mom did stuff for optics, like PTA. It was all about how SHE looked, and I couldn't do things that might make her look bad."

Darla looked away in thought. "I remember this one guy. He didn't last long. They were sitting out on the back patio, mom in her gauzy wrap. I think he was naked. I didn't go out there and he was sitting so I could not see if his junk was out, but the screen door was open so I could hear. Dude couldn't get a word in edgewise. Mom was talking about how lazy black people are, and how they give less money to the church than white people. Just horrible stuff. That's when I figured out dudes will do most anything to get laid. I looked out the kitchen window at them sitting by the pool, and his shoulders were all bunched up and tight. He did not like what my mom was saying. I could tell. He put up with it so he could screw her again later. Mom is a babe, even now. She LOOKS good, I mean. Pretty outsides to hide her horrible insides."

"That sounds really awful." Morgan said.

"I can't wait to go away to school. Never coming back to this shithole. I'll wash dishes at a coffee place on an Island somewhere first. Fuck: Changing my name too." Darla sounded truly angry, and Morgan could not blame her.

"Means, Motive, and Opportunity. All here. I just can't do anything about it. Your mom has powerful friends in the department. I can stand in front of a judge with all of my evidence and thinking, and I will never get a search warrant to find that gun, assuming she still has it." Morgan said "But thank you for giving me this additional background. It convinces me that I am correct."

"I think you are too. I think she did it. You can't get her at all?" Darla asked, looking slightly shocked at that revelation.

"There are these people in the department that agree with your mothers' views on ethnicity. I call them 'The Cabal', but they are always trying to tell me who I can be with too. Same as your mother, but a bunch of nameless, faceless men. I do not listen to their directives, but they can block me on something like this. They told me to leave your family alone, and Sam and I have reached the end of the line. We KNOW your mom bought a .22, but it is just not enough. Not with these guys in the way. Also: the person selling illegal firearms is not going to be a credible witness in court if we could even get him there, which we promised him we would not." Morgan said.

It was Sam's promise, but that made it Morgan's as well.

"So? You are giving up?" Darla asked.

"No. Of course not. I just do not have any way forward at the moment. I have to ask, you seem to be remarkably unhappy that I CANNOT arrest your mother for murder." Morgan asked.

"She killed three guys I liked. I already hated her. Now I am afraid to be NEAR her." Darla said.

"I am sorry. Perhaps you have a friend you can stay with? If not, you will be eighteen soon, and able to move out and get your own place. If they try and stop you, I can help."

"You can get me an apartment... On a cop's salary." Darla said sarcastically.

"Yes." Morgan agreed, without explaining. She was not overly proud of her trust fund, but this would be a good use for a tiny bit of it.

"What if I helped you, instead?" Darla asked.

"I cannot put you in danger." Morgan said with finality. "You cannot search for and find the gun without suspicion being equally upon YOU, either. The killer was your height, for example. That is also your mothers' height, but that turns into a you against her thing. Not safe. Your mother strikes me as one that would throw her own daughter under the bus rather than admit her guilt."

"You know my mom well. Fuck." Darla said. "Hey. How about this. I fuck another black guy and tell her, and when she goes after him, you grab her? She brings the gun and everything, right?"

"Darla..." Morgan started.

Darla cut her off. "No, Detective. This is perfect. You can't stop me, but when I DO it, I tell you, and you have to protect him."

"Give me a moment?" Morgan said. "I need to think about this?"

Morgan had an idea. Based on Darla's idea, but one that did NOT put another kid in danger and that probably would raise the Richter scale of Deedee's response.

CHAPTER TWENTY-FIVE

Planning

"Hi, Wendell. Bad news: This is not a booty call. Good news, if you do not get killed, it might become one." Morgan started.

Wendell chuckled. "Morgan, you know how to start a conversation like no one I have ever met. What is up?"

"Sit back. This is going to take a while to explain." Morgan laid it out. The murdered boys, the motive for their deaths, the problems getting past the Cabal, the need to have the murder weapon brought to them by the murderer, the trap Darla came up with on the fly and that Morgan wanted to modify.

"So. You want to have Darla tell her mom that she met an older man. A black cop. That she is in love, wants to move in with him. Maybe even have his little baby. Just over-the-top, layered on bullshit so that this woman gives him a call and arranges a back alley meet for love and bullets. Oh. By the way, this poor black cop is me."

"Yep." Morgan agreed.

"I assume you will give Darla a picture of me to sell this charade?"

"Also yep. It would be better if I could do a little two-shot of you and her in some romantic place, but I want it so you two never actually have ever met. I don't want to take the time to gin up a fake either. I want to land this bomb in Deedee's life before she has a chance to dump the gun."

"Why no two-shot?" Wendell asked, knowing Morgan had a reason.

"Court. Cabal. You name it. I want it so they cannot say that you two actually WERE lovers. Not that it should matter, but ... Cabal. Who knows what they will do?"

"Kill you?" Wendell asked.

"Maybe. They had a chance in my bedroom when they were after my phone. I do not think they want me dead. I think they want me to be a good little girl."

"I guess what they want in their good girls and what I want in mine are two different things." Wendell said.

Morgan reacted to that possessive usage instinctively. "I don't know. I have never met any of your other women."

Wendell paused. Thought. Correctly deduced the reaction. "Well, they are all exceptional people." He said. "All that I date in fact. You want to be with me, you have to be amazing. You barely got in, frankly."

"Good to know." Morgan had a smile in her voice. This is a thing she really liked about Wendell. He understood her, and the little twist of the knife at the end was well done. Ken would have just shut down or changed the subject. "I think, for a kid, Darla, despite being a complete mess, is pretty amazing. She just has never had a chance in life. Another reason to keep you two apart."

"I am not sure I LIKE you being the opposite of a matchmaker here. What if Darla is my true love? Maybe I DO want her to move in?"

"If so, by the time this case is over, she'll be eighteen, and you can work that out without my help. I only aid you into MY bed for booty calls. After that, you are on your own."

"Fine. I will try to live with that restriction." Wendell said, Faux-resigned.

"I will call you after I get it set up with Darla." Morgan said.

"OK." Wendell agreed.

After they hung up, Morgan wondered for a very brief moment how many other women Wendell was seeing. Not out of jealousy but rather equity. She would not like the idea that she was seeing other people and he was not. At the same time, she admitted that was none of her business either.

In further self-examination, there was also some fear there. Morgan did not have to choose but if she DID have to, Wendell was right up there at the top. His primary negatives being that he is a 'morning person', a gym rat, and lived too far away. The 'morning person' point was really irritating.

Morgan called Darla. "Can you talk?"

"Yeah. I am in my room in the Mansion that greed built. Dad's at the office, probably fucking Cathleen. Mom is 'out', and by that, I think that means she is off seeing a lover too. One great big happy sexually satisfied family around here. Except for me, because my mom keeps killing my lovers." Darla said, and this was the most bitter Morgan had heard her become over this so far. Reality setting further and further in.

"I set everything up with your new fake lover. He is on board. I will get you a picture of him. Also, the name and phone number to put into your phone's address book. I will not tell you how to sell this: You know your mother better than I. Perhaps a twist of the knife? That you are thinking about moving in with him because your lovers keep getting killed, and he is a Cop? You think you and he would have cute babies? Something of that nature?"

Darla gave that some thought asked "Tell me about him. Why do YOU date him?"

"Well, I like him. He is smart. Funny. A great cop. He followed my lead perfectly in an interview once, and that meant a lot to me. Why I gave him a second look: A man not threatened by a successful woman. A strong, smart woman. He finds those things about me sexy. His male ego is intact and not threatened by me, and that is not a thing I come across all the time." Morgan explained. As she reviewed Wendell, she was smiling, caught herself doing it, but left it on. So what if he makes her smile. Big deal.

"Is he good in bed?" Darla asked.

"Why do you ask?" Morgan almost just told her none of her business, but Darla had enough shit like that in her life.

"I am trying to sell my mom that WE are lovers. That I want to move in with him. I need to SELL it." Darla explained.

Morgan was not sure there was not still some prurient curiosity involved. "He is to my way of thinking, excellent. Not about technique so much as following my lead. He can tell what I am after, and he goes there. Sex is not always or even frequently about banging the headboard against the wall. I am not saying he reads me like a book, but if he starts doing something I am not enjoying, he pays attention. He tries a different thing. Since I do not always want the same things, he runs no script. He figures it out from my responses, or if I say one word, or do one little thing to direct his attention to a current... Interest."

"Oh my god." Darla said. "Can I have him when you are done with him?"

"Get your own. Or grow one. You said Neil was good, so it seems to me that you have the ability to find good lovers." Morgan told her.

Darla sighed. "Do you know how hard it is to find female-to-male full post-op transsexuals in this city?" Darla exclaimed.

"No." Morgan admitted. "Though it is my understanding that being transsexual is NOT about the genitals. Male is male, even if perhaps they have not gone through the surgery. You know that procedure is not only expensive but has a high level of pain and an appalling failure rate. Many rightly choose not to endure it."

"No. Never really thought about it. Still, after Neil, I may be looking." Darla said.

Morgan had to ask again. "Darla. Seriously. We are planning to create a situation that results in your mother being arrested and possibly spending the rest of her life in prison. Are you sure this is something that you want to live with for the rest of YOUR life? I can find another way. I usually do."

"Detective. It was my idea. I am not being impulsive here. It is not just that my mother is a bitch of epic proportions. She killed three people. Three KIDS. She needs to go away. As I said, I'll do it myself if I have to, but I like your plan much better."

Morgan knew Darla well enough to know she would do it, and in a much less controllable situation. Also, Darla's way put a fourth young man at risk.

Morgan considered. She could arrest Darla for what she planned to do, though the charges would not stick, and it was a private, off the record conversation. It would poison her relationship with Darla, let the cat out of the bag to Deedee that they were on to her. Morgan could find no upside to that idea. Morgan did not like the idea of leveraging Darla like this, but it was the best of several bad situations.

"I'll meet you at Mr. MgGoo's after school?" Morgan asked.

"Yeah. Sounds good." Darla agreed.

"Darla: Completely unrelated question: Do you know why they call that hangout 'Mr. MgGoo's?" Morgan asked.

"No. No one does, and the owner won't say." Darla said.

"Weird." Morgan commented.

CHAPTER TWENTY-SIX

Busted

The hardest part of setting up this sting had been getting the location Deedee picked for the meeting set up. They needed to put in camera's, hidden. The same with directional microphones. Deedee had to think that she was walking into the same kind of unmonitored situation she had preferred for the other killings. This had taken finesse on Wendell's part. Set the meet, but allow enough time between the call and the meet to get to the place, look it over, and figure out their options.

The selected spot was not an alley like Derek Jefferson's meeting place or a loading dock like Neil Snyder's. It was a park, similar to the one Ailani Aquino had met his death in, though it was much smaller. The problem for the technical squad in this location was power. The park had none except for the occasional working overhead light, so all the monitoring equipment had to be battery powered. This park was due for renovation. The local tree planting commission intended to make the place over. Fix the gardening, and was doing fundraisers to get the walkways and lighting repaired. Ironically, or perhaps not, the New Covenant Abundant Light Church was a named sponsor on the project, and perhaps that is how Deedee Odean knew of the suitability of this particular location for her next planned homicide. Like almost any park in Houston, there is a counter-movement to take the park away from its use as green space for the community and make it into commercial or residential property because Houston has far less use for parks than places to stuff residents or businesses. Like liberty itself, maintaining a green-space area in Houston requires eternal vigilance.

In its current largely unmaintained condition, the park was exactly the kind of place Deedee Odean liked to meet her victims in. Easy to sneak into and out of unobserved. Away from street cameras and with the bonus of poor lighting.

Wendell had played it nicely, messaging Deedee, pretending to be Darla, that he had to work a double that day because he was covering for a buddy who was sick, but he could meet her late that night. A late night rendezvous was exactly what Deedee wanted so Deedee bought it. The team Sam and Morgan assembled for the operation had eyes on Deedee all day to be sure she went nowhere near the park while they bugged it.

To keep the Cabal away from this, the entire operation was being staffed with people that Sam and Morgan knew and that JJ had some sway with, in one way or another. It is likely the hidden Cabal would get wind of it anyway, since it was using enough people as to be noticeable, not to mention a fair amount of technical equipment. To succeed, everything was a balance of last-minute notifications and setup, with contingency plans for everything. If one piece of gear they required for the operation was checked out or access blocked somehow by the Cabal, they knew where another was to replace it with, and a third behind that. The same with the personnel. A sick kid requiring one officer staying home at the last second being covered by another trusted officer.

Active intervention by the Cabal would also give Morgan clues as to the outlines of that organization, so while she wanted them to leave her operation alone, she was also ready to reap additional benefits.

Deedee cooperated with the team assigned to tailing her by going to the gym, and then she went to an apartment complex where she met a man. Quick checks on his apartment number pulled his name, Àlex Wells, his occupation, architect just getting started professionally. The check showed he was also a member of the gym. Morgan assumed Deedee was coping with pre-murder jitters by smoothing them out with amorous distraction. It was not like Deedee needed to do a great deal of planning. She had to know where to park, and to bring her loaded gun.

In the office, Morgan was checking over Wendell's gear for the night. Wendell was looking at Sam with eye rolls and faces to indicate what he thought about Morgan in her full on protective Mother Bear mode.

Morgan checked the ballistic groin protector, looking Wendell directly into the eyes as she did so, daring him to say ANYTHING about it.

"I appreciate you helping us with this op, Wendell. I really do.

However, do not think I do not see the stupid faces you are making over at Sam. You are going in as protected as I can make you. Deal with it, Wendell." Morgan told him sternly and underlining how deadly serious she was by using his name twice. "Also, no jokes about this covering the only important body part that needs protecting."

"I was NOT going to make that joke." Wendell said, aggrieved at the unjust accusation. He tapped his shoulders and the upper arm protectors. "It's a damn .22 Short, Morgan. Even if she HITS me with it, as long as its not a vital organ, like my brain, I'll be fine."

"You remember we have a date coming up soon?" Morgan asked.

"Of course." Wendell said, aggrieved again.

"Do you think it will be a fun date if you have holes in your body?" Morgan asked. She checked the throat protector.

Wendell scoffed. "I won't HAVE holes in my body. She is not getting that close to me."

"Famous last words. You get hit by ANYTHING I could not strap a shield over, instead of the date being fun, it will be less fun. For one thing, I will be smacking the bullet hole with the palm of my hand with metronome-like regularity, and asking you if it hurts."

"Now I can insert the joke I was not going to make." Wendell said.

"Nope." Morgan said. She handed him a windbreaker. Black. "Here. Need to see if you look like the Incredible Hulk with this one. Not that Deedee knows what you look like yet anyway."

Wendell slipped it on, and Morgan stood back to observe. "Ok: Now the sweat pants." She said, handing him those. They were also black.

Morgan considered. Gave her approval. "Not too bad. You and I know you are a slender, muscular guy, but now you just look bulked up. Lots of gym time. Your pretty face and neck I cannot do anything about... Make SURE she does not get close."

Wendell face-palmed himself. "Morgan! Oh my god! I get it. I read all your and Sam's reports. I know her MO is to get beside or behind me. Chill!"

"When you are a mother, are you going to be like that with your kids? Because I will pay to see you getting your kid ready for their first day at school." Sam asked with a huge smile.

"No. I get it." Morgan turned on full and deadly sarcasm. "Nothing to worry about here. Deedee Odean is a little bitty slip of a woman that only works out three hours a day, and took down three young and healthy kids. One a runner even. She bought and used a Saturday night special and made it look like a professional hit, even though as near as we can tell, it was her first time. Why the hell should I worry about you? There are other fish in the sea, after all. Sure, you getting shot will be a LOT of paperwork, especially since you are Galveston County and they will want to know why I got their dumb ass overconfident cocky officer shot, but whatever. Why we have computers, right? Just print two copies of everything!"

Morgan glared at Wendell. "You know what, you dressed like that against me? You would be dead. You'd never know what hit you. But hell: She is not me, is she? So excuse the hell out of me for trying to give you a fighting chance."

Morgan pointed at Wendell's crotch with a stabbing motion. "You know what? I am the idiot here. You are right. You should just waltz into the park naked. See if you can distract her attention that way instead. You can do that Le Bare thing. Walk up and just spin your hips. Spin your money maker like a tassel. I don't think it matters if you are spinning it clockwise or counterclockwise when you are trying to hypnotize her. She will be all goo-goo eyed anyway, correct? And if she tried to shoot at the moving target, how much damage could a .22 even do to you, anyway? Why they invented strap-ons. I think it is right there on the package: 'Adults only, for use only by women and male cops that are too damn stupid to listen'. It is right there! Black and white. Big font."

Acid dripped from her every word. Wendell was holding up hands and waving them at her to stop.

"Wendell: You better do whatever she says." Sam commented wryly. "You do NOT want her to escalate that attitude. Trust me. That won't be good for anyone. I already can't get that out of my head."

Wendell looked properly chastened. "I will hit whatever marks you tell me to, and dress however you say, Detective."

"Good: because I was thinking I was going to be looking for a new date soon." Morgan said, crossly.

"No. Not a chance. You are going to owe me for helping you, remember?" Wendell said.

"Not if she shoots your dumb ass." Morgan said.

"Let me see. Choice one: Get my dumb ass shot, and my date canceled. Choice two: not get my ass shot, go on the date with the detective that is just trying to protect me. Humm. Which of THOSE am I going to choose? Can I get back to you on that?" Now Wendell was returning the sarcasm.

"Sam: Are YOU the detective in that scenario?" Morgan asked.

"Not me." Sam said, "He is too skinny."

"I am not skinny. I am svelte." Wendell said. "Except when I am wearing full body armor, of course, and I am not sure I like the idea of a date that requires full body armor."

The three-unit tail on Deedee reported that she was headed to the park. She had left the apartment, driven to her house, and had been seen dressed in dark clothing and getting into her car at midnight. It seemed Deedee wanted to be there early since the meet was set for 12:45 AM.

Dressed also in dark clothing and wearing full face masks, Sam, Morgan, and three other cops were spread through the park. Their earpieces kept them apprised of Deedee's exact location. Deedee parked her Black BMW 7 Series well away from the agreed upon meeting location and also nowhere near any traffic cameras.

The cars that had been following Deedee parked in various places, and the plainclothes cops spread out in a second cordon. The last car to park after Deedee had walked well away from the BMW came right up against her back bumper to preclude Deedee having an easy and quick escape. She was far enough from the car ahead of her that with some backing and filling she could still get out, but this would slow her down if it came to it.

'Next time, bring a car immobilizer' Morgan mentally noted.

The designated rendezvous point was a park bench alongside some old pine trees. Deedee's dark figure placed herself into the trees, to be able to watch the bench. Having anticipated that, Morgan and team were secreted behind other, further away trees, as well as a ramshackle building that park supplies were stored in.

On cue, Wendell walked up to the bench, looked around. Looked at his watch. He was directly on time.

"She is in that tree line behind the bench" Morgan whispered into her microphone. Wendell could hear Morgan in his earpiece, hidden by his black baseball cap. Wendell responded to that message by making a show of pulling out his phone to see if there were any messages on it.

The bench, if he sat down to wait, would put his back to the trees, but Wendell was clearly mindful of how much shit he would be in with Morgan if he tried to lure Deedee out by looking vulnerable. Instead, he leaned against the back of the bench, holding his phone in one hand, and glancing at it now and then.

After ten minutes of waiting, Deedee went to her next plan and made her way along the trees out of sight of the bench, but in sight of an officer placed behind her. "Suspect moving, to her left." He reported.

Once she had gone a ways, she walked out of the tree line quickly, to the sidewalk, and walked slowly back.

"Suspect headed back to the bench." Came the report.

Wendell started, as if he saw the approaching figure from a ways away, turned and faced her, acting like he was peering into the dark. "Is that you, Darla?" he asked

"No: Darla sent me though. She said her dad was still up and she was going to be delayed. Asked me to come here and tell you."

Wendell held up his phone in his left hand. "Why didn't she text me?", then he added suspiciously "Also, who are you? I can't see you very well in the dark."

"I'm just a friend. From school. Darla said she really wanted to see you tonight." Deedee improvised.

"OK. Well. Thanks. You must be a good friend to come out here this late." Wendell improvised right back at her.

"She said you were worth it." Deedee said. "How long have you two been together? She didn't say."

That went into a prepared and practiced line. "Oh, a while. I'm a cop, and I pulled her over once when she was driving erratically. It was because this young man was going down on her while she drove."

"Oh." Deedee absorbed that. She paused, then asked: "What did he look like? Do I know him?".

Morgan found it interesting that Deedee was making her voice slightly higher than her normal range, and assumed this was to try and sound younger.

"I don't know. I was not looking at him. Just a young brother. Not sure where from, you know? She likes her dark meat I guess."

Morgan asked Wendell if he was going to be OK delivering a line like that one, and he said he was.

It made her bilious. It was meant to elicit a response from Deedee though, and according to Darla, this was mild when compared to Deedee's vocabulary of hate.

"Yes." Deedee said. "Yes, she does. Why she is fucking you, I guess?"

"I guess. I don't know. She never talks about why she does things. She just lets you know she wants to do things. She's an adult, so I'm OK with it."

"Of course you are." Deedee said.

Deedee had walked to the sidewalk side of the bench to start but was inching her way around to get on the same side, trying to look very casual about it.

"You interested in anyone besides her? I mean: she's going to be a while..." Deedee said, and she opened her dark jacket to reveal a form-fitting white top that left little to the imagination. The hood was still up so all Wendell could see was her gym-trim upper body and prominent breasts. "You like big boobs?" Deedee asked.

"I like real ones. Big or small or in between. Darla's are nice though." Wendell offered back.

Morgan winced. That was provocative. Clearly aimed at pissing Deedee off.

"Yes: Not all of us got Darla's tits. Some of us had to improvise, you know? Still, these aren't bad. I haven't had any complaints." Deedee was irritated but kept it smooth.

"Ok. The proof is in the pudding: take 'em out and show me." Wendell said. Since one hand was in her jacket pocket where her .22 almost had to be, that was a move to get both hands into view.

"Why don't YOU take them out?" Deedee countered. Morgan winced. Improv gone wrong. "You take out my boobs, I'll take out your dick. Is it big? Darla didn't tell me."

Deedee inched closer and had one hand out as if she was going to push down the sweat pants. Wendell backed up. "You know, I don't think I want to cheat on Darla. I like her. She likes me. I kinda want to keep it that way. If we take it to the next level like we are talking about, better to not have cheating with her friend hanging on my conscious."

Morgan liked that line.

Deedee stopped her forward inching and dropped her hand. "I don't care if it's big or not. I was just curious is all. I like a normal size guy, you know? Who wants to be all stretched out?"

OK. Deedee was assuming the reason Wendell backed up was some sort of performance anxiety. Morgan filed that away in the Deedee personality bag.

Wendell stuck to his story. "Yeah, that's cool. Darla likes me like I am. I just want to keep it cool with her."

"What if I told you Darla said I was supposed to keep you entertained? You know how she is at parties. She said I should at least give you a blow job. I like blow jobs, so I was willing. She said you were really cute. I can't really tell in the dark... But hey. Darla is my friend. She wants me to blow a cute guy, I'll blow a guy, you know? We've shared before. You know how she is."

"Actually, Darla and I kind of keep us on the down-low. We never go to parties. She is worried what with me being older and black might be a problem with some people. She likes to stay in when we're together." Wendell returned to script with that one.

"You don't want a blow job?" Deedee persisted.

"Just from Darla..." Wendell replied. "Nothing personal miss. I am sure you are very good at it."

"The best." Deedee said, sounding actually wistful. "Look, if I can't get your pants off, I guess I have to do this the hard way." Deedee said, and Morgan tensed.

Deedee pulled her hand out of her pocket in the dark "I could have made this easier on you, darkie. You are NEVER putting that thing in her again. You are NEVER going to make your little mixed race babies. Not with anyone..." As Wendell backpedaled with forewarned and extreme rapidity, Deedee fired her .22.

Cops converged at the 'Go go go!' imperative, and Morgan herself accelerated from behind the building and headed to the bench at her best speed. She had studied the ground ahead of time to be sure there were no hidden obstacles. No sprinkler pipes or roots or other things that would literally trip her up.

There was a second shot. Not even a flash in the dark, as the .22 short cartridges were propelling their 27-grain bullets directly away from Morgan and directly at Wendell.

There was no third shot. Morgan went high and tackled Deedee, Morgan's arms tightly around her shoulders. As the pair of women skidded to a halt on the grass, Morgan was already sitting up on Deedee's back, her service SIG out, and pressed to the nape of Deedee's neck.

"Deedee Odean. You are under arrest. Wendell? You OK?" Morgan shouted as cops skidded in from all sides, guns out.

Deedee went limp under Morgan. She was unable to move, her arms were pinned under her, and she felt the cold muzzle against her neck.

Sam, behind her, reported in clipped tones "I have the .22. She dropped it when you went all Refrigerator Perry on her ass. Nice distance on the skid."

Morgan did not engage in Sam's light tones. She stayed deadly serious. "Deedee. I am going to take my 9mm gun off your neck, but it is still here in my hand, safety off, and it is still pointed at the back of your head."

Morgan looked up into the dark, then back at Deedee."Wendell. What is your status?" Morgan said in command tones.

"I'm here." Wendell said, walking up to the figure on the ground.

Morgan, not taking her eyes off Deedee this time said sharply "I said your STATUS, mister. Report!"

"I am unharmed. I cannot find anyplace where she hit me with either shot. Still looking." Wendell said, chastened by her tone with him. He was not used to Morgan speaking to him like that: At least not before tonight. Morgan was not even his boss, but he felt like he just got busted back to cadet.

Morgan looked around quickly, found an officer near Wendell. "Officer Jones: Could you help Officer Jackson assess his damage, if you please? Sam, can you point your gun at Mrs. Odean while I cuff her?" Morgan tapped the base of the skull very lightly to indicate where to aim, but mostly so Deedee would feel her gun's cold muzzle.

Morgan was narrating and tapping so that Deedee knew that when Morgan was cuffing her, she could still be shot.

"Done. She is covered." Sam said moving alongside them and making a point of clicking his safety off audibly. Morgan slid back down Deedee's body to her legs, pulled out cuffs, and then applied them one wrist at a time, reciting the Miranda warning as she did so.

"Do you understand these rights, Deedee Odean?" Morgan asked, underlining that Morgan knew exactly who she just arrested.

"Yes." Deedee said. It was a single word, and not at all meek.

Sam and Morgan pulled Deedee Odean to her feet, and then Morgan patted her down very completely. The .22 now in Sam's gloved hand was her only weapon. She had no ID. No car keys. The minuscule white top was matched with a white g-string, and Morgan had to wonder if the plan was to use sex as a distraction if required. Either that or Deedee planned to return to her lovers' apartment after the murder.

Deedee looked sourly on as Wendell took off his windbreaker and removed his upper body armor. "Fucking hell. You were a setup this whole time. Darla was never fucking your nigger ass?"

Hearing the ugly word required Morgan shoving her anger down so that she did not do something to undo this arrest. They were still on camera. Instead, Morgan pushed Deedee toward two cops that had a squad car nearby. "Would you guys take Mrs. Odean to the house and in-process her, please? I do not think I can stand to look at her just yet.

Sam and I will be by for the initial interview soon."

The two officers reached out and lightly took an arm each. "Absolutely, Detective Olsen. It will be our pleasure" said one.

"Don't TOUCH me." Deedee shouted, to no effect. Morgan presumed that as officer Guerra was Hispanic and officer Constantin was black, Deedee was unhappy.

Deedee confirmed that when she said as they walked to the car "Jesus Christ. Are there NO fucking white cops in this city besides that bitch?"

To their credit, neither said a word or accidentally tripped her in the dark.

"Huh." Sam said taking off a glove and looking at his hand in the darkness.

"You are more peach than white." Morgan told him. "Lovely complexion, really. I know a modeling agency..."

CHAPTER TWENTY-SEVEN
Interview

Morgan and Wendell arrived at where she had parked her truck, and he placed the body armor in the bed, ready to be returned to the armorers. Morgan drove them back to the station. He was subdued and Morgan was willing to not fill in the silence. She was fighting her anger at Deedee down still and was grateful for the mental space.

Back under control, Morgan looked at Wendell sitting there quietly. "I am sorry she called you that."

Wendell looked over at Morgan. Smiled. "Yeah: She's a bitch. No worries." Wendell said.

He lapsed back into being quiet.

"We got her. Success. What is wrong?" Morgan asked.

"I just never heard you like that before." Wendell said.

"Like what?" Morgan asked.

"I felt like a kid being chewed out by his mom in front of his friends." Wendell said

Ahh. Now Morgan understood. It was not Deedee's ugliness, it was Lead Detective Morgan Olsen that was bothering him. "Oh. Yes. Well. I would apologize... But I won't, Wendell. On mission, I am on task. Who I am. Thought you knew that about me."

"Morgan: It is one thing to know that, in your head. I was even right there in the room when you worked Hector. Still: for all that it is another thing to be on the receiving end of the worlds shortest dressing down, and realize that in two sentences you can reduce me to feeling like a damn child."

"Wendell. Deedee shot at you. Twice. I needed to know immediately if you were OK or if I needed to get an ambulance rolling. You were fucking around. I appreciate you coming up here and risking your life and working with me. I do. You were excellent. Even when you were riffing on what she was saying and having to go off our script, you were perfect. However, sir: when I want to know the status of an officer, ANY officer, on my Op, I expect a crisp answer. There is a time and a place for everything."

That got a glance over to Morgan. "You ever do that to Sam?" Wendell asked.

"Yes. Ask him. He liked it about as well as you just did." Morgan said.

"Respect, Sister. Respect. You are an awesome cop." Wendell said.

"Thank you. That means a lot to me. Also, as we are in my private truck, and no one is around, I intend to kiss you before we get out of this truck as a preview of later things to come."

"You make my brain hurt." Wendell said.

"Really?" Morgan asked. "I just view it as being able to maintain a firewall between my personal and professional lives. I am a cop. I am a woman. Do you disagree with my approach?"

"Really... You do that for sure, he says as the kid you just verbally sent back to grade school." Wendell assured her. "And NO. I do not disagree. I think we all should take a page from your book in that area."

The interview room at the city jail is pretty much like one would expect. Table. Chairs. Rings for cuffs. Lights covered under grates. One way glass wall. Steel door with wire mesh embedded in the glass window. Microphone for recording. A video camera behind the one way glass.

Morgan, Sam, and Wendell entered after Deedee had been brought in, cuffed to the table, and left. Morgan knew one of the games cops play is leaving an interviewee in the interview room for a while, alone, but she did not think that was going to be effective with Deedee. She expected having Wendell in the room might be more enlightening, but told him before they entered that it could get a little rough.

Wendell nodded. "I understand, Detective" he replied, and that caused Sam to raise an eyebrow.

"She is good at the operational discipline thing, isn't she?" Sam said.

"Drill Sargent good." Wendell agreed with some emphasis.

Deedee glared when she saw Wendell. "What are YOU doing in here?"

Morgan did not answer, nor did Wendell. Instead, Morgan said

"Deedee Odean, you know who I am already, but for the record, I am Homicide Lead Detective Morgan Olsen. This is my partner, Homicide Detective Sam Parker. With us is Officer Wendell Jackson. Deedee: We arrested you, advised you of your rights, and charged you for the attempted murder of Officer Jackson. He identified himself to you as an officer of the law during your conversation this evening, and you shot at him twice. We have video, audio, and eyewitnesses to all of these things, so these are not allegations but documented facts and you are going down for your actions. Further, you used derogatory language when referring to Officer Jackson, indicating that your actions were ethnically motivated. This adds 'hate crime' to the charges. Are you with me so far?"

Deedee gave Morgan a withering look. "I am not stupid, Detective."

"Excellent. Because it was not our intent this early morning to even HAVE these particular charges against you." Morgan said.

That caused an eyebrow dance on Deedee's face. "Oh. What were you and your pet cop trying to do, then?" Deedee asked, acidly.

"Is that a reference to Officer Parker or Jackson?" Morgan asked, looking over at them as if she was not the confused one.

"You know who I am talking about. No need to be a bitch about it." Deedee said.

"I really do not." Morgan said. "No matter. The reason I wanted to have Officer Jackson meet with you this evening was to see if you would bring that particular 22 caliber short cartridge revolver along. I wanted to give it to my ballistics people. While I do not approve of you shooting it at my officer, I do appreciate you having it along with you and in such a circumstance that I can legally relieve you of it, and have a long forensic look at the weapon. I knew you HAD it. Detective Parker found the man that sold it to you. I know it is not legally registered as neither you nor your husband have any registered weapons at all, so I could have taken it on sight, but you kept it in your pocket. Very uncooperative of you. Then, for some reason, you pulled it on my Officer and solved that conundrum for me, while adding a new one. You tried to kill my officer!"

When she said the phrase 'my officer' Morgan made that overtly possessive. She wanted Deedee to completely understand exactly who was running the show tonight, but it had a second level to it.Under the table and out of sight of the camera, Morgan touched Wendell's leg lightly. Not possessively or sexually, just signaling the second level of meaning to her words.

Deedee barked a laugh. "You are so cute. Sending that fucking negro in and have him pretending he was fucking my daughter, so I'd pull the gun out. My daughter telling me she and this... Person, were going to move in together and have children. All of it. So clever."

"I never asked Darla to tell you any specific thing. I only asked her to sell the idea that she was seeing my officer. I am sorry Officer Jackson. Knowing Deedee's previous homicides, I would never have had her think you and Darla were going to have children, as I would, after her killings, known how the very idea of herself as a grandmother to ethnically mixed grandchildren would set her off." Morgan apologized, her eyes fixed on Deedee.

"Oh, fucking hell, girl. Give it a rest. Stupid game. Sure, he isn't as dark as some, but a white girl like you should know better. But you do, don't you? You are just screwing with me. I pulled a gun and shot at your damn pet. Why are we here? You saw me do it." Deedee was imperious.

Morgan drew herself up. "I, ma'am, am not white."

"What? Jesus Christ, you are full of it." Deedee was swerved over to disgusted, which was not a long trip from her previous attitude.

Sam offered his first comment. "She isn't, Mrs. Odean. Detective Olsen, despite that last name, is American Indian. Apache, I believe."

"What? With those dark blue eyes? Bullshit." Deedee said. "What is the game here?"

"Well, the game, as you called it, was as I said. I wanted your gun." Morgan said.

"Why?" Deedee asked.

"Because, in the parlance of my trade, it has three bodies on it. At LEAST. Maybe more."

Wendell asked Sam in confidential tones "Does that mean it was used to kill at least three people?"

"Yeah: When you are the lead detective, you have to take classes in sounding like that." Sam whispered back. "It's when they do the lobotomy and take out the backbone too."

"Hell: They forgot to do either of those things to her!" Wendell said back.

"I know. It's SO annoying." Sam grinned.

Deedee watched and listened to the byplay with pure, unmitigated disgust. "You all think you are SO funny."

Sam pointed. "She got YOU, didn't she, Mrs. Odean?"

"I'll be out of here in no time. Attempted murder ain't going to stick.

That damn gun can't hit the broadside of a barn."

"Oh, I know." Morgan agreed with a nod. "Why you kept trying to get in close, wasn't it? Probably would have given him the oral sex you promised him if you had to in order to get the revolver to point blank range, which is its only effective range."

"Oh, fuck no! Nigger cock in my mouth?" Deedee shuddered.

Morgan hated every time she used that word. Every time she did, Deedee was digging her hole deeper.

Morgan laughed instead. "Sure, Deedee. Protest all you like. You were angry, because apparently you thought Darla was going to present you with mixed ethnicity grandchildren. You could not have that, could you? You would have done whatever you had to in order to get your gun in close. You were about to undress right there in the park. Show him your breasts, at least until he said he did not like your breasts. Why did you say that?" Morgan asked Wendell.

"Because she kept inching closer, and I wanted her to stop that. Her hand was in her pocket the whole time, even when she unzipped her jacket. I knew you were after that gun, so I figured it was in that pocket, and it was." Wendell explained

"I see. OK. Smart." Morgan said. Of course, she already knew that, but this was for Deedee's and the recording's benefit.

"So smart." Deedee mocked. "I'll have you know, not that YOU'LL ever see them, that this is the best boob job money can buy. They look real as all hell."

"I am sure your fellow inmates at Huntsville will enjoy them." Wendell said.

"I am never going to see the inside of that place, but YOU might." Deedee asserted.

"Oh?" Wendell asked.

"When my lawyer is done with you all, you are going to wish you had never been born, which in YOUR damn case, and all your race, is something we all wish." Deedee said, looking at Wendell.

"Daniel Moritz, of Moritz, Grant, Neumann, and Moritz?" Morgan asked.

"Exactly!" Deedee Odean looked triumphant, and when no one looked particularly moved by that revelation she added "When he is done with you all, you will be sued for false arrest, entrapment and god knows what else. I am an upstanding member of one of the largest churches in Houston. You all are grubby cops looking for a cheap headline. He will destroy you." She stabbed her eyes at Wendell. "A negro, in his twenties, a cop or not, having sex with my underage daughter. No jury..." She trailed off there.

Morgan had hoped that Deedee Odean would count on her connection, via Moritz's firm, to the Cabal inside the department to help her out, and that might lead to her being overconfident and angry, and it was working better than she dared hope. With everything they had on record this evening and the number of people that had been involved, the Cabal would have difficulty burying it. Morgan decided to keep digging in.

"You seem remarkably incurious as to the fact I was after your gun." Morgan noted.

"First time I ever shot it was tonight. I don't know what the gun was used for before I bought it." Deedee said.

"I know the exact date you bought that gun, thanks to Sam and his contacts. With this arrest, I will have the grounds required to find where and WHEN you bought the ammunition for it, as the gun dealer you bought it from did not stock .22 shorts. If there have been deaths caused by this weapon before that date of purchase, you are correct in that you will not be charged with them. As it pertains to you, I am after the three deaths that occurred AFTER you bought it. Also, I need to correct something you just asserted. Age of consent in Texas is seventeen, not eighteen. In theory, and I emphasis that word here, in THEORY, Darla is free to have sex with, and for that matter children with, whoever she damn well pleases. In this case Officer Jackson has he ever had sex with Darla, despite the fact it would be legal for him to do so, because he has never even met Darla. Never met her. Not once. Knows what she looks like because her face in on YOUR billboards. The people I am concerned about and that you killed with your illegal . 22 caliber revolver are Derek Jefferson, Neil Snyder, and Ailani Aquino."

"Who?" Deedee asked.

"Deedee: You are not being clever with that denial, as you knew exactly who they were when we were at the church. I have a witness to that. Cathleen? Remember? You have been very clear and with very MANY people as to your views on ethnic social and genetic mixing, so no one here is going to buy that you were happy when you learned FROM Darla that she had consensual sex with these young men at a party. Do not pretend you do not know WHO. I have Darla on record telling you who she had sex with, and how it made you angry. I have YOU knowing the transsexual status of Neil Snyder, which was a very well guarded secret. I have all sorts of evidence regarding how well maintained that secret was. You literally could not know any way OTHER than Darla telling you. There is also another boy from that party named Shawn Pascolla that you did NOT kill because he is ethnically Caucasian. Your problem with Neil was not his ethnicity but how he came to be his gender. You are an equal opportunity bigot, Mrs. Odean."

Deedee shook her head. "You can't prove any of that."

"I have your gun." Morgan stated.

"It's a .22! God! Why do I have to explain shit to you?" Deedee exclaimed

"The caliber does not matter, except that it is the same exact weapon that killed all three boys."

".22." Deedee said again.

"Do you think being a .22 short, we can't get ballistics off of it?" Morgan asked. "Because we can. Not just which gun fired it, but we can chemically match the powder burns to the manufacturer of the cartridge. We have GSR off you tonight, and it will match as well. We have your fingerprints on the murder weapon, and ONLY your finger prints. Once we knew it was you that killed the boys, we can now prove it is YOUR car was in the area of ALL the murders. Traffic Cams. Sure, you were clever on your site selection, but it's a big city. You drove YOUR car. Your gun. Your hatred. Three young boys are dead because YOU did not like something about them."

"Neil or Neilette they should be called was NOT a boy." Deedee said.

"He was, but so? What do YOU mean?" Morgan asked.

"She was a woman, with an inflatable cock. My daughter fucked a woman. Not a boy."

"You literally know nothing about gender dysphoria or transsexualism," Morgan said, with a disapproving shake of the head.

"I have never met a fucking liberal cop before." Deedee answered, in a way Morgan found to be an utter non sequitur. "You don't even know who runs this place, do you?"

"I'm sorry? We are not discussing politics. We are discussing medical conditions and murder. You seem to be conflating things. Do you know what conflate means?" Morgan asked as if she was concerned about Deedee's educational level.

"Oh, fuck you, detective. I am not saying another word till my damn lawyer gets here."

Morgan stood up, and Sam and Wendell followed suit. "Very well. Have a lovely evening. We have all we need. With any luck, we will see you at your trial, though a word or professional advice: you would be better served to take any deals the DA might wish to offer you. In a Courtroom, with our evidence, EVERY jury would convict."

"You will be seeing me all right. In your nightmares." Deedee said.

Reports take forever. Sam and Morgan worked until ten in the morning on Sunday, and Wendell called into his job to let them know the weekend operation was a success and that he would be back on regular duty tomorrow. He then sat in the guest chair and nodded off. Cops learn to sleep about anywhere. Morgan envied Wendell the snooze.

Once everything was filed, Sam and Morgan both peeked into JJ's office. JJ was in over the weekend because of the Op.

"All the reports are in. Evidence logged. I checked: Everything in from the team too. DA notified. We are toast, boss: headed home." Morgan said.

JJ nodded. "You think they are coming after you for this one?"

It was clear from context JJ meant the cabal. Morgan sighed tiredly. "Maybe. I do not know. We tied this one up and put a cherry on it. Deedee Odean was so cocky in the interview she gave us motive times about ten. We have the gun now. It is not an us-against-her thing either: So many witnesses. Cross-agency task force even. These guys are powerful. They can make bodies go missing from County morgues, but this is a lot of stuff to bury, and the papers are going to have it too, more than likely."

JJ smiled at that. "Oh. They do. I called the Chron and fed them the whole thing on deep background. Kept your names mostly out of it, because I know you hate that. Be in the evening edition... If they still have that. In the morning for sure."

"Wow. Thanks, boss!" Morgan said. She really was not used to JJ treating her well yet.

"Go home. Get in your eight. See you tomorrow for whatever fresh hell you are going to get me involved with, Morgan. Sam." JJ waved them out of his office.

First names even.

Morgan smiled over at her partner as they returned to their shared cubicle "Goodnight Sam. See you tomorrow. Call me if you need anything but I hope we have a few hours of calm before the storm."

"Good work tonight... Well... This morning, Morgan. Well done. You played Deedee Odean like a fiddle. It was a thing of beauty to watch." Sam returned the smile.

Morgan smiled more broadly in acknowledgment of Sam's complement. "Thank you, Sam."

Morgan touched the sleeping Wendell's shoulder. "Your ride is leaving."

Wendell stood up, looking brighter eyed than Morgan thought he had any right to. "Really? You sleep in the chair and now you look chipper already?" she complained.

"Sorry." Wendell did not sound sorry.

In the Dodge, and headed home, Morgan was glad the morning go-to-church traffic was over. She rubbed at her burning eyes. "I cannot decide if I want a shower, then bed, or bed then a shower."

"Personally, I suggest shower, then bed. Then shower. Then bed. Three or four times." Wendell offered.

Morgan gave him a dark look. "As long as I have a REASON to take all those showers."

"I promise you, Detective: Cooperate with my evil intentions and you will."

"Also that I get some sleep between them..."

"Some. Let's see. Eighteen divided by four is four with two spare hours..." Wendell offered math unconnected to anything and yet, of course, his thinking clear.

"I can be a little late tomorrow. I worked all weekend, after all." Morgan said.

"And I have a mid, so..." Wendell looked at her. "As I am apparently YOUR officer, Detective, I await your orders."

"I already dressed you down. Now I think I will just undress you." Morgan said. "After I sleep." She added.

CHAPTER TWENTY-EIGHT

Closure

"Homicide. Detective Olsen." Morgan answered.

"We told you to leave the Odean's alone. You did not listen." Came the distorted voice.

"Yes. So? I thought it clear I never listen to you. I solve homicides. I do NOT take orders from you, whoever the entire bigoted hell you are. You do not like it, have people stop killing each other." Morgan said. She would have said 'We solve cases' but Sam did not need to be included in this Cabal shit.

Sam was alerted immediately to who this call must be from, based off her tone and the conversation and listened closely.

That elicited a distorted laugh, which was just ugly after it ran through the device disguising their voice. "In this case, you came up smelling like a rose, Olsen. Odean is NOT unhappy with the outcome. It was, in fact, the perfect outcome. Now he can get the divorce he wanted anyway, and socially no one will question that. We thought you would like to know that by your ignoring us, you did us a favor."

Joseph Odean was connected to the Cabal, via Daniel Moritz. Morgan was sure of it, based off their reactions when she had forced them into the interview room AFTER she was warned. Deedee was obviously NOT as covered, and that was interesting in that Deedee was the one that shared their repugnant values about ethnicity. Darla said Joseph Odean had even had sex with a church member that was not completely white. So had slave owners though, so Morgan was not sure that had meaning other than there being a double standard.

Deedee was the wrong gender, it seems.

Morgan said nothing. She was not sure what she could say that would not make the caller happy. Damned if she did or did not. Being totally silent probably would not going to help either. She finally said "I caught the killer. All I care about."

"Good Work, Detective. You may not be more trouble than you are worth after all. Nice story in the paper too, although they neglected to put your picture in. We'll get that fixed. We'll be in touch." And they hung up.

"What?" Sam asked. Morgan relayed the short conversation.

"Fuck." Sam said.

CHAPTER TWENTY-NINE

Epilog

Morgan opened the back door.

"Hi, Darla. This is unexpected. Come on in." Morgan shifted Nakoma to her other hip to make room for Darla to pass by.

They went through the mudroom to the kitchen, then on to the left to the Rec room, where Angel sat at the huge bar.

Morgan did the introductions. "Darla, this is my dear friend, Angel. This munchkin here is Nakoma."

"She is so CUTE. I did not know you were a mother." Darla enthused, looking at the baby with a grin, wiggling a finger at her, but not touching. Good baby manners. Nakoma grinned back.

"Co-Mother. Angel gets to take her home at night, the witch." Morgan said. "She says my job is too dangerous to let me keep her."

"It is." Angel said calmly. "Hello, Darla. Nice to meet you. I, of course, know about you. You must be tired of that." Angel stood and shook Darla's hand, and Morgan could see Angel absorbing the young woman in that odd way Angel had.

"Yes. It gets old." Darla agreed. "Though Morgan is all over the news too, even now. Barely mentions Sam. He is a quiet guy though."

"Yeah: I gave no interviews. Took no pictures. The damnable PR department put all that garbage out. They never ask me about it." Morgan waved at her glass. "We were just having Iced Tea and talking about where to go to lunch. Would you like some? Unsweetened."

"Thank you, yes. That would be nice." Darla agreed.

Angel said she would get it, and went to the kitchen.

"Sorry to drop in unannounced like this. I am headed off to school next week, and I wanted to say goodbye." Darla apologized.

"I know I am not in the book: how did you get my address?" Morgan asked, curiously. Darla had her cell number and Morgan said Darla could call any time. This physical visit was not something she should have been able to manage.

"It's nice being rich sometimes. I asked Moritz. He knew. Dude's getting rich off my mom's defense, so it was the least he could do, ya' know? Besides, I think he liked the idea after you kind of put him in his place in the interview room at getting back at you. In his head, I am a pox upon your house." Darla explained.

Morgan considered that. Since Moritz was clearly tied into the Cabal, she was not really shocked he knew her address. After all, the missing dead man not only knew where she lived, but that Morgan slept upstairs. That was even a recent change, to catch breezes on cooler nights, whenever those happened along. Not often in the Gulf Coast.

"Not at all a pox, of course. Did you decide where you are going to school?" Morgan asked.

"I am taking your advice. I have learned I should listen to you. I'm a legacy at Harvard if you can believe that, so I am going there. Far away from here. Far away from Dad and his church, and all the bullshit. I am just so tired of it all. You see the papers. On and on the scandal goes."

"Yes. I am sorry. I predict that once the divorce between your parents is finalized and a year or so goes by, we'll be seeing articles about how God brought your dad a new love, to heal his life here on earth. A gift from God. All that." Morgan grimaced.

"Oh, you KNOW it! Probably Cathleen too." Darla said. "Dad did not have NEARLY as many chicks as Mom had dudes on the side. Other than being a lovesick fool, Cathleen's OK. I like her better than either of my parents." Darla grinned. "Guess Bio-mom is going to have to stock up on that screwing now, given where she is going."

Angel returned with a large glass, and they pushed the barstools around to make a triangle. Darla looked over at the bar as they did so. "This thing is amazing. It looks real."

"It is real. I am not sure which Saloon it came from yet. Been looking into it. I fell in love with it during a case. Had to have it." Morgan explained.

Darla looked down at her glass. "I talked to mom the other day. I guess you know she's out on like a million dollar bond, and they took away her passport and put an ankle bracelet on her. I... I asked her why she did it. It was awful. So much hate. She deserves what is going to happen to her. I know that sounds really bad: a daughter saying that about her mom and shit, but... She killed three guys because they were the wrong ... something. Race. Gender. She says they defiled me. Shawn, the white boy? That one was OK. He could defile all he liked."

"Race is not a thing." Morgan said. "Just so you know. Well, it is a thing in the sense that it is the same thing as 'species'. Not trying to be pedantic here, but I think this distinction makes what your mother did worse. She killed over ethnicity. Because a fellow human's ancestors lived in the, by her lights, wrong part of the world. She did not just kill, it was a hate crime. Killing Neil when she KNEW he was transsexual? Hate crime. Add to all of that the attempted murder of a Cop as well. That is going to make her sentence much longer. Even on good behavior, I doubt she is ever free again. I hear the DA took the death sentence off the table as part of the plea deal, but I am not sure that is done yet. If it goes to trial, she'll more than likely get the death sentence. With automatic appeals, that means she would spend decades on death row. In Texas, they do not issue clemency on Death Row that I have ever seen. I am sorry about that. I hope she takes the deal."

"Yeah. I get it. Not your fault, Morgan. You didn't kill them." Darla frowned. "Neil. That one pisses me off even more than the other two. Weird, right? Mom killed him because he was born the wrong sex. He was such a super nice dude. I would have liked to see him some more, and not JUST because he could last forever and made me have a great orgasm, just to be clear." Darla looked directly into Morgan's eyes. "I know I have a rep."

Morgan returned the look and gave Darla a smile. "Not with me you do not."

"I know during the course of a case, you can't get personal, but let's just say that Morgan has her own string of suitors. Like that guy. And that one. Also, that one." Angel pointed at a few pictures here and there in the room.

Darla looked around as Angel pointed. "You date another black guy?" clearly not recognizing Wendell. She was not near it, and the picture Morgan had given her of him was pretty lousy. Drivers license photo bad.

Morgan shrugged "More than one, but yes, although not because they are a particular ethnicity. I don't care about anything like that. It is not that I can't see it, it is just that it does not matter. For me: I just have to like a man. As Angel ever so helpfully pointed out and you can see, I am not exclusive with anyone at the moment. Why I use protection at all times. I hope that you are?"

"I haven't fucked anyone since then, actually." Darla said. "Finding out my mom kills dudes she does not like because to her warped mind they 'defile me' sort of put me off, ya know? Not sure what guy the reads the news would want to get near me while she is out anyway. On the other hand, I hate giving her that kind of control."

"Understandable." Morgan said. "Still, whenever you DO re-engage in sexual activity, please consider what I said. I really do want to see you alive and well years from now. Some of the range of sexually transmitted diseases can be asymptomatic for years. A great deal of it can in fact, and if you are asymptomatic, you can transmit the disease without knowing you are. Part of how STD's are so successful is their ability to be stealthy."

Darla nodded. "Yeah: I read up on it after you talked to me about it. I heard you. You get that shit from your parents, and you just stop listening. Get it from YOU, and I hear it. I went and got tested at the Doctors office. I'm clean still. Next time I don't use a condom will be if I find 'the one', if that is even a real thing. You think you are ever going to find 'the one'? Or will you always date around?"

Morgan shrugged. "Who knows the future? Not me. I just know if this theoretical person or persons exist, I have not met them yet. Maybe. There is one guy right now that tempts me sorely. To try a committed relationship thing, I mean. Have him move in here. All the tropes. Not there yet though."

"Will it be a dude? Does it have to be?" Darla asked.

"Like you and Karen?" Morgan asked.

Darla narrowed her eyes. "How did you... Never mind. It's you. You never said you knew about that."

"It was not important to the case and therefore not any of my business. Only I know. Not even Sam." Morgan said, waiting to see where that took Darla.

"Yeah. Like her. I like Karen. She is so fucking talented, but I can't see being with just a woman. If I could get her AND a nice dude? That would fucking rock. My perfect world. Her parents would shit bricks though."

"They are traditional. Yes." Morgan considered for a moment. "Perhaps when you are away at school, and she is as well... Harvard to Juilliard is what: a three-hour drive? Four? You could have weekends, though her practice schedule will be brutal."

"Just stir in a dude for when she is practicing. Nirvana. So. You did not answer. What about you. You are open minded... Obviously." Darla returned to her question.

"I assume 'the one' is a male, yes. I have never sexually been with a woman, so I don't want to say that with absolute certainty. I only recently found out I could find some women attractive at all. Her." Morgan pointed at a picture on the bar. A group photo.

Darla asked, "Can I see it?"

Angel, the closest to the picture handed it over. "When she met me, I was naked, but I am not her type, it seems."

"I just met you and I'd do you in a heartbeat." Darla said offhandedly. She looked at the group. "Who are these people?"

"Some people I met during a case we closed a while back. Death of an exotic dancer. Those people work at an exotic club called 'rox'. We did a group photo after a party. Janie is the earth mother looking one there" Morgan reached over and tapped Janie's image. "You have to see her naked to get her impact. In that picture, she looks pretty normal. Naked, she has a real sexual presence. For me, in any case."

Angel agreed. "Oh, yes. Janie is really something. Top dancer at 'rox', and for a reason. Morgan absolutely should try her, except that Janie doesn't do chicks either. That is too bad because they would be good together."

Morgan waggled a finger at Angel. "Janie said she and I were going to try someday."

"To be a fly on THAT wall." Angel grinned back.

Darla nodded, pointed at another face. "Who is this hottie?"

Angel answered "Mike. Bouncer and bartender. One of Morgan's lovers. They are still just getting going."

Darla looked at Morgan "Oh, wow. He is a babe. Is he as yummy as he looks?"

Morgan not being one for oversharing, said simply " The first time with any new lover usually is awkward. Takes time. Mike was used to the preferences of the women in his orbit. Exotic dancers and professional sex workers, plus some gym ladies. He was not tuned in at all to my preferences." Morgan shrugged. "Part of making a relationship work is listening to your lover. He heard me when I told him what I wanted. That he listened and did not just fold up camp is good. Most men are not able to get a, shall we say, 'bad review' and stay with you to try again. Ego. It is not a one-way street either. It is just that so far he has come to like my preferences over his former ones. Our first time was not, as you put it, 'yummy'. It rarely is. It is much better now, for both of us."

"Except Wendell. He got it right the first time." Angel said unhelpfully.

"Thank you, Angel." Morgan glared. "Yes: Wendell is the exception that proves the rule."

Darla hopped off her barstool and went to a good copy of the picture that the Cabal had sent her, this one of Morgan and Wendell on their bikes, and Morgan looking back at him and seeming to be so happy. Morgan loved that she took something meant to intimidate her and then framed it and put it in her Rec Room. A complete 'screw you'. She also liked how happy she looked in the picture.

"Ah yes. I recognize him. This is my supposed cop lover guy. Wendell. Wow. You look like you are having a good time. This is a better picture than the one you gave me to show mom. Is it hilarious that the guy I was pretend-screwing you really are? God: He is cute! You only date babes? I'd do him for sure. Or the bartender guy. Shit, I think I might be horny." Darla asked.

"As I said, I just have to like someone, Darla. Ken, for example, over there." Morgan indicated a picture on the wall of her and Ken with drinks."Mexico trip we took together. Geologist. Smart. Kind of nerdy. We often play Trivia on our dates. Tall, but not a gym denizen like Mike or Wendell. A super nice person I enjoy being with. We have been lovers for a long time."

"Ken would marry her instantly except Morgan has made it very clear that is not a welcome question." Angel noted. "Mike would too, not that he'll ever say it. Morgan could take him out of circulation for sure. For Morgan, that would be the shortest romance she has ever had. Now Wendell. He is different: He would marry Morgan too, but he worries about the shit the Cabal would give her over him." Angel opined. "However, that is what stops him from being her one committed relationship. Even in working hard to not give them power, they still have it."

"The Cabal?" Darla asked, "Those guys you mentioned at Mr. MgGoo's?"

"Yes, them. Thank you, Angel..." Morgan glared again. "Also, yes. Wendell is the man I would consider committing to, to the exclusion of the others. I may ask him still. Time will tell, and I do have to be the one that asks. Just how it is set up right now. Being committed means having to not be with other men, and I know I am not quite ready for that yet. I have not been with Janie yet. Maybe I will like your idea of having a matched set of live-in lovers? Who knows?"

Angel responded to Morgan's approbation. "Not like YOU are going to tell her about the Cabal, Morgan. Darla needs to know this kind of shit. Your life is not simple. Every choice you make takes you to places where you have to be stupidly brave sometimes, and she needs to understand that about you and your life. You are important to her, Morgan. She needs to know when she is at school that is OK to be herself, especially since she is planning on trying to be like you. Smarter about her choices, but still a free spirit. What she thinks you are, she wants to become. She is smart and has never really had a female role model that informed her HOW to be a smart woman in this world. So: if you won't tell her things, I will."

Morgan had no idea what to do with that, but Darla was looking at Angel with a slightly open mouth.

"Huh... I guess I kinda am...?" She said, ending on an upward inflection.

Angel told Darla "It's OK to try on being Morgan for size. Your mother is hardly the female role model you need, is she?"

"No. Really not." Darla agreed with fervor.

"Pick a good person, like Morgan. It is not like I'd let my little girl idolize just anyone, you know." Angel said, smiling at the girl on Morgan's hip, currently chewing on her hands. "You'll figure out who you are from there, but it's like Morgan says: You are a good person. So modeling another good person? All to the better."

"Wow." Darla said.

"Wow indeed. Join us at lunch?" Angel asked. "We can tell you about the Cabal, and men that try to run your life by remote control."

Printed in Great Britain
by Amazon